Wishful Thinking

MELISSA HILL

POOLBEG

This novel is entirely a work of fiction. The names, characters and incidents portrayed in it are the work of the author's imagination. Any resemblance to actual persons, living or dead, events or localities is entirely coincidental.

Published 2005
by Poolbeg Press Ltd
123 Grange Hill, Baldoyle
Dublin 13, Ireland
E-mail: poolbeg@poolbeg.com
www.poolbeg.com

1 3 5 7 9 10 8 6 4 2

A catalogue record for this book is available from the British Library.

ISBN 1-84223-222-3

Typeset by Type Design 11.3/15
Printed by CPD, Wales

www.poolbeg.com

About the Author

Melissa Hill is originally from Cahir in Co. Tipperary, and now lives with her husband Kevin and their dog Homer in Co. Wicklow. She is the author of *The Irish Times* No. 1 bestselling novel *Never Say Never*, as well as previous bestsellers *Not What You Think* and *Something You Should Know*, all published by Poolbeg.

For more information, visit Melissa's website at www.melissahill.info

Acknowledgements

Huge thanks as always to the following people:

My family – Mam, Dad, Amanda and Sharon – and also my friends, who have all been wonderfully supportive and are always there for me. To Homer who keeps me from turning into a couch potato.

To Poolbeg – Kieran, Emma, Claire, Lynda, Conor, Gaye and Paula who all work so hard on my behalf. And a big welcome to baby Leo!

To my fantastic agent Sheila Crowley, and all at AP Watt who look after me so well.

To booksellers throughout the country who have given my books such amazing support and who are incredibly welcoming whenever I visit – thanks so much.

Likewise a special thanks to all who buy and read my books, and continue to send me feedback and lovely messages of support through my website www.melissahill.info Do keep them coming, as they certainly keep me going! I really hope you all enjoy *Wishful Thinking*.

And last – but certainly not least, much love and thanks to my long-suffering hubby Kevin. I really couldn't do any of this without you.

Also by Melissa Hill

Something You Should Know

Not What You Think

Never Say Never

To Kevin
Thanks for five great years

PROLOGUE

Late Nineties

Thursday October 20: 8.40 am

She was not going to miss this, she told herself. Come hell or high water, she was not going to miss it.

But the rumbling was getting louder by the minute, so, despite her spiky heels and slim-fitting pencil skirt, she had no choice but to make a run for it – an extremely awkward run, that no doubt made her look as if she were competing in a three-legged race.

Very classy.

But she'd already been late twice this week and once again the previous week, so she knew that if she missed the train today she was in big trouble. It looked as though she wasn't the only one running late this morning either, she thought, seeing another harried-looking commuter rush towards the ticket office.

Luckily, she already had a travel-pass and once inside the train station, she scurried through the barrier and breathed a huge sigh of relief to find that the train was still at the platform. Just in time.

Breathing heavily as a result of her sprint, she nipped inside the double doors just seconds before they shut – and nearly catching the hem of her precious John Rocha pink trench coat in the process. Now that would be a disaster!

1

But the person behind her hadn't been fast enough and, as the train pulled off, she felt for the unlucky commuter who would undoubtedly have to wait some time for the next train.

She shrugged and repositioned her handbag on her shoulder. Such was life.

The morning service to Dublin was a busy run, and by the time the train reached this station there was normally only standing room in the carriages. But to her immense relief, today there was an unoccupied seat a little way down, one that the other commuters obviously hadn't yet seen. She smiled softly to herself and quickly made her way to the seat, thrilled to be able to sit down – especially after all that running. But as she pushed through the standing crowd, her handbag slipped off her shoulder and down along her arm before falling awkwardly onto the ground. Typical! The one time she decides to bring her precious Orla Kiely bag to work and she has to go and drop it on a dirty floor! Inelegantly, she bent down to try and pick it up – the train's forward movement, as well as the weight of the briefcase in her other hand, unbalancing her.

"Here you go!" Another passenger, a young blonde girl sitting nearest the aisle, had retrieved the bag for her. She gave the pretty pink and white-patterned bag a blatantly appreciative glance before handing it back. "Orla Kiely, isn't it?"

"Yes – thanks a million," she replied breathlessly, and with relief continued on towards that precious seat, which at this stage she needed very badly.

The backs of her thighs were already aching from their unaccustomed exertions, and as she sank gratefully onto the seat and put her briefcase on the floor and her prized handbag on her lap, she reminded herself once more that she really should start going to the gym.

As she dusted off the bag, she shuffled exaggeratedly on her seat, trying to give a not-so-subtle hint to the man beside her to move his things so she could sit comfortably. She'd noticed a bit of extra padding on her backside lately but this was ridiculous – the man and his belongings were sprawled all over the place! Eventually, Mister got the message and grudgingly, she thought, moved his jacket and laptop to give her some more room.

She caught the eye of an older lady sitting directly across from her and the woman gave a slight conspiratorial smile as if to say 'typical men!'. She was reading one of those fluffy romance novels and, judging by her age and the relaxed manner in which she carried herself, was most likely the only person on the train today not on her way to work. Then again, she decided, catching sight of some guy in a tracksuit (not your typical besuited professional) trying to push his way through the standing crowds, who knew what people might be doing?

Lucky thing though, she thought, eyeing the older woman enviously and trying to remember the last time she had been able to lose herself in a cosy read. Speaking of which . . . she reached for her briefcase and, groaning inwardly, withdrew the documents that needed going over for this morning's meeting. Cosy reading it wasn't.

Flicking through the documents, she began to read, but soon found that she couldn't really concentrate. Her mind absently kept going over what the love of her life had said to her the night before.

"We need to talk," he'd announced. God, that was such a cliché, but they knew each other inside out, and seemed to be getting on really well lately, so what on earth could be wrong? Her mind raced as she tried to come up with a few possible scenarios – was he going off her, had he decided that they shouldn't be together after all or . . .

And then it hit her. Of course! He was going to propose! Thinking back on it now, it hadn't been a serious 'we need to talk' – it was more of a nervous 'we need to talk'! So after all this time, he'd finally cottoned on to the fact that he couldn't live without her! She hugged herself excitedly, crumpling her work papers in the process. But at a time like this who cared about work?

She could be wrong, of course, and could very well be jumping to hasty conclusions, but somehow deep down she knew she was right! She had to be! They had a fantastic time together, and were madly in love, so what was the next step only marriage? Thinking of proposals and engagement rings, a horrified thought struck her. Please, please may he not have picked out the ring himself! The man was perfect in every other way, but God love him, he had terrible taste in jewellery! She remembered the time he had given her this absolutely hideous, tacky-looking silver chain one Christmas – it looked as though he had picked it up in –

3

Just then, her thoughts were cut off by this tremendous . . . incredibly overpowering . . . ear-splitting . . . screeching sound, and she instantly put her hand to her ears to try and block it out. What was going on?

Then, all of a sudden, the train began to shudder, and although she had no idea what was happening, her body tensed and the hairs on the back of her neck stood up. She looked wildly around the carriage, wondering if everyone else had heard it, or was she the only one? No, the older woman across from her looked terrified, confused . . . everyone looked bewildered . . . and then there was this incredible roar, a sound so deafening it was unlike anything she had ever heard before, so loud it was as though it had invaded her mind, her body, her entire being. Her heart hammered, her brain flooded with this other, even more excruciating noise . . . and then her seat jerked forward . . . and for a strange few moments, it seemed as though time had slowed to a crawl and everything was happening in slow motion. Surreally, the entire carriage seemed to have lifted off the tracks, and the train was now travelling on thin air. But that couldn't be the case, could it, she thought absently, as a tremendous force winched her out of her seat.

Trains couldn't fly, could they?

* * *

Thursday October 20: 10.10 am

The normally self-assured and flawlessly composed Clare Rogers today looked ragged and white-faced. She stared unseeingly into the camera, as if she wasn't quite sure where she was and what she was doing.

When she spoke, her words sounded panicked and uncertain – totally inappropriate for a professional TV journalist – but then again, she thought, when had she ever needed to report something like this?

In her earpiece she heard the voice of Richard Heffernan speaking live from the RTE news studio.

"Our correspondent, Clare Rogers, is at the scene of this morning's train derailment on the east coast. Clare, can you tell us anything concrete at this stage?" he asked.

Clare began slowly. "Well, Richard, the emergency services have just

4

arrived at the location, so details are very sketchy at this time." Her voice trembled slightly as she spoke. *"All I can confirm is that this train is a very busy commuter carrier serving the east coast to Dublin city centre. However, it seems very likely that the route suffered a signalling failure, which resulted in the train's derailment here near Merrion Gates."*

"And is there any indication as to what might have happened to cause this derailment?" Richard prompted.

"Again, Richard, we can't confirm anything at present. I do know that Rail Ireland will be making a statement in due course, so we should know more then. However, before we went on air, I spoke to a number of witnesses – commuters sitting in traffic and waiting to pass through the gates – who've helped me reconstruct the scene. They saw, or rather heard the train braking loudly from some distance, which would suggest that the train driver may have spotted traffic passing through the crossing, and identified immediately that there was a problem with the signal. Seconds later, the train derailed a few yards from the gates. It then careered across the tracks and through a concrete wall before ending up on the strand here." Clare swallowed hard. "Luckily, there were no southbound trains coming the other way at the time," she added quietly.

"So the driver tried to stop the train in order to avoid crashing into the early-morning traffic?"

"Perhaps – again we're just not sure. No doubt there will be a full investigation, but at the moment, the emphasis is of course on the rescue efforts." Once more, Clare's professional façade dropped slightly, and her eyes betrayed her inner distress.

"Now, a signal failure, this is something that is most unusual for this country's rail network, isn't it?" Richard went on – evidently intent on getting to the bottom of the situation.

"That's right," Clare confirmed. "Derailments can unfortunately be quite common for our neighbours in the UK, simply because of the fact that there are a number of rail companies operating and using the line network there. The system is well organised, but signals can get confused. Which," she said, once more struggling to keep her voice even, "can lead to accidents like this one."

"But we have only one rail carrier operating here in Ireland, Clare, and as a result mistakes are very rare, aren't they?"

"Usually, yes. But, Richard, over the last couple of months, Rail Ireland have been carrying out a number of upgrades throughout the network. Although it is only speculation at this stage – and, as I said, the company will be making a full statement soon – it would appear that the signalling system on this particular level crossing may have failed." She swallowed hard.

"Which would obviously have serious implications for the company," Richard finished solemnly.

Clare looked directly into the camera. "Very serious implications, Richard," she agreed, her voice grim. "At this time of morning, the train would have been full of commuters, regular users of this service, and – as I'm sure our viewers can tell from our camera footage of the scene – there will be a high number of serious injuries, and undoubtedly some fatalities."

"Thank you, Clare – we'll come back to you later for the Rail Ireland press conference." The footage of the wreck disappeared from the screen, and the picture cut back to the newsroom studio. Richard looked solemnly into the camera before adding, "Our thoughts go out to the friends and families of any viewers at home whose loved ones might have taken this particular train to work this morning. Stay tuned for further updates."

FOUR MONTHS EARLIER

CHAPTER 1

June 21st, 8.00am

Rosie Mitchell waited patiently at the platform. The train was a little bit late this morning, she thought, checking her watch. Not that it mattered to her. Unlike all the young hassled-looking people here, Rosie wasn't in any hurry. At this stage, she was long past her rushing-around days, and, unlike these poor misfortunates, had no big mortgage to worry about, or loan or car repayments to meet.

Thank goodness for the train all the same, she thought, otherwise these days she'd be really stuck. Martin had always been the one to do the driving, and God knows he went on at her enough to learn, but she never had any interest.

To be honest, she liked the train, enjoyed being able to sit back for the journey to Dublin and admire the beautiful views along the coast, gaze at the birds weaving in and out over the cliffs between Greystones and Bray, or stare in awe at the stunningly beautiful Killiney Bay. Or, if the day was cloudy, and the scenery not so spectacular, she would sit and read a book. Sometimes she'd be so stuck in the story she was reading that she wouldn't even notice the journey going.

So Rosie loved the train and she wouldn't dream of getting a car. What was the point? The station was a short walk down the road from the house and, with the train going three times a day to Connolly station, she had plenty of options. She could nip into town whenever she fancied a bit of window shopping, and the house in which her old friend Sheila now lived was close enough to the rail line, as was her daughter Sophie's place. For the moment anyway.

The train finally pulled into Wicklow Station, and Rosie stood back and waited until the cluster of younger commuters were happily seated before she herself boarded. The upside of this was that she wouldn't get pushed and shoved while stepping onto the train. Since putting her back out in a badminton match a few years back, Rosie's balance wasn't as sure as it used to be, and she liked to take her time for fear of slipping into the huge gap between the train and the platform. Of course, the downside of waiting until everyone else had boarded was that she was often left without a seat. But Rosie didn't mind. These people all had a hard day's work ahead of them whereas she didn't have a care in the world.

In fact, wasn't she the lucky one – a lady of leisure going off to view houses with her only daughter? She'd hate to have to face a day's work now like all her poor fellow passengers. You could almost see the tension in their expressions – all preoccupied with whatever awaited them at their jobs. It was a shame really, the lengths that people had to go to these days just to keep their heads above water.

It had been a lot different when she and Martin were starting out. Neither of them had to spend hours of their day commuting back and forth like that and, she thought, they were much the better for it.

Martin had worked in his father's gardening business since he was old enough to use a trowel, and Rosie had worked in the Civil Service, which of course back then was one of the cushiest numbers you could get. They'd bought the house in Wicklow Town so she could walk to work, while Martin went off in his van to wherever he happened to be working that day.

She smiled sadly as she thought of poor Martin. There wasn't a day that she didn't think of him, of course, and miss him dreadfully, but yet she couldn't really complain. They had had a wonderful marriage, two wonderful children in David and Sophie, and in their many years together rarely a cross word had passed between them. She and Martin

9

had both known for some time before his death that the day would soon come when she would be left on her own. High blood pressure was in Martin's family, and when he suffered two near-fatal heart attacks in his last year, it became clear that a simple change in lifestyle or the tablets he was taking weren't going to save him. But it was lovely that he had died doing what he loved, tending the roses out in the back garden – the evening sun just beginning to fade when Rosie found him.

So, eighteen long months ago, Rosie had buried the one great love of her life, having made him a promise that she would keep going, keep laughing and smiling and enjoying life in the same way she always did, so that it wouldn't seem all that long until she saw him again. At times it was very hard, but she was doing her very best to keep that promise.

Anyway, she was very lucky. Her two children were happily married and with good jobs, David to a lovely Liverpool girl named Kelly (although there were no sign of kids yet, and Rosie wouldn't dream of asking) and working as a builder over there. Sophie and Robert had little two-year-old Claudia and had good jobs, but were still searching for a house. Rosie shook her head. That was another real hardship for the younger people these days. The house prices in Dublin were legendary and it would only get worse!

Anyway, today Sophie was taking her to see a house she had her eye on out in Malahide. "Mum, it's perfect!" she'd enthused on the phone the day before. "You have simply got to see it!"

Rosie was delighted with her daughter's enthusiasm but couldn't help feeling a little bit disappointed that Sophie would want to live all the way out there, and so far away from her. It was far enough as it was with her living in Santry, and having to take the train and then a bus just to visit her.

Still, it would be nice to see the three of them settled in something other than the rented apartment they were in now. There wasn't much space, and what with Claudia hitting the terrible twos it couldn't be good for them all living in what was basically one big room. And the height of the place! Imagine if the child somehow opened or even *fell through* that big front window? Rosie didn't even like to think about it. No, it would be better for all concerned if this place Sophie wanted her to see today was a nice little tidy semi like Rosie's own house, with a safe back garden for Claudia to run around in.

The train emptied a lot of its passengers at Pearse Street Station, and Rosie sank gratefully onto a recently vacated seat. She laughed softly to herself, as she could almost hear Martin's lilting Wicklow tones jeering her. 'Jaysus, missus, you'd swear you were an oul wan!" But her back had been giving her a fair bit of trouble lately, and as much as she tried to tell herself otherwise, there was no denying that she was feeling the effects of it. And in all honesty, no matter how energetic and cheerful she might feel, she *wasn't* getting any younger, was she? She smiled. She was definitely *not* one of those glamorous granny types she often saw walking confidently around the town. With their coloured hair, perfect make-up and lovely up-to-the-minute fashions, these women looked for all the world as if they were still in the first flush of youth.

And apparently, these days a person could get injections to get rid of wrinkles – from your buttocks, no less! Good luck to them, but that wasn't Rosie's way. No, she was going to let her auburn hair go as grey as it liked, and her skin get as wrinkly as it wanted – weren't these things just marks of a life lived at the end of the day? Getting older was nothing to be ashamed of, and as much as you might like to, you simply couldn't outrun time.

But today, she wasn't running anywhere, she mused, getting off the train at Connolly Station and going to wait at the bus stop. It was a pity that Sophie's car was in having a service today, otherwise she could have come and collected her at the station, and she wouldn't have to wait in the cold for the next bus to Santry.

Because the train had been late in the first place, she had missed her usual connection but such was life. Rosie reached into her bag and took out the novel she was currently reading. Anita Shreve, a nice gentle read – not half as gripping as our own lovely Irish writers – but still, nice enough to pass a bit of time.

Finally the bus arrived, and twenty or so minutes later, Rosie reached her daughter's apartment building. She took extra care selecting the right buzzer, always afraid of her life that she'd push the wrong one and wake up some poor misfortunate sleeping off their night-duty or something. She shook her head. Originally from County Clare, and despite living in Wicklow for all of her married life, she still couldn't shake off the 'small village inferiority complex' as Martin used to call it. Rosie called it good manners and concern for a fellow human being. Outgoing and confident all his life, Martin didn't really understand.

Nor, it seemed, did Sophie. "Mum, I'm just drying my hair – can you hold on for five minutes?" her daughter's voice blared tinnily through the speaker.

"No problem," Rosie replied agreeably, although the cold was now making her fingers numb.

"Hi, Mum!" It was a good ten minutes before Sophie appeared downstairs, dark hair sleek and shiny as always and her make-up beautifully applied. Her daughter always looked stylish, and today she was dressed in a gorgeous fitted woollen suit, something that even Rosie's inexperienced eye could see had cost an arm and a leg. But then again, it couldn't have cost that much because Sophie and Robert were mad saving for this house, weren't they? No, knowing Sophie and her incredible talent for spotting a bargain, she had probably picked the suit up for next to nothing in one of those second-hand shops that seemed to be popping up everywhere these days.

"Sorry about keeping you waiting like that, but I think you were a little early – I said 10.30, didn't I?"

Rosie thought idly that if her daughter was occupied and couldn't come to the door, there was no reason why she couldn't have just buzzed her into the hall. But Sophie could be a little bit scatty sometimes.

"No, the train was late actually – where's Claudia?" Rosie stepped into the hallway, eager to get out of this cold. Although it was supposed to be summertime, the seasons in this country generally set their own agenda.

Sophie linked her mother's arm and steered her back outside. "At the childminder's of course! I couldn't bring her with us to the house – we'd have no peace with her wailing and whingeing and *touching* everything!"

"Oh." Rosie was disappointed. She had been looking forward to seeing her granddaughter. "Maybe we could pick her up afterwards?"

"Ah no, Tracy offered to take her for the day – she knows I need a break," Sophie answered dismissively. "And, of course, she won't say no to the money either."

Rosie nodded reluctantly. Perhaps Claudia could be a bit of a handful but . . .

Sophie chattered on. "Oh, Mum, I am just *dying* for you to see this place – it is truly incredible!"

"I'm sure it is, pet, but don't get your hopes up too much either, sure you won't? You know yourself that there's a lot of competition out there for nice houses and – "

"Mum, this is our house – I just know it is!"

As they walked towards the residents' carpark, Rosie had to smile at her daughter's enthusiasm. She had been the same as a young girl, always full of excitement and mischief.

Sophie and David had both been quite a handful when growing up really, and, while Martin had always insisted that she spoiled and sheltered them a little too much, she was proud to say that they had both turned out very well. 'A credit to them,' her own mother might have said, had she been alive today to see her grandchildren.

"And afterwards I thought we might go and have a nice lunch and have a chat about it all – what do you think?"

Rosie was thrilled. That sounded lovely actually. A nice old gossip with her daughter was just what she needed. Although they spoke often on the phone, she hadn't seen Sophie in a while, and she wanted to tell her all her news, and of course she wouldn't mind confiding in someone about how her back was starting to give her more trouble and . . .

Rosie jumped, as the flashy-looking sports car in front of them beeped noisily.

"What do you think?" Sophie grinned, proudly waving her keys.

"Is this yours?" Rosie gasped in surprise at the car. A brand new

13

car? Despite herself, she couldn't help feeling a bit hurt. If her car was no longer giving her trouble, and indeed it didn't look likely, why hadn't Sophie collected her from the station, instead of having her wait twenty minutes in the cold and then another twenty in the bus? And how on earth would they get a baby-seat into that tiny thing?

"Yep," Sophie confirmed happily.

"But what about the old one? The one that was giving you trouble?"

"Well, I told you the other car was having a service because I wanted this to be a surprise!" Sophie suddenly looked crestfallen. "Don't you like it?"

"Of course I do, love." Seeing the disappointed look on her daughter's face, Rosie felt guilty. For some reason, Sophie had decided that this new car would be a huge surprise for her mother, although why that would be the case, Rosie didn't know – well, it *was* a huge surprise but not an altogether pleasant one. Still, she'd better humour her. "It's lovely, Sophie – I can't wait to get a good spin in it."

"Well, you won't have long to wait!" Her good humour instantly restored, Sophie opened the driver door and sat princess-like in front of the steering wheel, while her mother eased herself into the passenger seat. She tilted forward the rear-view mirror and applied a fresh coat of lipstick. "Ready then?" she asked, turning the key in the ignition.

"Yes." Rosie's back ached from trying to manoeuvre herself into what in her opinion amounted to little more than a biscuit tin. Sophie's swerving and quick lane-changing all the way to Malahide didn't help much either.

About fifteen minutes later, they pulled onto a quiet tree-lined cul-de-sac.

Rosie was sure that behind all those large expensive wrought-iron gates, intercoms and granite stonework were equally large and expensive houses – houses that were way beyond the reach of a currently part-time insurance clerk and her department-store manager husband. There was a For Sale sign outside the one at the end, but surely Sophie wasn't even *dreaming* of . . .

But Sophie slowed the car in front of the house, rolled down the window and pushed the intercom button. "Sophie Morris – I have an appointment for an eleven o'clock viewing," she announced, in this strange haughty voice that Rosie had never heard her use before.

"Certainly, Ms Morris, I'll open the gates for you now."

"Sophie, surely you couldn't be thinking of buying a house like this? It must cost an absolute fortune."

"Well, in the scheme of things, it isn't that expensive actually," Sophie replied airily. "Anyway, I just want you to take a look at it first and see what you think. We'll discuss the rest later."

'The rest? What rest?' Rosie wanted to ask.

But just then it hit her. Just then she realised why Sophie was so eager to show her this house today, why her daughter had been so cheerful and attentive these last few weeks, ringing her often to see how she was. Rosie had to give her credit, to be fair. Sophie had bided her time and had waited until well after her father's death before she once again asked 'The Question'.

All of a sudden, Rosie felt sad and more than a little used. She supposed she should have known better than to think that Sophie had brought her all the way out here just to get her opinion on the house. Sophie didn't need an opinion – her mind was already made up.

Still, deep down Rosie knew that this time she probably *would* give in and let her daughter have exactly what she wanted. How could she not? In truth, she would have given in that first time, only Martin wouldn't have it. Rosie had thought it a sensible idea, but her husband had been dead set against it, and so that had been the end of it.

Until now.

As they approached the admittedly beautiful, but very expensive house, Rosie sighed inwardly. Martin would not be very happy with her – not very happy at *all*.

* * *

Almost two years earlier, Sophie, Robert and baby Claudia had visited Rosie and Martin in Wicklow one Sunday for dinner. Sophie's husband was a pleasant if rather quiet fellow whom Rosie liked well enough, but Martin didn't trust.

"I can't quite put my finger on it, Rosie – it's just a feeling I have," Martin had said, when Sophie and Robert had first become engaged a few years before.

"The same feeling you've had about every fellow she's gone out with over the years?" Rosie teased, knowing full well that Martin's 'feeling' was more than likely down to simple over-protectiveness of his little girl.

No, Robert was a nice enough lad. He wasn't exactly the chatty type, and normally he didn't say too much, so Rosie couldn't really fault him.

But on that particular day, it seemed Robert had plenty to say.

To Rosie's delight, Sophie had arrived bearing an enormous bunch of white lilies, her mother's favourite. Dinner was a lively, chatty affair, but as Martin said himself to Rosie later that night, it was obvious that there was 'something coming'.

Rosie had sensed it too, and was puzzled. It was highly unlikely Sophie was pregnant again; Claudia was only a few months old, and according to Sophie very 'tiring and troublesome'.

Rosie understood well how hard it must be for Sophie, spending all day on her own in that tiny apartment with just a small baby for company, and little or no support from friends or family. She and Martin did their best to help out, but because Wicklow was so far away, it was difficult.

Rosie felt for her daughter's generation, she really did. Back when David and Sophie were babies, most of Rosie's neighbours in the estate were also new mothers, and as a result there was a lot of shared support and swapping stories. Thinking back on it, it had actually been fun – nothing like today, when it seemed that new mums like Sophie had a huge struggle to try and juggle work and family life.

So, when over dessert, Sophie and Robert finally got round to what they had to say, Rosie was in exactly the right frame of mind to listen.

"Mum, Dad," Sophie began tentatively, "we were wondering if we could talk to you two about something."

"What is it, pet?" Martin asked, adding more chocolate sauce to his low-fat ice cream, and getting a stern look from Rosie for his troubles.

"Well, you know that Rob and I have been looking to buy our own house ... oh, for ages now."

"Oh, did you find something?" Rosie interjected, pleased. It would be lovely to see the three of them properly settled.

Sophie gave a huge exaggerated sigh. "We found lots of places, Mum, but ... it's just," she bit her lip in the same endearing way she'd done since she was a year old, "well, they're all just so *expensive*!" She looked mournfully at her father.

"Well, of course they're expensive, Sophie. When your mother and I got this place it was very expensive for us too. We hadn't much money, but we managed, didn't we, Rosie?" he said, smiling at his wife.

"Actually," Robert piped up, and gave a sideways glance at Sophie, "it's not so much that the houses are expensive – interest rates are so low now that what we're paying at the moment in rent would more than cover our mortgage repayments. The main problem we're facing, Martin," he added easily, "is the deposit."

Rosie knew by his expression that Martin was shocked – shocked because his son-in-law had never called him by his first name before, but also because neither of them had ever heard Robert say so much all at once.

Sophie nodded. "The money they want for a deposit is crazy, Dad. I mean, we've been saving for *years*, and still what we have wouldn't go next nor near what we need."

"So what are you saying – or should I say what are you asking? Because you two are *asking*, aren't you?"

"Well, we were wondering ... well, *hoping* that you and Mum might consider releasing some of the equity on this house to give us a hand with the deposit." Sophie smiled happily at her parents.

"Equity? What does that mean?" Rosie asked, looking at her husband for explanation. Being in business, Martin was well up in all these financial terms.

But Martin was stony-faced and instantly Rosie knew that whatever it was, he was not going to go along with it. "It means that because our house is now worth a hell of a lot more than we paid for it –"

"And because you've already paid off *your* mortgage," Sophie interjected in a faintly jealous tone.

"That we *supposedly* have this great big windfall that we can *supposedly* cash in."

"But you do, Dad! This house must be worth at least five or six times what you paid for it!"

That was true, Rosie thought. The neighbours were always going on about how much their houses were worth now compared to when they had bought them back in the seventies. It seemed to be the main topic of conversation these days.

"So the banks will just give us money on the strength of what the house is worth – just like that?" she asked, the whole thing now beginning to make a lot of sense. "And we can help the kids out with getting their house? Oh, Martin, I think that's a great idea!"

Sophie beamed, pleased that her mother was on side. "Look, we wouldn't ask, but everyone is doing it, and because everyone is doing it, then they all have a head start on us, and we're getting desperate because of course we now have Claudia to think about and –"

"No," Martin interjected solidly.

"What?" Sophie and Rosie chorused.

"I'm sorry, but it's not going to happen. I know that it's supposed to be difficult to get on the housing ladder these days, but, Sophie, it's *always* been difficult. Do you think that myself and your mother just dipped into our back pockets to buy this house? We did not. We scrimped and saved for the deposit beforehand, and then went without for years just to keep up with the mortgage repayments."

"But, Dad – "

"Pet, I'm sorry but no. You said yourself that interest rates are very low these days. Well, they weren't low in our day. Yes, house prices are crazy now compared to back then, but the price of everything is crazy now compared to back then, and it's all relative. You just have to sacrifice what you have, to get something you want even more. That's the way life works."

18

"But, Dad, didn't you hear me? *Everyone* is doing it! All my friends' parents are giving them a leg-up! Caroline and Nikki and – I can't *believe* that you won't do the same for me! And with Claudia and everything ..." she trailed off, the tears beginning to show.

"Martin, let's not make any hasty decisions just yet," Rosie said gently, the mention of Claudia piercing her heart. "Let's think about this some more. It does sound like a good idea, especially if we have all this money –"

"But we *don't* have all this money, Rosie, that's the point. It's just moving figures from here to there. It's more borrowing on the strength of what the house is worth."

"Oh." All of sudden Rosie felt silly. Of course it wasn't going to be *free* money, was it?

"Obviously, we would pay you back," Robert said matter-of-factly. "Maybe we didn't make it clear from the outset, but this would be nothing more than a temporary loan – just something to give us a head start rather than having to save for years, and seeing all the good places snapped up."

"Robert, I'm sorry but that's the way it goes. Again, when we were younger and we wanted something, we had to save for it. These days, it's all credit this and credit that, and 'I want it now'. Instant gratification. In a way, that's why things are as crazy as they are now, and I'm sorry but I won't do it. After working hard enough all these years to pay off my own debts, I'm not about to go down that road again for someone else."

"Not even for your own daughter or your *grand*daughter?" Sophie challenged tearfully.

"Now look here," Martin began, and by his tone Rosie knew that this had really angered him, "over the years, your mother and I made a lot of sacrifices for you and David. For the first few years, we didn't have a car, let alone one each," he added pointedly.

"But my car is an old banger, Dad – you know that!"

"Sophie, if a six-year-old car is an old banger, then I've been driving them for the last twenty-odd years."

"But you know what I mean ..."

19

"Pet, I know it's hard for you to understand now, because you never wanted for anything when growing up – your mother and I made sure of that. But we made a lot of sacrifices for you and David. We rarely had a holiday, and if I remember correctly, you've had *two* sun holidays already this year, haven't you? Don't you think that the money would be better spent on saving for this supposedly impossible deposit?"

"But we *needed* those holidays, Dad! I don't know if you understand how hard we work, and how tiring it is looking after a new baby. We *had* to get away!"

"Maybe I understand more than you know, love," Martin's tone softened. "Now, I'm sorry, but you also have to understand that your mother and I just aren't in a position to get into more debt. I know the house might be worth X amount but we still have to live too."

"I suppose." Sophie, it seemed, had finally given up, although the disappointment in her tone was breaking Rosie's heart.

The kitchen was silent for a few minutes then, each of them lost in their own thoughts.

Then Robert spoke up. "I can understand your reluctance to get into more debt, Martin, and I'm very sorry that we put you in that position."

Martin nodded graciously.

"But there is another way," he continued, and Sophie looked at him with renewed hope, "a way that you wouldn't need to get into any debt at all." He sat forward as if the thought had just occurred to him. "Apparently, parents can also guarantee a child's mortgage, simply by letting the bank or building society hold onto your deeds. So if we buy a house, they have both yours and our deeds to cover the loan should we default. Which of course, would never happen," he added quickly. "But the important thing is, there would be no money involved, only assets." He sat back then, sure that he had made a valid point.

Martin studied his son-in-law. "You seem to have put a lot of thought into this, Robert."

He shrugged modestly. "Sophie and I are reaching breaking point. At this stage, we have to examine our options, especially for Claudia's sake."

"And does examining your options mean that you've also asked your own parents to contribute their deeds?"

Robert reddened. "Well, that's a little bit different. As you know my parents' house wouldn't be worth anywhere near ..." Robert's parents lived up north where house prices had yet to reach the dizzying heights of the Dublin suburbs.

"I see. So, it's just myself and Rosie that would be put at risk."

"Oh, for goodness sake, Dad, there would be no risk! Rob and I would never default! Don't you see? There is no way that we can possibly afford to buy a five hundred thousand euro house in Dublin without your help – no way!"

"And therein lies the problem, Sophie," Martin said, his tone weary.

"What?"

"You and Robert have good jobs – you admitted that yourself. You also admitted that interest rates are low. You seem to have plenty of money to buy fancy clothes and go out for fancy meals and the like. It seems to me that the two of you should have no problem getting the deposit together for a nice starter home out in Lucan or Meath or somewhere like that."

"But we don't want to live in some poxy estate, Dad – we want to live in Dublin –Malahide or Portmarnock, somewhere *nice*."

"Lucan is a lovely place."

"But we'd have no friends out there! All our friends are here! Caroline Redmond's parents gave her a hand, and now they're living in this fabulous mews in Malahide, and Nikki Cassidy and her husband are about to move to –"

"The answer is no, Sophie," Martin said quietly, and by his tone, Rosie knew that there would be no turning with him.

"Thanks, Dad," Sophie said, looking petulantly at Robert. "Thanks a bloody lot."

* * *

"Couldn't we give them a hand, Martin?" Rosie asked him, later on that evening, when the kids had gone back to Dublin. "It must be tough on them all the same."

"Love, at this stage in our lives, we don't need any more debt. Jesus, I worked like a demon over the years to get rid of it – we both have. Sure, we'll be lucky if our pensions keep us going, never mind going off on foreign holidays and getting widescreen TVs like they do." He sighed. "And, Rosie, you and I both know that my health isn't improving. If anything happens to me – "

"Sssh, don't say that," Rosie interjected, although she knew deep down that Martin was right. He'd only just got over his second heart attack and all the warnings were there. So, it wouldn't be right for them to take on more debt, not at this stage in their lives.

"Anyway, didn't we already shell out a fortune for that big wedding of hers two years ago? I know we had a great time, but honestly, all that money for just one day!"

"I know." Rosie herself couldn't believe the colossal amount that Sophie had racked up for her wedding. Martin had insisted on paying for most of it but, in more ways than one, neither had budgeted on their daughter's expensive taste, nor the swanky hotel she'd chosen for the reception. And Rosie only knew a fraction of the two hundred and fifty guests she'd invited. Still, it had been a great day, Sophie was their only daughter and being the last child they'd never get to do it again so ...

Still, Sophie's comment about how all her friends' parents were helping out unsettled Rosie. It did leave them at a disadvantage. And now with Claudia to think of, they really did need a decent roof over their heads.

She could understand too, Sophie's reluctance to live all the way out in Lucan. Sure, Lucan was a different county!

And of course there was little prospect of them moving down here to Wicklow, although it would be lovely to have them close by. But Wicklow house prices were just as bad as the ones in Dublin, if not worse. And at the end of the day, she couldn't blame Sophie for wanting to live near her friends, especially now that they were all starting to settle down and have kids. Sophie needed the support, and wasn't Rosie the very same when she first had David?

It was such a pity Martin couldn't see things from his daughter's point of view. But the problem was that once Martin made up his mind about something, then that was the end of it. And Rosie wouldn't dream of forcing her husband to do something he genuinely didn't want to do.

Still, lying in bed that night, unable to sleep, Rosie couldn't get her daughter's devastated expression out of her head.

And for the first time in her life, she wondered if she and Martin had let their daughter down.

CHAPTER 2

"So what did you think?" Sophie enthused. They were having lunch in a very nice hotel close by the house they'd just viewed, and while Rosie felt ill at ease with these sumptuous surroundings, Sophie, her sunglasses perched fashionably on her head and in her fancy suit, looked as though she'd been frequenting this kind of place all her life.

Although very nice, the house had been a humongous, hugely over-elaborate mansion – Rosie's house in Wicklow would have fitted in the entrance hall alone. The décor was very American what with all these marble tiles and stone pillars – dangerous enough for a fully-grown adult, let alone a young child like Claudia.In Rosie's opinion, it was totally over the top, and a small family like Sophie's had no need for a house like that.

"Well, it was nice –"

"Nice? Mum it was *fabulous*! Didn't you see that amazing American oak floor and the incredible Acacia kitchen? And weren't the K glass windows just divine?"

Rosie felt a bit lost. How did her daughter *know* about these things? The kitchen did stand out as being very nice indeed but, to be honest, wasn't too far off a version of the one Martin had put in himself back

24

home with a few bits and pieces from the local builder providers. And what on earth were 'K glass' windows and how did they differ from ordinary windows? In truth, Rosie felt a bit threatened. Was she that behind the times these days? *Should* she know about American oak floors and brushed steel handles and granite flooring?

"And, apparently, the houses were designed by J. Sparks Architects," Sophie added reverently, as if again this was something to get excited about.

Rosie looked blank.

"The famous award-winning architects?"

"Oh, right, those ones." Rosie feigned comprehension, wondering why this made such a difference.

"Nikki will just *die* when she sees it. She's been after a Sparks house forever and will just go apoplectic when she finds out I'm thinking of buying one."

"Look, are you sure this is really the right house for you, pet? It's a huge place – think of what the heating would cost, let alone the mortgage."

Sophie sighed. "Well, Mum, this is the thing," she began, reaching across and softly touching Rosie's arm. "Rob and I have been doing the sums and ..." she paused dramatically, "remember when we came to you and Dad before? Looking for help?"

Rosie nodded, her earlier suspicions verified. "And now you'd like me to help you out," she confirmed, quietly. She'd expected Sophie to ask, of course, but still she couldn't help feeling a little pressurised, especially when Martin had been so against it. But yet, if she didn't agree, Sophie and Robert and the baby would be stuck in that rented apartment so ...

"Do you think you could consider it?" Apparently unaware of her mother's discomfort, Sophie's eyes shone eagerly.

"I don't know ..."

"Mum, you're our last hope." Now her daughter's eyes shone with tears and Rosie's heart melted. "You have no idea how difficult it is trying to get enough money together for a deposit – let alone the fact that the bank won't lend us enough on the basis of our salaries. We're spending so much money on rent as it is that we're practically living hand to mouth!"

Hand to mouth? Almost instinctively Rosie's glance moved to the window and the carpark, where Sophie's brand new sports car was sitting proudly.

"We would be so grateful, Mum, you know we would. We can't ask Rob's parents because these days he and his dad don't really get on. And I know Rob would rather live on the street than ask him to help out," she added bitterly. "But luckily, you and I don't have that problem, do we, Mum?"

"No, no, of course not." Rosie couldn't concentrate properly. She'd never heard anything about Rob not getting on with his parents before.

"So as I said, you're really our last hope – ours – and Claudia's . . ."

And at the mention of her granddaughter, Rosie actually understood what it felt like to have her heartstrings tugged.

"You saw yourself the size of the back garden," Sophia went on. "Claudia would be in her element out there."

"But it is such a big house, Sophie. Surely you don't need five bedrooms for just the three of you. You'd be lost in a place that size."

There was a brief silence.

A moment later, Sophie cleared her throat. "Well," she said looking sheepish, "I didn't want to say anything, but ... well, Rob and I were talking the other night, and we decided that if we *did* get this house ... well then we'd start thinking seriously about a brother or sister for Claudia."

"Oh." After all the giving-out her daughter did during pregnancy, and especially after childbirth, Rosie would have put her life savings on Sophie *never* having another baby. But wasn't it true what they said, that over time every woman forgets the pain and hardship? And it would be lovely for Claudia to have a little brother or sister, or indeed for Rosie herself to have another grandchild. She smiled, the thought of it all delighting her enormously.

Sensing she had hit the bull's-eye, Sophie sat forward. "So, we were hoping to start trying as soon as we could but, of course, we couldn't even *dream* of it until we were settled in a house of our own – a big enough house of our own and ..." she let the remainder of her sentence trail off.

Rosie exhaled loudly. "Well ... I don't know much about those kind of things," she said, shrugging a little. "Your father was the one who looked after all of that and – "

Sophie almost leapt out of her seat. "Mum, you wouldn't have to do a thing! Rob will sort it all out ... well ... I mean he could help *you* sort it all out!" She looked fit to explode with delight. "But to begin with, we need to have your house valued, you know – just to see how much the bank will lend against it." She smiled conspiratorially. "By my reckoning, it should easily be good for about three hundred and fifty thousand. So then, with your equity guarantee, and what the building society give us, we should be well able to afford this place!"

Her eyes shone happily, and just then Rosie knew that despite her misgivings about what was actually involved, she wouldn't dream of refusing her. Granted, she didn't understand a lot of what Sophie was saying about guarantees and equity and all that, but she was sure Robert would help her get to grips with it all.

And sure, these things were par for the course now too – weren't they always saying it on the News how hard it was for couples to get a foot on the ladder nowadays? In all honesty, it delighted Rosie's heart to think that she'd be able to help her daughter out when she needed her. Wasn't that what parents were for after all?

"Mum, I can't believe it – our very first house!" Sophie enthused, her eyes shining with delight. "Oh, I can't wait to tell Rob!" Quick as you like, she whipped out her tiny mobile phone and pressed a button. "Darling, hi, it's me. Mum's agreed!" She grinned happily, and Rosie couldn't help but grin too. "I know, isn't it fantastic? Yes, well, why don't you phone the estate agent now and get an offer in. Great! Well, look, I'll see you tonight and we'll talk more about it then. Oh and Rob?" she added, giggling girlishly. "Don't forget to pick up some VC on the way, OK? *Ciao!*"

Rosie sat back in her seat, relaxing a little. "You should tell him to get that new Russell Crowe one that's out now," she said, as Sophie put her phone back in her bag. "Myself and Sheila were watching it last week, and I must admit I really enjoyed it. He's a fine cut of a fellow, that Russell Crowe."

"What?" Sophie looked as though her mother had suddenly gone dotty.

"Well, I wasn't trying to listen in or anything," Rosie was embarrassed, "but I couldn't help hearing you tell Robert not to forget to pick up a video on his way home. I just thought that —"

"Oh, Mum!" Sophie burst out laughing.

"What?" Rosie didn't know what was so hilarious.

"Mum, you're a ticket! VC doesn't stand for video, it stands for *Veuve Clicquot!*"

Again Rosie looked blank.

"Champagne?" Sophie supplied helpfully.

"Oh."

"Well, it's not every day a girl gets a chance to bid on a J. Sparks home, and that certainly calls for a glass of bubbly or two, doesn't it?"

"Oh ... oh, I see." For about the third time that day, Rosie wondered if she and her daughter actually inhabited totally different worlds.

"God, Mum, our very own home!" Sophie was still gushing. "I have to admit I really didn't think it would ever happen, and at one stage I was feeling so desperate that I really thought we'd end up raising poor Claudia in that shoe-box we're in now." She smiled winningly. "Mum you are absolute treasure for helping us out like this. You know that, don't you — an absolute treasure!"

"Not at all love," Rosie basked in her daughter's praise, surer than ever that she had made the right decision. "Not at all. And if you can't rely on your parents to get you out of a spot, sure who can you rely on?"

* * *

The next week seemed to go by in a daze. A daze of estate agents, valuations and lots and lots of talk, most of which went completely over Rosie's head.

28

Today, the three of them were on their way to Sophie's solicitor in town, to 'sign everything over'.

Rosie knew she wouldn't understand half of what was going on, but luckily Rob and Sophie were there to fill in the forms. All she'd have to do was sign her name, they'd told her.

Rosie hated filling in forms – it was something that had always overwhelmed her, even back when her eyesight had been perfect. Martin used to laugh at her staunch resistance to even the simplest of paperwork, like writing a cheque, or even a birthday card, but it was all right for Martin, at least he had finished school. Rosie had left school and went out to work when she was fifteen years old, and while she was no by means illiterate, she just wasn't confident enough about her reading and writing abilities to get involved in it all. Martin had always done what was required, so she had little need to get involved.

Anyway, it looked like she was right to be wary – weren't the brats always in the news lately for swindling and overcharging people, and wasn't Rosie better off looking after her own money? The final straw had been when poor old Sheila – or rather Sheila's husband, a builder – had been accused a while back of holding one of those illegal off-shore accounts, and had to pay the taxman a small fortune as a result. The problem was that Jim had been dead for years, Sheila had never known anything about it, and the poor thing had to hand over most of her life-savings to pay the bill.

Now, sitting in this swanky office, in front of an even swankier-looking solicitor, Rosie didn't like all the questions he was firing at her about title deeds and insurance policies and the like. Robert and Sophie sat on either side of her, and although Rosie knew they were sitting like that to make her feel more comfortable, in truth she felt a little stifled.

"So, Mrs Mitchell, you're content to let the building society take a lien on your title deeds in order to fund your daughter's mortgage?"

Rosie blinked.

"Mum, he's simply checking that you're happy doing this, and that you don't have any objections to helping us out."

"Oh, right." Feeling silly, Rosie reddened a little. "Of course I'm happy to do it. I wouldn't be much of a mother if I wasn't, would I?" she said, with a little laugh.

"Great," the solicitor smiled. "But I take it you're aware that if there is any default in repayment, your own property may be at risk of repossession."

"There won't be any default," Sophie interjected sharply, and Rosie looked at her, confused. "He's only letting you know the worst-case scenario, Mum," she soothed. "Don't worry. Rob and I can well afford to make the repayments. The banks are just trying to cover themselves, aren't they, Mr King?"

The solicitor smiled. "Certainly, and I'm sure everything will go very smoothly. However, it is my duty to point out the consequences of what could –"

"It'll be fine," Sophie reiterated, gritting her teeth. "Rob and I have explained everything, haven't we, Mum?"

Rosie smiled nervously. They had tried to explain everything, but again, she hadn't really understood much of it, other than the fact they were 'unbelievably grateful' she was making it possible for them to have 'the house of their dreams'.

"Yes, I'm sure it's all grand," she said, smiling at the solicitor.

"Terrific. Well, all I need now is for you three to sign this little lot –" He pushed a sheaf of papers across the table, and immediately Rosie stiffened. "There you go, Mrs Mitchell," he said, handing her a pen and adding playfully, "We'll let you be the first to sign your life away."

Sophie gave him an irritated look. "As if," she said conspiratorially, rolling her eyes at her mother, and instantly setting Rosie at ease.

The way this fellow was going on, she thought, you'd swear Sophie and Robert were asking for the clothes off her back and not just the deeds to her house! But that was solicitors for you, a pack of scaremongers the lot of them. Rosie scrunched up her eyes, searching for the place she should sign her name.

In all honesty, there was no need to be concerned. Sophie was her daughter, her own flesh and blood. She and Robert wouldn't *dream* of doing anything that would put her home in jeopardy, would they?

CHAPTER 3

June 21st, 5.00pm

Dara Campbell watched with interest as the room fell silent, and the man stood up to speak. She sat forward and took a tiny sip from her glass. This should be interesting.

"Um, thank you all very much for coming here today," the groom began, his voice shaking nervously, his complexion deathly white against his fair hair. "I, ah – really hope you all have a great day."

A pause – a very *long* pause, Dara thought, feeling for him. The room remained silent, and the guests watched him expectantly.

Eventually he spoke again, this time his voice barely audible. "Um, thanks to the hotel for providing this nice food, and ah – thank you all for coming. I hope you have a great day."

Red-faced, he sat down to faint uneasy applause from the guests and, Dara noted, plenty of raised eyebrows.

She could almost read their minds. That was it? They were thinking. That was *all* Mark Russell had to say on a big day like today? On his own wedding day? What about thanking his beautiful bride, or telling some romantic story about how they met, and reiterating how he was the luckiest man in the world to be spending the rest of his life with her? Oh, and not to mention thanking the priest for such a lovely ceremony! Never mind the bride, forgetting the priest was a serious

31

no-no, and by the sour look on the man's face, Dara noted, Fr Deegan wasn't at all impressed to have been overlooked.

But something told Dara that this was all they could reasonably expect today from the anxious groom. The poor thing was so nervous he couldn't even remember his vows throughout the ceremony, let alone the most basic wedding-speech clichés!

"Oh, and before I forget!" Mark again leapt up out of his seat.

Dara could almost hear a collective sigh of relief from everyone in attendance. This mightn't be such a total disaster after all.

"Thanks very much to the bridesmaids!" he spluttered, as if relieved to have something worthwhile to add. "I think you'll all agree that they look, um – they look um, very –" finally the word came to him, "they look very nice!"

There was a short stunned silence, but eventually Mark was rewarded with another bout of weak applause, and a look that would cut diamonds from the bridesmaids, each of whom, Dara knew, had that morning spent two hours at the hairdresser's, another hour at the beautician's, and untold time in front of the mirror to look that 'nice'.

She smiled.

Then, instead of sitting down alongside his bride, the groom slipped away from the table and, moving as fast as his long legs could carry him, headed straight for the bathroom. Incredulous, all eyes in the room followed his every move. Poor thing, Dara thought, shaking her head in mild amusement. Mark wasn't at all used to public speaking, and her heart really went out to him.

Again there was a low murmur, and a slight shuffling amongst the crowd. The best man, a good friend of Mark's, and a man who himself wasn't the best at public speaking, quickly picked up the microphone and tried his best to lighten the mood by reading out some supposedly witty emails from friends.

Listening absently, Dara sat back in her seat and fiddled with a slice of wedding cake. She couldn't help imagining what kind of speech Noah would make, had it been their wedding day.

Confident and utterly charismatic, no doubt he would begin by telling the guests some silly story about the early days of their relationship, before launching into a romantic and heartfelt account of his feelings for Dara – something that would have every woman in the room – and possibly some of the men – in tears.

With a flash of those intense green eyes and just a few simple words, Noah would make each guest feel as though they were taking part in something hugely important – and, she thought with a grin – he'd make doubly sure the bridesmaids were suitably complimented! The word 'nice' just didn't feature in his eloquent vocabulary, and she could only imagine how he'd describe her on the day. Cheesy as it might seem, Noah always had a way of making Dara feel as though she was the most beautiful woman in the world.

And, of course, Noah wouldn't look too bad himself all dressed up in wedding gear, she thought, trying to ignore a slight shiver of desire as she imagined how amazing one of those starched white shirts would look against his tanned skin, or how the tailored jacket would really emphasise those broad shoulders. She sighed inwardly. Yes, he would look utterly incredible.

Still, there was no point in thinking about Noah Morgan at a time like this, Dara told herself. No point at all.

The best man had just finished speaking, and a sharp nudge from Amy on her left brought her thoughts right back to the present.

"I can't believe he said we looked *nice*!" her sister hissed, incredulous. "Nice! What kind of a word is that? Does he not *realise* these dresses are Maria Grachvogel?" Gritting her teeth, she added, "Does he not appreciate how much bloody *effort* it took to fit into them?" Normally a size sixteen, Amy had found it particularly difficult to lose weight for the wedding, and today she'd expected to be suitably commended for her efforts.

"I'll give him 'nice'!" agreed Serena, equally miffed. "Although I suppose we were lucky to get a mention at all. He said nothing about Fr Deegan, and he completely forgot to thank Mum and Dad for welcoming him into the family!"

Dara repositioned the neckline of her dress. "It's not easy to stand up and speak in a roomful of people like that, you know," she said gently. "I think he did quite well, considering."

Amy tut-tutted once more as the three girls watched the groom make his way back to the top table. The best man immediately began teasing him about 'having to make an urgent telephone call' and now the guests were laughing, the early awkwardness having diminished somewhat.

"Well, maybe he *was* a bit nervous," Serena whispered, "but that doesn't give him any excuse to forget about you. I mean, how could he *not* mention you?"

"It doesn't matter, Serena," Dara shushed her as the groom approached, looking somewhat relaxed and much more like his normal self.

Mark took his seat alongside his bride and gave her an apologetic smile. "I'm sorry – I really made a mess of that, didn't I?" he said gently.

"Don't be silly," Dara soothed, smiling back at her new husband. "You were absolutely fine."

* * *

As she and Mark danced their first dance as a married couple, Dara studied the smiling faces of the people around the dance floor – her sisters, her married friends, her mum and dad. It was a little disconcerting to find that, not only did they look pleased and delighted to see her and Mark together, they also looked a damn sight relieved.

Did they know she still had thoughts about Noah, she wondered, panicking a little. Did they know that only just last night she had to talk herself out of pulling out of this wedding altogether?

But no, she thought, irrelevancies like a lost love or pre-wedding nerves wouldn't really matter to most of Dara's friends, or indeed her family. Such nonsense was only the stuff of romantic novels and soppy Hollywood films. No, this was the real world, and in fairness, having turned the dreaded age of thirty-four, Dara should count herself lucky that she had found a man, never mind one who actually wanted to marry her! And even better, a man who didn't seem to mind the fact that she was one of those high-powered career women who'd run rings around you, and unlike most of the married thirty-somethings in this country – and due to the aforementioned high-powered career – had actually been able to afford a home of her own.

But Dara knew well that a guy like Mark would never be threatened by the things that seemed to really bother some of her old friends and her family. Mark loved her independence, he appreciated her work ethic, and understood her better than her oldest friends – most of whom had become decidedly distant in the last few years, when one by one they'd all taken the matrimonial plunge, and she had been the only one who remained stubbornly single. Not to mention the only one who'd remained as attractive as she'd been at eighteen.

With her long dark naturally curly hair, pretty face and curvy figure, Dara was a good friend and all that, but really, when any sane married woman thought about it, she was way too much of a temptation to have around. At least, that's what one of her married friends Clodagh had informed her a while back, after one too many Tia Marias.

And up until today, Dara's single state had been the bane of her mother's life. Hannah Campbell just couldn't understand how a girl as attractive as her oldest daughter couldn't attract a decent man. She and Eddie had begun to despair that there was something seriously wrong with Dara, that maybe God forbid she swung the other way! Of course, they wouldn't dream of mentioning something like that out loud, but privately, each had their own suspicions.

Never once did they suspect that Dara's single state might be self-imposed, and that she might be perfectly happy with everything she'd achieved in life so far. She'd studied for years to become a solicitor, and now worked in a well-respected Dublin law firm. She loved her apartment, a cosy modern duplex situated near Sandycove, boasting fantastic views across Dublin Bay. Luckily she'd bought it early in her career just before the explosion in house prices, and she knew she was sitting on a nice piece of equity. She'd made some good friends in Dublin, and although many of them were married too, they didn't seem to feel the same urgency as those back home in Wexford to get her married off. And then, of course, she had the perpetually single

Ruth, who hadn't been able to come today and, Dara thought wryly, probably wouldn't have come anyway. Her friend, a die-hard romantic, had made no secret of the fact that she seriously disapproved of what was happening today.

For a very long time, Dara had been quite content being single and had no great need or desire to be part of a couple. She conscientiously ignored her mother's loaded remarks and digs about her being 'too independent', and after a while, she learned to laugh off her friends' sympathetic glances and pointed questioning. She knew well that some of them had settled for men they wouldn't normally dream of accepting for fear of being left on the shelf. Some of them had even admitted it.

"He's a nice guy, and there aren't too many of those left these days," one of her oldest friends, Sinead, had told her, shortly after her engagement to the slightly dull but pleasant Nick. "I'm tired of going out to nightclubs and looking for the man of my dreams, Dara. And lately, I've begun to understand that maybe there really is no such thing. Anyway, what's wrong with good old-fashioned fun and companionship? It doesn't all have to be bolts of lightning, you know."

At the time, Dara had been horrified. Surely Sinead wasn't thinking – wasn't *dreaming* of settling? Why would anyone do that? But back then, Dara had been twenty-eight years old, and back then, she still believed in fairytales.

At the time, she had been lucky enough to experience those bolts of lightning, and had found the man of her dreams. OK, perhaps she had made a mistake in letting him slip through her fingers, but as she told herself afterwards, the timing had been all wrong, and they had been a bit too young. But there was no doubt whatsoever in her mind that Noah Morgan was the man she was eventually going to marry, and no matter what the others might say, she knew they'd be together again. All she had to do was wait for him to come back to her.

So until that happened, she'd had no intention of settling for second-best, no intention of wasting her time on other men, none of whom could live up to Noah anyway. Sinead was an idiot for even thinking about marrying someone who didn't make her weak at the knees. Dara would never, ever do that, she was certain of it.

But, she reflected now with a slight sigh, she'd been certain about a lot of things back then. And how wrong had she been?

"Dara, are you OK?" Now Mark was looking at her worriedly. "You seem miles away."

She smiled. "I'm fine," she said, offering up a silent prayer that Mark couldn't read her thoughts just then. Because if he could, her new husband would have discovered that Dara had eventually given up on the fairytale – and, in the end, had little choice but to settle for reality.

CHAPTER 4

"Wow, look at that!" Mark said to his wife a few days later, as awestruck, he tried to take in the extraordinarily all-encompassing sight of Rome's magnificent Colosseum.

It was truly spectacular, Dara had to agree – especially lit up at night like this – and evoked everything noble and majestic that she'd ever imagined about the city's ancient history. The grand amphitheatre stood imposingly at the top of the Via Claudia, and she and Mark stared out of the taxi-cab in wonderment at their very first view of the world-famous landmark.

She had finally made it, she thought, exhilarated at the thought of exploring the city and all the reminders of its glorious past. Having been fascinated by the history and splendour of ancient Rome for as long as she could remember, she had always dreamed of visiting the famous seat of the Empire. And just then, catching sight of another incredible Roman landmark, the Arch of Constantine, she wondered why on earth it had taken her so long to come here.

The answer niggled in the back of her brain. *You know exactly why,* she argued with herself. She hadn't come here before because she'd always thought her first visit would be with –

"Wow!" Typically eloquent, Mark couldn't contain his amazement.

"I mean wow, Dara. I had no idea this place would be so cool!"

Dara had to smile. Yes, it had taken a bit of convincing to persuade her new husband that Rome would be the perfect place in which to spend their honeymoon. She knew he'd had his eye on somewhere more exotic and much more luxurious, like the Caribbean or the Maldives. In fact, it was only when she intimated that they might get tickets for a football game at the Olympic Stadium to watch Roma or Lazio thrash out a pre-season soccer game, that he had been at all enthusiastic.

But from then on in, Rome was the place, and Mark had thrown himself with gusto into finding them a suitable hotel central to all the sights – perfect for the hours of exploring he knew his wife would insist they do. He had no interest in history or ancient sights – as far as he was concerned, if they were gone, what good were they?

"History is grand and all that, but what's in the past is in the past. You can learn from it, but you shouldn't let it dictate the future," he'd said, when Dara had raved exuberantly about Rome's ancient legacies, and the importance of being able to tell Leonardo from Michelangelo.

Still, Mark knew that these things were important to her, and she knew that he would allow himself to be dragged to this museum, and stand for hours staring at paintings in that gallery, as he'd done many times throughout their relationship.

He was like that, though, she thought, smiling affectionately at her new husband, his face animated as he looked excitedly from left to right. Mark was so laid-back, so easy to please and rarely one for confrontation. In fairness, even if the city didn't have a famous football stadium to keep him happy, she was certain he would have gone along with her preference anyway. In Mark Russell's carefree world, the less hassle the better, and Dara didn't think she had ever come across anyone less selfish.

It had been this facet of his personality that had endeared him to her in the first place, she thought, remembering how a mutual friend had introduced them just less than two years before. She hadn't been actively searching for a relationship, and didn't think much would come of it, but Mark was such good fun and so easy to be with, that they sort of 'fell into' a relationship of sorts.

And now here they were, on their honeymoon – and in Rome, of all places.

* * *

A day or two later, Dara was sitting alone drinking espresso outside a small *trattoria* at the Piazza della Rotunda, the afternoon Italian sun gently warming her face.

Mark was back at their hotel room – a charming boutique hotel he'd found not far from the Trevi Fountain – having a well-earned nap. He'd been terrific company so far, and had really enjoyed their visit to the Colosseum and the Roman Forum the day before. In particular, he'd been completely fascinated by the remains of the Circus Maximus – the 300,000-seater stadium in which – the guide informed an impressed Mark – a variety of old Roman competitive sports, including chariot-racing, had been held from the fourth century BC.

He had *not* been impressed however, by the catacombs at San Callisto where they had been led through a series of eerie passageways stacked with thousands of ancient human bones. Dara had found his discomfort amusing – a sports physiotherapist by profession, she had been sure he wouldn't bat an eyelid at the sight, but instead he'd found it all decidedly creepy.

But this morning, the newly-weds had gone to visit the Vatican Museum and the Sistine Chapel, and after the first few hours of wandering around looking at sculptures and paintings, and then standing for ages 'just looking at the ceiling' Mark admitted he'd had enough. "I think it's the crowds that are wearing me down more than anything," he'd said apologetically, before kissing Dara on the forehead and letting her carry on alone with her 'staring'.

Dara had to agree. She knew Rome would be busy – it was, after all, one of the most visited capital cities in the world – but even she had been taken aback by the number of tourists on the 'Dan Brown Trail'; people visiting the sights and locations made even more famous by the

American thriller writer's immensely popular novel. From where she sat, just across from Giacomo della Porta's fountain, with the Pantheon to her right, she could, at that very moment, make out at least three different people studying a copy of the bestseller, and looking up at the Pantheon with delighted interest. Notwithstanding the crowds, she thought it was wonderful that a simple book could get so many people interested in European history and architecture.

Dara had always been interested in history. In school, she'd been fascinated by stories of Egyptian scribes, Roman emperors, and Italian painters and sculptors – much to the anxiety of her mother, who didn't think it right that her eldest daughter should be interested in ancient gladiators and such like, when it would be more in her line to read about princes and princesses and happily ever after.

But Dara found it *all* incredibly romantic, these ancient and glorious accomplishments and exotic languages; she couldn't get enough of it. In class, she loved hearing about the European conquistadors who set off around the world hoping to discover new lands and cultures, and the powerful popes and kings who commissioned beautiful paintings and sculptures that still stood the test of time. Upon visiting the Sistine Chapel that morning and seeing for the first time Michelangelo's famous ceiling fresco above her – still there six hundred years after Pope Julius II first commissioned it – she had been completely awestruck. Mark agreed that it was very nice indeed, but also pointed out that it 'needed a bit of touching up'.

Studious by nature, and having achieved record marks in her school exams, it had been Dara's father who suggested she put her talents to good use, and take up studies in Law or Medicine. She had very much hoped to study the Classics at university, but he had put the kybosh on that notion from the very beginning.

"What would you get from that rubbish?" he'd said at the time. "What kind of living could you make knowing nothing about anything other than all these nancy-boy painters and chippies who are long dead? You need to learn a good trade, Dara, something useful." Eddie Campbell remembered only too well the periods of unemployment this country suffered for over a decade, and if he could help it, no daughter of his would ever have to join that soul-destroying queue to the dole office.

"At least until you get married, pet," her mother added, quickly. If Hannah could help it, no daughter of hers would ever be one of those high-powered career women who had no time for looking after their husbands or raising families.

"But it's what I love, Dad," a teenage Dara had protested, but no-nonsense Eddie wouldn't have it. So, reluctant to go against her dad's wishes, and still herself unsure what she wanted to do with her life, Dara acquiesced. Being rather squeamish by nature, Medicine was out, so she thought that at least if she studied Law, her near-perfect grasp of Latin might stand to her in some way. And despite herself, she found she enjoyed studying the intricacies of the legal system, and her natural work ethic suited all the long hours of poring over old cases and judgements – which really, she supposed, could be considered ancient history of sorts.

So, with typical diligence, Dara settled happily into her chosen career, and put aside her worthy but futile interest in the humanities, at least until Noah Morgan came along.

A bit of a romantic, Noah too seemed to share her fascination with the past, her wonder at the scientists and artists who lived and died for their creative endeavours. While he'd studied English and History in university, he had absolutely no interest in any specific career. He got a job when it suited him, and when it didn't, he simply moved on to the next one. This sustained Noah's main passion in life, which (apart from Dara) was travel.

For Dara, their mutual interest in all things historical was a revelation, and merely increased her assurance that she and Noah had something special, that they were truly on the same wavelength, that they were meant to be together.

But, Dara thought now, as she – a newly married woman – sat in the city that she and the love of her life had sworn they would one day visit together, she had been wrong.

CHAPTER 5

The following Monday morning, Dara waited patiently at the station for the commuter train to Dublin. It was back to reality now, back to work, and Dara supposed – as she eventually boarded the train along with the usual throng – probably back to an earful from Ruth too.

"So, how did the wedding of the year go?" her colleague asked sardonically when Dara arrived at the offices of Cullen & Co Solicitors. Due to her own sister's wedding taking place on the same day, Ruth hadn't been able to attend Dara's, but even if her workmate had been free, Dara didn't think she'd have gone anyway. Ruth knew all about Noah Morgan and, unfortunately for her, knew even more about Dara's hidden – but enduring – feelings for him.

"It was a lovely day – we had a great time," Dara replied mildly, sitting down at her desk with a heavy heart, spotting a high pile of paperwork that threatened to topple over.

Ruth, whose desk was situated parallel with Dara's, swivelled around in her chair to face her. "Best day of your life and all that?"

Dara smiled softly, thinking of Mark's dreadful nerves, her mother's fussing, her sisters' histrionics. "Close enough."

Ruth shook her head. "I still think you sold out," she stated matter-of-factly. "In fact, I *know* you sold out. And I'm disappointed in you."

43

"I did not sell out, Ruth," Dara said through gritted teeth, not wanting to go through all this again – and especially not now. She wished she'd never told her anything. Ruth could be like a dog with a bone sometimes.

"Of course you did. Mark Russell is a lovely guy, but he's not the one for you."

"Who says he's not?"

"You did, dearie. Don't think I've forgotten our little tequila binge many moons ago."

Dara flushed, and idly switched on her PC. "I told you that was just the drink talking. I didn't mean any of it."

Shortly after she and Mark got engaged, Dara had one night, over a bottle of tequila, drunkenly told Ruth all about Noah – her one true love. Stupidly, she'd also confessed that although she loved Mark dearly, he really didn't hold a candle to Noah. A born romantic, but paradoxically pragmatic, Ruth had been horrified.

"Then how can you even *think* of marrying the guy?" she'd asked.

"Well, I love him, but I'm not *in* love with him," Dara had slurred.

"Bullshit! Either you are or you aren't."

"But I am. I like his company, I like his sense of fun, his reliability – "

"Next you're going to tell me he has a nice personality."

"Well, he does."

"But?"

Dara sighed exaggeratedly. "But he's just not Noah."

"Look, Dara," Ruth insisted, "if this Noah was so bloody perfect and the right guy for you, then how come you two aren't still together? What the hell happened?"

"I was an idiot," Dara shook her head ruefully. "It was all my fault. I made a total mess of things."

Ruth got up and poured another shot of tequila. "Tell me everything," she implored. "And start at the very beginning."

Dara did.

* * *

Like most women, Dara had always had a pretty good idea of the kind of man she'd like to meet and fall in love with. He'd be attractive, of course, charming, considerate, funny, and with any luck he'd be also be very romantic. Dara was no extreme feminist; in her eyes a dollop of old-fashioned romance was essential in a relationship. Pulling out chairs, opening doors, all those things made her go weak at the knees, and while it mightn't have been fashionable to admit such a thing in these days of so-called equality, Dara didn't care.

But Noah Morgan ticked all those boxes and more. With intense green eyes, jet-black hair and a smile that could make him a living in Hollywood, Noah was so attractive it should have been illegal. He had the power to make Dara – and quite possibly every other woman within a hundred-mile radius – go completely weak at the knees.

Yet for some reason, he seemed to have taken a fancy to her in return, and from the very first moment they'd laid eyes upon one another, the two of them had been inseparable.

Considering their passionate and romance-filled relationship, they'd met in the least romantic of circumstances. Dara had popped out one evening to buy an emergency packet of tampons in the little shop near her rented flat, and was standing in front of the checkout when she realised she'd come out without her purse. To her utter embarrassment, the fine thing standing behind her insisted on paying on her behalf. Dara had been unable to determine which was more embarrassing: the entire shop knowing her menstrual workings, or Mr Sex-on-Legs seeing her at her worst in baggy track bottoms, no make-up, and greasy, unwashed hair.

But this hadn't deterred Noah Morgan, and when a blushing Dara insisted he walk back to the flat with her so she could repay him, he duly followed and then promptly asked her out. After that, they were rarely apart.

The relationship was fantastic and every day Dara pinched herself, wondering what she'd done to deserve someone like him – someone who was drop-dead gorgeous, but who was also funny, intelligent, *faithful*.

The early days had admittedly been challenging for her – Noah's fun-loving personality, brooding good looks and magnetic appeal to other women being almost too much for Dara to bear. But after a while, after coming to terms with the fact that *she* was the only one he wanted, much of her jealously dissipated.

And Noah was different to most men she'd met in that he was quite unashamedly romantic. He loved grand gestures, and would think nothing of sending a dozen roses to Dara's office on any given weekday, or whisking her away for romantic weekends for no apparent reason. And she'd loved his devil-may-care attitude about work and careers. To him everything was transient, and to Dara this facet of his personality made him all the more enigmatic. Noah had a way of making real life seem so unimportant, had a way of reducing things like career and money to the most mundane.

When it all started to go wrong, they'd been together for as long as she could remember, and at the time Dara was sure they would be together for good.

To this day, she still couldn't figure out why she'd pushed the self-destruct button.

Of course, she could see *why* it happened, but at the time she'd had no idea what she was really doing.

It had all started when Clodagh Thompson, Dara's best friend at the time, became engaged to her boyfriend Simon. The girls were in their late twenties then, and although she and Noah had been together for some time, and shared a flat in Dublin together, before then Dara had never *properly* considered marrying or settling down with him. They were having lots of fun going out weekends with the gang, taking life as it came, just enjoying being together. And because none of the others had gone down the marriage road, it hadn't really been an issue. Because they'd been together for so long, and they were so much in love, somewhere in the back of her mind she'd assumed it would happen eventually. He loved her, she loved him, they were a perfect match, so why *wouldn't* they end up together?

But as Dara became more and more involved in Clodagh's preparations for the wedding, she – almost unconsciously – became more and more interested in the dresses Clodagh tried on, in her choice of wedding cake, the flowers, the hotel – all the fun stuff. Before Dara knew it she'd been bitten by the wedding bug, totally enthralled by the fairytale.

Then, hardly aware that she was doing it, she began dropping tiny wedding-related hints to Noah.

Dara cringed when she thought about it afterwards – how she kept filling him in on every detail of Clodagh's wedding preparations, about how Simon was so looking forward to their buying a house and starting a family.

Before she knew it, she'd somehow got into the habit of picking up bridal magazines with her weekly shopping, and getting estate agent brochures sent to the flat. And then, to top it all off, while on supposedly fun nights out in town, she'd taken to not-so-subtly dragging Noah to jewellery store windows and pointing out expensive diamond rings glittering attractively in the darkness. Within a few months of her best friend's engagement, Dara had turned from a fun, easy-going, take-things-as-they came girlfriend, to a desperate wannabe bride.

Noticing that her best friend was by now on first-name terms with the city's best bridal designers and that her typical topic of discussion was how many high-street shops they'd get through on any given Saturday, Clodagh had no choice but to eventually pass comment.

"Have you and Noah talked about getting married, too?" she asked one day when Dara was at Clodagh and Simon's new house.

"Nope, why?" Dara replied absently, all the while flicking through one of Clodagh's bridal magazines. God, that colour would look amazing on Serena, she thought. With her fabulous sallow skin, Dara's sister could wear any colour she wanted. But it wouldn't look too bad on Amy either – although her younger sister couldn't seem to lose her teenage puppy fat. Hmm, it would be tough to get them to agree really, but –

"Then why do you keep marking pages on my bridal magazines?" Clodagh picked up an article entitled 'Top Ten Beauty Tips for the Big Day'.

Dara shrugged guiltily. "I dunno, I'm just keeping up to date with

47

things – for you. I know you can't do everything, so like any good best friend should, I'm making sure I know as much as I can, so I can help as much as I can." She wouldn't meet her friend's eye. "And I happen to find all this wedding stuff very interesting, you know. Considering I've never really thought about it before and all that."

"Dara," Clodagh began carefully, "I appreciate all your help, you know I do, but if I were you, I wouldn't go on to Noah about how 'interesting' all this is. Simon is bad enough when I talk about it, and he's the one who suggested this wedding in the first place, so if Noah's hearing a lot of it from you –"

"Don't be silly. Noah knows that as your best friend and bridesmaid, I'm just keeping myself informed on the most up-to-date developments, that's all." She lifted her chin defiantly.

"Are you sure?" Clodagh moved across to sit beside her on the couch. "Are you sure that you aren't getting a teeny bit over-involved in all this? Making it a little more personal than you think?"

"What? Of course not! Anyway, I'm sure Noah and I will be getting married eventually, Clodagh. So it's no harm to have some of the groundwork done, is it?"

"The most important groundwork of all is to have a willing groom on the day," Clodagh shot back, and seeing her friend's wounded expression, instantly wished she hadn't. "I'm sorry – I didn't mean that as it sounded. But, men can be a bit funny sometimes," she added quickly.

"Not Noah," Dara insisted. "He knows what I'm like. And I don't think he is one of those funny men you're talking about. I mean, what other guy do you know quotes Shakespeare to his girlfriend when he gets drunk?"

Clodagh laughed. "Maybe you're right. Maybe Noah Morgan is the one guy who *could* take all this wedding talk in his stride!"

But, one evening shortly afterwards, Noah arrived home from work, took one look at Dara, and promptly sat her down for a chat.

"We need to talk," he said gently.

Dara almost burst with optimism. He was going to do it, he was going to propose! He'd finally decided that they were ready to make the move. Fantastic! Did he have the ring with him, she wondered, unable to prevent a grin. He knew how much she loved that oval solitaire, didn't he? The one she'd pointed out that day in Appleby's? Or if not, he could always get that similar, but less expensive one from Fields' – had she shown him that one too? Yes, she was sure she'd mentioned it one time while shopping in town. The only snag was, he'd just started a new job, so she really couldn't expect him to fork out for a big diam–

"Dara, listen to me," Noah was saying, his voice ultra-serious as he lightly caressed her hand.

Oh wow, she thought – knowing Noah, this was going to be *incredibly* romantic! He was so thoughtful, always leaving little love-notes around the place when he was away, always bringing her little presents for no particular reason. His proposal was bound to be spectacular – but why hadn't he taken her to Paris or even Rome for a special occasion like this? Considering how much they wanted to visit …

Still, what did it matter where it happened? It was *happening*, wasn't it?

"Yes, Noah?" Dara squeezed his hand, and looked at him expectantly, the beginnings of tears in her eyes.

Oh, God, she was going to remember this moment for the rest of her life! She was going to remember what she was wearing, what he was wearing – which happened to be a manky sweatshirt and ripped jeans – such a shame he couldn't have dressed up a little. But then again, maybe he'd just been struck by the moment! Maybe it was because she was looking particularly – ahem – bride-like today, dressed as she was in one of Clodagh's 'rejects', which incidentally fitted her like a second skin.

They had been shopping for bridal dresses that day, and the boutique had allowed Clodagh to take the dresses home for a time to try them out with shoes and accessories. Dara had to take them back into town tomorrow, and when Clodagh left she couldn't resist trying on one of the wedding dresses. The dress was low-cut and slinky and Dara, unlike her friend, had the boobs to fill it.

But she definitely wouldn't go for a veil, she decided absently. No a veil wasn't really her thing. Now she couldn't *wait* to get out there and start picking out her own dress – her own style! Clodagh would be thrilled to hear it.

"Dara, I need you to listen to me, to pay attention to what I'm saying," Noah said, and he tugged at her hand a little.

"Sorry, darling, I am listening," she said breathlessly. "Go ahead ..."

Should they have a double wedding? No, no, that wouldn't be fair. Every girl's Big Day was *her* Big Day, and *she* should be the centre of attention. Anyway, Clodagh had most of the arrangements already made, whereas Dara had so much to do! Now, she'd see what Noah had to say, but to her mind, they should probably leave it for another year or so, just until she was fully settled in her new job. After all, she had barely started her solicitor's apprenticeship and –

"Dara, honey, you have to stop this," Noah said gently.

"Stop?" she repeated, confused. "Stop what?" Did he mean stop being his girlfriend and become his fiancée? Well, she would – if he'd just get on with it and ask the all-important question!

"All this trying-on of wedding dresses," Noah went on. "All this talk of engagement rings, and bridal fairs. Not to mention all this pointing out 'romantic' wedding chapels every bloody time we go for a drive!" He seemed to be trying to hold back his irritation. "Dara, I know you're having a great time helping Clodagh with her wedding preparations, but just try and keep in mind that these are not *your* preparations."

Dara felt her throat close over.

"Honey, unlike Clodagh and Simon, I'm not ready to get married. I love you very much and we've always had great fun together, but lately you've turned into somebody else – somebody I don't particularly like spending time with. You're fixated on weddings, weddings and more weddings. It's all you can talk about, and from what I can make out, all you can think about. It's not the kind of thing that keeps a guy interested," he added quietly, his voice full of meaning.

"What are you ... what are you saying?" Dara struggled to get the words out. "Are you saying you don't want to marry me?"

"I'm just saying I don't want to be *forced* into marrying you. I won't be forced into anything. Dara, over the last few months, you've changed from my fun-loving, happy-go-lucky girlfriend into some deranged, desperate Bridezilla." He shook his head. "I don't know what I want any more."

All of sudden, Dara realised how idiotic and pathetic she must look sitting there in one of Clodagh's wedding dresses. Worse, she realised how it must look to Noah. But didn't the sight of her in the dress move him at all? Did it not make him a little emotional seeing her all dressed in white like that? She was so sure that seeing her in the dress would finally convince him to make his move.

"But don't you want to marry me?" she asked again, knowing deep down that she shouldn't be saying it, she shouldn't be pushing it. But she'd been so wrapped up in the idea, so sure that they would end up walking down the aisle that she hadn't been able to think straight. They'd been together forever – they were the perfect couple. There was fun, romance, passion – everything you could want in a relationship, and Dara knew that Noah was the one for her – her Mr Right – so what was the problem?

Until then, Dara had never entertained the possibility that Noah might not feel the same way. Until then, she'd believed their relationship was indestructible.

She was about to find out just how wrong she'd been.

"Dara, I think you and I should take a break," he said quietly, and she felt her heart sink to her stomach.

She tried to speak, but again the words wouldn't come.

"I don't know," Noah went on. "Maybe I'm overreacting, but all this talk of weddings has made me reassess things. Dara, settling down and having a wife and kids is so far away for me at the moment ..." His voice trailed off. "You know I want to travel, see a bit more of the world. I want to experience it all, different cultures, different ways of life. Up until a few months ago, I thought you felt the same."

"But that was before I ..." Dara managed. That was before I fell in love with the fairytale, she finished silently. Before I began to envy Clodagh and Simon and their plans of a life together forever.

51

Somehow, silly things like travel and adventure seemed immature and frivolous – like something a pair of students would do – not two adults who had decent jobs, and should really be saving their hard-earned money for a deposit on a house.

Her head was dizzy, her mind still in shock at his words. 'Take a break?' How could it have gone from planning weddings to taking a break so quickly? What had happened?

But no, no, no, he was just overreacting – so he wasn't quite ready for marriage – then that was fine, she'd just have to wait until he was. Get the travelling out of his system, and then when he'd seen 'the world' he'd be more than happy to settle down for good. All of a sudden, Dara realised the error of her ways.

"Look, I think a break might do us good," Noah was saying. "You know I'm not happy in that stupid job, and I was thinking of taking off somewhere for a while – to Asia or Australia – I've always wanted to see that side of the world."

"I'll go with you!" Dara cried eagerly. It would be perfect. They could go away together, and while they were away she'd convince him that she'd just been going through a phase. She'd lay off on the wedding talk for a while – until their relationship was back on an even keel. Then he might a bit more receptive. She bit her lip. "Now I don't know if work will give me the time off. I haven't been in the job all that long. And then there's my exams." Dara had recently secured a junior solicitor's position at a legal practice in the city centre. "How long do you think we'll need? Two, three weeks at the most I suppose and –"

"I didn't mean a holiday, Dara." By now, Noah was looking at her strangely. "I meant I wanted to go away – really travel. And," he added, pointedly, "I was planning on going on my own."

"On your own?" Dara was horrified. "Why would you want to do that? Won't it be very boring? Not to mention dangerous. I mean, there are always stories in the newspapers about backpackers being stabbed, and murdered and – "

"I didn't mean that. I meant without you," he clarified. "Charlie's coming with me."

"What?" Dara's blood went cold. "You mean you've already planned this?"

He nodded shamefacedly. "Look, over the last few weeks, I've tried so many times to talk to you about this. But you were too busy dropping hints and poring over wedding magazines that you barely noticed I was here, let alone what I was saying."

"Well, for some strange reason, I thought all these years together meant something!" Dara shot back, hating the way he made it all sound so pathetic, made *her* sound so pathetic. "I thought telling someone you loved them, and always wanted to be with them meant something!"

"It did," Noah said, before adding gently, "at the time."

She looked at him, stunned.

"But people change. People start to want different things and move in different directions. Over the last few months, I've come to realise that you and I want totally different things, Dara. You seem to have your heart set on settling down, whereas I'm the complete opposite. I can't see myself doing that for a very long time."

"Then what the hell were you doing with me all this time?" Dara said hoarsely. "Why did you tell me I was the one for you? Why did you keep going on about how lucky we were to find one another, how well suited we were, how you couldn't see yourself with anyone else?"

"I meant every word of that, Dara," he said. "We were well suited, we were lucky to be together, and I did feel that you'd be the one I'd end up spending the rest of my life with."

Dara realised that he was speaking in the past tense. Did all of that mean that his love for her was past tense too? Stupidly, she asked the question.

"Don't you love me any more?"

Noah sat forward and took both of her hands in his. "I do love you. But things have gone a bit weird lately, and I really think we need some time apart. For both our sakes."

"But how much time? If you go off travelling with Charlie, who knows when you'll come back? And when you do decide to come back, what makes you think I'll still be sitting here waiting for you?"

She knew she sounded petulant and childish, but she couldn't help it.

"That'll be up to you," he said.

But something in the way he said it made Dara decide he didn't really care one way or the other. With that, she went on the defensive.

"Well, go then, Noah Morgan! Go off on your big round-the-world trip! Go to Asia and India and wherever you like! You can go to bloody hell, as far as I'm concerned!"

It seemed Noah had also reached the end of his tether. "Fine!" he countered. "I will! To be honest, anywhere would be preferable to sitting here listening to you going on and on about bloody wedding bands, and 'dinky invitations'!" he mimicked cruelly. "Jesus, Dara, you should hear yourself sometimes. These days, you've turned into a bloody psycho!"

"A psycho!" she countered. "A psycho! Well, now that I think of it, perhaps you're right! Maybe I *am* a psycho, because only a psycho would put up with someone like you, Noah Morgan. Someone who after three years of a bloody good relationship could just up and leave like that. Someone who says 'Oooh, I want to take a break, Dara! I feel trapped, Dara!' You never had any problems being trapped when it suited you though, did you?" she accused angrily. "You never had any problems being trapped when you decided to quit yet another job that didn't suit, and your *psycho* girlfriend had to pay your rent for you, did you?"

With that, Noah picked up his coat and headed for the door. "Talk to me when the rant is over, Dara," he said caustically and then, giving her a final appraisal in her wedding dress, told her. "Talk to me when the Dara I fell in love with comes back."

With that, Noah slammed the door behind him.

For a very long time afterwards, Dara sat on the couch, stunned and defeated, hot salty tears running down her cheeks, and staining the delicate satin of her 'borrowed' wedding dress.

CHAPTER 6

"So, what happened then?" Ruth asked, hiccuping slightly when Dara had finished recounting her mortifyingly embarrassing 'Bridezilla' story. Although, she had to admit, the ensuing years (and the few tequilas) had dulled the humiliation somewhat.

"What?"

"Well, surely that wasn't the end of it," Ruth went on. "I mean, if the two of you had such a brilliant relationship, then surely you had it all out properly before Noah went away."

Dara shook her head. "Not really."

Notwithstanding the fact that she'd been ashamed and embarrassed by her behaviour, Dara was also incredibly hurt by Noah's rejection of her – his rejection of a real future together. "He phoned a few times and left messages with Clodagh, but I didn't want to talk to him." She sighed. "I was playing mind games I suppose, stupidly thinking that if he knew how upset and hurt I was, he might not go away." When Ruth made a face, she tried to explain. "I know, I know, it sounds pathetic and incredibly childish. But our relationship was a bit like that. More often than not, my little sulks and tantrums worked because Noah normally hated arguing with me." She smiled, remembering. "He was always the one to give in and be peacemaker.

Stupidly, I presumed the same thing would happen then."

"But he didn't give in," Ruth finished.

"No, not that time. As I said, he did try and contact me, saying things like 'I don't want to part on bad terms', things like that, but I didn't want to hear it. And up until a week or two after he left, I was still convinced he'd come back to me."

She shook her head sadly. "About six weeks into his travels, he sent me a letter, basically saying that he'd forever treasure our time together, and it was a shame it had to end badly."

Ruth sighed dreamily. "I can see now why you're kicking yourself – he *does* sound perfect."

"He was," Dara said quietly, "but I was an idiot."

"But that was what, ages ago? Surely, you've seen him since? Surely he's come home since?"

Dara shook her head. "I can't be sure, but I don't think so."

"He never returned at all? For Christmas, holidays – nothing?"

"Not that I know of. And given his circumstances after that I doubt it," she added cryptically.

"So what happened?" Ruth implored. "Why did he stay away? Or *did* he get kidnapped or stabbed or … Sorry," she added quickly, when Dara glared at her. "Seriously, what *happened*?"

Dara shrugged. "He just settled elsewhere."

"Look, you said that letting him go was the biggest mistake of your life. Well, for someone who made such a big mistake, you didn't exactly bust your backside trying to rectify it, did you? When you finally came to your senses or should I say – when you finally *grew up* – sorry –" she gave Dara a winning smile, "why didn't you go after him – or try and contact him – *something*?"

Dara sighed. "It was too late by then."

"But why?"

Then Dara told her how, upon finally realising that she had made a huge mistake, she'd tried to find some way of contacting him, perhaps an address, mobile phone number, email address – anything.

She'd made a few cautious enquiries of Noah's parents and discovered that he was still travelling, but as far as they were aware, perfectly fine. He was by then nearly six months into his travels and 'probably in the middle of the Outback somewhere', his mother had told her, and apparently they hadn't heard too much from him recently.

"And did he say when he'd be back?" she asked, trying to keep her voice neutral, not wanting to push it. It was obvious by Carol Morgan's clipped tones on the other end of the telephone that she wasn't going to give Dara too much information. Noah's mother obviously had some idea of the reason they'd split, and she probably didn't want this desperate madwoman following her son halfway across the world, trying to get a ring on his finger. It had been mortifying, but Dara had to know.

"He's staying away for another six months – probably longer – that's all I know."

"Oh." Dara was disappointed. She'd hoped a year away travelling had meant just that.

So, for the time being, she told Ruth, she could do nothing other than simply wait for his return. She couldn't follow him, as she didn't know where in the world he might be – she couldn't contact him, because according to Carol Morgan, he didn't stay in any one place long enough to have a base.

In the meantime, she got on with her life, she worked long hours at her new job, saw some of her friends get engaged, and a few of them get married, while all the time her mothers' spinster-related comments got louder and more annoying. But Dara had no interest in going out with other men and wasting her time and theirs, when she knew in her heart and soul that Noah was The One for her. She just hoped that when he did eventually come back, he'd feel the same way. It was a hell of a chance to take, but what else could she do?

But when a further year passed, Dara began to get tired of waiting for his return and decided to take matters into her own hands. If his mother wouldn't help her, then she'd find a way round it. She'd find some way of contacting Noah.

One day she hit on the idea of running his name through the Google search engine, hoping to find an email address or perhaps some mention of him. Yes, it was a very long shot but it was worth a try. And there couldn't be *that* many Noah Morgans in the world, could there?

She was wrong. There were hundreds of them, most of them American – and Dara spent ages trawling through pages and pages of links, trying to find some mention of a Noah Morgan from Ireland. Eventually, she narrowed the search terms by including the words 'Ireland' and 'Irish'. *Duh!*

Seconds later, a list of links popped up. Great! Dara thought, optimistically. She'd was bound to find something here …

But as Dara read down through the links, one about halfway down the page knocked her for six.

'*Maria Brown from Manchester, pictured at The Spanish Steps with her Irish groom,* **Noah Morgan**.'

As if in a daze, she clicked onto this link, and almost immediately the website of some company – some online *wedding* company – appeared onscreen.

'*Paradise Weddings . . . your dream wedding abroad . . . beach weddings, themed weddings, romantic weddings in paradise. Let us know your requirements and we'll help make the dream come true,*' read the website description. The link featuring Noah and this – this *Maria,* was under their 'Recent Clients' section.

Dara's heart was already racing, but it almost stopped as she studied the faces in the accompanying picture. The full graphic took a while to download, but there was no mistaking the face, no mistaking that square jaw, that lovely smile and those extraordinary green eyes. There he was, all tanned and even more gorgeous than she remembered, standing with this – this strange woman on The Spanish Steps. It was her Noah all right.

And he was married.

Not only that, but he was married in Rome, in Italy – in *their* place. Dara couldn't comprehend the sense of unbearable disappointment and defeat she felt at that very moment. It was as though her entire world, all her wonderful memories of the past, all her optimistic hopes and dreams for the future had come crashing down all at once.

There he was, the love of her life, the man of her dreams – but now he was married to someone else.

And it was all her own stupid fault.

* * *

"So, what did you do?" Ruth poured another shot of tequila. "Did you just give up?"

"Of course!" Dara cried. "What else *could* I do? While I was sitting at home, stupidly thinking he'd come back to me, convinced we were meant to be together, he'd met and married someone else! So, I just had to come to terms with that."

In the weeks and months that followed, she tried her very best to deal with it, to put it behind her and move on, but stupidly, a small part of her clung to the idea that she and Noah were meant to be. How could he have fallen for someone else so quickly, when only a year earlier he'd repeatedly told Dara that there would never be anyone else for him?

She remembered thinking then that there had to have been something – something else – that would make him marry that girl and forget all about her. Was he on the rebound, perhaps?

But no, she decided then, that was just wishful thinking, and she was clutching at straws. Maybe Noah really did love this Maria person, maybe she made him happy and loved him the way he deserved. And, unlike Dara, maybe she knew a good thing when she saw it.

After that, she heard nothing more from or about Noah Morgan. In truth, she didn't want to know more, she knew her heart couldn't take it. Noah was gone – gone for good. And Dara had to come to terms with the fact that she'd had her chance. From that day onwards, Dara gave up on the notion of the perfect man, from then on in she began to understand what Sinead and Nuala and her other thirty-something friends were saying. Maybe there was no such thing as the right guy, the perfect other half – it was simply the stuff of fairytales, and Hollywood chick-flicks.

Maybe the best any girl could hope for was a kind, decent, reliable man – someone like Mark Russell.

"It's as close to true love as I'll ever get now," she'd tried to explain to Ruth that night.

But Ruth wasn't having any of it. "That's a pile of crap and you know it. So what if the Noah thing didn't work out? That doesn't mean it was your only shot at it."

Dara looked at her as though she was mad. "You don't know how it was. There could never be anybody else like that, anybody else like him. What we had was special and …" she shrugged, "I fucked up."

"So instead you just go and settle for the first guy that looks at you?"

"That's not how it happened. And I'm not settling, I'm just – "

"You *are* settling. You said yourself that Mark's a nice enough guy but there are no sparks – no bolts of lightning."

"Did I say that?"

"Yes, you did. But didn't you ever stop to think that maybe *Mark* deserves something more? That he deserves a woman who loves him honestly and completely and who doesn't go around telling people how 'reliable' he is?"

Dara grew quiet. "I have thought about that."

"And?"

"And I tried to explain my feelings to Mark before, when we first met. I tried to explain that I'd been hurt by somebody – somebody I cared a lot about. But he understood."

"He did?"

Dara nodded. "He said of *course* my feelings for him would be different. If I'd been hurt in the past then it was only natural I'd be a bit cautious about him. He reckons that anyone our age is bound to bring a certain amount of baggage into a new relationship."

"So he knows he's second string, then?"

"He's not second string, Ruth," she sighed. "I do love him. It's just … it's just not the same as it was with Noah, that's all. Mark makes me happy, and although it's different, it's still good. With him everything is simpler, steadier and there are no surprises." She thought about it for a moment. "With him I feel … safe."

"'Safe'?" Ruth repeated, her brow furrowing. "And do you think that feeling safe is enough of a basis for marriage? For both of you?"

"I'm not sure," Dara answered truthfully. "But I certainly hope so."

* * *

Thinking back on it now, as she began opening her work mail, Dara supposed that her decision to settle for Mark had to do with a number of things other than just giving up on Noah.

But no, it wasn't really 'settling', she corrected herself quickly. Settling was the wrong word. It implied things like 'desperate', and Dara hadn't been remotely desperate. At that stage, she was just tired. Tired of waiting for happily ever after, tired of wondering if the elusive 'One' would ever come along. And finally realising, that perhaps he had – and what had she done? Only gone and lost him!

Second and third choices were there for a very good reason, she told herself. When deciding on a university place – essentially deciding on a career – it was mandatory to include a second or third choice if the first choice wasn't to be, wasn't it? So, surely, the same applied in other instances in life?

Surely it wasn't all hearts and roses, boy meets girl and lives happily ever after, was it? What if – like in her case – the timing was all wrong? Boy did meet girl, but girl went a bit mad for a bit, they took a break, and boy went on to live happily ever after with someone else. How did the Hollywood scriptwriters deal with that scenario, she wondered.

So, when she hit her thirties, and her mother started making loaded comments about 'eating dinner out of cartons' in front of the telly at weekends (which was in fact true), Dara started to think seriously about where she was going with her life.

Were the great job and the fancy apartment enough? Would the nights out with the girls – what single ones were left, that is – keep her going for the rest of her days? Was female friendship and companionship enough? Did a girl really need something to come home to at the end of every day? Something other than the cat?

In the years immediately following Noah's departure, Dara tried not to analyse it too much. Anyway, she was having too much fun enjoying life to think seriously about it. Yes, she'd had her perfect man but she'd lost him. She'd get over it. She'd messed up, she knew that, but it wasn't the end of the world. There would be other men.

And there were – lots of them. But none of them came close to Noah. There wasn't the same sparkle, the same fun, the same attraction. The men she met were bland and superficial in comparison.

And soon, everyone else's reaction to Dara's single state began to get on her nerves. All the loaded remarks from her family, the not-so-subtle questioning from her married friends, the whispering behind her back. The way they went on, you'd swear that hitting the age of thirty without a man was something to be ashamed of!

"I know what you're doing," Serena informed her one day over lunch, after Dara's latest romance had gone by the wayside. "You're still waiting around for someone to live up to *him*, aren't you?" Her younger sister sat forward. "Dara, someone like that doesn't exist, not outside your mind anyway. So you have to let go and start looking for someone who makes you happy, and who you make happy in return. It doesn't all have to be hearts and flowers and weak-at-the-knees stuff. If you just forget about your high standards, then you might be in with some chance of finding a guy that'll live up to bloody Noah Morgan!"

But Serena was wrong. Dara didn't have high standards, or any standards at all – no measurement existed that could live up to Noah.

Eventually though, she did begin to wonder. If it had been so easy for Noah to move on and forget about her, so easy for him to live his life with somebody else, despite what they'd had, then maybe she too should think about moving on.

So when Mark with his boundless optimism and happy-go-lucky personality began to take a determined interest in her, Dara left herself open to the possibility of a real future with him. She couldn't go wrong, could she? He was respectful, warm-hearted, reliable … an all-round nice guy, who she knew instinctively would never let her down.

No, he didn't have the same animal magnetism that Noah did, but you couldn't have everything.

So was her sister right after all? Was that enough? Could she go through life without the passion and romance that fuelled her relationship with Noah? Did she need the grand gestures, the fiery arguments, the overwhelming feeling of wanting to be near him all the time, of being lost without him?

Perhaps not.

With Mark, well, they had fun, they shared a few interests, they had a similar outlook, and she knew that she could trust him implicitly. Again, there was no great passion, no sense of overwhelming desire, but it was better than nothing, wasn't it?

"What? What planet are you on?" Ruth had almost taken her head off, when one day at work, Dara had innocently aired her feelings on the subject.

Both manless for long spells, the two girls spent many hours bemoaning their single state, and many more hours trying to do something about it. At the time, Dara hadn't been seeing Mark all that long and Ruth knew nothing of her still-lingering feelings for Noah. All Ruth knew back then was that Dara had been in a serious relationship a few years back, but it had ended badly.

"'Any man is better than no man?'" Ruth cried. "Have you been so brainwashed by that backward family of yours, that you now feel subhuman just because you're not married?"

Dara smiled. Ruth had an endearing tendency to overstate things at times. "Look," she began, "you and I both know that this so-called independent-women thing – in this country anyway – is a complete cod. It's all a big cover-up. Yes, we can earn our own money, buy our own houses, and change our own spare wheels, but no matter what way you look at it, deep down we're all still judged by whether or not we have a man at our side."

"Speak for yourself," Ruth said huffily.

"Look, we all grew up on the Prince Charming fairytales – we all believed our 'special someone' was out there, didn't we?" Dara shrugged her shoulders. "All I'm saying is that maybe in real life, that's not the way it works."

"But I still believe that!" Ruth cried. "Otherwise, I've wasted years waiting for the perfect man, waiting for the perfect relationship when many times over I could have settled for less. I've given up on relationships that were good, but not great – because all the time I was sure there was something better – do you know what I mean?"

Dara knew. Except for her, things had worked in reverse. She'd had the perfect man from the very beginning, and it was only recently that she'd experienced the 'good, but not great' phenomenon. "Look, all I'm saying is that lately I'm getting tired of being the odd one out. I look at my friends and even my younger sisters are paired off." Amy and Serena both had serious boyfriends. "So eventually you start to wonder, why isn't it happening to me? What's wrong with me that I haven't found my special someone? And soon, you begin to feel lonely and vulnerable and a bit … worthless. And the only thing that'll solve that problem for you is a man – any man." She sipped her coffee. "I'm sure it happens all the time. People get tired of looking, tired of waiting for the perfect man. Maybe he doesn't really exist, Ruth. Maybe it's all a big lie – yet another occasion dreamt up by the Hallmark Greeting Card Corporation."

"Now I'm depressed," Ruth said, meaning it.

Dara laughed. "I didn't mean to depress you, but what I'm saying is that perhaps what I've got with Mark Russell now is enough. I had my Prince Charming and I lost him. I don't think there's another one out there, so maybe I should just cut my losses and get on with my life."

"But what if that guy wasn't really him?"

"What?"

"The thought's never even crossed your mind, has it?" Ruth said, shaking her head. "And I think this could be part of the problem." She looked at Dara meaningfully. "What if that old boyfriend you're talking about wasn't really The One – the man of your dreams? What if you got it all wrong?"

Dara said nothing. She didn't even want to consider that prospect.

"Life works in mysterious ways, that's all I'm saying." Ruth sat back and folded her arms across her chest. "So if you settle for nice, reliable Mark in the meantime, then you're not just cutting your losses, you're also obliterating your gains."

"Spoken like a true woman of the law!" Dara said, lightening the mood, and immediately discounting everything her friend had to say.

Mark was a good guy, and perhaps they would be very happy together. All Dara had to do now was convince Ruth of that fact, and everything would work out just fine.

CHAPTER 7

June 21st, 11.50 am

Louise stared at the passport photograph for a very long moment, wondering why the face looked so familiar. She knew this guy from somewhere, didn't she?

Then again, she thought, setting the document back down and fiddling with a strand of blonde hair, didn't she *always* think she recognised the people from this particular file? It was just one of those strange things, that was all.

"You're too sentimental," her mother used to say, and Louise knew she was right. She *was* too sentimental – and, by rights, she should feel nothing other than detached sympathy for the names on the photocopied passports that crossed her desk from month to month. But instead, she always felt incredibly sorry for them.

She did a quick search on the individual's name through the computer, but nothing came up, no account information, no outstanding lending, nothing. This guy wasn't one of theirs then. With a short sigh, Louise ticked off his name, and went onto the next name on the list. Right from the very beginning of her job here, she'd found it difficult to probe into a newly deceased person's financial affairs – there was something slightly tawdry about it. But probate investigations were not only part of the job, but also necessary by law,

66

and every financial institution in the country, including Advanced Credit Services had to co-operate.

But Louise still hated the idea.

She felt a slight rumbling in her tummy and looked up the clock. Almost twelve o'clock and she was due to go to lunch at one. With the way she was feeling today, she'd love to break out and have a nice bar of chocolate or a packet of crisps, but no, those days were well and truly over. A girl had to make sacrifices to stay a size eight and, boy, did Louise make those sacrifices!

Speaking of passport photographs, she really should get some new ones done. Her passport would be out of date soon anyway, and it would be nice to have a new glamorous and thin photograph of herself, instead of the podgy-faced eleven-stone person that was on it at the moment.

She smiled. She'd definitely have to get her passport sorted if she was going to go on that big Christmas shopping trip to New York the girls were planning in December. That would be great fun. Louise had always wanted to visit New York – it seemed like such a glamorous, lively place. Still, she thought with a faint unease, if she wanted to go she would have to cut down on the late nights for a while, otherwise her finances wouldn't get her as far as Kildare!

"Louise!" Fiona's head appeared above the partition of Louise's work cubicle. "Guess what? Jigsaw are having a twenty-per-cent-off sale – today only! Let's grab something from a deli and go straight down there at lunch-time – what do you think?"

Fiona's dark eyes shone with exhilaration, and Louise knew why. Jigsaw had a fantastic range this season.

Despite herself, she was tempted. She'd love to go clothes shopping. "I don't know, Fiona, the finances are a bit low this month and – "

"But you don't have to buy anything if you don't want to, do you?" Fiona teased, knowing full well that on Grafton Street, this was almost impossible. "But I really need something new – I've nothing for Thursday night. What are you wearing by the way?"

"Thursday night?" Louise looked blank.

"The hen night? Don't tell me you'd forgotten about it?"

Shit, yes, Louise *had* forgotten about that. And she really wished Fiona hadn't reminded her because yet another night out on the town drinking apple martinis and champagne cocktails with the girls – never mind the clubbing afterwards – was really going to put a massive dent in her finances.

"You *did* forget, didn't you?" Fiona laughed at her workmate's expression. "Better not tell Gemma that – she'd be very upset!" Gemma was another work friend who was getting married soon. But the get-together Thursday night was only a precursor to the main event at the weekend – a four-night hen *weekend* in Marbella.

Louise was really looking forward to that, and as she didn't know Gemma all that well, was especially pleased to have been asked. So, as an invited guest, it would be very rude of her to duck out of the *pre-*hen night, wouldn't it? And knowing the girls, who spent cash like it was going out of fashion, all this was really going to cost her a fortune. Louise did a quick mental calculation – she'd already paid for the tickets to Spain and the hotel, so all she needed was enough for drinks and food and then, she remembered, her stomach turning ... then there was the outlay for attending Gemma's wedding.

"Sorry, Fiona," Louise said with as much firmness as she could muster, all the time knowing that her friend would not be impressed. "I'd love to go shopping with you at lunch-time, but I really am strapped for cash."

Fiona's animated expression changed immediately. "I really don't know *what* you do with your money, Louise Patterson," she said huffily. "You get paid the same as the rest of us, and *we* all manage fine, so where does all the money go? Anyone would think you had gambling debts or something!"

With that Fiona turned on her heel and marched back towards her own cubicle at the top of the room.

For a long moment, Louise stared unseeingly at her computer monitor, her mind going over Fiona's last comment. Her friend wouldn't fall out with her over something as simple as not going shopping, would she? Though Louise supposed she was lucky that Fiona was her friend at all – it wasn't all that long ago that someone like Fiona wouldn't look twice at her. So, she really should count herself lucky that she had a friend in Fiona, because without friends, what else did she have?

"Fiona, wait!" Louise stood up and called after her. "I'm going with you. Meet you at the escalators at one?"

Fiona swung around and her features broke into a large smile as, walking backwards, she nodded. "Good woman!"

Sitting back down at her desk, Louise took a deep breath and allowed herself a little smile. To hell with her finances! She'd go shopping at lunch-time and if she saw something she liked, well, she'd go and buy it. And if, with all that was happening over the next few weeks, her finances got out of hand, well, she could always just top up her loan, couldn't she? After all, she worked in the right place for that!

Yes, Louise decided, trying to push the guilty thoughts that were threatening completely out of her mind. So what if she was in debt? Life was too short for worrying about something as stupid and inconsequential as money, wasn't it? Of course it was – way too short. Something she herself knew only too well.

* * *

It had happened almost three years before, shortly after Louise's twenty-first birthday, and well before she moved to Dublin.

Still attending university, she'd been living at home in Cork at the time, and one evening she was on her way home from her part-time job in Roches, the busy city centre department store. It was getting close to Christmas, so late-night shopping was in full swing, and while Louise didn't usually work late nights, the overtime rate was great, and the additional cash would be much needed to pay for Christmas presents and the like.

The evening was dark, cold and wet and Louise didn't remember much other than standing shivering at the lights at Patrick Street Bridge, while waiting for the red pedestrian light to change to green. Her sister Heather was duty manager in the Metropole, a popular hotel on the other side of the river, and was also due to finish work shortly. So, that evening, instead of having to wait in the cold for a bus out to the suburbs, Louise would be getting a lift home in her sister's ancient – but warm – car. She couldn't wait.

The pedestrian light finally changed to green, and stupidly – she remembered thinking afterwards – without looking, she immediately stepped out onto the road.

Right into the path of a speeding car.

The next thing she remembered was waking up in Cork University Hospital, bound up and in traction, Heather's earnest and worried face looking down at her. Heather was Louise's only sister and her only remaining family member – the girls having lost both parents to cancer in Heather's late teens. Roger had gone first and Bridget – her illness greatly exacerbated by her husband's death – had died a year later.

"You're awake!" Heather cried in relief, and went to embrace her. But Louise was too full of morphine to even sense her older sister's touch, let alone understand what had happened to her.

Apparently she had broken an arm, fractured her hip and thigh 'with a shattered fibula thrown in for good measure,' the doctor explained. The driver, a Dublin businessman in an apparent hurry (and with a few drinks in him) had failed to stop at the red light, and had thrown Louise five feet into the air.

This had resulted in a two-month stay in the hospital for Louise, but as the driver had been charged with drunk and dangerous driving, the insurance company very quickly paid out a sum to go towards her hospital bills. While the guy had admitted liability, what had really hurt Louise was the lack of an apology or even a simple 'get well' card from him. Apparently, he was such an important man that he wanted the episode dealt with as quickly as possible, and had little time for such pleasantries.

At the time though, Louise was in college at UCC and was barely scraping by on her part-time wages, so the insurance payout had been a godsend. Heather, although doing well in her chosen hospitality career, had also been unable to contribute much to her sister's hospital

70

and rehabilitation bills, so they were both grateful the insurance company had paid out so soon. Additionally, Heather was due to get married in the New Year, and had postponed her big day as a result of Louise's prolonged hospital stay.

What the girls hadn't bargained on, though, were some additional complications – namely a recurring back injury, some ten months after the crash. Louise needed further rehabilitation, and much to her disappointment, was deemed by the doctors to be unable to continue with her Physical Education degree in college.

As the insurance company had already contributed to her initial hospital bills, Louise had no choice but to take on a large Credit Union loan to pay for her additional medical costs. At twenty-two, personal health insurance was the last thing on Louise's mind, and much as it bothered her, she eventually agreed to Heather's tentative suggestion that they sell the family home to help make the repayments. The decision was greatly helped by the fact that Heather had in the meantime married her Welsh boyfriend of three years, and was then making plans to move to Cardiff with him.

So, denied of her initial choice as a result of her injuries, Louise set about finding herself another career. Although she was greatly tempted to stay in Cork where all her friends were, she found that due to her back injury in particular, potential work choices were limited. Then, when she was offered what seemed like a most attractive opportunity to work flexible hours at a new Dublin company, Advanced Credit Services, Louise found she really couldn't turn it down. Also, after the difficulties she'd had recently, the idea of packing up and starting afresh in another city – as Heather was doing – appealed to her enormously.

So, Louise, no longer quite as bashed, but still a little bruised, moved to Dublin to start her new job and her new life, leaving her home town – and, she hoped, her recent run of rotten luck – far behind.

CHAPTER 8

That Thursday night after work, Louise went out with the girls to celebrate Gemma's forthcoming nuptials. She was sitting with the others, enjoying her drink and minding her own business, when someone caught her eye.

Someone who was really, really cute and who was looking at ... was he looking at *her*? Louise wasn't sure.

It was a bit weird. Usually when they were out on the town, the good-looking lads nearly always made a beeline for Fiona, her long shiny almost jet-black hair, exotic looks and pretty heart-shaped face making her stand out from the rest of the girls – especially Louise, who was at *least* a stone overweight and ... No, Louise admonished herself quickly, you must stop thinking like that. You are no longer the overweight one here – in fact, according to your beloved sister, you are least half a stone *under*weight for your height.

Of course, when she'd had all those additional problems after her accident, her weight had dropped off considerably, although not enough to make a major difference. But the bits that *had* dropped off made Louise doubly determined never ever to let them back on again.

It wasn't very pleasant being overweight, really. When she'd moved to Dublin at first she had very little self-confidence (not that she'd had much to start with, she thought wryly), few friends, and practically no social life. In the beginning, she'd convinced herself she didn't mind really; after all, she was happy enough as she was getting her little bedsit in Rathgar decorated, and settling into her new life, so the lack of company didn't matter too much.

It was only after a few months living in Dublin and working at ACS that she realised she didn't really know anyone. So much for her great new life!

So, in order to get out and about and try to stop herself from feeling lonely, when the bright evenings came in, Louise began to go out after work for long walks around the area. It made her feel great. There was always lots of life around the place and, for once, Louise felt as though she was really part of it.

After that, when the evenings weren't so bright, she got a bit braver and decided to join a gym. Not one of those trendy, noisy spots that looked like a nightclub, though – Louise wouldn't feel at all comfortable in one of those. No, she joined a small, old-fashioned-type place, which was really more for the locals – a place with only a handful of treadmills and not a stepper in sight. Thankfully, Louise's gym didn't have any of those *He-Man Master of the Universe* types looking over your shoulder, and banging on about your fat-to-muscle ratio either. No, in her gym, nobody looked over your shoulder unless they wanted you to hurry up and get off the place's only shaggin' treadmill so *they* could have a go.

So that was how Louise almost overnight (it took her months overall, but overnight sounded better) went from twelve and a half stone down to nine and a half stone, which for someone as tall as Louise made a hell of a lot of difference – in more ways than one.

Despite the fact that she had that huge loan for the hospital bills hanging over her head, she couldn't resist going out and buying clothes that she had never in a million years believed she would ever wear. Things like halter-neck tops (the bulgy arms were gone), satin pencil skirts (the bulgy thighs too) and, although it was only a short mad phase, belly tops (self-explanatory).

But after a while she developed taste, and although it took her absolutely ages to pluck up the courage to go into those lovely boutiques in the Georges St Arcade – the lovely fancy ones where the shop assistants asked, "Hello, can I help you with anything?" instead of just narkily nudging you out of the way like they did in the shopping centres. Once she did that, Louise really didn't look back. She had a bit of an eye, not so much for fashion, but for what suited her. Why else were the girls at work constantly complimenting her clothes and trying to find out where she 'picked up these *fabulously* original pieces'?

Fiona O'Neill, the office's self-proclaimed fashionista, seemed particularly interested and one day Louise suggested taking her shopping – well, in retrospect, Fiona had *insisted* Louise take her shopping – but that wasn't the point.

From then on in, she and Fiona became firm friends, and they went shopping … oh, about every week or so. No, Louise thought biting her lip, they went shopping … oh, about every *day* or so.

Working just off Stephen's Green, so close to the shopping Mecca that was Grafton Street didn't help. And then of course they'd booked that shopping weekend to New York, which was coming up soon. God, Louise wondered then, as friends did she and Fiona do anything else *but* shop?

Still, she couldn't help it. And although Fiona could be a little bit bossy sometimes, she was great fun, and if it weren't for her, Louise wouldn't have much of a social life. And she certainly wouldn't be invited on girlie nights out or to Gemma's hen weekend, her wedding or indeed tonight to her pre-hen night.

Louise gave another quick look to where your man was standing on the other side of the room. He seemed to be on his own, which was usually a very bad sign – namely one that proclaimed weirdo, as Fiona would say.

But it wasn't all that long ago that Louise had been on her own, only she didn't have the confidence to go out to pubs on her own, much as she was often tempted. But it was easier for men to get away with that kind of thing, wasn't it?

Anyway, she really wished he'd stop staring at her like that; it was becoming a little scary and she was beginning to wonder what on earth was wrong. Why didn't he stare at Fiona, who looked fantastic tonight in her purple sequinned top and skinny blue jeans, both of which she'd bought in the Jigsaw sale the other day.

Louise wasn't going to, but Fiona had persuaded her to buy the multicoloured wrap dress she had on tonight, and while it was expensive – even for a sale – she had to admit it was a lovely fit and she'd probably get great wear out of it. She bit her lip – after spending nearly two hundred euro on it, she'd want to.

Just then, the bride-to-be or 'The Hen', as she insisted being called tonight – so much so that she wore a huge sticker proudly proclaiming same – poked Louise hard in the ribs. Louise wore a much smaller sticker announcing that she was a 'Hen-Nighter'. Which wasn't strictly true actually seeing as –

"Your shout, Louise! Most of us are dry," Gemma declared, waving a glass in front of her. The others looked at Louise expectantly, empty glasses all round.

Now, Louise wouldn't really mind, but there had initially only been seven girls here when they met up first, but since then, five more had joined the party. So was she also expected to buy –

"Bellinis again – for everyone?" she enquired, hoping that the others might let her off the hook, or if not, at least ask for something less expensive. But her heart sank when everyone with the exception of Fiona (who gave her a sympathetic wince) nodded energetically. Louise loved champagne cocktails as much as the next girl, but what would *twelve* of them cost – especially here!

Oh stop it, she admonished herself as she got up out of her seat. Don't be so bloody stingy – it's just the luck of the draw that you got stung for this one. And wouldn't it all come out fair and square in the end? Although, the next round would be Fiona's, and knowing Fi as well as she did, Louise knew she'd probably take them across the road to Paddy Cullen's, or at least somewhere more down-to-earth, and probably a hell of a lot cheaper than here.

Right. Knees trembling at whether she'd have enough cash for this round, let alone for the rest of the night, Louise cautiously went through to the bar.

"Twelve Bellinis, please," she announced, and even the middle-aged barman, who was no doubt well used to extravagance here, looked a little surprised.

"You're sure?" he enquired. "It won't be cheap."

"I know." Louise smiled airily as if this sort of thing was par for the course. Fiona was always saying that in places like this, you should always give the impression that you were used to this sort of life – that you belonged there. Then, remembering her watch, she quickly dropped her arm to her side, lest the barman spot the cheap Swatch and see right through her self-assured façade.

The barman moved away, wondering what on earth he was doing working twelve-hour shifts in a bar, when some young one half his age could order a dozen champagne cocktails in the Four Seasons Hotel without blinking an eye. Soon they'd all be asking for those diamond Martinis they had over in New York – the ones that literally had diamonds in the drink, and were ten grand a pop. He shook his head as he searched for fresh raspberries. But that was the Celtic Tiger for you.

At that very moment, Louise was doing mental calculations in her head, trying to figure out how, after tonight, she would be able to pay her rent – let alone be able to afford food. Well, she supposed, at least there was no question of the dreaded weight creeping back on!

Just then, a tall figure appeared alongside her. It was *him*, wasn't it? Louise realised, faintly excited. The cute one with the lovely brown eyes who had been looking at her earlier, although for the life of her she still couldn't figure out why. God almighty, she hoped he wasn't some weirdo. For some reason she always attracted the odd-balls, the ones that nobody else wanted to talk to. Whatever it was about her – probably her natural inquisitiveness or inoffensive open personality – strange people often approached her. Sure, when she came to Dublin first, she had to get out of the habit of saying hello to everyone she met on the street, the way she used to back home. Everyone seemed to think that *she* was the weirdo!

"You girls seem to be having a good night," he said amiably, and Louise was almost afraid to look at him, in case he was talking to someone else. That was another thing that often got her into trouble – she had a habit of staring at people and wondering about their lives: where they lived, if they were married, if they were happy. She enjoyed making up her own little versions of their lives, always had. It was a throwback from the early days in Dublin where she knew nobody, and wondering about other people had been her greatest pastime.

Anyway, it seemed your man *was* talking to her, because now he was smiling at her.

"I'm sorry, maybe I got it wrong," he said quickly when she didn't reply. "You're *not* having a good time?"

"No, no," Louise shook her head, "we're having a great time. It's my friend's hen night, you see. Well, no, it's her pre-hen night actually," she clarified.

"*Pre*-hen night?" he repeated, baffled. Louise knew exactly how he felt.

"Yes. We're off to Spain for the real hen-night – I mean hen-*weekend* – tomorrow after work."

"Hen-weekend – I see," he said, nodding benignly, as if the dressed-up group of girls had been let out of the mental hospital for the weekend. "So, she's making the most of her last few days as a single woman, or," he said, pausing slightly, "maybe *you're* making the most of your last few –"

"Oh God, no!" Louise laughed, cutting him off. "*I'm* not getting married!" She turned and pointed towards the girls. "She's ... see the tall, red-headed girl sprinkling glitter over everyone? That's her." Louise idly wondered what the management of the five-star Four Seasons Hotel would feel about having to get *Miss Selfridge* body glitter out of their lovely furniture tonight. Not too happy, she decided, suddenly feeling a little gauche.

"I'm Sam, by the way," he said, extending a hand and flashing a friendly smile.

With his lovely brown eyes and wavy brown hair, he was very good-looking, a bit too good-looking to be using that smile on the likes of her, and again she couldn't figure out why he was bothered with her when every other woman in throwing-distance was probably a million times more attractive than she was.

77

But, he was still smiling at her, so she supposed she might as well enjoy it.

"Louise," she said shaking his hand in return, and right away noticing that it felt lovely – really smooth and soft. Judging by his hands, Sam obviously worked in an office job or something, not like the last guy she went out with.

Max was a brickie, and his hands were as rough as sandpaper and covered with so many blisters and cuts that Louise often wondered if he had a second job as some sort of serial killer or something. Once the thought had entered her mind, the relationship hadn't had a chance really.

But Sam seemed really, really, nice and not at all serial-killer-like.

The barman had placed twelve long-stemmed martini glasses on the bar in front of Louise, and having poured the champagne and added the schnapps, he was now balancing berry-loaded cocktail sticks across the mouth of each one. They looked fantastic, all twelve glasses attractively filled with sparkling rose-coloured liquid, and topped off with raspberries, but when he handed her the till receipt, Louise nearly fell down.

"Thanks," she said just recovering in time to hand him her Visa card – her already-so-overloaded-it-might-spontaneously-*combust* Visa card – and prayed like hell the transaction would go through.

Even Sam seemed surprised. "You lot are *definitely* all out to celebrate tonight," he said, eyes widening. "I was going to offer to buy you a drink, but ah … I think I left my gold-card at home!"

Shit, Louise thought, as the barman offered to help her take the drinks back to the girls. Now, he thinks I'm one of those flashy, loaded 'It' girls – or whatever the Irish version was anyway. '*Cailíní Anseo*,' maybe?

Little did he know.

"Well, it's not usually like this," she said grimacing, as the barman went off with the first tray, "but somehow I got stuck for this round and – "

"Some round. I thought my mates were whores for the drink, but at least beer doesn't cost the same as Africa's national debt!"

OK, OK, don't remind me, she wanted to say. But at least she wasn't the only one who thought this was going way overboard. Then, catching sight of Gemma approaching, she quickly altered her features into something resembling a carefree smile.

"What's taking so long, Louise?" Gemma demanded. "We're all parched!"

Sam laughed. "She's trying to come up with something to pawn off so she can pay for your cocktails!" he teased.

"What?" The bride-to-be eyed Louise, her expression like thunder. "Louise, if you didn't want to buy me a drink, all you had to do was say so," she said huffily.

Louise wanted to murder Sam. Now it looked as though she was a right stingy so-and-so!

"Don't mind him," she said, mustering another carefree smile. "Of course I've no problem buying you drinks. Sure, isn't it your big night, after all?"

"Well, look, hurry up with those, will you? The girls are getting impatient. Sasha, Stephanie and Tania can only stay for this one – they're on the night-shift tonight – and Fiona wants to move somewhere else soon."

Typical! Louise groaned inwardly as she watched Gemma sashay back out to the others, tiny flakes of glitter falling off as she moved. She shook her head. Crafty old Fiona would avoid not only an expensive round in the Ice Bar, but would also get away with a much smaller one too! At times like this, Louise really wished she could be more assertive. Fiona was always saying she was way too soft. But for some reason, Gemma was one of those people that you just couldn't say no to – especially not on her hen night anyway. Although, Fiona had no problems saying no . . .

"Looks like you lot are in for a hectic night then," Sam stated, and Louise wasn't sure but she thought she sensed a slight disappointment in his tone. He wasn't really that ... oh no, perhaps she'd read it all wrong. Perhaps he was interested in one of the other girls, maybe Tania or even Gemma, and he was just getting friendly with her so as to work his way into their company. That had to be it. God, she was such an eejit really, thinking that someone like him could be –

"It's a pity, really," he went on. "That you're on a hen night, I mean – otherwise …"

"Otherwise?"

"Well," he looked nervous all of a sudden, "you're on a girls-only night tonight – and a very important *pre*-hen night." His eyes twinkled and just then, Louise noticed he had a lovely smattering of freckles across his cheeks. "So, I can hardly ask you to leave them and come for a drink with me, can I? Much as I've been dying to since you walked in the door," he added meaningfully.

Louise looked at him blankly, wondering what the punch line was going to be.

But Sam just looked right back, obviously waiting for her to say something.

"I … I …" God, you are such an idiot, she admonished herself. This guy is lovely and he's just asked you out in a roundabout sort of way, so say something! Anything!

"Um … Bellinis are lovely, aren't they?" was all she could think of.

Sam looked disappointed. "I don't know – I've never tried one, to be honest."

Louise couldn't think of anything else to say – she was too busy kicking herself for acting like a numbskull.

"So," Sam tried again, "seeing as you're otherwise engaged tonight, would you consider going out for a drink with me some other night?" He blushed slightly. "Um, we could have Bellinis if you want, I don't mind, but I should warn you, I'm only a lowly paid office dogsbody."

Louise couldn't believe her ears. Of *course* she'd go out with him!

"I'd love to," she said, before adding, "For a normal drink though – not one of these."

"I'm still a bit worried about what women call 'normal' drinks these days," he said laughing.

Out of the corner of her eye, Louise saw Gemma, Fiona and the others beckoning frantically at her. They must be leaving soon, she thought idly, waving back at them. Pity.

"I think your friends have already polished off their drinks," Sam said. He fished in his pockets and brought out his mobile phone. "Can I get your number? I'll give you a call next week some time maybe – seeing as you're abroad this weekend. Would that be OK?"

"What?" For a moment, Louise didn't know what he was on about. Then she remembered – Gemma's hen weekend! God, now he really must think she was one of those mad socialites, poor little rich girl and all that. She'd better set him straight soon, otherwise he'd expect her to pay for their night out!

But more importantly, there *would* be night out. Brilliant. He seemed really, really nice and it was such a pity that she was going away this weekend otherwise –

"So can I have your number, then?" Sam's voice brought her out of her reverie.

"Oh – oh, sorry." Louise recited her number and watched him input it into his phone. She wondered if he really was going to call her, or if it was just another one of those waste-of-time exchanges. But at the same time, *he'd* approached *her* at the bar so –

"Louise, come on – drink up!" Gemma approached and, after giving Sam one of her most seductive smiles, grabbed Louise by the arm, almost knocking her drink over in the process. Just then Louise realised that while the others had finished their cocktails, she'd barely touched hers. The thoughts of throwing it back in front of Sam now would make her look like a right lush so …

"I think I might just leave it," she said, putting the nearly full glass back on the bar. Then thinking of something, she smiled at Sam. "Or maybe you'd like to finish it? Seeing as you said you've never tried one and all."

Sam looked delighted. "Well, if you don't want it … I must say I didn't expect to be downing swanky cocktails when I came out tonight but …" He trailed off and gave Louise an appreciative look. "But then again, I didn't expect to meet such an attractive lady either."

Gemma rolled her eyes, either unimpressed by your man's smooth chat-up lines, or distinctly unhappy about being ignored.

"Sorry I have to rush off like this," Louise said apologetically.

"No problem – have a good night," Sam said smiling. "I'll call you next week?"

"Sure," she replied casually but, as she turned to follow the others out to the lobby, her mouth broke into a huge happy grin. Spotting her friend's delighted expression, Fiona conspiratorially teased her: "Having a good night?"

Louise smiled back. "Having a *great* night," she replied happily.

CHAPTER 9

The weekend was even better, and although Louise felt incredibly guilty about yet *again* having to increase her overdraft to pay for this little break, it was almost worth it.

Marbella was fantastic. Lots of warm sunshine, fabulous beaches, and their hotel was a lot more sumptuous than Louise was normally used to on holidays. Upon arrival, and although they were only there for three days, Gemma immediately drew up a plan of action for getting a tan, with a military precision that would be the envy of the US Special Forces.

"Right girls, we start at seven am, break for food at twelve, and then it's back on the beds until five," she announced. "So, I need a list of volunteers to get up early and nab the sunbeds. Obviously, *I* won't be doing it so ... "

There was usually nothing voluntary where Gemma was concerned, and Louise hoped desperately that she wouldn't be chosen as one of the misfortunates who would be getting up at sunrise and blearily traipsing downstairs with an armful of towels. But luckily, this time the bride's teenage sister Mel ended up drawing the short straw, and Louise escaped that particular chore.

Not that she minded helping out, but sunbathing was normally way down on her list of priorities. With her typically Irish skin, Louise had long since given up hope of ever getting a golden glow, but now that she was thinner, she supposed it would be nice to be able to wear a bikini without having to worry about her figure.

Worrying about her scars however, would be a different matter. She had quite a few slash marks, as she liked to call them, on her abdomen and of course the skin grafts on her legs tended to catch the eye. But blast it, she was on holiday, and judging by the amount of the unnaturally big-busted women on the beach here, Louise wasn't the only one to have 'gone under the knife'.

The afternoon of their arrival, and under Gemma's strict instructions, the girls managed to grab some empty sun loungers, and settled down for a few hours' relaxation around the pool. Louise had been dreading exposing her body for the first time, but luckily the girls didn't seem at all interested in or bothered about her war wounds – they were too busy worrying about how they themselves looked *au naturel*.

Although someone like Fiona didn't need to worry, Louise thought, glancing enviously at her friend's sallow, unblemished back, her faint colour set off by a white string ensemble. Fiona only had to look sideways at a holiday brochure in order to turn a deep golden brown. Louise sighed and reached for her Factor One Million, glow-in-the-dark sunscreen which she'd applied only twenty minutes earlier, knowing that if she waited any longer she'd end up a fetching shade of cerise tonight.

Just once, Louise thought dreamily, as she sat up on her sun-lounger, just once she'd love to return home from abroad triumphant and tanned – with a bronze glow that would cause everyone to remark enviously, "I see *someone's* just back from the sun!" instead of the usual, puzzled, "You were away? Where? Galway, was it?"

But Louise knew from experience that she could get burnt waiting for the transfer bus at the airport – *Dublin* airport, so despite Gemma's stringent sunbathing routine, getting a tan would strictly remain wishful thinking. No, she'd need a year in the sun to make a difference and, even then, she'd be lucky if she came out in freckles!

She looked around the hotel grounds and spied a group of thin, leggy, Britney Spears clones wandering self-assuredly around the pool, chattering at the top of their voices in a distinctive, confident twang. Americans, she decided.

Now how did *they* all get to be so gorgeous, she wondered, particularly when Americans were all supposed to be descended from places the likes of Louth and Limerick? Why didn't they go all pink and freckly in the sun, like normal, decent Irish people did? Oh, well, it was definitely the luck of the draw, she decided, slathering on her sunscreen, hoping they wouldn't spot her and start making smart comments about her elephant skin.

"Can't you stay still for one second?" Fiona piped up a little testily. "You haven't stopped jumping up and down since we got here! What's up with you? Oh let me guess, you're still mooning over that guy you met the other night, aren't you?"

Louise looked at her blankly.

"The cute one with the nice brown eyes?" Fiona clarified, grinning.

"Oh!" Louise reddened slightly, but chances were Fiona wouldn't know the difference – her skin was nicely flushed as it was. She hadn't been thinking about Sam just then, but in truth had thought of little else since meeting him that night. He seemed lovely and hopefully he would ring her. "I'd forgotten all about him," she lied.

" Mmm, I believe you."

Louise wished Fiona would stop teasing her about Sam. There was a very good chance that he might not ring at all, so there was no point in getting too excited over it.

Still, it was difficult not to be excited. He was so cute and he did seem genuinely interested, didn't he?

She lay back down, and closed her eyes, deciding that she would definitely not allow herself to be sunburned on this holiday, especially now that Fiona had reminded her of Sam. Scaly, peeling skin was definitely not a good look. And sure, she could always break out the St Tropez when she got back, just in case Sam thought she'd lied about going to the sun this weekend.

That night, the girls – some of them miraculously already bronzed

– got dressed up to the nines and went on the rampage once again. As they flitted from cocktail bar to cocktail bar on the marina, ordering elaborate and pricey concoctions that Louise had never heard of, she once again couldn't help thinking about how much all of this was going to cost. Yes, it was great fun and as Gemma kept repeating tearfully, going out with the girls was 'what life was all about', but it also was, quite literally, haemorrhaging Louise's finances.

She had a meeting with her solicitor next week though, so hopefully Mr Cahill would have something positive to report – namely a date for the court hearing – but in the meantime, she was still up to her eyes in debt.

At her doctor's suggestion, Louise had a few months earlier made enquiries about getting some form of compensation from the driver who'd knocked her down. She'd been horrified by the suggestion initially – after all, the man's insurance company had already paid out for it.

"They paid out a pittance, Louise – barely enough to cover your treatment and enough to cover their own backsides," Dr Cunningham had said during one of her periodic consultation visits to Cork University hospital. "You should have a chat with a personal injury solicitor in Dublin, and see where you stand. But in my opinion, that driver got away scot-free – considering the damage he did."

So, upon her return to Dublin, Louise consulted the Golden Pages and shortly afterwards ended up in the offices of James Cahill, a solicitor whose ad proclaimed that personal injury claims were his 'speciality'. Cahill had been amazingly upbeat about her chances and even better, had offered to take the case on a no-win, no-fee basis. The actual term was 'no *foal*, no fee', apparently, but the whole situation was confusing enough without trying to grasp the meaning of that expression. The solicitor asked her a few questions about the accident and about her subsequent injuries and then, quick as you like, suggested filing a civil suit against the errant driver. "Seeing as the cut-off date for making a claim is rapidly approaching," he'd explained. Additionally, it seemed that Louise was actually *lucky* that her accident occurred when it did, as only just recently, the government had introduced a system whereby all new personal injury claims had to go through some specially appointed board, whereupon, Cahill informed her acerbically, "You wouldn't get tuppence".

So with any luck her solicitor would soon get a date for a hearing and there might be some light at the end of Louise's current debt-strewn tunnel.

Still, this wasn't the time to be thinking about it, she thought then, jumping up and joining the girls in an impromptu cancan, otherwise what was the point of being alive at all? Hadn't she spent long enough alone in her bed-sit with no friends and nothing to do, she thought, kicking her legs as high as they would go. And wasn't she lucky to have a life like this and great friends to share it with?

"Louise, you're bloody useless!" Gemma, on her right-hand side, informed her. "Your timing is way off!"

"Oops, sorry!" In fairness, her rhythm had never been the best, but of course since her hip injury –

"Oh, forget it, there's no point!" Gemma petulantly dropped her arm from around Louise's waist, and bowed out of the line-up, leaving Louise still kicking madly trying to keep up with the rest of them.

Back at the table, Vanessa, Gemma's best friend, gave Louise a withering look. "What is *wrong* with you?" she asked.

"Wrong? What do you mean?"

"You've been sitting there all night with a face that would trip a jackass! It's Gemma's special weekend! What's the problem?"

"There's nothing wrong – honestly ..." Louise trailed off, puzzled. She hadn't been making it that obvious, had she? Oh no, she had never intended to let her money problems ruin poor Gemma's hen weekend. She really should cop onto herself – and to hell with the blasted money! "I'm sorry, I didn't mean to upset anyone – "

Was she really acting a bit strange? she wondered, deciding she'd better ask Fiona if she'd thought that. Although, at that moment her friend was being chatted up by some good-looking guy at the bar, so Louise didn't like to interrupt her. She'd ask her later. "Just because you're the only one who didn't get a tan this weekend doesn't mean you should take it out on the rest of us!" Gemma accused tetchily.

"What? I didn't – "

"Well, you haven't stopped complaining about it since we got here, have you? 'Lying out in the sun is a waste of time, I'll never get anything here'," she mimicked. "In fact, you haven't stopped complaining about everything since we got here. And don't think I didn't see your face earlier when everyone chipped in to buy me dinner."

Well, yes, Louise *had* been shocked certainly – as had Fiona. Of course she had no problem chipping in for Gemma's meal – again. But she had been a bit taken aback because Gemma had ordered and happily polished off a big platter of fresh lobster. At forty euro a pound ...

But still, she really hadn't said or done anything that would make them think –

"Look, I'm really sorry if I'm a little bit off form, Gemma," she said gently to the other girl. "But to be honest, I do have a few things on my mind and –"

"But it's *always* the same with you, Louise – you're always off in dreamland somewhere! And if you didn't want to come with us, you should have just said so." The bride-to-be paused for dramatic effect and, soon after, tears magically appeared in her eyes. "If you weren't interested in celebrating the most important occasion of my life with me…"

Your *hen* night? Louise thought, startled. What about your wedding? "Of course, I want to celebrate with you, Gemma," she said, hoping to mollify her. "And I do know how important this is to you. I'm sorry if I upset you, I really didn't mean to. Tell you what," she stood up, "let me make it up to you. Would you like another drink or …?"

Gemma smiled gratefully, the tears disappearing almost as quickly as they'd arrived. "One of those passion-fruit cocktails would be nice. What do you think, girls?"

Louise groaned inwardly. Great, looked like she was stuck for another round! Then, just in time, she stopped herself. It really wasn't fair to poor Gemma, and she really had no idea they considered *her* the life and soul of these things. She didn't even think she and Gemma were that close, but if the girl was that upset over her not joining in the fun ...

"Fifteen passion cocktails it is, then," Louise announced magnanimously, and Gemma beamed.

Louise smiled back. She obviously had a lot more friends than she'd thought!

CHAPTER 10

Rosie stared out the window, watching the scenery whiz by as the train travelled towards Dublin. She had brought a book with her as usual, but try as she might she just couldn't concentrate – not today, and certainly not after the surprising phone call she'd received the night before.

She wondered what Sheila would make of it all when she told her. Sheila was brilliant like that – so perceptive and intelligent, always great for getting to the bottom of things. Not that what her friend thought mattered that much really, Rosie told herself. The decision had already been made.

She sighed, trying to feel a bit happier about it all than she did. How had this happened? She had thought that her job was done, and done well. She had thought that her children were finally settled and happy. How hadn't she seen it coming?

But then again, how *could* she have seen it coming? It wasn't as though she knew all that much about her children's day-to-day lives other than what they told her, was it?

Thinking of Sophie, she sighed again, as a familiar sense of disappointment – no, *rejection* – swept over her.

Since moving into her famous new house in Malahide a few weeks before, Rosie had barely seen or heard from her daughter. Of course she understood that Sophie would be busy, and moving into a new house was bound to be stressful, but if she would just let Rosie help! Not by signing forms and visiting solicitors and the like, but normal everyday help like cleaning and decorating and keeping Claudia occupied while her mother tried to get organised.

But no, Sophie had insisted that she was fine, that things were going very well, but couldn't her mother understand that for the moment she just wouldn't have the time to bring the child for a visit on Sunday afternoons. Instead, she'd need the time to visit furniture stores and garden centres and what not.

"But Mum, when everything is done, and we've settled in fully, you can always come and visit," Sophie had said on the phone recently, while fobbing off her mother's offers of assistance for about the fifth time.

Rosie supposed she couldn't blame her – moving into your first house with your husband and child was a huge occasion, and something for the family to savour, but wasn't she family too? And hadn't she heard time and time again that she, Rosie, had made it all possible for them in the first place?

She shook her head. Oh, she was being silly, really. It wasn't fair of her to hold Sophie and Robert to ransom like that. The whole point of helping out wasn't to get something back; it was to make someone else happy in the first place, wasn't it?

And that after all was what mothers were for.

Rosie snapped out of her trance, realising that the train was about to approach her stop at Blackrock. She got up from her seat and smiled a brief recognition at the woman standing by the doorway, also waiting to get out here.

Like herself, the woman usually got off at this stop at around the same time on a Thursday morning – in fact you'd often see the same people getting on and off at the same station at the same time. Rosie often speculated about where they might be going and what they might be doing. Was this particular woman's visit or errand specific to Thursday mornings, she wondered, or did she take this journey every day?

In Rosie's case, Thursday morning was her morning for visiting Sheila and also for visiting the hairdresser's, a lovely place in Blackrock village that, in her opinion, did the best blow-dry in the country. On Thursday mornings between nine and ten, the salon did a special half-price offer, which she usually availed of before heading down the road to Sheila's for a short visit. It was a nice morning out, and something she really looked forward to each week.

Her old friend had had a bad run of health in the last year or so, and as a result had moved away from Wicklow to live with her eldest daughter and her young family. Rosie thought it was lovely the way Gillian had insisted on taking her ailing mother in and looking after her. She smiled knowingly. Somehow, she couldn't quite imagine Sophie doing the same for her, should the occasion arise.

Rosie would have preferred to visit her friend more than once a week, but at the same time she didn't want to be annoying Sheila's daughter, or getting in her way. But between her own sisters and three very good children, Sheila was never stuck for visitors and, in all honesty, Rosie probably looked forward to these visits more than her friend did.

Today, Sheila looked fresh and well and was sitting up in the living-room reading a book when Rosie arrived. Gillian let her in, and they all chatted easily together for a while before she left the two friends on their own. Then they settled in for a proper chat.

"So, has the princess held court at her castle yet?" Sheila asked acerbically, referring to Sophie and her refusal so far to let Rosie visit, let alone help.

"Ah stop it, you," Rosie said with a slight grin at the 'princess' reference. Sheila had known Sophie since she was a baby, and although her friend would never admit it out loud, Rosie knew that Sheila thought Sophie spoilt and a little selfish. Despite herself, Rosie couldn't help but begin to think along the same lines. "She's just been very busy, and she doesn't need me in the way."

"Mmm, she wasn't too busy to come and ask you to sign your house deeds over to her, was she?" Sheila shot back.

In addition, Sheila didn't approve of what Rosie had done for

Sophie, holding a similar view to Martin's in that 'we all had to work hard and make sacrifices to afford *our* houses when starting out'. But Sheila's children were all well settled with nice places of their own, so she never had to worry about them in the way that Rosie did about Sophie.

Or the way she was worrying now about David.

"I got a phone call from David last night," Rosie said casually, but her tone let Sheila know that this wasn't just any call.

They both knew that Rosie's son wasn't exactly the best for keeping in touch, and Sheila had made no secret of her annoyance at David when he'd swanned back to Liverpool immediately after his father's funeral that time, pleading work as an excuse. It was true that Rosie didn't hear from him too often, but it was different with boys – he wasn't going to be on the phone to his mammy every day of the week, was he? Anyway, as she'd told Sheila time and time again, David had his own life to live and was doing very well over in Liverpool.

Or at least that was what Rosie had thought.

"Oh? How is he?"

Rosie's brow furrowed. "He and Kelly are splitting up," she said, as if admitting something shameful. "I just can't believe it – they've only been married a few years and I thought she was such a lovely girl."

"You *thought* she was? What happened? Did she go off with someone else or –"

"I don't honestly know, but reading between the lines I think so," Rosie replied sorrowfully. "All he said was that they'd had a trial separation, which is now looking like a full separation, and probably divorce." She wrung her hands together in her lap. "I never saw it coming, Sheila. I thought they were so happy together, and Kelly was such a dote."

David's wife was a pretty, bubbly Scouser who rarely stopped talking and had a lovely warm way about her. Everyone adored her.

Rosie recalled her and Martin's first ever visit to Liverpool a few years back when David and Kelly first got engaged. While the men went to a game of football, Kelly and her mother – a woman the spit of Kelly in both looks and personality – had insisted on showing Rosie around the sights and taking her shopping. Rosie had enjoyed herself immensely in the lovely friendly city where everyone seemed eager to chat in the same attractive lilting Scouse tones that Kelly and her mother had.

Even the shop assistants, upon recognising Rosie's Irish accent, wanted to know all about her, asking why she was visiting Liverpool and hoping that she liked it – instead of simply grabbing her money without a please or a thank-you, as they tended to do in the shops here these days. "And be sure and come and visit us again, love," they'd insisted, smiling and saying goodbye as she went away with her purchases.

So touched was she by the genuine camaraderie of the Liverpudlians, that by the end of the trip she had almost felt at home in the place. When Kelly heard this, she had laughed, gratified that her mother-in-law-to-be had experienced a little of her home city's famous hospitality.

Having liked her from the very beginning, it was hard for Rosie to reconcile her own image of Kelly with one of a woman who would cheat on her husband – cheat on David. But then again, you just never knew, did you?

"Oh, Rosie, I'm sorry," Sheila soothed, knowing well how much Rosie adored her daughter-in-law. "But if it's not meant to be, it's not meant to be."

"I know, but that's only part of the problem," Rosie said, looking strained and recalling how, having explained that he and Kelly were splitting up, David outlined the rest of his plans.

"So, Mum, I've decided to come home," he'd said and Rosie had almost dropped the phone.

"Home? Home here to Ireland?"

"Yes ... and I was thinking," and, instinctively, Rosie knew what was coming, "I was thinking I might stay with you."

"With me?" Rosie parroted.

"Yes." There was a trace of irritation in David's tone. "I've just split up with my wife, Mum. I don't exactly have anywhere else to go."

"No, I don't mean you're not welcome, or anything like that,"

Rosie said quickly. "It's just ... I'm sorry, love. It's just come as a bit of a shock to me, that's all."

"It's been hard going for me too, Mum, believe me, but I've had a chat with Sophie and she thinks –"

"Sophie? You've already spoken to Sophie about this?"

He cleared his throat slightly. "Yes, she's known about it for a while."

"Oh." This surprised Rosie. David and Sophie weren't close – in fact, they didn't get on well at all – never had. And Sophie hadn't said a word about it. Not that Rosie would have expected her to really. After all, David had probably told her in confidence, but still, this was all coming as such a big shock to her now. It would have been nice to have been more prepared.

But thinking of it now, well, wouldn't it be wonderful to have David back home and staying with her? She didn't see enough of him as it was, and had really missed him when he moved away to Liverpool.

It really was the perfect solution, she decided then. David would have a bit of time and space to get back on his feet without having to worry about starting all over again here in Ireland. God knows, it wouldn't be easy for him either to buy a place of his own in Dublin, should he decide to stay for good.

And it would be brilliant for Rosie too, to have another person in the house, someone else to worry about whether the door was properly locked at night, or if the upstairs window had been left open. Silly little things that Rosie had taken for granted when Martin was there, but were most important while on her own.

And having David around to chat to would stop her from feeling restless during the dark winter evenings, when she mightn't get out for as many walks as she did now. Winter that first year was when Martin's death had hit her the hardest. Until then, Rosie had been able to keep busy, going out and about and meeting people down the town and or along the seafront. But, come winter, it had begun to hit home that she was well and truly on her own.

Still, she thought fondly, she'd managed to get through it – thanks in no small way to a little cocker spaniel called Twix. The dog had come into Rosie's life quite by accident. One evening not long after Martin's death, Rosie had been feeling very down, and in order to get herself out of it, she'd decided to pop down to the shop and pick up a few bits and pieces – and maybe a bit of chocolate while she was it. She'd just seen an ad for a Twix bar on the telly and decided that this would go down very well indeed – especially with a nice cup of tea. On her way down the road, she'd thought she spotted a small animal peeking from behind the bushes but didn't think too much of it, until, upon reaching the shop, she turned around and spied a little lump of golden fur close on her heels – tongue out and tail wagging vigorously. The dog was female, obviously a young pup and an adorable little thing. But she was very likely lost and obviously belonged to someone, seeing as she was clearly pure-bred and much better-looking than most of the other mongrel-type scamps around the estate.

The pup waited outside while Rosie was inside the shop, and then accompanied her on the way back to the house, all the time jumping up on Rosie and and nipping playfully at her feet.

The dog looked hungry and, her heart going out to the little thing, Rosie brought her inside and gave her some leftovers from her dinner. Then, with a wistful goodbye, she put the excitable spaniel out the front and sent her on her way. No doubt her owners would be frantic looking for her.

But when the next morning Rosie opened the door to the postman and nearly fell over the little dog, it seemed she'd found a new friend. Over the next few days, she pored over the newspapers in case anyone was looking for her, and put up a few notices in local shops, but no one came to claim the playful doe-eyed spaniel, who by then Rosie had tentatively named 'Twix'. "It was the first thing I took out of my shopping bag that night, and seeing as it was what brought us together in the first place, I thought it would suit," she informed her next-door neighbour, good-humouredly. At the time, little Twix had been a godsend, particularly throughout those long dark evenings after Martin's death. Without her little friend, Rosie didn't know how she would have coped.

"So Sophie insisted you would jump at the chance of a bit of company," David said then, bringing his mother back to the present.

Rosie couldn't help feeling a little annoyed. Yes, she'd enjoy having him around but 'jump at the chance' was overstating it a bit! And yes, of course she still felt lonely after Martin, and would no doubt always feel lonely after Martin, but at the same time, she was beginning to enjoy her independence. She went out for walks with Twix three times a day, had played badminton until only recently when her back had started giving her trouble, and was always nipping up and down to Sheila on the train. The way her children were talking, you'd swear she was sitting at home pining for someone to talk to!

"Well, I'd enjoy the company of course but, David, I do have my own interests too," she said, with a slight edge to her tone.

"I know that, Mum, and to be honest I'd rather I didn't put you out, but Sophie's trying to get settled in her new house, and I know she doesn't want me in on top of them. In fairness, I didn't really expect her to but –"

At this Rosie's eyes widened. "So you asked Sophie if you could stay there first, did you?"

"Well …" David backtracked a little. "No, no, I asked her what she thought might be best … for everyone . . . and we both agreed that my going to stay with you in Wicklow might be it."

"I see." Rosie felt a little miffed that all these decisions were being made without consulting her. But in fairness, she thought then with a sigh, Sophie was probably right. She and Robert and Claudia were a young family trying to enjoy their brand-new house. It probably wouldn't do her daughter's marriage much good to have her newly separated big brother shacking up with them!

Although he could certainly have helped fill one of those five huge bedrooms …

"So, I was hoping to come home soon – probably sail over in the next few weeks," David continued. "Hopefully I'll be able to fit most of my stuff in the car, but if not, I can get it sent on and –"

The next few weeks? He'd be there before Rosie even had the chance to get used to the idea! While of course she was looking forward to having him home, she really didn't think she would have such a short space of time to do so!

"But what about Kelly?" Rosie asked. "Are you sure you two can't still work it out between you? Are you sure there's no going back?"

But by David's tone when he answered, Rosie almost wished she hadn't asked.

"I can assure you it's over," he snapped. "There's no going back to that."

And Rosie decided there and then that she wouldn't dare raise the subject again any time soon.

Now, she turned to Sheila. "So it seems I'm getting my son back," she said.

"And how do you feel about that?"

Rosie shrugged. "He's my son, and from what I can make out he's been through a tough time of it. I'm not going to have him out on the street."

"Of course not, but still, this will be a huge change for you," Sheila said. "You have your own life now, and your own independence. David has been gone for nearly ten years, and then out of the blue he just decides to up sticks and come home. Has he even thought about what he's going to do when he gets here?"

"I suppose that's his business. He can do what he wants."

"But what about you, Rosie?" Sheila insisted, suspecting that her friend wasn't completely happy with the situation. *She* wasn't happy with the situation. David and Sophie had been taking their mother for granted for as long as she could remember and it just wasn't on. "What about what *you* want?"

"I want what's best for my children, Sheila," Rosie said, shrugging. "At the end of the day, isn't that what every mother wants?"

CHAPTER 11

The train was late – again. Dara's bones ached as she stood on the crowded platform at Connolly Station. She knew she could hop on the next Dart to take her back as far as Sandycove, but the beauty of the train was that it didn't stop at every station along the way. Psychologically as well as physically, the train was a whole lot faster, so really, she convinced herself, it was worth the extra few minutes' wait.

Finally, the train pulled in and the impatient passengers piled on all at once, Dara included. Her face fell when she realised the carriage was already packed to the gills and there wasn't a hope in hell of her getting a seat. She groaned inwardly. It was the same in the mornings. This train seemed to be getting busier and busier and the rail company should seriously consider putting on some extra carriages. It would be more in their line to do that, she thought groaning, than all these track upgrades they continually seemed to be doing.

Still, however bad the trains might be, at least it was better than sitting in slow-moving traffic for hours on end. Dara had more than once suggested to Mark that instead of using a shamrock for the country's national symbol, a traffic cone would be more appropriate, seeing as there seemed to be several million of them on Irish roads at any given time.

Mark was lucky though. Working as the resident physio for a nearby rubgy club, he didn't have to keep to nine-to-five hours, nor try to get from A to B at the busiest commuting times. As a result, he tended to drive everywhere. Still, the flipside of that was that Mark often had to work weekends and some evenings, whereas Dara loved having weekends free for shopping, dinner with the girls, or simply flaking out in front of the TV with a stack of chocolate and a mountain of crisps. Mmm, flaking out sounded like a very tempting prospect just then, and she was really looking forward to getting home and resting her aching joints.

Mark was making dinner when she returned. He was brilliant like that; Dara could hardly make a cup of tea without getting into a frenzy. For some reason, she'd been born without the cooking gene – or indeed, she thought, grimacing at the dust on the coffee table – without the housework gene either. Oh, sod it, she'd do it sometime. Anyway life was too short to stuff a mushroom as someone once famously said, and despite the fact that it wasn't quite Shakespeare, Dara thought it just might go down as the best quote in history.

"How was work?" Mark asked, adding a myriad of different ingredients – most of which Dara didn't recognise – into the blender. Great, he was making some of his famous Italian sauce, she thought, her stomach growling approvingly. When it came to Italian cooking, Mark's stuff could often be ten times better than what you'd get in a restaurant. She reached over and gave him a quick kiss on the cheek. "Busy as usual. Still catching up since the holidays, really." With one hand, she kneaded the small of her back, trying to ease the low throbbing.

"Well, this won't be too much longer. Sit down on the couch, and I'll call you when it's ready."

"Thanks, hon." Dara smiled gratefully at him and toddled off to the sofa. Instantly, she kicked off her uncomfortable shoes, something she'd been dying to do all day. At one stage on the way home on the train, she was half tempted to slip her aching feet out of them, but she suspected that wouldn't have gone down well with the other passengers!

Soon, dinner was served and as usual Mark had come up trumps.

As soon as they'd finished, he raised a subject that Dara suspected had been on his mind for some time.

"How would you feel about moving?" he asked, as she put utensils into the dishwasher. "I know you love this place, but it's a bit too small for the two of us." Before they moved in together, Mark rented a much smaller apartment in the city centre. Unlike Dara, he hadn't had the foresight to invest in a place of his own before the property market went crazy, and she knew he was anxious that the two of them settle down somewhere permanently. Dara's two-bed apartment was fine for the moment, but once they decided to start a family ...

"We can't stay here forever," Mark went on, as he poured them both a cup of coffee and handed one to Dara, "so we might as well start looking sooner rather than later."

"I know." Dara bit her lip. The problem was that she really loved this apartment and was proud of the fact that she'd bought it herself. It was something to show for all the months and years she'd spent working like a demon, and trying to forget about ... trying to forget about her mistakes. "But at the same time, I'd hate to sell it."

"Then don't," Mark replied easily, taking his coffee into the living-room area and sitting on the sofa, stretching his long muscular legs out in front of him. "Hold onto it and rent it out. You'll have no problem getting tenants for it – not here anyway."

Dara sat beside him, pondering on what he had said. He was right. And they would need to think about something bigger, particularly for when they started a family, which by rights they should be thinking about very soon. They'd both decided to keep the first year of their marriage to themselves before they started trying for a baby. Dara was thirty-four now, and as much as she hated to admit it, time was beginning to run out. She grimaced, thinking how Ruth would probably pounce on this idea as yet another unacceptable reason for her decision to 'settle'.

"OK, we'll have a think about it," she said. "We should have a look on the internet later – see if anything jumps out at us. I'd love something around here though, a gorgeous Georgian place with a sea-view and maybe a balcony or – "

Mark laughed. "I think you're in the wrong job then – you should have trained to be a barrister! And unless I get a job with the national rugby team in the meantime, you might just have to settle for a sensible semi – especially if you don't want to sell this place."

"We'll see," Dara said, thinking that if they found the perfect house, she might just be persuaded to part with her beloved first home. She finished her coffee and set her mug down on the floor beside her. "Ah, that feels good!" Mark had swung her legs onto his lap, and was now expertly massaging her aching feet. "Mmm, that feels even better," she sighed dreamily and then laid back and rested her head against the arm of the sofa. Mark was terrific at massage. Being a sports physio, he'd have to be, but his talents were also very much appreciated at home.

"I've told you before that those heels are doing dreadful damage to your posture," he scolded.

"I know, but I can't exactly turn up at court wearing trainers, can I?"

"Why not?" he teased. "Would the judge strike the case out just because he didn't like the look of your Reeboks?"

Dara giggled at the thought of it. "No, but my clients would probably strike *me* out!" she joked, thinking of what someone like Leo Gardner might say if his legal team appeared in anything less than perfect attire. Thinking of Gardner, she sighed deeply.

Mark noticed her change of mood immediately. "Now *that* wasn't a sigh of pleasure," he said. "What's the matter? Work?"

Dara nodded and rolled her eyes. "Oh, bloody Leo Gardner is driving me mad – again."

Gardner, an arrogant, self-important TV producer, was one of Cullen & Co's most important clients and – primarily because of his abrasive personality – was also one of their most frequent. Dara did a lot of work on his behalf, but in truth she hated having anything to do with the slimy git.

Mark nodded sternly. "Look, if he even thinks about laying a hand on you again, let me know. After I'm finished with him, he'll have to think very seriously about it again."

Gardner was also a male chauvinist pig who often had trouble keeping his hands to himself. Dara smiled at her husband's protectiveness; she'd love for Mark to put someone like Gardner in his place.

"It's not just that," she said sighing. "Nigel and I had a meeting with him this afternoon, and no sooner was he in the door of my office than he asked – no *ordered* – me to go and make tea. Tea! I'm in line for a partnership, Mark, yet the bloody Neanderthal sees me as good for nothing but making stinking tea!"

Mark shook his head in disgust, having heard much of this before.

Dara went on. "Throughout the entire meeting he gave me as much respect as he would one of those lap-dancers he visits on a regular basis! Actually, wait, no – he probably gives those girls much more, because at least they supposedly 'know their place'." She rolled her eyes.

"There's no way you can pass him over to someone else? Give all his stuff to Nigel, maybe?"

She sighed. "No, he creates too much work, which is great for Cullen & Co, but not so good for the likes of me or any other females in the office." She thought wryly of the time Gardner casually slapped Ruth's behind one day while passing through the office. Ruth had there and then threatened to take a sexual assault case against him, but quickly changed her mind upon realising that her own employer – and indeed Dara – would be the one ending up defending it. Dara almost wished somebody *would* take such a case against the creep, because she'd be seriously tempted to try and throw it.

When she told Mark this, he shook his head. "I still can't figure out how you can continue working on his behalf, then. Surely there's a conflict of interest?"

Dara shrugged. "I don't necessarily have to love all my clients. And at the end of the day, it's just work. It's what I do. Same as what you do. You know that fly-half you're always complaining about? The sleazy one that gives you the eye – the one you reckon definitely swings the other way?"

"Yep," Mark shuddered, and Dara smiled.

"Well, if he pulls a groin strain, you have to help him out, don't you? No matter how much it might repulse you, no matter how much you hate doing it, you still have to ... attend to his groin." She laughed at Mark's nauseated expression. "It's your job, isn't it? Isn't it?"

"Ugh, can we change the subject please?" he said, shaking his head. "I don't want to be thinking about some hairy, ugly idiot's groin, not now anyway." He gave her a meaningful look and clasped her ankles together. "Not when my gorgeous wife is in such close proximity to my own."

Dara's eyes widened. "You dirty little devil," she teased, trying to wriggle out of his grasp.

"It's no use," he said, using one hand to tickle her feet, which he knew always sent her into fits of laughter. "I have you caught – there's no getting away from me!"

The tickling sent her into fits of convulsions, and try as she might, Dara couldn't escape. Eventually, things grew a little more serious, and soon Mark began to kiss and caress his way along her body, covering her in tiny, feathery kisses. He was a wonderful lover, she thought. Always so considerate, gentle, loving. And when they were together, it was good – in fact it was very good – but, as she'd tried to explain to Ruth, her and Mark's relationship just didn't have the same fiery, passionate intensity that she and Noah had. They didn't seem to have that incredible, uncontrollable lust for one another. It was, like the rest of their relationship, good, steady, enjoyable.

And, Dara once again reassured herself, there was absolutely nothing wrong with that. Mark might not set her world on fire, but fiery passion wasn't everything, was it? Although, she thought, recalling her uncertainties about the future of their relationship in the early days, it had taken a bit of convincing before she accepted that idea.

* * *

What had really helped Dara let go of her romantic and idealistic notions about the perfect relationship was a conversation she'd had with her father back when she and Mark first got together.

Her parents knew she was seeing someone, but she purposely hadn't told them all that much about Mark or how the relationship was going. Still, upon hearing that Dara was in a romance at all, her mother behaved like she'd won the lottery. Finally, poor old Dara had found a man for herself! Finally, they could stop worrying about her and stop wondering what the hell was wrong with her. Oh, wouldn't it be lovely if at thirty-three years of age, she finally settled down and concentrated on something other than her precious career! And wouldn't it be even better if she could land this Mark fellow for the long haul and ended up getting married! In Hannah's opinion, a ring on the finger fixed *everything*.

But what Dara had wanted to find out was if those two things had fixed everything for her mother – if the wedding and the husband had meant happily ever after for her parents. This was something that she could never be quite sure of. Her parents had been together for the best part of thirty-five years so they must be happy, but still, she wanted to know if things had changed in their relationship over the years.

And as she and Hannah didn't have that sort of rapport – you could never get a straight answer out of her mother – she went instead to Eddie.

Like any child, Dara had always taken it for granted that her parents had met and fallen passionately in love, got married then went on to have much-wanted children. But she wanted to know if the passion was still there, if the fire still burned. In other words, she wanted to see if her long-held romantic ideals about love and marriage were valid. Where better than to start with the marriage she knew best – or did she?

They were sitting in the local pub one Friday night, Dara sipping white wine, Eddie nursing a creamy pint of the black stuff. Hannah, who wouldn't be seen dead inside a poky little pub, and who was much more at home in hotels where she could show off a little, had stayed at home. Typically, she'd expressed her disapproval when Dara told her that she and her father were going out for a while.

"What would this poor Mark think about you gallivanting around pubs behind his back?" she said.

Dara fought the urge to roll her eyes. "Mum, I'm going across to Brady's with Dad for a quiet one. It's hardly gallivanting."

Hannah sniffed. "I don't think it's right, a girl of your age going out drinking with oul fellas in pubs like that. People could get the wrong idea."

Aha! So it isn't Mark you're worried about then, Dara thought, gritting her teeth. It's the fact that your decrepit thirty-three-year-old daughter might be seen as being left on the shelf! Bloody hell, did everything always have to be about what people thought? What about what *she* thought?

"Let them think what they like," she replied artlessly. "But if it's gone to the stage where I can't go for a quiet drink with my own father – "

"Ready to go, love?" Eddie interrupted, trying to head off the inevitable battle of wills between the two women. It had been this way since Dara had turned thirty, and he couldn't understand for the life of him why, in Hannah's eyes, his daughter's unmarried state was such a shameful thing. Of course, he'd love to see her settled, but only when it suited her and certainly not just for the sake of it.

Hannah harrumphed. "Don't you come back here full to the scut with Guinness either. I don't want to have to listen to you moaning and groaning all day tomorrow."

Dara shot a look at her. Anyone listening would think Eddie was a raving alcoholic! Surely, after a hard week's work, he deserved to go out and relax over a drink or two. And it wasn't as though he went out very often – the way her mother went on, you'd swear he was never out of the pub!

"I won't, love," Eddie replied dutifully.

Dara shook her head. Would it be too much to ask that her mother should simply wish them both a good night out? But no, she had to get in the few digs and lay on the guilt trip. God forbid that they might go out and actually enjoy themselves!

"So, how's himself?" Eddie asked later, once they were on their second drink and had settled in for a chat.

Surprisingly, no one in the premises had recoiled in shock at the sight of the local spinster out for a drink with her father. And incredibly, they didn't seem to notice the thick cloud of 'desperation' that Hannah was so sure Dara would emit.

"He's fine," she replied. "He and the rugby team are up north this weekend."

"He's sounds like a nice lad," Eddie went on. "Dependable too, I'd say." Then he laughed a little. "Sorry, love – that sounded a bit like something your mother would say."

"It certainly did!" Dara laughed too. It was exactly like something Hannah would say, but coming from her father it didn't sound so loaded. Still, seeing as he'd brought the subject up … "He's lovely Dad, and I like him a lot, but . . ." She reddened a little, wondering if her father was the right person to talk to about this after all. Then she faltered, deciding that no, he probably wasn't. "Yes," she finished, "he's great."

Eddie looked at her. "I think I heard a 'but' in there somewhere."

She grimaced. "Better not tell Mum that. She'd have a heart attack. As it is, she thinks Mark's 'my last hope'." She made quote marks with her fingers.

"Don't mind your mother – she only wants the best for you – we all do."

Dara sat back, the second glass of wine relaxing her a little. "Is it really that awful, Dad?" she asked, trying to keep her tone light. "Having an unmarried daughter at thirty-three?"

Eddie looked embarrassed. "Not at all, that's not what I meant. I meant the opposite actually. I know you get a hard time from your mother, and I've tried to talk to her about it, but," he shrugged, "you know as well as I do that I might as well be talking to the wall. Anyway, I don't think she means it, it's just her way, and behind it all, it's her way of showing that she worries about you."

"But why does she worry about me? I've got a good job, my own house, a great life – it's not as though I'm stuck in some bed-sit somewhere destitute and with no friends! Why is having a man the be- all and end-all for her?"

Eddie shook his head. "I suppose it's different nowadays, but back when we first met, being married *was* the be-all and end-all. Nobody thought too much about what would happen afterwards. Sure, I know myself that a lot of those marriages weren't necessarily a good thing for the people involved."

He paused then, and for a brief second Dara wondered if he was speaking from personal experience. It wouldn't have surprised her. Hannah was a difficult woman to live with, she knew that only too well. But at least she could get away from the nagging and the little digs. Did her father have to put up with it all the time? Did he fall madly in love with a woman very different to the one they'd left at home? Had his marriage turned out differently from what he'd expected?

Dara knew that they'd met in one of those old dance halls that were all the rage in Ireland back in the sixties and seventies. Apparently they'd gone out together for a year before getting married and then, nine months later, Dara had arrived. With barely two or three years between each subsequent child, her parents hardly had the time to enjoy just being together as a married couple. When she asked her father about this – about whether they'd had enough time together as a couple, Eddie smiled softly and shook his head.

"That kind of notion didn't exist back then. How it worked was you met someone you got on well with, you got married and then had a family soon as you could. It was the same for everyone as far as I know."

"So, when you met Mum at the dances, did you know right away that she was the one for you or ..." Dara felt strange talking to her father like this, but what he'd said about everyone else at the time following the same path intrigued her.

Eddie laughed. "It wasn't really like that either. She was a fine-looking woman, we got on well and, well, I suppose, after a while, it was inevitable that we'd mosey along together."

"Inevitable? It sounds like you didn't think too much about it. Either she was the one for you or she wasn't."

Eddie sat back in his chair. "Dara, that was the way it was in those days. We didn't spend half our lives pondering over every decision like ye seem to do now. I'm not saying there's anything wrong with that, mind," he added, when he saw his daughter's expression. "It was just the way things were, but in fairness, I think it made life much simpler. Myself and Hannah got married, moved into the new house and soon afterwards, you came along and after that the other two. Your mother always wanted a few children, particularly girls, so she was delighted when we had you."

Didn't last long, though, did it? Dara thought sadly. These days her mother was as far from delighted with her as she could get.

But what her father described was so far from her expectations, so far from the thunder bolts she was so sure existed, that in a way it was strangely comforting. He hadn't spoken about Hannah the way they often did in those old black and white movies, reminiscing about how from the first moment they met, they just *knew*. She'd never heard her mother wax lyrical about their courtship either – if anything it had come across as all very sensible and down-to-earth. There was certainly no mention of knocking knees or butterflies in the stomach as far as Hannah was concerned.

Eddie went on. "To be perfectly honest, I think maybe there's so much divorce around these days because people *do* think about it too much. They want instant perfection and if the one they're with doesn't live up to the ideal, they go off looking for one that does. But, love, there's a lot to be said for someone who's reliable and dependable, and who doesn't have any fancy notions about the ideal romance. But these days, people are too busy chasing rainbows to realise that." Then he looked at her, a mischievous glint in his eye. "It's nearly closing, but I must say I'm enjoying our little chat. Will we have another one?"

Dara nodded, deciding in that instant that her father's words made a whole lot of sense.

Was that what she was doing then, she wondered, when Eddie had gone to the bar. Was she simply chasing rainbows, wishing for something that wasn't there? Making herself unsure and unhappy by waiting around for someone who could make her go weak at the knees, when in her father's time, any sensible woman would have settled down with someone like Mark long ago?

Perhaps she'd wasted years waiting around for the Hollywood fairytale, waiting around for the perfect man – the elusive One. Waiting around for someone who could live up to her idea of perfection – Noah Morgan. So perhaps she should give up on the fairytale, give up on the childish idea that she could find another Noah, and just be damned grateful for what she did have.

CHAPTER 12

The following Friday evening, she and Mark were invited to a family dinner at his sister's house. Gillian, the oldest of the Russell children, lived in Blackrock with her husband and two young children. Mark's mum also stayed there, Gillian insisting on caring for her mother when her father died and Sheila's health began to fail. It was a wonderful selfless gesture, and Dara admired her for it, not sure if she could ever see herself doing the same with her mother. They'd end up strangling one another!

Gillian had always been polite when they met, but for some reason, Dara had never really warmed to her. She couldn't quite put her finger on what that was, but there was something about the other woman's manner that made her uneasy.

The other sister Linda, though, was a different story. Sweet, pretty and a little bit shy, at twenty-six she was the baby of the family, and Dara liked her enormously. Linda worked and lived in the city centre.

She and Mark hadn't seen the family since the wedding, and she knew he was looking forward to catching up with them all.

Dara loved the way the Russells were so close and seemed so relaxed and at ease with one another, and where Mark's mother was just as likely to make a witty comment or hilarious joke as Mark was.

Sheila treated all her children like adults, a very far cry from the Campbell household, whereby Hannah treated all her children as though they were undisciplined idiots, sure to embarrass her at any given moment.

So, she was particularly looking forward to this dinner, despite her misgivings about Gillian.

"Well, if it isn't the honeymooners!" Gillian's husband Jeff greeted them effusively at the front door. They had taken the Dart from Sandycove for the short hop down to Blackrock. "Come in, come in – Dara, let me take your coat." He winked at her. "So, any sign of an old niece or nephew for me yet?"

Mark rolled his eyes to heaven. "Jaysus, give me a chance! I have to recover from the wedding yet!"

Used to her brother-in-law's playful teasing, Dara laughed. Although, she thought, she'd better get used to those sorts of comments. No doubt the questions would soon start at home too, taking the place of the ones she'd had to listen to previously about getting married. She groaned inwardly. Sometimes there was no keeping people happy!

Following Jeff into the living-room, Dara waved a greeting to the others. "Hello, all!" The twins were nowhere to be seen and Dara deduced they must have already gone to bed. Pity, they were great kids and Dara enjoyed spending time with them. Although perhaps it was just as well. Gillian could be a bit of a baby bore and while the toddlers were very pleasant, it was not so pleasant hearing every tiny detail of their latest exploits. Out of sight, out of mind hopefully?

"Hi, Dara!" Linda stood up, and gave her a warm hug. "You're looking fabulous – and typical, you've managed to keep your lovely Italian tan!"

"You're looking great yourself," Dara replied, meaning it. Then catching sight of the handbag her sister-in-law was holding her eyes widened. "Linda! '*Is this a Fendi which I see before me, the handle toward my hand*'?"

Linda laughed. "Fake, I'm afraid." Grinning broadly, she handed Dara the bag for further inspection. "So, I take it you studied *Macbeth* in the Leaving too?" she added, raising an amused eyebrow.

"No, she's one of those weirdos who actually *likes* Shakespeare," Mark quipped, outwardly mocking his wife. "She's always spouting that stuff to me too, although unfortunately not in the way you'd think. Only last week I made dinner, and she comes into the kitchen, wrinkles her nose and says, *'There's something rotten in the state of Denmark!'*" He mimicked her tone perfectly, and Dara elbowed him. "Denmark? It took her half an hour to explain to me that it was a quote from Shakespeare and what it was supposed to mean!"

The others laughed and just then Gillian entered the room. "I knew a girl like that in college," she said dryly. "She was also doing that, seemed to love trying to make other people feel inadequate with her fancy words and fancy wardrobe."

Instantly, the buoyant mood changed.

Dara couldn't believe Mark's eldest sister hadn't even said hello before getting a dig in. "Well, I was actually trying to give Linda a compliment," she said, smiling tightly and trying not to betray her embarrassment.

"Go away out of that, Gill – we're only having a bit of *craic!*" Sheila laughed, giving Dara an encouraging wink. "Anyway, we all know how intelligent Dara is. Isn't she entitled to show off a little?"

Yikes! Definitely the wrong thing to say, Dara thought, wincing, particularly as Gillian seemed to be in one of her moods. She had long suspected that the other woman's apparent dislike of her stemmed from the fact that she felt somewhat threatened by Dara's supposed high-flying job and education. Yet, Dara respected Gillian enormously for the wonderful sacrifice she had made in looking after her mother – something that she herself knew she could never do. In her opinion, every woman's circumstances were different and all anyone could do was respect another's choices. It seemed Gillian wasn't prepared to do that.

Dara knew well that the two of them would never be close, but stupidly she'd thought that things might get easier once she and Mark were married. Although, the fact that Dara hadn't automatically taken Mark's surname as her own after the wedding was another lost

Brownie point where Gillian was concerned. Dara didn't have a strong opinion about it one way or the other, but because her professional name was Dara Campbell, and people were used to that, it seemed easier just to keep it that way. And Mark didn't give a damn either way. But, apparently, this was something that really got up Gillian's nose.

Still, it wasn't fair of the woman to imply that Dara was being patronising tonight. It was a stupid habit really, and one that she'd had for ages, but Dara couldn't help it that she had a habit of throwing the odd Shakespearean quote into conversation now and again.

"Well, something smells *gorgeous* tonight," she ventured generously, determined to keep things upbeat. "Can I give you a hand with anything in the kitchen, Gillian?"

"No, it's fine – I've got it all under control."

"You're right not to let her near the place, Gill," Mark interjected sardonically, "especially if you still want the house standing tomorrow. Did I tell you about that time she tried to do a shepherd's pie for me, and we had to call out the fire brigade?"

Dara looked at him, all innocence. "You're wasted in physio, Mark Russell. For the life of me, I can't understand why you didn't go into dramatic writing."

Truthfully, Dara hated her domestic shortcomings being aired in front of Gillian, who – judging by the wonderful aroma coming from her kitchen – was obviously Nigella Lawson's long-lost twin. She had a bit of Martha Stewart in there too, she thought, eyeing the corners of the room, which looked strangely conspicuous by the absence of a single cobweb. And there wasn't a speck of dust anywhere. How did Gillian keep up with it all, she wondered, thinking of the never-ending cleaning that needed doing in her apartment. Never-ending, because she rarely did it.

Sheila laughed, and regarded her son shrewdly. "You know, you *do* look like you've lost a bit of weight recently. So, my daughter-in-law hasn't been feeding you properly then?"

Dara grimaced, wishing they'd change the subject. "Sorry, Sheila."

"Mam, I don't know where I got her," Mark was saying. "And here's me thinking I'd end up going for a woman like my mother."

"Well, in my opinion, you did a lot better!" Sheila laughed, hobbling along in front of them towards the kitchen.

They all took a seat around Gillian's huge farmhouse table in her huge farmhouse kitchen. Gillian obviously took great pride in her cooking and mothering skills and seemed totally at home with entertaining. Dara had always envied that, envied those women who could quite effortlessly cope with cooking huge dinners for more than four people, and who didn't get flustered as she did by trying to entertain them while at the same time having to get everything ready all at once. Her mother was the same. Hannah hated having visitors, probably because she spent the entire time wondering what her visitors were thinking of her, if they noticed the carpet was a bit threadbare in places, if her children were behaving themselves.

But it seemed Gillian was a whiz at that kind of thing. There she was balancing a couple of plates on each arm, dishing out the starters along the table as though she did it every day. Which in a way, Dara supposed, she did.

Picking up a mouth-watering prawn wrapped in perfectly cooked filo pasty, Dara once again marvelled at Gillian's domestic prowess.

"This is fantastic," Dara knew it was rude to speak with her mouth full but she couldn't help it. This stuff deserved it.

Gillian was temporarily mollified. "I know my darling brother loves them," she replied, before adding, "and since Mark tells us you're not feeding him …" Her tone was light but there was no mistaking the barb.

"It was a joke, Gill," Mark interjected, annoyed. "And I'm perfectly capable of feeding myself."

Jeff, it seemed, also felt his wife had overstepped the mark, and he deftly changed the subject. "So, Linda, how's the social life these days?" he asked, smiling warmly at Gillian's sister.

Linda reddened a little. "I wouldn't really know. I haven't been out much lately."

"Why not?" Mark asked.

"Ah, money's tight at the moment, and to be honest, it gets a bit boring after a while."

"You'll never meet a man sitting at home at weekends in your pyjamas watching the *Late Late Show*," Gillian pointed out.

"Maybe I don't *want* to meet one," her sister replied testily and Dara suspected that this was an old and well-worn conversation. "Anyway, it can be like a meat-market out there sometimes, and every man I meet these days seems to be just after the one thing. Sorry, Mum," she added, when Sheila looked worried.

"I can only imagine," her mother agreed, "and to be honest, I'm a little relieved that I've brought you up wise enough to see it. There's no point in going out and throwing yourself at fellas for the sake of it."

"Linda, at your age you're mad to be sitting at home on your own!" Gillian continued, ignoring her mother. "You have to start getting out there, meeting people. So, you have to kiss a few frogs before you find your Prince Charming but so what? We all had to do it."

"I don't think it's quite the same any-more, Gillian," Dara ventured, speaking from experience. As far as she knew, Gillian and Jeff had been together since their schooldays and had married relatively young. Gillian had been lucky enough not to have to kiss too many frogs. "I know what she's saying. It can be hard to meet people these days." She'd been deliberate in using 'people' rather than 'men', knowing full well how pathetic this could make a girl sound – or feel. Anyway, Linda was way too young to be made feel odd for not having a man. She was only twenty-six for goodness' sake!

"Exactly the reason she should be putting herself out there. If you're not careful, Linda, you'll end up missing the boat and where will you be then?"

Dara noticed Linda's knuckles had gone white.

"Work is very busy at the moment, Gill." Linda worked for the Revenue Commissioners, and she'd been recently promoted to officer level. "Most of the time, I don't have the energy to go out chatting up men. Anyway, I'm not like that. I don't like throwing myself at people."

"I don't like the idea of you throwing yourself at people either," Mark piped up protectively, "and I agree with Dara that it isn't easy to find someone decent these days. It took us long enough, didn't it?" he laughed.

Dara didn't laugh. She was too annoyed at Gillian for making Linda feel exactly the way her own family used to make her feel, before she'd joined the club and married Mark. What was it with families that they had to stick their oar into everything? What business of Gillian's was it whether or not Linda had a man?

"You'd want to be careful not to turn into one of those high-flying career women," Gillian said, and again Dara sensed there was a dig in there. "You might have a great job and lots of money but what good is it if you have no man and no friends to share it with?"

"But I'm only twenty-six – "

"Exactly. I was twenty-two when I got married and I had my first child at your age. Time is moving on and – "

"Gillian, do we need more salad?" Sheila interjected, evidently trying to change the subject and take the heat off Linda. Why she didn't challenge her daughter directly, Dara didn't know, although, in fairness, as a permanent guest in Gillian's house she wasn't exactly in a strong position to start acting the matriarch.

Clearly uncomfortable with the conversation, Linda stood up. "Excuse me, I need to use the loo," she said quietly. "Back in a second."

The poor girl obviously couldn't take any more of her sister's intrusive and dismissive comments. Dara couldn't blame her either.

"Gillian, are you really suggesting she should sacrifice her career for the sake of finding a man?" Dara asked when Linda had left the room. She knew she was overstepping the mark – this was a family conversation after all – but Gillian's comments had got right up her nose.

"Well, we all know what these hard nosed career women can be like. Too busy doing power lunches, having meetings and obsessed by money to even think about anyone other than themselves. I don't want Linda to turn into someone like that. What good is money to her if she's left on her own?"

Dara was so annoyed she could hardly speak. Hard nosed career women? Why were career men always described as hardworking, but career women as hard *nosed*? Gillian's attitude was exactly the small-minded and pathetic approach her friends had taken with her. *'Don't be so obsessive about work, Dara! Men don't like neurotic career women, Dara!'* Yet, almost as soon as she'd married Mark, the comments stopped and everyone gave a collective sigh of relief. Ah, great, Dara's married now. At last she's one of us – she's normal.

Sensing his wife's annoyance, Mark spoke up. "Gill, you and Jeff were very lucky to find one another when you did. But it's not that easy for everyone, especially these days – regardless of your career or lifestyle," he added diplomatically.

"But she doesn't even try!" Gillian persisted. "She said herself she's too tired to go out these days. You can't order in a boyfriend like you can a pizza, you know."

Dara resisted the urge to roll her eyes.

"And I know most of her friends are attached now, so it'll get to the stage where she'll have nobody at all to go out with."

"Why? Do your friends automatically stop being your friends once they become attached?" Dara enquired.

"Well, no, but it is different. No couple wants a single girl hanging around with them when they go out, especially a good-looking one like Linda. It's not good for the relationship."

"I see. So, a single girl, any single girl – even a good friend – is a threat all of a sudden?"

Unfortunately, she knew well where Gillian was coming from. Some of Dara's married friends had stopped asking her on nights out once it became apparent that there was no sign of her following suit and getting married.

"Well, not exactly, but at the same time ..." Gillian's words trailed off as Linda came back into the room.

The younger girl smiled shyly as she resumed her seat at the table.

Mark licked his lips exaggeratedly. "I can't wait to see what you've got for the main course, Gill," he piped up. "Cos this will be very hard to beat." He nudged Dara under the table, and she knew he was trying his utmost to drop the subject and keep things upbeat. "Seriously, why can't *you* cook like that?"

Because I'm one of those poisonous hard nosed career women, Dara wanted to say, but instead she followed her husband's lead.

"I can actually," she teased, with a surreptitious wink at Linda, "but I don't want to spoil you too much, otherwise you'll go all soft on me!"

Gillian went straight in for the kill. "There's nothing wrong with spoiling a man," she said, smiling beatifically at Dara. "In my book, it's a woman's duty."

Dara harrumphed. Well, your book must have been written in the last century, she said to herself.

And you certainly won't find it on my bookshelf.

* * *

"That really wasn't fair of Gillian to go on at Linda like that," Dara said to Mark on the train home. "I know it isn't really any of my business, and she is her sister but ..." she let the rest of her sentence trail off.

"Look, don't mind Gillian – she's always been a bit of a bossy boots and is never afraid to make her feelings known. To be honest, I think she acts the mammy more than Mum does. She was the same with me before I met you, always making comments about finding a good woman to look after me."

Dara grimaced. "She must be thrilled with me then. I don't think I'm quite what she had in mind for you."

"Do you think I care what she thinks? I've told her often enough to keep her nose out of my affairs. The problem with Linda is that she's too soft to do the same."

"I got the impression that tonight wasn't the first time she'd been needling Linda about it. Thinking of it now, I did wonder why she seemed so apologetic about bringing one of her girlfriends to the wedding instead of having 'a proper date'." She exhaled deeply. "I wouldn't have got so annoyed, only I know exactly how the poor girl feels. I never heard the end of it from my crowd until I met you."

"Really?"

"Yes, you know that. I've told you often enough how Mum used to drive me mad with all these loaded comments and little digs. She couldn't rest until she saw me married. The strange thing was she never seemed that bothered about Serena or Amy as they always seemed to have boyfriends. But I went through what you could call a dry period a few years ago, and once I hit thirty poor Mum thought there was no hope for me. She started saying novenas – anything to help the cause."

Mark guffawed. "No wonder she was all over me when I came to the house that first time."

It was true. Hannah had fawned over Mark so much that day Dara wondered if she had actually taken a fancy to him herself. But no, Hannah had been on her best behaviour so that they wouldn't frighten away such a decent prospect. It was pathetic.

When Dara had announced that she was bringing her new boyfriend home for Sunday dinner, she could almost hear the popping of champagne corks in her mother's brain.

At last! And a nice respectable lad, a normal down-to-earth fellow, it seemed – not a bit like that Morgan layabout Dara had spent so long pining over. Who ever heard of taking off and travelling the world like that. And at his age!

Mark had immediately won over her parents, and indeed the girls with his unassuming, easy-going manner. He just chatted away about normal, everyday things and there was no high falutin' talk about seeing the world and 'not being ready' for marriage and kids.

And best of all, he seemed mad about Dara, and didn't seem at all threatened by her high-powered career and her fancy wardrobe. Somehow, Mark seemed to understand how women were these days.

"So you're a physiotherapist then, Mark?" Hannah began, nice as pie. "Some kind of doctor, is it?" Dara could see her mentally working out how to bring this impressive piece of information about Dara's new man into conversation at the following week's farmers' market. A doctor, no less!

"Well, no, not a doctor," Mark replied amiably. "What I do is quite specialised and I trained specifically for it. It's a great job though, and I love it."

"It sounds very interesting indeed," Eddie said agreeably.

Dara knew he wasn't sizing Mark up as a prospective son-in-law as much as trying to determine if he liked him.

"So, you're doing well for yourself then?" Dara's mother ventured.

"Well, it's hard work at times, but sure what isn't these days?" Mark said with his trademark mischievous grin – the one that had won Dara over in the first place.

Hannah's head bobbed up and down approvingly, and inwardly Dara groaned. Great, another point scored in Mark's favour.

She could almost hear a collective sigh of relief when they left the house that evening and the phone call that followed the next day was full of talk about how Mark was a lovely guy, so respectable and such a great catch for her.

"Yes, my mother certainly was all over you that first visit," said Dara dryly. "In fact, she actually used the words 'great catch' when she phoned me the next day."

Mark stifled a grin. "Well, wasn't she right?" he teased, standing up as the train pulled into their station. "I *am* a great catch."

Dara smiled at him as they alighted from the train. "I suppose you are in your own way," she said, tucking her arm into his as they walked out of the station and back towards their apartment. "Still, I can't help but feel sorry for Linda – no, I take that back, I *don't* feel sorry for her because I used to hate the fact that people felt sorry for me. What I mean is I feel bad for her that she has to listen to that sort of rubbish from Gillian. If she starts to feel bad about herself, it'll only make things worse."

"What do you mean?"

"Well, if she starts feeling the pressure from people to find a man, then she won't be at all relaxed and at ease with herself if she does happen to meet someone she likes. She won't be able to just take things slow and see how it goes. Instead she'll be constantly wondering 'Is this Him? Is this The One?'." She shrugged. "I did it myself for long enough – I know how it works."

"And men sense it too, I suppose," Mark nodded. "I came across that myself a few times before I met you." He looked at her sideways. "That's what got me interested, you know."

"What did?"

"The fact that you didn't seem all that bothered about me. You didn't give off that whiff of desperation that some women did. I liked that about you. It made things much more interesting."

"Ah, you liked the chase." Little did he know that the reason she didn't give off that whiff of desperation was simply because she wasn't desperate. And, at the beginning, she wasn't that bothered. It was only when they'd been together a while and they'd become good friends that she'd seriously considered him romantically.

"So why weren't you bothered about me?" Mark asked, as if reading her thoughts.

Dara reddened a little. "Of course I was. But that was different. You were Sinead's friend so – "

"And you didn't realise that Sinead was trying to set us up?"

"Of course, I bloody realised. How could I not?"

Sinead had been on a mission to find a man for Dara back then. Mostly because she was always the odd one out at get-togethers and nights out. So when she met Mark at one of Sinead's 'Fix Up Dara' dinner parties, she reluctantly admitted that this time her friend had made a good choice. At that stage she was sick to the teeth of her friends' obsession with finding a man – *any* man – for her, so when Mark turned out to be relatively normal and seemed good fun, she opened herself to the possibility of a few dates with him.

And as some of her married friends had been giving her a not-so-subtle brush-off whenever she invited herself on nights out, at least if she was with Mark they wouldn't worry so much.

Anyone would swear that she'd turned into this exotic femme fatale, she thought dryly, recalling the way the girls had clucked so possessively around their husbands in those days. Simon and Nick were nice enough, but in fairness, Dara wouldn't go near either of them with a bargepole. And as far as she knew, the feeling was mutual.

But when she and Mark got together properly, Dara finally stopped being the odd one out at dinner parties or the uneven number at get-togethers. And amazingly, once she was more officially attached, the invitations and suggestions for nights out returned. Dara was 'one of them' again. She'd joined the party – properly. She was safe.

Now it seemed the same thing was happening to poor Linda, at least where her family was concerned. She didn't know about Linda's friends, but from what she had said earlier, most of them were already attached.

When they were back in the warmth of the apartment, and Mark had put on the kettle for a late-night coffee, they discussed Linda's situation once more.

"I always found that the hardest bit to take," Dara said, recalling her not-so-distant single days, "the way my married friends used to always be a bit wary of me around their husbands – men who happened to be my friends too."

"I know what you mean, but I do think it's mostly a girl thing. None of my mates batted an eyelid if I chatted with their wives or girlfriends or whatever." Handing her a steaming mug of coffee and a plate of warm buttered toast, he joined her on the sofa.

"But why is that, I wonder?" Dara continued between mouthfuls. "What about trust? And I don't just mean between men and women, but what about between *women* and women? I was friends with Sinead and Clodagh for years, and even if their husbands happened to be say … Josh Hartnett or even Matthew McConnaughey, I wouldn't look twice. They're off limits!" Although if they looked like those two, she might just be tempted, she thought with a grin.

"Matthew McConnaughey, eh?" Mark said, rubbing his chin thoughtfully. "Now that you mentioned it, I've been mistaken for that fella a few times myself."

"You wish," Dara grinned. "No, wait, scratch that – I wish!"

"Think about it," he insisted, draining his coffee mug. "The slightly ruffled fair hair, hunky tanned body, smouldering come-hither eyes." He raised one eyebrow suggestively.

Dara had to laugh at his antics. "I'm really having trouble seeing the resemblance here," she said, mocking him, "but if you say so." Mark was fair-skinned and quite good-looking in his own way and he did have nice enough eyes. But God love him, he was no movie star.

"I sure do, darlin'," he drawled then, in an almost perfect imitation of the actor's sexy Southern accent.

Dara burst out laughing. "That was really good!" Then, putting her mug on the coffee table, she sidled up alongside him and smiled her most mischievous smile. "So, will you talk to me like that later – in bed?" she asked, fluttering her eyelashes at him in blatant exaggeration.

"Why later?" Mark replied huskily, keeping the accent going, and then – taking her completely by surprise – he put an arm around her waist, and deftly pulled her beneath him. He lowered his mouth to hers, the smell of coffee still fresh and warm on his breath. "And who needs a bed?"

Dara giggled and kissed him back.

CHAPTER 13

Louise was barely home after that fabulous weekend in Marbella when, incredibly, Sam phoned. She was unpacking her weekend bag on Monday evening when her mobile rang, and she grinned with delight when she recognised his friendly tone at the other end of the line.

"Remember me?" he asked.

"I think so," Louise sat down at the edge of the bed, her palms sweating with nerves, her heart thumping in anticipation. He phoned!

"So, was it a good weekend?" he enquired. "Worth missing a date with a handsome bloke like myself?"

Hearing this, Louise practically danced around the room with delight. She couldn't believe he was so interested! Did being skinny really make that much of a difference? Yes, she looked a hell of a lot better than she had a year ago, but there was no getting away from the fact that she was still pretty ordinary and unexceptional-looking, by anyone's standards. Still, maybe it was true what they said about beauty being in the eye of the beholder and all that. Maybe Sam wasn't interested in her because of her looks. Maybe he just liked her personality.

"It *was* a great weekend," she replied, trying to keep her tone measured and slightly aloof, but failing miserably.

"And the other bit?"

"What other – ?"

"The bit about it being worth missing a date with me," he repeated mischievously.

"I don't know that yet, do I?" she replied, her own forthrightness shocking even herself, "Seeing as I haven't actually *been* on a date with you."

"Yet," he finished.

"Yet."

"So how about it, then?" he went on, and Louise mentally hugged herself. "Do you fancy doing something tomorrow night?"

"Oh, that would be nice but . . ." Louise paused, debating the matter.

On the one hand, she was *dying* to go out with him. It had been ages since she'd been on a date – a proper date – not counting the dopes that Fiona tried to palm off on her while actively hunting their typically good-looking mates – and for once, this was someone who had approached *her*. It would be madness to say no. Yet, at the same time, shouldn't she play it cool, like the others always did? Coming over like an eager beaver wasn't such a good idea.

"I don't want to push it or anything," Sam was saying, sounding embarrassed now, "it's just . . . well, we got on so well the other night, and I'd really like to see you again."

"Oh . . . I'd like to, Sam. It's just I think I might have something on tomorrow night – hang on a minute there while I check . . ." She laid the receiver down. Oh, God, that sounded stupid! As if she wouldn't be sure if she had something on tomorrow night or not!

Oh, what should she do? There was also the fact that she was just back from a hectic weekend away and had spent so much she'd planned on living like a monk for the rest of the month. But she couldn't say anything like that to Sam. The other night, he'd been led to believe she was a sophisticated, self-sufficient woman of the world, someone for whom drinking champagne at the Four Seasons was par for the course. What would he think if he learned that she had barely enough to survive on for the rest of the month? No, better say nothing about the money situation, and try and put him off a bit. For once, she'd play the interested but I'm-oh-so-very-busy card. Not the dying-to-but-I'm-actually-broke card.

She picked up the receiver again. "Sam?"

"Yeah?"

"Um, I'd love to go out with you this week," she began, trying to affect a nonchalant tone, "but I'm afraid I already have something else on."

"All *week*?"

He sounded suitably surprised – or was it impressed? Louise certainly hoped so.

"Yes, I'm meeting friends for dinner tomorrow night, and then – then there's this autumn fashion event in Harvey Nichols on Wednesday night," she blustered, one of the many flyers she'd picked up with the post on her way in catching her eye. "Ten per cent off all designer items," she recited authoritatively.

"Designer … oh, you mean you're going shopping?"

I wish, Louise groaned silently. "Yes. Well, it is an *event*," she informed him gravely, as if these things really deserved to be taken seriously.

"I see."

Now he sounded a bit put out, and Louise wondered if she'd taken things too far. It was all very well trying to maintain a cool distance, but at the same time she didn't want to come across as some airhead fashionista either.

"Oh, I probably won't buy much," she added quickly. "It's just an excuse for a night out with the girls to be honest."

"You and your friends do go out a lot, don't you?" he said, sounding disappointed.

Wow, he must be really interested! Louise laughed gaily, thinking of their most recent exploits. Clothes shopping on Monday, cocktails and clubbing on Thursday, and sunbathing in Marbella at the weekend. It *did* sound good, didn't it? "Well, you're only here for a good time, not for a long time!" she replied, borrowing Fiona's oft-used phrase – generally when she was trying to convince Louise to buy yet another expensive outfit, or go out on another night on the town.

Yes, yes, this was good. She really did come across like someone with a bubbly, carefree attitude to life, someone with lots of friends and a whirlwind social life – in short, someone definitely worth getting to know.

"That's one way of looking at it," Sam replied.

"And then of course, I have Gemma's wedding at the weekend so …" She trailed off, as if having such a busy social calendar could be *so* tiring. She giggled happily, thoroughly enjoying her inspired performance. By next week, he'd be *dying* to go out with her.

But on the other end of the line, Sam remained oddly silent. Oh dear, had she overplayed it? Had she come across as *too* fun-loving?

"Look, why don't we arrange something for next weekend?" she suggested quickly.

"Are you sure? You don't want to check your diary first?" he replied, and this time Louise thought she could definitely detect a tinge of irritation in there.

"No, it should be fine," she replied, meaning it. Of course it would be fine, any weekend would be fine, as she had vowed she wouldn't be putting her nose outside the door until wages day! But that would be a long time yet, and in fairness she couldn't put her life on hold until then. Not when a very good-looking and totally charming man was showing such an interest in her.

"OK, well, I'll give you a call sometime next week, then," he said, sounding much more like his initial friendly self. "Enjoy your friend's wedding."

"I will," she said, having visions of herself stuffing her face at the meal – the only decent one she was likely to get in the next few weeks, let alone days.

* * *

That Wednesday afternoon, Louise showed up for her appointment with her solicitor James Cahill.

"So, how have you been?" he asked, when the two were comfortably ensconced in his office.

Louise found she was never really sure how to answer that question – especially when asked by him. She was feeling great these days, and apart from the odd twinge in her back now and then, she couldn't really say there was anything wrong with her.

Which made her feel doubly guilty about what she was doing, she thought, biting her lip. Then, just as quickly, she remembered the rapidly increasing loan sitting in the bank waiting to be paid, the massively maxed-out credit card, and the overdraft that just kept on giving. It hadn't just been her spending habits that had got her finances in this state.

"Not too bad," she replied, her expression non-committal.

"You're sure? Any back pain at all?"

She shrugged. "A few twinges now and again, but nothing serious."

"I see." For some reason Cahill didn't sound very happy.

He seemed to expect Louise to tell him she was crippled. Yes, the doctors had agreed that as a result of the accident, she would forever suffer from chronic back-pain but luckily for her, this pain wasn't continuous. Still, when it hit, it hit very badly and there were times when she could barely move. According to the doctors, this would gradually worsen with age, and it was likely she would suffer for the rest of her life.

"Well, I've been looking over the file, and we really do have a very strong case," the solicitor went on. "Dr Cunningham's injury report is comprehensive and very convincing, and I would be confident that we should get a decent judgement come October."

Louise sat up. "So, you have an actual date for the hearing, then?"

"We certainly do."

"That's good news." In truth, it was terrifying. Louise was dreading the hearing, dreading having to go through with the case. Recouping the cost of her medical bills would be lovely, of course, but from day one she wasn't happy about Cahill's insistence on claiming for diminished earnings as a result of her injuries.

She wasn't a bricklayer, she'd told him, so it was most unlikely her back problems would affect her at work, wasn't it? And as long as she could sit comfortably at a desk, she should be fine.

"So, there are no diminished earnings really," she'd explained.

"But Louise, your first-choice career was Physical Education and because of that accident, you're stuck working in an office," Cahill argued. "Think of what you'd be earning if you were working in your qualified field. Without doubt there's a case of diminished earnings here. I think any judge in the country would agree with that."

Louise bit her lip. She didn't like the idea, especially when everyone and anyone seemed to be suing people these days. There were always stories in the papers about it. '*Soldier sues army for being too strict*' or '*Woman sues for distress because tomato soup is green*' or something. And then there was that mad American one that sued the TV station for emotional damage when Janet Jackson exposed her breast at the MTV awards that time. It was all a bit mad really.

To Louise, it just didn't seem right. OK, maybe an office dogsbody in ACS wasn't the career she thought she'd have, but she had a job, didn't she? In fairness, wasn't she lucky to be alive at all afterwards, let alone go running to the courts crying for compensation? And it wasn't as though the driver had intentionally knocked her down – it was an accident and accidents happened. People couldn't be constantly going around with the hand out, just because there were a few stones on what was supposed to be a sandy beach, could they?

And there was no denying the notion that perhaps she'd been at fault too. The idea had crossed Louise's mind more than once over the last couple of years. Yes, she had the green pedestrian light and was free to walk, but maybe she should have given a quick look just to make sure nothing was coming. But no, at the time, she was too busy day dreaming about what Christmas presents she was going to buy. So maybe she was just as much at fault as the driver was.

She explained all this to Cahill.

"For goodness' sake, Louise, don't ever say that in a courtroom!" Cahill admonished testily. "There is no question that you were anyway at fault. The driver drove illegally through a red light, and he was way over the speed limit. Not to mention the fact that he had a few drinks in him at the time. Louise, the guy was an idiot who could have killed you!"

"But he didn't kill me, that's what I'm saying," Louise argued. "And look, I have no problem with your asking him to pay my medical bills, because to be perfectly honest, that's the only way they'll ever be paid," she grimaced ruefully, "but I'm just not comfortable with the earnings thing."

"Trust me, Louise, our doctor's report is irrefutable. It's almost impossible to calculate the damage that man did to you – *financially*," he added, when Louise opened her mouth to protest that she was fine now. "And it's certainly much more than that miserable insurance payout."

He made it all sound perfectly reasonable but still Louise couldn't help feeling as though she was pulling a fast one. Yes, the thought of having the loan for her medical bills paid off sounded fantastic because, with her measly wages, it wouldn't be paid off anytime soon. And of course in the meantime she had to live.

So, eventually she'd relented. Although to this day, she still felt guilty about the diminished earnings part of the suit.

Now, according the Cahill, the case should be all done and dusted by Christmas.

"Our office received confirmation early last week. As I said, the case will be heard in the Four Courts in October. The judge is a good man, can be a grumpy old sod at times, but fair. I've also engaged an excellent barrister, Donal O'Toole, who should do a very good job for us."

"Mr Cahill, are you absolutely sure we're doing the right thing?" Louise asked again. The thoughts of getting rid of all those loans by Christmas sounded fantastic but something deep down told her that this was all wrong. She really didn't like being part of this litigious, money-grabbing section of Irish society. It just didn't seem right. Shouldn't you just be happy with what you have? OK, so she might get a good verdict, but what if it brought her nothing but bad luck?

"Louise, we've been through this before. You haven't done anything wrong here. As far as I'm concerned this is an open-and-shut case.

There's no question of liability – the driver's already admitted he was at fault. All we're asking is that you be suitably compensated for your injuries, and the lifestyle you're resigned to as a result of those injuries. Nothing more."

"I suppose." Still, she wasn't convinced. "But, Mr Cahill, what if the judge thinks I got enough from the insurance company in the first place? What if he thinks I'm just chancing my arm looking for another payout?"

"Louise, I've spent months working on this case trying to prove beyond doubt that you didn't get nearly enough – far from it. Now, I can't tell you that we're definitely onto a winner – in all my years as a solicitor I've never told *anyone* that – but what I can tell you is that we have a very good chance of success."

"But if we don't win ..."

"Louise, trust me," Cahill persisted. "Everything will be fine."

* * *

The following morning at work, while Louise was still trying to put her imminent court case out of her mind, Fiona approached her with a very timely and most intriguing suggestion.

"I have a fantastic idea!" she declared, plonking herself on the edge of Louise's desk.

Please, please don't let it be another shopping trip, or another big night out, Louise prayed silently. After Gemma's ultra-expensive nuptials the previous weekend – and of course, all the associated wedding-related celebrations – she really couldn't handle it. And she was being so good lately too. She had barely put her nose outside the door since and, much as she was tempted, particularly with all those fabulous party clothes in the shops these days, she hadn't been near Grafton Street.

"Go on," she said, almost afraid to ask.

"Well, you know the apartments me and Becky were looking at – the ones on the Marina Quarter?"

Louise nodded. Fiona and her flatmate Becky had decided that living in the Dublin 6 area 'with all the students and refugees' was no longer cool, and that modern apartment living was now the 'in' thing.

Following a massive construction effort along Dublin Bay, a large number of high-rise and high-spec waterside apartments had been built near Dun Laoghaire in an area now christened the Marina Quarter. The apartments had been sold within minutes of going on sale, mostly to investors, and as a result there was a fantastic selection of rented accommodation available in the area, ideally suited to discerning Southside professionals. The Marina Quarter was being heralded in the newspapers as Dublin's new bohemian district, with all its new galleries, trendy bars and restaurants – perfect for any self-respecting fun-loving single girl. Fiona had fallen in love with the place on first sight, consumed with the idea of living the *Sex and the City* lifestyle, albeit in boring old Dublin.

Louise had recently gone with Fiona one Saturday morning for a viewing, and could see why her friend wanted to live there. The apartments were chic, modern and infinitely glamorous – a million miles away from Louise's shabby matchbox in Rathgar.

"You haven't changed your mind, have you?" she asked, thinking it was unlikely. But having said that, it would be nothing new for Fiona. The girl was known to do complete turnarounds on anything, be it the colour of her hair or the men she fancied. So, if she'd suddenly decided that living in mud huts was the next big thing, Louise wouldn't have been too surprised.

"Of course not! Louise, you saw the place overlooking the Marina, the one with the floor-to-ceiling windows, with that incredible view out across the bay ..." She sighed dreamily.

"But I thought that one was too expensive," Louise replied.

Fiona's eyes gleamed. "It was – for two of us," she added pointedly. Louise looked blank.

"But not for *three* of us!" Fiona declared, as if it were the most obvious thing in the world.

"For three of ..."

"You don't really want to stay in that horrible little room forever, do you, Louise? Three of us could get a much bigger apartment, a lovely, big airy one with a room each. Can you imagine what it would be like – three single girls living right in the heart of it all, the trendy bars and clubs, the restaurants, those fab little boutiques ..." She grinned excitedly. "We'd have a fantastic time! But, in order to get the bigger place, me and Becky need a third person – Louise, *you* could be that person." She announced this better than the one who did the voice-over for the Lottery.

Louise thought it about it. She could imagine *exactly* what it would be like. She'd never get out of debt; she'd be spending money constantly if she lived somewhere like that. And speaking of money ...

"I don't know Fi," she said shaking her head. "A place like that –"

"Please?" Fiona begged, and just then Louise understood how utterly desperate she was. Fiona *never* begged.

"So what happened to you and Becky getting a place, just the two of you?"

Fiona sighed. "We couldn't get a two-bed for love nor money, as it turned out. But the letting agent rang this morning to say that a three-bed has just come up. We couldn't afford that with only two, but with three of us it would be no problem. The thing is, we need to move fast, Louise, so ..."

It did sound tempting, but Louise knew she just couldn't afford it. Her own bed-sit was originally supposed to be just a stopgap until she found something better but, as it turned out, she couldn't afford anything else. But wouldn't it be lovely not to have to live all alone any more? Louise hated that bit. She'd never been happy with her own company, had always felt a bit of a saddo. Now Fiona, her good friend Fiona, was asking her to move in with her – and to a lovely modern place in a lovely to-die-for area. What more could any girl want?

And there was always the possibility that if Louise didn't agree, then Fiona might hold it against her. She was really desperate to get this place, and Louise didn't want to be the one responsible for her losing it. She might end up losing her best friend as a result. But there was still the very important matter of whether or not she could afford it.

When Fiona eventually quoted the rent, Louise was a bit taken aback, but not as much as she'd expected. And it would be a million times better than where she was living now.

"It's not terribly expensive considering," Fiona persisted. "And, of course, we can share all the bills – not there'll be too many," she added quickly, when Louise looked worried. "Just have a little think about it and let me know by the end of the week, OK?"

Louise nodded. She would think about it, but in reality, there was just no way she could afford it – not with the way things were going now. Then again, if her court case went as well as Cahill was so sure it would ...

She smiled longingly. Wouldn't it be wonderful though, sharing a flat, no wait – an *apartment* – with someone like Fiona? It had taken her long enough to make friends when she came to Dublin first, so she really should try to hang on to the ones she had, shouldn't she? And in fairness, wasn't Fiona doing her a huge favour in getting her out of that run-down kip in Rathgar? Although, she wouldn't be able to walk to work from now on, would she? No, she'd have to start taking the train into town and back each day but that wasn't really a problem ...

"Well," she said, breathing deeply, "I'll have to give notice so – "

Fiona almost leapt into her lap. "Oh, Louise, you are fantastic! Becky will be thrilled! She really likes you, you know, and the three of us will get on like a house on fire! Oh, Louise, I can't wait! This will be absolutely brilliant!"

It would be brilliant, Louise decided, thrilled that she'd made her friend so happy. Forget the bloody money – at the end of the day wasn't friendship *much* more important?

CHAPTER 14

Rosie was shattered. Her back ached like never before, and after all the dusting and polishing she'd done that morning, she sorely wished she could lie down for a few hours and let the pain wear off.

But unfortunately, this was out of the question. This afternoon, David was coming home, and Rosie wanted everything, including herself, to look fresh and clean when he arrived. She smiled happily at the thought of her only son's impending return. She had given the place a good scrub, and if she did say so herself, the house was looking wonderful. Now all she had to do was prepare David's special welcome-home dinner.

Having finished polishing the furniture in the living-room, Rosie gathered her cleaning utensils and made her way into the kitchen to wash her hands.

Twix looked expectantly up from her basket, and wagged her tail.

"Honestly, Twix, aren't you ever full?" Rosie scolded her good-naturedly. She went to the cupboard to get her a small doggie biscuit and, as if to prove a point, Twix gulped her treat at lightning speed, and happily licked her lips.

Rosie looked around the room, trying to view it through David's eyes. His house in Liverpool had a lovely modern kitchen with brand-new appliances and every time-saving gimmick you could think of. David had always been very interested in gadgets and technology, whereas Rosie preferred to do things the traditional way. The only gadgets she had in her kitchen were an electric kettle, a toaster and a microwave – and none of these new-fangled juicer and blender things that David and Kelly seemed to like so much.

She hoped that he wouldn't find it too difficult settling back home, but then again, the place hadn't changed all that much since the last time he'd lived here.

The kitchen was still Rosie's favourite room, and had probably been the main reason she and Martin had bought the house in the first place. Very bright, it got the light for most of the day, and the buttercup yellow they had chosen for the walls along with the traditional pine cupboards and matching table and chairs, gave it a lovely country-cottage feel. Rosie had expanded on this theme by choosing a blue gingham tablecloth and decorating the walls with dried flowers, handmade ceramics and traditional copper cookware. Sheila called Rosie's kitchen 'the bistro'.

But for Rosie the room's greatest attraction was the wonderful panoramic sea view which swept right down to the harbour, and out over Broadlough towards Bray Head. As the majority of housing in Wicklow town was built along the hillside above the harbour, a sea view wasn't unusual, but she and Martin both agreed when viewing the house that this particular room was perfectly positioned to make the most of the spectacular coastline views. The two of them would often spend long afternoons sitting quietly reading or in Martin's case, *snoozing* in front of the window. Because it was such a warm, inviting and restful spot, they rarely spent any time in their living-room, neither of them being great television fanatics. The living-room was quite comfy too, and grand for watching the news or a half-hour of *Coronation Street*, but Rosie could count on one hand the number of times she'd spent an evening in there since Martin's death. She much preferred curling up in the armchair with a good book, Twix resting contentedly on her lap, or by her feet. No, the kitchen was her choice, her room, and the place in which she felt totally relaxed and at ease with life.

But today, there was no time for relaxing in the kitchen, not when there was a homecoming dinner to prepare. David would be driving down directly from Dun Laoghaire ferry port, which was very handy as he wouldn't have to be dragging all his belongings too far.

Rosie smiled again, the thought of his arrival cheering her enormously, her initial unease about it long forgotten. Despite what Sheila had been saying about the possible difficulties of having someone living with her again – as if David was some strange lodger or something – Rosie was really looking forward to it.

So, her first-born child would soon be back living under her roof, and in order to give him a proper welcome, she was going to prepare his favourite dinner of fried steak, onions and mushrooms and some of her own-recipe gravy. David would get a kick out of that, she thought affectionately. When he first moved to Liverpool, he was always saying that the beef just didn't taste the same over there. So this was as good a way as any to put him at ease, and try to forget – for a little while anyway – the reason he actually was coming home. She'd been down the town earlier, and had picked up a lovely bit of sirloin from the butcher's so …

The phone ringing in the hallway put a stop to Rosie's musings and, grabbing a towel to wipe her wet hands, she went to answer it. She hoped it wasn't David ringing to say that the ferry had been delayed or anything. The last thing the poor crature needed was more hassle in his life at the moment and …

"Hello?"

"Hello, is that Rosie?"

Rosie immediately recognised the warm, melodic, Scouse accent.

"Kelly, hello," she said, slightly discomfited. Why was David's wife ringing her? Was she hoping that Rosie would help convince him to come back? Was she looking for forgiveness? Well, David hadn't told her much, so Rosie didn't know what had happened and didn't really want to get involved …

To her surprise, Kelly began to weep. "Rosie, I just wanted to say how sorry I am that all of this has happened. And I'm sorry it had to come to this. I love David, and you know I really liked you, and, of course, Martin and –"

"Kelly, love – you don't have to apologise to me," Rosie soothed. "Now, I don't know exactly what happened between you and David and, to be honest, I don't particularly want to know. Obviously, you two have been having serious problems, so –"

"I just couldn't do it any more, Rosie," Kelly sniffled. "I couldn't live with it any longer. I tried, honestly I tried, but it was too difficult. *He* was too difficult, and no matter what I did, no matter how much I tried to change, it just wasn't good enough."

Rosie's eyes widened. What was all this 'trying to change' business? From what David had said, Kelly had cheated on him, and from what the girl was saying now, it obviously wasn't just the once. Rosie held no tack with that attitude. If a person cheats at all there is something seriously wrong and, as the old cliché went, a leopard never changes its spots.

"He was just so hard to live with, and, Rosie, I know he's your son, so maybe he'll be different with you, but I just feel I should warn you, and again tell you how sorry I am for putting all of this on you."

Warn me? Warn me of what?

"But when I told him to leave, when I told him I couldn't take it any more and I wanted him out of the house, I thought he would go and get a flat in town or something, I really didn't think he would go home –"

"*You* told David to leave?"

"Well, yes," Kelly calmed a little, "I thought you knew … oh no, please don't tell me he's trying to blame all of this on me." She began to cry again. "Oh, Rosie, I don't want to have to put you through this. It's not fair! And he is your son after all but … Rosie, he's changed! He's not the same David I married, not the same David I fell in love with. He's … I don't know … he's just … different."

Rosie's head spun. It was inevitable that Kelly would be upset and bewildered that her marriage was over, but what was all this she was saying about David having 'changed'? Of course, people changed, and particularly when they got married. People got older and wiser and more settled. Kelly was by her nature an outgoing and sociable kind of girl, but Rosie had always believed she was sensible with it. Was the root of the problem that David had wanted to settle down to married life and Kelly still wanted to be out at weekends enjoying the lively Liverpool nightlife? If that were the case, then yes, it would certainly lead to problems.

Particularly if Kelly had being enjoying her nightlife a little too much.

Still, the fact that she seemed so upset about it all meant that there might still be a chance for them, didn't it?

"Kelly, again, I don't know what happened between you two, but I was under the impression that," she chose her words carefully, "that one of you had maybe met someone else or something." When Kelly said nothing, she went on. "I'm sure mistakes were made on both sides but, obviously, the two of you aren't quite ready to call it a day. I think that David coming back here for a while and the two of you taking some time apart might be a good thing in the long run. Who knows how you'll both feel after a little while? Things might look very different."

"Rosie, I'm sorry but it's more complicated than you think. If for some reason you think that I cheated on him or anything like that, you are completely mistaken. I would never *ever* cheat on David. I still love him." Then her voice broke. "But I just can't do it any more. I've tried and tried, and it's just too hard. This constant walking on eggshells, wondering whether or not he's going to explode ..."

Explode? But David didn't have a temper.

"Whatever do you mean? Explode?"

Kelly recollected herself. "Look, I just hope that he doesn't act the same around you ...oh, I suppose I'm being stupid. After all, he is your son and you know him best, but ... I just wanted to let you know that I did try my best. I did try, but there's only so much you can take before you realise that it's not right."

Rosie felt bewildered. "Are you sure that the two of you can't –?"

"I'm sure, Rosie. And again, I'm sorry that it had to end like this. I'll miss you a lot."

At this Rosie felt very saddened. Kelly was still the same kind, soft-hearted girl she knew well, and it was obvious from listening to her that she still loved David. And she'd just told Rosie that she *hadn't* gone off with some other fellow either, like she had first suspected. She believed her too; Kelly wasn't an underhand type of person, and Rosie was certain that had it been the case, the girl would readily have admitted it.

So what on earth had gone wrong for them?

* * *

A few hours later, when the steak was perfectly cooked medium-rare – exactly how David liked it – and the gravy was almost ready, the doorbell rang. Perfect timing. Rosie almost couldn't contain her excitement. He was here!

To her surprise, she'd felt almost nervous in the last half hour while waiting for his arrival, as if David was just some stranger coming to dinner, and not her first-born coming home after ten long years away. But everything would be fine, and with a nice home-cooked meal waiting for him on the stove, soon it would be as though he was never away.

As she went out to greet him, Rosie tried to put the earlier telephone conversation with Kelly out of her mind. She wasn't going to stick her nose in – if David wanted to discuss his problems, that was all well and good, but she certainly wasn't going to say anything of her own accord. It wasn't her place to.

Beaming from ear to ear, she flung open the front door to find her beloved son standing on the doorstep, an irritated look on his face. Poor crature, the ferry crossing must have been tough on him was her first thought, the second being how pale and wretched he looked.

"Hello, love," Rosie said merrily. "Welcome home!"

David was still scowling. "Did you tell the whole country I was coming back this evening, or something?" he said, by way of greeting.

"No, I only told Maureen next door – why?" Rosie replied, slightly stung by his sullen demeanour.

"Because there's a shower of biddies having a good old gawk for themselves over there," he said, cocking his head to where some of the older neighbours stood at one of their gates having a chat, as was often their custom.

"They're always standing around there, love – and I don't think they're looking at you at all. Look, why don't you go inside, and I'll help you with your luggage later."

"All right," he replied grudgingly, as he stepped into the hallway. "But I really don't appreciate the welcoming committee."

"Well, it had nothing to do with me," Rosie answered, a little annoyed that he hadn't even said a proper hello. Still, this was bound to be difficult for him, wasn't it? Returning home to Mammy after the break-up of your marriage couldn't be good for the ego, never mind the mood, and Rosie couldn't really blame him for being glum.

Still, she thought, her spirits lifting as she closed the door and followed him inside, once he sat down and got a good dinner into him, the two of them could have a proper chat, and …

"Jesus Christ!" David stopped short at the kitchen doorway and turned to look at her, disgust written all over his face. "What the fuck is that smell?"

"Smell?" For a moment, Rosie didn't know what he was talking about. She hoped the drains in the small bathroom under the stairs weren't acting up again but … Oh, surely he didn't mean …? "David, it's your dinner, your favourite dinner – steak and onions. I knew you'd be hungry after all that travelling, so I got a lovely big bit of meat down the town today and –"

"For Jesus' sake, Mum, do you not have any cop on?"

"What? But I – "

"I don't eat bloody steak. I don't eat bloody *meat!*" His nose wrinkled in disgust, his expression the same as if he had just come across an open sewer, David marched into the room and began roughly opening the kitchen windows as far as they could go.

Rosie watched him, bewildered, and in truth also a little frightened by his behaviour.

"What are you talking about, David? You love steak. Isn't it your favourite?"

"It might have been my favourite when I was too young to know

142

any better, but it's been shagging years since I've eaten that stuff! I'm a vegetarian, Mum. I thought you knew that!" David brushed right past where his mother stood, shocked, in the hallway.

A *vegetarian*? Rosie didn't know that, had never heard anything about it. When had this happened? Yes, he had mentioned once that the meat in England wasn't as nice but … Come to think of it, no wonder he looked so drawn and pale – obviously he wasn't eating the right foods. And all that lovely dinner that she had so painstakingly prepared in order to get everything just right …

"I'm so sorry David. I really didn't know that," she said to him, feeling very uneasy all of a sudden. This wasn't exactly the homecoming she'd imagined. "But you'll eat the potatoes and broccoli, won't you? And the mushrooms and onions should be fine so – "

"Knowing you, you've probably cooked them all in the same frying pan as the meat, so of course they won't be fine!" Clearly agitated – considerably more agitated than the situation merited, Rosie thought – David ran a hand through his hair. "I'll bring my stuff in, and then I'll go down the town and get something," he said. "Hopefully the stink will be gone by the time I get back."

With that, he strode out the front door while Rosie just stood there immobile and in disbelief.

Who was this angry person? It certainly wasn't her David, the well-behaved and well-intentioned David she and Martin had so lovingly raised until he left to make his own way in the world. Why was he so annoyed with her? Yes, she could maybe understand him being angry about the steak, especially if he thought she knew that he was a vegetarian, but surely he wouldn't think she'd done this on purpose? Why would she do that? Why would *anyone* do that?

Trying to calm herself, and also to stay out of David's way while he brought in his luggage, Rosie went into the kitchen and sat down by the window. Her head spun and she felt icy cold. By now, the cold air coming in through the open windows had begun to diffuse the earlier cosy warmth of the room, but the chill Rosie was feeling wasn't as a result of the room temperature.

She tried to get a grip on things. In fairness, it was inevitable that this wasn't going to be easy for him, wasn't it? The end of a marriage was no picnic for anyone; so really, she had been a bit stupid to expect this grand homecoming, whereby she and her son would sit having dinner and chatting as if nothing was wrong. Of course, it was going to be difficult and, as David's mother, she really should have understood that. But she supposed she just couldn't see past her delight at having him home and looking after him again.

So, she should just give him a few minutes to calm down, and maybe then he'd realise that he was out of order. David had always been good like that, and while he was never one to shy away from confrontation – he and Sophie having had a right few barneys when they were younger – he was also never afraid to admit a fault and offer an apology when he was in the wrong.

So, she'd just give him a bit of time to calm down. Yes, it was a bad start, but they'd sort it out. They'd have to, wouldn't they?

A few minutes later, Rosie heard the front door slam again, the sound reverberating loudly through hallway. She remained sitting there for some time, stunned and motionless with Twix in her lap, the little dog having sensed Rosie's anxious demeanour and jumped up in an attempt to cheer her up.

David had gone out to get something to eat – gone out without a word, an apology, nothing.

Who was this person? What had happened to her son?

* * *

"The little so-and-so!" Sheila was apoplectic. "He lost the rag at you – all because *he*'s turned into an oddball?"

Rosie nodded, a little ashamed at admitting what had happened. "A vegetarian. But I suppose I should have asked really –"

"Nonsense! It's bad enough him coming home and landing himself on top of you – let alone looking for special menus!"

In a way Rosie was sorry she'd said anything to Sheila, but in the last day or two since David's return, she'd been beside herself with worry. After the outburst that evening, he'd later returned to the house, having picked up some odd-smelling takeaway somewhere. Brushing off Rosie's apologies and feeble attempts at smoothing things over, he eventually went upstairs to unpack, dashing her hopes of a nice one-to-one chat.

Rosie had barely seen him since. Early the following morning, he had taken off somewhere in his car and, as he didn't yet have a house key, she had stayed in all day not wanting to leave him locked out. Of course, she hadn't been able to put her nose into the kitchen without Twix whimpering and rolling over, begging to be brought for a walk. But Rosie was afraid to nip out even for a half an hour – thinking that typically it would be just the time David *would* come back. As it turned out, he didn't return until much later that evening, but she was heartened to find that there was a slight improvement in his manner when she offered him her spare key.

"I suppose he's just trying to re-familiarise himself with everything," she said to Sheila. "The place has changed a lot in the ten or so years he's been away. It can't be easy for him."

"It can't be easy for you either, but he doesn't seem to think of that, does he? 'Stink' my foot! What a lovely way to greet your mother!" She shook her head disbelievingly. "God, I'd choke him if I had him – who does he think he is?"

Rosie sighed. "He's a newly separated man, Sheila, and I think that could be part of the problem. It's hard to blame him for acting a bit odd. Any of us would be the same." That had to be it. David was acting all strange and standoffish because he was suffering deeply over his marriage break-up. All she had to do was give him a little bit of space and some time to adjust, and then everything should work out all right.

Sheila harrumphed. "I still think you shouldn't let him get away with being rude to you like that."

"It's just David's way," she replied softly. "I'm sure he'll get over it, but in the meantime, I have to make allowances."

"Let *him* make allowances! If I were you, I'd start laying down some ground rules. And let him know that he can't just swan in and out of the place whenever he feels like it!"

"He's a grown man, Sheila, not a wayward child," she replied, faintly amused at the thought of treating David the way she did when he was a teenager. But in all honesty, he had been a well-behaved teenager. Sophie had been the one who was difficult to control and, in a way, she thought with a faint smile, she still was. But, of course, Martin never let either of them away with much and David had always ...

Then it hit her. Of course! That had to be part of it. Not only was David grieving the loss of his marriage, chances were he was still grieving his father too. Returning home to live in the same house would probably aggravate that grief. She didn't know why she hadn't considered that before. It wasn't all that long ago since Martin died, and he and David had been very close, so that must be it. Rosie wished she could ask him, or talk to him about it, but he was so withdrawn at the moment that she didn't really want to chance saying anything.

"Nevertheless, you're entitled to a bit of respect," Sheila went on. "I know that he might be going through a bit of a bad patch now but, don't forget, you're the one who came to his rescue by letting him run back home to you."

"'Run back home?' Saying something like that is really going to endear me to him, isn't it?" she said wryly.

"Oh, you know what I mean. But don't be afraid to show a bit of backbone! Princess Sophie might have you wrapped around her little finger, but the Rosie I know doesn't suffer fools gladly."

Rosie's eyes widened theatrically. "Are you calling *my son* a fool?" she said, affecting her most pretentious tone, and Sheila laughed, this being a long-standing joke between them. Both women had raised their families in the same estate, and greatly amused by the petty competitiveness of some of their neighbours when boasting about their children, they often joked amongst themselves about 'my David' and 'my Gillian'. Although much to Sheila's amusement, 'my Gillian' had turned out to be just as boastful when it came to her own children.

"No, but at the moment, his mother is starting to look a bit like one," Sheila retorted crabbily. "Now go home and sort him out – let him know that he won't get away with that carry-on."

Sheila was only teasing but at the same time Rosie knew that there was real concern behind her friend's words. But she had no need to be worried, she thought, her spirits lifting enormously now that she'd cottoned onto what might be wrong with 'her' David. Suddenly things didn't seem so troubling. In a way, the realisation was a bit of relief, as in the day or two since his return she had wondered if she was somehow at fault. Granted serving medium-rare steak to a vegetarian had been a bad start, she thought wryly, but things could only get better from here on in.

No, Rosie decided, feeling much more upbeat and positive on the train journey back to Wicklow, David would be fine.

And in all honesty, things certainly couldn't get much worse, could they?

* * *

Later, laden down with heavy shopping bags, Rosie struggled up the path towards her front door. Through the window, she spotted the television blinking in the living-room. Good, David must be home then.

She'd go in and start the dinner, the right kind of dinner this time – Rosie had picked up lots of vegetables down the town – and maybe afterwards, the two of them could sit down and watch one of those crime programmes that seemed so popular these days. She was sure David would love those.

Like herself, he had always been an avid reader, but instead of the light, cheery romances Rosie read, David was mad into those 'find the serial killer' type stories. Rosie shuddered as she put the key in the door. She'd picked one up once when she was stuck for something to read, and couldn't imagine why anyone would want to read stories about people being stabbed and chopped up and the like. But the crime programmes on the telly weren't that graphic, and she'd sit through them if it meant that the two of them could spend a bit of time together.

"Hello, love," Rosie called a tentative greeting as she came into the hallway.

"Hi, Mum," David replied, in what could be considered a relatively cheerful tone, and Rosie realised then that, up until his response, she had actually been holding her breath. Feeling silly, she hung up her coat and went into the front room.

"How's everything?" she asked conversationally. "Are you sleeping OK? Is the bed comfortable?"

"Everything's fine, Mum, thanks," he replied with an easy-going smile.

Rosie's relief was almost palpable. Today he looked and sounded much more like the real David. She held up her shopping bags. "I did a bit of shopping on the way for the dinner, and I thought I'd make –"

David waved her away, his gaze fixed on the television. "Nothing for me. I got something earlier."

Her face fell. "Are you sure? I bought a lovely selection of vegetables and –"

"Honestly, Mum, I'm fine. And look, don't worry about cooking for me. I'll do my own thing."

"Oh." For reasons she couldn't quite fathom, Rosie felt injured. Granted, she'd made a mess of it first time round, but there was no reason for David to feel he had to cook for himself. Earlier, before going out to visit Sheila, she'd bought a book on vegetarian cooking to read on the train, and had this evening planned on doing one of those vegetable stir-fries for him. She wouldn't touch it herself, of course – no, Rosie couldn't miss out on a bit of meat at dinner-time. But because she didn't want David to be affected by the smell of cooked meat, she'd bought one of those pre-cooked chickens – something she'd never done in her life. It probably wouldn't taste half as nice as a fresh one, but sure, if she didn't like it, then it would do for Twix.

"Well, then, let me know what time you want to eat tomorrow evening, and I'll do you a stir-fry."

"Mum, seriously, I'll do my own thing," David repeated, this time with a slight edge to his tone. Then he turned to look at her. "Look, like yourself I'm used to my own routine. There's no reason why you should have to change things round to suit me. You just eat when you normally eat, and I'll do the same. Honestly," he added, when Rosie looked unsure. "I really don't want to put you out."

"But you wouldn't be putting me out at all. I enjoy cooking for you, and it makes no difference to me when I eat."

But it was a losing battle, and Rosie knew it. David was obviously used to his independence and didn't want his mammy running around after him. Which was fair enough, she supposed.

"Listen, while I think of it," David said then. "I was wondering if it would be all right for me to do some decorating in the bedroom, maybe touch up the walls a little."

"In the bedroom? Your old bedroom, you mean?"

"Yeah, well, it still *is* my bedroom, isn't it?"

"Oh, of course," Rosie interjected quickly. "I'm sorry, I didn't mean … Of course it's still your bedroom and, yes, of course you can do some decorating in there if you like. It probably needs it actually. Your father had planned to do up the bedrooms, but then with his heart getting so weak …" She smiled sadly.

"I know that, Mum."

"So yes, of course, do what you want," Rosie repeated. "You get the materials you need and I'll sort you out afterwards."

"Don't be silly, there's no need."

"Of course there is!" Rosie said, buoyed by the fact that they were actually having a decent conversation. "Aren't I only too delighted to have you to do it, otherwise I'd have to get someone in. And that would cost ten times more."

"Well, if you're sure … because until I get settled and find a job, I don't have a whole lot to spare and –"

"Oh, David," Rosie was mortified she hadn't thought of that before. "Why didn't you say something? You know I'd only be too happy to help out." She quickly reached for her purse. "Here," she said, thrusting a small bundle of notes at him. "That's all I have on me at the moment, but my widow's pension is due in next week so –"

"Mum, I can't take this."

"Of course you can – I'm just sorry I didn't think of it before." The poor thing, of course he'd be stuck for money! And Rosie was only too delighted to help out, delighted to help make him happy.

"Well, as soon as I get work, I promise I'll pay you back." David was suitably gracious.

"There's no rush, no rush at all," Rosie said. "And another thing, let me know what bits and pieces you'll need for those dinners you like. You can make them up yourself if you want but write me a list, and I'll get one of the girls in the supermarket to pick them out for me. Knowing me, I'd probably pick up the wrong thing and poison you!" She laughed gaily, delighted that they were getting on so well.

"Would you mind? I'd go shopping myself this week, only I'm planning to go into Dublin to see if I can get work on a building site somewhere."

Rosie's heart lifted. He was obviously planning to stay around for a while then.

"I'd say you'd have no problems there. With the amount of cranes in Dublin these days, I think they're planning on building apartments all the way to the moon!" she said jokingly.

"Well, hopefully I might get lucky then."

"You'll be fine," she reassured him. Then she paused slightly before continuing, almost afraid to push it but also unable to resist asking. "So, you and Kelly are definitely …?"

Quick as a flash, David's manner changed, and his expression hardened. "Definitely," he said.

Rosie felt like kicking herself. Why had she opened her big mouth? "Grand." She stood up then, and almost backing out of the room added, "I'd better go and start the dinner then."

"Right." David's gaze returned to the television.

"One of those crime programmes is on telly tonight, isn't it?" she added casually, hoping to change the subject, and with any luck, regain the nice cordial atmosphere of minutes before. "When I come back from walking the dog, we might –"

"I'm going out soon," was David's sharp reply, and Rosie knew that once again, she had lost a battle.

150

CHAPTER 15

A week later, David left a bill from the local hardware shop on the kitchen table. Rosie spotted it when she returned from her walk with Twix, and she had to admit she was a bit taken aback when she read the final figure. He had spent almost four hundred euro – on a simple thing like paint!

But Rosie didn't dare question him about it, not when lately her son was going around with a smile on his face and a spring in his step. It was as if making the bedroom his own had brought him out of himself, so in truth, a few tins of paint and – Rosie squinted again at the bill – a shelving unit, bedside locker and lamp were a small price to pay for making David happy in himself again.

There had no been no mention of Kelly again since and as far as Rosie knew she hadn't phoned, so it seemed that it really was the end for them. Such a pity, she thought sadly. Especially when they'd seemed so perfect for one another. But it was none of her business so …

Hearing footsteps coming downstairs, Rosie tucked the bill into one of the drawers and quickly busied herself with something else.

"Hi, Mum!" David bounded into the kitchen and almost immediately Twix let out a low growl.

Rosie threw an amused glance at her. Twix was doing that a lot lately. When David first arrived, she had tried all her usual doggie tricks to try to get him to play with her; lying at his feet with her paws in the air hoping to be petted, and jumping up and down whenever he entered the room.

But despite her playful antics, David didn't take to her at all and, in fact, behaved as though she wasn't even there. So, unhappy with being ignored, Twix had obviously given up on David, and had since decided he was actually the enemy. Rosie thought it hilarious the way she tried to act the big bad dog whenever he was around, because in reality she wouldn't hurt a fly.

But David obviously didn't share Rosie's opinion.

"Little shit!" he said, aiming a kick at her, and quick as a flash the little spaniel scampered into her basket in the corner, her huge eyes mournful and hurt.

Rosie looked at him, shocked. Did he really do that? Did her son just try and kick a poor defenceless little dog? "David, she's harmless – she wouldn't go near you!" she exclaimed.

He scowled. "That's what they all say," he said bad-naturedly, "and then before you know it the little fucker's taken a chunk out of your leg. They're animals and they're all bloody vicious as far as I'm concerned."

Rosie was unnerved. "David, I promise you, Twix wouldn't touch you or anyone else. Look at her!" She glanced over at Twix, who was trembling nervously in her basket. "She's only a slip of a thing!" Hurt by his behaviour and by his attitude towards her harmless little dog, she couldn't resist adding, "Anyway, she only growled at you in the first place because you keep ignoring her."

David's eyes widened. "Ignoring her? Jesus, what do you want me to do, say hello and goodbye and please and thank you to the thing! Mum, she's only a stupid little mutt!"

At the sound of David's raised voice, Twix cowered even further into the corner of her basket, and tucked her face closely in to her body.

Much as she was tempted to, Rosie decided against informing David that the 'thing' might be a little mutt but she was Rosie's mutt, and had been an essential companion, a lifeline even, after his father's

152

death – when David had gone back to his nice life in Liverpool and Sophie to hers in Dublin.

Twix had been the one who, in her own little way, had tried to comfort Rosie when her mistress felt sad and lonely. She had read somewhere before that dogs had an innate sense for human distress or sorrow, and it did seem as though Twix instinctively knew when Rosie needed her close. Some days, she would jump up on her lap and lick her face and, on occasion, Rosie's tears.

In the weeks and months after Martin's funeral, Rosie knew she would have been lost without the little dog's company. Indeed, the first piece of advice she'd give any newly bereaved man or woman was to get themselves a dog. Having the animal around, even if it was just a tiny thing like Twix, seemed to somehow lessen the inevitable emptiness that permeates a house immediately after a death.

But mentioning Martin's funeral at a time like this might well be treading on dangerous ground, and Rosie decided that there was little point in bringing it up.

"She's a good little dog," she said, trying to bite back her uncharacteristic annoyance, but his dismissal of poor Twix had really upset her, "but I suppose she needs a bit of time to get used to having you around."

David snorted. "It has the run of the place, that dog, and it leaves its bloody hairs everywhere! All over the armchairs, all over the floor – everywhere!" He shook his head. "It's not hygienic to have a dog in the kitchen either."

Again Rosie struggled to hold her tongue. "A bit of hair never did anyone any harm and anyway, she's an inside dog so she's very clean, aren't you, Twix?" she said, and instinctively, but decidedly cautiously, the little spaniel's tail began to wag.

David grunted, his earlier good humour now well evaporated. "Speaking of clean, I thought I might give this place a bit of a going-over while I'm at it."

"A going-over ... what?" Rosie was confused.

He frowned again. "The kitchen. It needs freshening up. So, when I'm finished upstairs, I thought I'd start on this." He looked around the

153

room and his gaze rested on the walls. "If you could get rid of those ancient old plates and stuff, that would be a great help. I've a few nice pictures from my old place that would look well up there. And, of course, those manky old armchairs will have to go too."

Rosie didn't think it was possible to feel any more shocked than before, but yet she did. Those 'ancient' plates he was talking about were Rosie's pride and joy – and this was her kitchen – her room! She had no objections to it being repainted or touched up, but there was no way she was going to let him redecorate completely! And to think he wanted to get rid of her armchair, her favourite reading chair on which she had spent many a cosy evening curled up with a cup of tea, a good book and some chocolate biscuits. Not to mention the fact that the other 'manky' armchair had been Martin's!

"I'm sorry, David, but I think the kitchen is fine the way it is," she said, trying to keep her voice even. She didn't want a disagreement or an argument, the *last* thing Rosie wanted was an argument and she hated any kind of confrontation but, like Sheila said, she couldn't just let him come in and take over her home. Yes, he was her son and she wouldn't have him homeless but, in reality, he had to realise that she was doing him a favour by letting him stay here.

"Mum, it hasn't been touched in years!" Then David's tone softened slightly when he saw her hurt expression. "Look, you said yourself that Dad wasn't able for doing things, and nobody would expect you to be going up and down ladders. But the fact is that this house will go to rack and ruin if someone doesn't take it in hand. And seeing as I'm fit and able to do it, and I'm not working at the moment, why can't you let me help?"

Rosie blinked. Since when had it turned into her needing his help? The kitchen was fine as it was, although it could probably do with a repaint but …

"Look, Mum, we can keep the pots and stuff if you like, although I do think that in this day and age it's all a little bit dated-looking. You've seen those property programmes on the telly, haven't you? Aren't they always saying that a fresh, modern house is the one that keeps its value?"

"Its value? David, I don't know what you're talking about because I'm certainly not planning to sell this place," Rosie cried, her heart pounding faster now. All this talk was beginning to make her feel incredibly threatened. First Sophie expected her to sign over the deeds to the house, and now David was talking about selling it! What in the Lord's name was going on? "Anyway, I can't sell it, not while Sophie's building society has the deeds and –"

"What?" David asked sharply, and Rosie noticed Twix again cower backwards into her basket. "What do you mean? What's Sophie got to do with this?"

"Well ... I helped her, you know," Rosie didn't like the look of dark suspicion he was giving her all of a sudden, "I helped her with getting the mortgage for her house. All I had to do was sign –"

"The devious little bitch!" David exclaimed venomously. "So, she did manage it after all, then!"

What? What did *that* mean? Rosie felt as though the ground was opening up beneath her, as if her world was turning and there was some strange conspiracy going on that she knew nothing about.

"So, you just signed over the deeds to this place, knowing full well that Dad didn't agree with it when she asked before. And with good bloody reason! Mum, do you not realise what you've done?"

"Of course," Rosie explained, trying to keep things calm, although her voice shook. What was he getting so upset about? Martin must have told him about Sophie's request that time before, but as far as she was concerned it wasn't really any of David's business because at that stage they had all thought David was settled.

And anyway, she had no choice but to make the decision herself, because Martin wasn't around any more, was he?

"I was helping her – I had to help her. David, you probably don't realise how expensive the house prices are over here. Without my help, Sophie and Robert would never have been able to –"

By now, David's face was red with anger. "Mum, you had no right – *no* right to do that without asking me first!"

Asking him? What did have to do with him? "But it's – it's *my* house, David," she reiterated, confused. "Mine and your dad's."

"Yes, but what about when you're *gone?*" he shot back and, instantly, the blood drained from Rosie's face. "It's supposed to be split two ways – *two* ways, Mum! Of course, it's all right for Sophie, thanks to you she's well sorted for somewhere to live. But what am I going to do? I'll have nowhere, now the smart little bitch has gone and taken the place right from under me!"

And then, without another word, David marched straight out of the room.

For a long moment, Rosie couldn't breathe. Heart spinning and weak with shock, she eventually slumped down on her favourite armchair, her legs feeling like jelly. Then, having first checked that David was gone and that the coast was well and truly clear, Twix promptly hopped up on her mistress's lap. Instinctively, and now desperate for some kind of comfort, some sense of reality, Rosie began to softly stroke her fur.

What about when you're gone? The question David had barked kept repeating over and over again in her mind. *When you're gone.*

He didn't give a hoot about helping Rosie decorate the house. He was simply making sure the place was well maintained and looked after, quietly ensuring it kept its value, all under the pretence of being a dutiful and helpful son. But hearing that Sophie had already made use of the property's value had really shown his true colours.

The realisation of what David was really up to hit hard and it hurt – desperately. And perhaps he was right. Perhaps Sophie had been devious. She too had made a great show of being a dutiful daughter in the weeks leading up to the big favour. And having got what she wanted, Rosie had hardly seen her since.

How had this happened? How had her children turned out so heartless, so selfish? Had she done something wrong? Had she been a bad mother? Had she made some major mistake in their upbringing?

If she had, she didn't know what it was. All she'd done was love them desperately; all she'd ever wanted was for them to be happy. All her married life, she had lived for the children and for Martin – her family was the most important thing in the world to her.

And, even though Martin was gone, up until today Rosie really believed that she still had a family, that her children loved her just as much as she loved them.

But, she decided, she had been stupid, she had been very wrong.

Her daughter had taken what she wanted and now couldn't be seen for dust, and after only a short time at home, David was waiting patiently for his mother to go off and die for herself, so that he too could begin to enjoy his inheritance.

CHAPTER 16

The morning was unseasonably cold and miserable, and Dara was delighted to get to the office. She'd been out meeting a client first thing that morning, and was just checking for messages with Breda, the receptionist, before heading upstairs to her desk.

Just then, a client approached the desk. Dara politely moved aside to the other end of the counter, while the man announced his appointment.

"Hello, I have a meeting at two o'clock with Paul Owens," he said confidently.

Dara was too busy reading through her messages to really listen, but afterwards she couldn't understand why she hadn't recognised the voice.

Immediately.

Breda smiled at easily the best-looking client she'd seen in all her ten years working here. "Mr Morgan, is it?" she confirmed. "Just take a seat and I'll let him know you're here."

At the mention of the surname, Dara's head snapped up, and as the man turned his back she gave a quick surreptitious glance at him. It wasn't … it couldn't … could it be?

She stood rooted to the spot, almost afraid to move.

158

No, no, her mind was playing tricks on her. Of course it couldn't be him. Still, her head grew dizzy all of sudden, and she had to hold onto the high front of the desk for support.

"Dara, are you all right?" Breda asked in a very low whisper. "You've gone a bit white."

"I'm … I'm fine," Dara managed to say. But she wasn't fine. Just then she was about as far from fine as she'd ever been.

"Dara?" came a voice from behind her. "Dara Campbell, is that you?"

And then, Dara turned around and came face to face with the man she was so sure she would never see again.

"It *is* you!" Noah said. "I don't believe it! I had no idea you worked here – I thought you were still at Brophy's."

"Noah, lovely to see you," was all Dara could manage, afraid that Breda could tell exactly what was happening, exactly what was going on here. Because she was certain her feelings were written all over her face. "No, I work here, now."

"Fair play to you," he said, gently. "I'm delighted you've done so well." Then he smiled, the same incredible smile that melted her heart in the same way it had all those years before. "So how have you been?"

"Very well, thanks," she replied, trying to keep her voice even, trying not to betray her utter astonishment and disbelief at seeing him here.

"Mr Morgan? Come this way, please," Paul Owens' assistant appeared in the doorway and Dara's heart stopped, realising something. Paul Owens specialised in family law. Separation agreements, child support – *divorces*.

Noah looked at her speculatively, those magnificent green eyes probing, searching, almost reading her mind. "Maybe we could have a chat when I'm finished here?" he suggested casually.

And before she could stop herself, Dara nodded.

"It would be great to catch up," he went on.

"Sure, let Breda know when you're ready," she replied, a little out of breath, and Noah smiled.

Dara moved like a zombie on the way up the winding stairs back up

159

to her office, having left instructions for Breda to buzz her when Noah was finished with Paul. What on earth had just happened?

Of all the solicitors' firms in all the world ... she couldn't comprehend it. How, *how* had Noah Morgan ended up at this one? It was fate, wasn't it – it had to be fate. Because things like that just didn't happen, other than in the movies. Things like that didn't happen, unless it was for a very good reason.

At the thought of seeing him and talking to him, spending time with him again, after all this time, Dara's heart soared.

Noah Morgan – the love her life, the man of her dreams, the one who got away – was back.

* * *

The sex was even better than Dara had ever imagined.

She hadn't been able to help herself. Once she'd seen him standing innocently in the lobby like that, once they'd laid eyes on one another once more, Dara knew deep down that it would come to this. It was just a matter of when.

Noah was all she could think about when she went back upstairs. The next half hour or so passed in a blur until finally Breda buzzed to let her know he was waiting out front for her.

Dara tried to calm herself, she tried to keep her legs steady as she walked outside but, once she came face to face with Noah, all right and reason went straight out the window.

She wanted him, she wanted him so much that had he taken her in his arms there and then in full view of the whole street, she wouldn't have cared. The desire was so great it was almost unbearable.

"Hi," she said softly, and when Noah looked at her she could see it in his eyes that he felt the same way. The look he gave her made her head spin and her legs turn to jelly.

They walked for a little while, each saying nothing, until eventually the incredible magnetism between them was just too much to bear.

Then, without a single word passing between them, Dara let Noah lead her into a nearby alleyway – the back of some stationery company the office used.

Then, he lifted her in his arms, pinned her against the wall, and without saying a single word, without planting a single kiss on her mouth, Noah positioned himself between her legs.

Her arms clinging tightly around him, Dara couldn't comprehend how anything could feel so good. As Noah's breathing deepened, and his thrusting grew deeper and then faster, she held on tight, praying that he would never, ever stop. She was drunk on him, drunk on the feel of him inside her, drunk on the notion that he was here – really here. She remembered thinking that it all had to be a dream, some dangerous, delicious dream, one from which she didn't want to awaken.

Finally, Noah bent his head and kissed her fiercely and, as he did, she cried out inside his mouth in sheer ecstasy. It was the most incredible pleasure she had ever experienced.

After that, and still without saying a word, they went straight to the nearest hotel, Dara dazedly asking and paying for the room. Once upstairs, they roughly undressed one another and spent the entire afternoon drinking in each other's bodies. All throughout, she wondered why on earth she'd given him up, how she'd ever convinced herself that another man could be any sort of a substitute.

Noah's body was toned and hard and that afternoon, it seemed, in a permanent state of arousal. He was totally insatiable, but they were in perfect harmony – each knew exactly what the other wanted, what the other one needed. It was just as good as it had always been between them – raw, passionate, ferocious – yet the intervening distance made it seem a million times better.

Noah had obviously learned a lot on his travels.

Since leaving Dara's office, they'd barely spoken at all – they'd simply let their bodies do the talking. There were no questions, no answers, nothing but the two of them, wrapped in some timeless bubble, locking out the rest of the world.

For Dara, it felt as though she was under the influence of some powerful mind-altering, pleasure-inducing drug, and she had absolutely no control over what her body was doing. Her rational mind didn't get a look-in, let alone her conscience. She just had to have him, to be with him again.

When she'd seen him standing there in the lobby, in the flesh again after all those years, it was almost too much to take, and she hadn't given Mark a second thought. It was as though he'd never existed and –

"Dara, Dara, Dara ..."

Now, he was calling her name over and over again and she felt his lips lightly brush her cheek. She didn't think she'd ever get the chance to hear him utter her name like that, to be with him like this. But then, for no apparent reason, he started ... he started *shaking* her all of a sudden. What was wrong with –?

"Dara! Dara! Come on! You're going to be late for work!"

"What? Where ...?"

Dara's eyes fluttered open, and she stared up at the ceiling, groggy and disorientated.

Then somewhere above her head, Mark's face appeared out of nowhere and ... *Mark!*

Instantly, Dara leapt up, horrified.

"That must have been some dream!" Mark laughed easily and sat down at the edge of the bed. "You were thrashing around like something from *The Exorcist*."

Dara burned with embarrassment at what she'd been dreaming, at what she'd been *thinking!* OK, it might have just been her subconscious, but still! What the hell was she doing – dreaming about making love to another man while her husband slept soundly beside her? Had Noah's reappearance the day before got to her *that* much?

"I ... I ..." Dara couldn't find the words. "It was a nightmare," she blurted eventually, before getting up and heading straight for the ensuite bathroom, still a little disorientated and very, very guilty.

And it was a nightmare. It was a *hell* of a nightmare to think she'd been so affected by seeing Noah that she'd been having a dream about it – that kind of dream. Shit! She undressed and turned on the shower.

Mark was chuckling. "Some nightmare," he called after her. "Was it the usual one? The one where you keep getting shot?"

Dara winced. That was one way of putting it!

"Something like that," she replied vaguely. She was so guilt-ridden she could hardly answer him. God, how embarrassing!

All of a sudden, Mark put his head around the door, startling her. He gave her an odd look. "Was it *that* bad?" he asked. "You look like you've seen a ghost."

"I'm fine. I'm fine. Sorry – still a bit groggy, that's all." She attempted a half-hearted smile.

"Well, I have to head off now, but I'll see you later, OK?"

She nodded. "Talk to you soon."

He closed the bathroom door behind him, and she stepped into the shower, hoping that the hot water might somehow wash away her still-vivid memory of that utterly embarrassing dream.

* * *

On the train journey to work, Dara recalled the previous afternoon's events.

After Noah had finished his meeting with Paul Owens, they'd arranged to meet for lunch, and mercifully, she thought wincing, the encounter had been nothing like last night's mortifying dream.

There was certainly no venturing into grubby alleyways or anything like that – what was she *think*ing?

Dara made a mental note there and then to bin her Mills & Boon collection when she got home that evening – those books had obviously sent her imagination into overdrive. That was it, she decided, her mind resting a little easier, the sexy, virile man she'd been … ahem … *dreaming* about had not been Noah Morgan. No, it had been some rugged hero from *The Italian Stallion's Baby* or something. Yes, that was definitely it, she reassured herself, and it was only pure coincidence that he happened to look a little bit like her old boyfriend.

And *far* from spending the afternoon having a passionate tryst in some hotel room, she had simply gone back to work and tried not to think too much about meeting Noah again. She was married to Mark now, and she had missed the boat where Noah was concerned. She couldn't forget that. So, there was no point in driving herself mad thinking about it, was there?

Even though Noah was still as charming and gorgeous as ever, and his eyes were still a fabulous Mediterranean green, and the years had made his strong jaw-line more pronounced and sexier than ever and –

Stop it! Dara took a deep breath, and willed her thoughts to stop wandering. That bloody dream had really unnerved her. Thank heavens someone hadn't yet invented a gizmo allowing people to read one another's thoughts, otherwise poor Mark would have asked for a divorce there and then!

But despite her best intentions, her mind couldn't help but replay the details of yesterday's meeting with Noah. They'd had lunch in a small café near the office, and over a couple of (very *unsexy*) paninis, Dara discovered that she'd been correct in her assumption about his visit to Paul Owens. He and Maria, the girl he had married in Rome, were in the process of getting divorced.

"What happened?" she asked, trying not to sound too interested.

Noah shrugged, his toned and broad torso clearly outlined in a tight-fitting T-shirt, which really, Dara decided, men like him should never be allowed to wear. It was way too dangerous. Stop it, stop it! she admonished herself, trying desperately not to notice things like Noah's incredibly attractive chest. Mark had an attractive chest too, so try and think of Mark. *Think of Mark. Think of Mark*, she chanted silently to herself.

But no, that was no good – if she tried to think of Mark then, of course, she felt guilty about being here with Noah in the first place. Not that she was doing anything wrong or anything, but still.

That was it! Happily, Dara hit on the perfect solution. In order to focus her mind and stop being distracted by Noah's painfully obvious good looks, she could try and pretend he was simply a client – an ugly, unpleasant client like say … Leo Gardner or someone. But no, that wouldn't do either; Leo Gardner was so unattractive, so nauseatingly repellent that she wouldn't be able to maintain the fiction. Oh, forget it, there was no chance of her forgetting how gorgeous he was – no woman with a pulse would be able to do that!

Noah was telling her about his marriage.

"It was never right," he admitted gently. "I met her while travelling around Australia, we got on well, and one day, in a moment of madness, I proposed." He looked at her directly then, the weight of his gaze almost pinning her to the seat. "I hadn't really thought seriously about it before but ... but we'd been together a while, and I thought I loved her but ..." His words trailed off.

Dara felt something then, something that felt uncomfortably close to relief, optimism, hope. Noah said he'd *thought* he was in love. Did that mean then that ... no, no, don't even think about it, she told herself silently. It simply meant that he thought he was in love, nothing more. It certainly did not mean that he was *actually* in love with someone else, someone like her.

"We came home a few months later, but almost as soon as we came back, everything changed. It was weird, but it was as though we'd been living some kind of fantasy life while we were away. There were no responsibilities, no bills to pay, no mortgages. And once reality hit ..." his words trailed off and he shook his head. "It fell to pieces within a few months of our coming home. We rented a house for a while here – a nice place in Swords, but Maria couldn't settle. Eventually, she decided to go back to Manchester, where she's from. I think deep down, we both knew it was for the best. We weren't making one another happy. Chances were we weren't really in love at all – it was just an impulsive thing, a moment of madness really."

"I'm sorry," Dara said, meaning it. Such a shame to have it all fall apart so quickly.

"Ah, we were foolish to get married in the first place. She's a wonderful person, and I still care about her but ..." he paused and held Dara's gaze, those mesmerising green eyes almost boring into hers. Then, he dropped his eyes to the tablecloth before adding quietly, "It was never the same as ...the same as what we had, Dara."

At the moment, with those words, Dara felt as though someone had taken her heart and danced all over it. Was he saying …? Was he admitting …?

"That was a long time ago, Noah," she said, swallowing hard. "And we were young." She couldn't get into this; they couldn't talk about it. Not now, not after all this time. And she was *married* now, for God's sake!

"I know things were a bit strange between us before I left, but why didn't you answer my letters, Dara – or return my phone calls? The way we left things … it was awful. I knew you were upset but – "

"I wasn't just upset – I was embarrassed – mortified! Even now, thinking back on how stupidly I was behaving, how pathetic I must have looked …" She cringed again, remembering.

Noah smiled. "Look, you were just caught up in Clodagh's wedding. I know that. I knew it at the time. But I couldn't understand why you were so upset that night, I couldn't believe that you all but cut me out of your life afterwards."

"*Why* I was so upset?" The shame of it all so clear in her mind, even now, Dara couldn't help but talk about it. "Noah, we'd been together for years, and then all of a sudden you tell me you don't want to marry me, that you didn't see a future together – why wouldn't I be upset!" She lowered her voice slightly, afraid that someone might overhear them.

"That's not what I said," he countered swiftly. "I never said we didn't have a future together. As far as I was concerned you were the one for me, the *only* one for me, and you were my future. But at the time, I wasn't ready. I wanted to do something more with my life, I wanted to see the world, I wanted *us* to see the world together, before we thought about settling down. That's all it was, Dara. It had nothing to do with not loving you, or not wanting to marry you. I just wasn't ready."

He leaned forward in his chair and lightly touched her hand. "I couldn't believe it when you didn't want to talk to me before I left. I couldn't believe that it was over. But when you wouldn't take my phone calls and reply to my letters, I realised that you were serious, that I'd really lost you." He shook his head. "For a long time afterwards, I could hardly function. I was gutted." Then he smiled slightly. "At one stage, Charlie was nearly giving up on me. We were in Bangkok, on Patpong Road, and everywhere you looked there were these fantastic-looking women – "

"You *hope* they were women!" Dara said, amused.

"Nah, it wasn't like that," he grinned. "But Charlie's eyes were nearly popping out of his head, and me ... well, I just couldn't get into it. I just wasn't interested. Eventually, Charlie got sick of my moping around and he told me straight to either cop on or go home. And I thought seriously about going home, so I wrote you one last letter to see if you'd mellowed at all, or if you'd really just given up on me."

Dara remembered, and her heart twisted like a piece of rope. "I didn't reply," she confirmed sadly.

"No, you didn't."

Dara couldn't comprehend what she felt just then. She had made such a mess of everything. Noah had just admitted that what had happened back then wasn't the end of the world. He'd admitted that the ball had been in her court, but stupidly, she'd stuck to her guns. She remembered thinking back then that, if he really loved her, he wouldn't have gone in the first place.

"And chances are he's enjoying his new-found freedom!" she'd said huffily to Clodagh, all the jealousy and suspicion she'd found so difficult to handle at the beginning of the relationship flooding back.

"If you say so." By then, Clodagh was tired of listening to Dara moaning about Noah. She had a wedding to plan, and had little time for plamausing her heartbroken friend, who – when it came down to it – was so stubborn she was her own worst enemy.

Noah was going on with his story. "So I gave up. I let it go. And after a while, Charlie and I were enjoying ourselves so much that we decided to stay away a bit longer. We picked up part-time jobs here and there to keep us going and, eventually, I came to terms with the fact that you and I were finished." He paused then, and his eyes twinkled humorously. "And seeing as you seemed so anxious to get married, I thought you might have moved on, and replaced me." He shrugged. "And so you have."

Dara sat back in her chair and tried to take it all in. This was, crazy, unbelievable, surreal – no, in fact there wasn't a suitable word to describe how she felt now.

"And after a very long time, I eventually moved on myself." He laughed when Dara's eyes widened. "Don't get me wrong, I didn't exactly live like a monk. But when I met Maria, it was different. We got on so well, had a good laugh and I don't know, as I said, life is different, easier, more carefree when you're away. So, we were together for a while, things were good and so we got married."

"I know." Dara remembered the crushing disappointment she'd felt when she found his wedding photograph on the internet. When she told him this, his face fell.

"Oh."

"So, why Rome?" she couldn't help but ask. She'd been hurt so much by that in particular, by the fact that he'd gone off and got married in what was supposed to have been *their* place. Not that she had any right to feel that way, but still she couldn't help it. It had been the deepest cut of all. "Why Rome, when it was supposed to be ..." she shrugged, embarrassed all of a sudden, "you know."

Noah studied her. "To be honest, it was Maria's suggestion. We were in Italy at the time, and it was easy to arrange. One of her mates at home put her in touch with this wedding company ..." He shrugged uncomfortably. "Then again, maybe, deep down ... I don't know ... "

"I did something similar," Dara revealed, and told him about her honeymoon there. "I suppose I needed to get it – get *you* – out of my system." She didn't mind divulging the truth to him now, and it was strange, but despite not having seen Noah in so long, she still felt as easy and comfortable with him as if they had never been apart.

But things were different now, she thought, feeling more than a tinge of sadness as she wiggled the gold band on her finger, things were very different.

Noah had known instantly that Dara was married – he'd spotted the ring on her finger at the office earlier.

"So what's he like?" he asked. "Are you two married long?"

Dara's stomach dropped. Had it really been that short a time?

"A few months," she told him, almost ashamedly. "But he's wonderful."

And he was. The problem was that however wonderful Mark was, he wasn't the one who gave her butterflies in her stomach, who made her go weak at the knees. No, Mark Russell wasn't the man who did that.

But the man who *did* was just then sitting directly across from her, and as they both tried to make sense of how it had all gone wrong for them, she felt an aching regret.

"I'd better go back to the office," she said eventually, realising that they couldn't go on talking like this. It was way too dangerous. Things had changed, and while it was difficult seeing him in the flesh, and even more difficult hearing how she had ruined it all for them, she knew she couldn't travel any further along this road. Too much time had passed. They were both very different people with very different lives. Chances were they had nothing in common any more, other than their shared past.

"I'd love to see you again sometime," Noah said then, his tone neutral and his expression unreadable.

"I'm sure we will bump into one another at some stage," Dara replied as airily as she could.

"That's not what I meant."

Oh God no, she couldn't do this. Much as she was tempted, she couldn't start meeting Noah behind Mark's back, like that. With the way things were going, it would end in tears, there were no two ways about it, and she wasn't so naïve as to think they could start seeing one another just as friends. There was still too much electricity, too much spark – any fool could see that.

"Noah, I really don't think it would be a good idea," she said, refusing to meet his gaze. She picked up her handbag, and slung it over her shoulder. "It was wonderful seeing you again, and I'm … I'm sorry that things didn't work out for you and your wife."

"Sure." Still his expression was unreadable.

"But Paul is a good solicitor, and I'm sure he'll do a good job for you."

Just then she realised that they could all too easily bump into one another again, seeing as Noah was now a client of the firm. And deep down, something that felt dangerously close to excitement raised itself within.

"I'm sure he will."

She smiled tightly. "Right, well, thanks for lunch and … all the best. Take care."

"You too, Dara."

With that, she left the café, and as if in a trance made her way back to the office. She was going to forget every single word of that conversation and forget every detail of Noah's face, his smile, his incredible presence.

Yes, it had been a shock seeing him again after all this time and hearing the things he said, but things were different now. She was married to Mark now, and Noah was just an old friend, just a distant memory. A memory that she had to erase from her mind once and for all.

But that hadn't gone well so far, had it? Dara thought now, as the train pulled into Pearse Street Station. She *hadn't* been able to erase the memory, otherwise she wouldn't have been dreaming about him last night. And she still couldn't stop thinking about him this morning, when by rights she should be thinking about her husband.

Then, the frightening but all-important question she had spent the last twenty-four hours trying to bury rose to the surface with a vengeance.

Why had she done it? she asked herself finally. Why had she *really* married Mark? Was it to get back at Noah somehow? To prove to him, or even to herself that she wasn't going to sit around waiting for him to come back to her? Yet she had convinced herself – she had *really* convinced herself that she had lost her chance with Noah – that he was out of her life for good.

She went over her list of reasons once again – all of which had seemed perfectly valid at the time. Time was moving on, she was sick of being single, sick of being made feel like some sort of social pariah because she was the only one who wasn't married. Tired of making excuses to her mother, tired of feeling embarrassed for being independent, and finally beginning to wonder if she might end up alone. There was the question of children too, wasn't there? She had always wanted a child but didn't relish the prospect of raising one on her own.

So she'd decided to settle for the next best thing and marry a man she enjoyed being with. Someone for whom she had great affection, but didn't *really* love – not like she loved Noah anyway.

Right then, Dara deep down began to properly question whether she had made a huge mistake in marrying Mark.

But if she had, it was a bit late to be thinking about it now, wasn't it?

CHAPTER 17

As she carefully applied her make-up, Louise couldn't remember ever feeling so nervous. She'd agreed to meet Sam in town for a drink and was so worried about it she'd barely eaten all day. Which wasn't a bad thing in a way; at least there was no danger of her bursting out of the slim-fitting jeans she planned to wear.

"Now be careful," Fiona warned, setting off even more butterflies in Louise's tummy. "You don't know this guy very well so ..."

So ...what? Louise wanted to ask. Sam didn't seem the axe-murdering type, although these days it was hard to tell. She was touched by her friend's concern though. Fiona had her moments, but she was a bit of a softie at the end of the day.

"I'll be fine," she replied. "And you met him too – did he seem odd to you?"

Fiona wrinkled her nose. "Not weird as such, it's just ... well, let's be honest, he wasn't your usual type, Louise."

"My usual type?"

"Well, he was a bit too suave, a bit too ... I don't know, too good-looking I suppose."

So my type is weird, ugly, blokes then? Louise thought, more than a little insulted. And surely there was no such thing as *too* good-looking?

172

When she said this to Fiona, her friend shrugged and said, "Sorry, I really didn't mean to freak you out but sometimes you can be too trusting for your own good. Just try to be careful, that's all I'm saying. Guys like that ... well, you just need to know how to handle them."

Now, sitting on the train on the way into town, Louise wondered if her friend might have been right. She didn't know Sam at all, really. Maybe she had been a little bit hasty in agreeing to meet with him in town like this, rather than somewhere closer to home.

But didn't you take risks with every guy you met these days? And she was a firm believer in going with her gut instinct. Sam was lovely that night at the Four Seasons, and he was even lovelier that time on the phone. And playing hard to get had been a brainwave on her part, she decided happily. The ball was well and truly in her court, and if she could just keep her wits about her, tonight she'd play it to perfection. She liked him – a lot, and for once she wasn't going to ruin it all by being over-eager. Men didn't like that. No, tonight, Louise would be the self-assured, happy-go-lucky independent woman all the magazines insisted every woman should be. And, hopefully, Sam would fall madly in love with her and ... well, no point in running away with herself at the same time, she thought, biting her lip. If they got on well tonight and Sam was interested in seeing her again, then that would be a job well done.

It was pouring out of the heavens, and by the time she'd walked from the train station to the pub, Louise was soaked. She'd agreed to meet Sam in a popular city centre bar, a trendy spot with lots of harsh lights, loud music and – maddeningly – beautiful, self-assured, clientele. The kind of place that made someone like Louise – raindrops (and make-up) running down her face, dressed in white jeans, beaded cerise pink top and matching pink shoes – stand out like a sore thumb in comparison to the bohemian, hippy-chick look common there.

Once inside the pub, she ran her fingers through her wet hair, hoping and praying it wouldn't go too frizzy. So much for spending all that time with the hair-straightener. She couldn't see any sign of Sam, so while waiting for him to arrive, she grabbed a table and tried to assume a cool-as-you-like posture, all the time trying to conceal her rain-spattered jeans and soaking feet under the table. In all honestly, she must look like a drowned rat. What had possessed her to wear white jeans and strappy sandals – in the rain? God, she was an idiot sometimes.

"Glad you could make it!"

Louise felt warm breath on her ear and, startled, she turned around to see Sam grinning from ear to ear.

"You're here!" She smiled back, delighted to see him again, and thinking he looked even better than she remembered. She loved those little freckles across his cheeks – it made him look so boyish and innocent and cuddly.

"I was standing at the bar and saw you come in." He looked her briefly up and down. "You look …um…great."

Her face fell. "Am I that bad?" she asked, all hope of looking the part of the poised, sophisticated girl-about-town rapidly deflating.

Sam tried to keep a straight face. "Well, unless you're trying out some new Goth look …" He made trail marks along his own cheeks, and instantly she understood.

"Oh shit – my mascara!" Louise leapt up out of her seat.

"Well, I wasn't going to say anything but –"

"Where's the ladies' in here?"

Sam indicated somewhere down the back, so Louise had to suffer the indignity of passing a group of stunning girls, each of whom it seemed achieved naturally what Louise had spent the last few hours trying to pull off – effortless perfection. She tried to make herself seem inconspicuous but when she reached the ladies' and spied her reflection in the mirror, she realised that this was next to impossible.

Oh, my God, she looked like one of those mad Curehead-types gone wrong! Her lovely Clarins bronzer seemed to have completely dissolved in the rain, and her mascara, which the label had assured Louise was waterproof, was now happily running down both cheeks!

What must he think of her? However attractive she might have appeared to him the first night, he would almost definitely be changing his mind now. Chances were he would have run off when she went back out there.

But amazingly – and once she had done a repair job on her make-up – when Louise went back to the table, Sam was still there. He smiled impishly at her, his lovely dark eyes twinkling mischievously as she rejoined him.

"I wasn't sure what to get you," he said, indicating his own Budweiser.

"A beer is fine for me too, thanks," she said pleasantly to the waiting lounge girl.

Sam seemed amused. "Are you sure? You don't have to slum it with me, you know."

Louise frowned absently. Slum it? What was he ... oh! She remembered then he was referring to those blasted overpriced, underfilled, cocktails. She smiled and shook her head. "Beer will do."

"So what have you been up to lately?" Sam asked, settling himself comfortably.

And Louise, feeling much better after fixing her make-up, began to relax a little. Yes, he was definitely still as cute as she remembered, if not cuter, dressed as he was in a blue and navy rugby shirt and stonewashed denims. His tousled dark hair curled attractively at the ends and when he smiled ... phew! Once again, she wondered what on earth he saw in her.

"Oh, not a whole lot," she began, "I ..." she trailed off, realising he'd be bored to tears within five minutes if she told him the truth, that she'd spent the last few days trying to sell finance packages to desperate financially overburdened families, desperate for some extra cash in the run-up to Christmas.

And that she had a court case coming up soon, which was worrying her to death, and that her friend Fiona had convinced her to move into a lovely, but very expensive seafront apartment . . . speaking of which . . .

"I'm planning to move apartment soon," she told him, thinking that he would be most impressed at this. In fact, now that she thought about it, the game would be up if he ever found out about her poxy bedsit, wouldn't it? Then he'd know damn well she was just an ordinary, boring, run-of-the-mill office worker and not the

175

sophisticated woman of the world he'd chatted up in the Ice Bar.

As she'd hoped, Sam's eyes lit up with interest. "Really?"

"Yep – into one of those fabulous new places out near Dun Laoghaire," she continued proudly. "The Marina Quarter." The Marina Quarter, her new address. It sounded good, didn't it?

"Wow!" As expected, Sam looked suitably impressed. "I've seen those advertised – they're fucking fantastic!"

She smiled coquettishly. "Well, as my friend Fiona says – you met her, remember? 'We're worth it!'"

Sam laughed along, but Louise could see something else behind the smile. What was he thinking, she wondered. Was he worried that maybe she was out of his league, that this girl-about-town was too much for him, that he wouldn't be able keep up with her? But if he was drinking in a place like the Four Seasons then he must be used to girls like her and . . .

"What about yourself?" she asked, quickly changing the subject. "Have you been busy? By the way, what is it that you do? I know you told me you worked in an office but – "

Sam took a sip of his beer, and rolled his eyes. "You don't really want to know – I guarantee it would bore you tears – and it's a bit complicated."

"I do want to know," Louise took a slug of her Budweiser.

"Well, if you insist – I suppose you could say that I'm a troubleshooter," he replied simply, his tone suggesting that most people hadn't a clue what he did.

Louise nodded immediately. She knew exactly what that meant. She'd needed assistance from people like him often enough. "Helping people find out what's wrong with things ... like in computers and electrical goods, things like that?"

He nodded. "Something like that."

"So you're a techie then."

"Well, not quite, but close enough," he said grinning. "And what about you?"

"Me?"

"Yep, what do you do?"

"Oh, my job's even more boring," Louise replied, rolling her eyes. "I work in finance."

Sam nodded. "Perfect! And handy for all these nights out, and holidays abroad too, I'll bet!"

You have no idea, Louise thought, groaning inwardly. "Very handy," she agreed, laughing.

All too soon, her glass was empty and Sam quickly called for another round.

They chatted some more and, as Louise felt herself relax and become more comfortable with him, she realised how much she really did like him. He was nice, really nice and not just nice in a one-date kind of way. He was the kind of guy she really could see herself getting to know. Despite his obvious good looks, he didn't seem at all vain, something that was all too common in good-looking guys like that. Fiona had it all wrong. Sam was as normal as they came, and there was something about him that told Louise she could trust him with anything.

She wasn't quite sure why – she just knew it.

* * *

Over the next few weeks, she and Sam began to see more and more of one another. They seemed to get on amazingly well and enjoyed doing the same things: cheap and cheerful Italian restaurants, Thai takeaways and nights out at the cinema. The only snag was that Sam had a very sweet tooth and his constant chocolate munching was playing havoc with Louise's careful diet. Crème eggs especially were his thing, and one night at the cinema, and to Louise's immense amusement, he'd scoffed five gooey eggs in quick succession! Gradually she began to fall for him. No, let's be honest, she thought grinning, she'd fallen for him right from the very beginning. In the meantime, she'd simply kept falling harder.

"You should bring him over for a visit sometime," Heather suggested one day over the phone. She tried to sound offhand about it, but Louise knew her sister would be dying to suss Sam out, and see what he was like, or more importantly, to see if he was good enough for her baby sister.

"Maybe soon," Louise replied, "but you might need a bit of coaching beforehand!" She went on to laughingly explain how she'd led Sam to believe she was some kind of high-maintenance girl-about-town.

But Heather's disapproval was almost palpable. "Why does he think that? And more importantly why are you *letting* him think that?" she asked, in her most annoying, big-sister tone.

Louise explained how she and Sam had first met, and how while trying to appear cool and uninterested, she'd kept up the pretence of being someone worth getting to know.

"But Louise, you *are* someone worth getting to know," Heather replied, exasperated. "You don't need to pretend to be anything other than yourself!"

"But I really like him, Heather. He's different to most guys I've gone out with. He's mature, sensitive, funny and I feel as though I can talk to him about anything."

"Well, if that's the case, what does it matter if he finds out the truth? That you're not some rich kid from a well-off background, that you're just an ordinary, decent, hard working person from a normal, decent, hardworking background. If he's as nice as you say he is, then I'm sure he won't care where you come from."

At this, Louise felt ashamed. Her sister was right. She had no reason to be embarrassed about her upbringing. Her parents, and indeed Heather, had always done their best for her, and here she was more or less trying to deny them. It wasn't right.

But, at the time, she hadn't seen it like that. She just thought it would be fun pretending to be the kind of girl she'd always wanted to be, a fun, confident, desirable woman of the world. And in truth, she'd enjoyed her little fabrications to the point where she almost delighted in coming up with something new and equally outrageous. She wanted to live that kind of lifestyle – the shopping, the holidays, the girly friendships.

It hadn't really been about her background at all; it had been more about the kind of life Louise wanted to live, and how she wanted Sam and everyone else to see her.

Which was why, in the meantime, she'd given in to Fiona's requests and moved with her and Becky into that fabulous apartment in the Marina Quarter, finally leaving behind that horrible student bed-sit.

And these days Louise *was* living the glamorous, city-girl lifestyle she'd dreamed of, so she wasn't really making it up, was she? Only the other night, she and the girls had blagged their way into one of the celebrity hangouts in town. It had been great fun. And there had been loads of really famous faces there – TV stars, sports stars, Irish models. Louise's eyes had nearly been out on stalks at the sight of people she usually only saw in the papers or on the telly.

"And guess who we saw there?" she told Heather, sure that her sister would be dead impressed by her glamorous social life.

"Who?"

"Troy Brophy-Hyland!"

"That tosspot rugby player with the highlights in his hair?"

Well, that was one way of describing him, Louise thought, and in truth he wasn't exactly God's gift, but he *was* a celebrity so … "Yes, and he smiled at me and Fiona when we were on our way to the ladies'!"

"*Ooooh!*" Heather gushed sarcastically.

"But it was Troy Brophy-Hyland, Heather!" Louise persisted, feeling vaguely disappointed that her sister didn't seem at all impressed by this. "He's really famous!"

"Famous for what? For his girly hairstyle, or the amount of Irish models he's screwed? It's certainly not for his rugby skills. Sure, he hasn't been picked for the Irish team in months."

Yes, well, Heather had a point there but –

"Louise, please don't tell me you've been taken in by all these posers and so-called celebrities. They're a shower of fakes! God knows I come across enough of them in the hotel over here, and they are so far up their own backsides it's incredible!"

Louise bit her lip. But they were all so glamorous, and so good-looking and so *important* – and most people would kill to get the chance to be in the same room as them, so –

"Look, just promise me you'll keep your feet on the ground, OK?" Heather went on. "I'm sure the Dublin party scene is great fun, but remember these people aren't your friends, and they never will be. They're brainless shallow idiots who worry more about posing for the society pages than they do about anything else. Don't fall for that crap, Louise."

"But I like being part of it all, Heather. It's really exciting and glamorous and – "

"What's exciting about it? And it's not glamorous – it's bloody pathetic. Why do you hold these people in such high esteem, Louise? What have they ever done for you? "

Louise sighed. Heather could be such a party-pooper sometimes. She just didn't understand the Dublin social scene, that was all.

When she told Heather this, her sister tut-tutted. "Just be careful it doesn't all end in tears."

"All what?"

"That new apartment, the expensive holidays and all these mad nights out. Listening to you, it does seem as though you're not telling this Sam too many lies at all. You do seem to be having a right old time of it." Then she paused. "Which is great, Louise, but ..."

"But what?"

"Well, how can you afford all this? Did you pay off the loan early, or something?"

Even though her sister couldn't see her, Louise blushed guiltily. *The* loan. Little did Heather know that where there had once been one loan, there were now two, as well as credit cards and an overdraft, of course. But it would all be sorted once the court case was settled, wouldn't it? And wasn't everyone always saying that you couldn't take it with you?

Anyway, Louise didn't want to spend the rest of her life living in a dingy bedsits, thinking about paying off loans, while all her friends were going out and living life to the full. And seeing as she had a boyfriend now, she grinned happily, she couldn't be sitting in every night, worrying about money, otherwise she'd end up old and grey –

and worse, on her own. Everyone knew how difficult it was to find someone these days, let alone someone nice, and she couldn't risk her budding relationship for the sake of paying off an overdrawn credit card, could she? That would be madness!

No, that was just the way things were these days. Fiona had *three* different credit cards, and with the way her friend spent money, she was probably *much* more in debt than Louise was. Heather just didn't understand how things were. She was ten years older, and had grown up in different times to this. Not to mention that she'd already found her man and was very happily married. So how could she possibly understand?

"No, the loan is still there, but Mr Cahill – "

"Louise, don't assume you're home and dry with that claim," Heather interjected, a warning tone in her voice. Her sister hadn't at all approved of the personal liability suit, believing, rather as Louise had at the beginning that no good would come of it. "Don't make the mistake of thinking that it will solve everything. God forbid, but if you lose…"

"I won't lose, Heather," Louise said defiantly. "Mr Cahill reckons it's an open-and-shut case. With all the complications I had afterwards – "

"I know that, pet," Heather's tone softened, obviously recalling that difficult time, "but you just never know."

"It'll be fine," Louise insisted, Cahill's words reverberating in her mind. "It's an open-and-shut case, we're certain of it. And it'll all be fine."

CHAPTER 18

In the weeks that followed, Rosie did her best to keep out of David's way. Thankfully, he had got a job as a plasterer on a building site in town, so these days she only saw him in the evenings. He had calmed down somewhat about the house since, although he had obviously had a go at Sophie.

"Just because he's dumped and homeless doesn't mean he should be taking it out on me," Sophie had whined down the phone the very next day. "And the nerve of him for suggesting that I would try to take the house from underneath him! Of *course* everything will be doled out fair and square – Rob and I wouldn't have it any other way."

On the other end of the line, Rosie waited patiently for Sophie to remember that her mother was actually still alive, and all this talk of 'doling out' was for at the moment totally irrelevant.

Not to mention hurtful.

It was hard to credit that her children were thinking this way. Perhaps it was inevitable – particularly once Martin died – that David and Sophie would begin to realise that their parents wouldn't be around forever, but what upset her the most was that this didn't seem to bother them all that much. If they realised she was getting on, surely the fact should make them appreciate her all the more?

Yet, Rosie was no martyr – she and Martin had raised their children to be self-sufficient and independent, and she certainly would never expect either of them to do what Sheila's Gillian had done by having them look after her in her old age.

Old age indeed! For goodness sake – they were behaving as though she was at death's door! And she was in good health apart, of course, from the arthritis, and the few twinges in her bones now and then. As far as she was concerned, she was a long way off being carted away!

But even having thoughts like these made her feel uneasy and pessimistic, and she didn't like that. She needed something to look forward to, something to lift her spirits and stop her thinking about how little her children seemed to think of her.

Which was why on her most recent visit to Sheila, Rosie told her friend she was taking up a new hobby.

"It's something I've always wanted to do," she'd said, purposely omitting the most recent 'confrontation' with David, and his outburst about his inheritance. There was no point. Sheila would only be worried about her, and would keep on at her to be more assertive when dealing with him.

But there was no point in aggravating the situation. David was obviously here to stay – and by the looks of things – for the long haul. They both had to live at the house together, and there was no point in her making things worse by creating tension between them.

So, instead, she resolved to stay out of David's way, her intentions of looking after him in his 'hour of need' now well and truly out the window. No, she'd do her own thing as normal, and let David do his, and hopefully there would be no more talk of what would happen to the house afterwards.

So when a brochure advertising a selection of evening classes came in the letterbox , she immediately decided to go for it. Her subject of choice was watercolour painting.

"What?" Sheila arched an eyebrow at this. "When have you ever been interested in that kind of thing?"

Uncomfortable with any kind of deceit, Rosie looked away. Sheila knew her too well. The truth was that she had no interest at all in 'that kind of thing', but the idea sounded pleasant enough, and as – unlike some of the other options – it didn't require any great amount of writing or studying, it should suit her down to the ground.

Anyway, it would get her out of David's way for one night at least, and that was the main thing. On the others, she could pop across to one of the neighbours for a chat, or maybe go down the town with Twix for a bit of a walk around. Still, the evenings were drawing in now, and as safe as the town might be, Rosie didn't want to run the risk of going down dark roads on her own. Twix might be great at acting the big bad dog, but in reality, she wouldn't be much protection, God love her.

On the nights that she didn't go out, she would leave David alone watching telly in the living-room, and she would stay in the kitchen, reading in her chair. She had stocked up on some great books and was looking forward to delving into them all.

Being without the television didn't bother her; she could pick up the news during the day if she wanted, and she was sure life would continue just fine without *Coronation Street*. It was all the same old storylines every week anyway, she convinced herself, and she'd get just as much drama from her books.

And with any luck, she might really like this watercolour painting and might end up losing herself for hours in the kitchen practising that. Rosie smiled. Martin would be proud of her. He was always a great man for knowledge, great for learning new skills and educating himself.

So, it was with a nice sense of achievement that, that same evening, Rosie presented herself at the school to take her first class in over forty years. She tried not to let the nerves show, especially when she walked into the classroom and instantly deduced that she was without doubt the oldest person there. By about twenty years.

The odds were stacked against her though, as it seemed that this particular class was under-subscribed, and there were no more than eight people in attendance. She had hoped there would be a few locals here, but she didn't recognise any of the faces.

Rosie smiled awkwardly around the room and just then her spirits lifted when another man, looking like he had a few years on her, came in just after her.

"Hello, everyone, and welcome!" the man announced in a strong, booming voice, and Rosie's heart plummeted when she realised that the older man had to be the teacher. Of course.

The man sat down, his long denim-clad legs facing the others; his face tanned and weathered-looking, as if he spent a lot of time outside.

"Welcome to 'Watercolour Painting for Beginners'. Now we all know why we're here – and by the looks of things there mightn't be too many of us," he added, his eyes twinkling humorously.

Rosie warmed to him immediately, and her demeanour relaxed slightly.

"So why don't we begin by introducing ourselves? I'm Stephen Dowd, and hopefully by the end of the next few weeks, I'll have taught you lot all there is to know about watercolour painting."

As Rosie was the nearest to him, he looked at her to continue with the introductions. She blinked nervously, and although it was many, many years ago, she remembered clearly feeling the same way on her first day at school.

"Em, hello," she began, her cheeks reddening at being the focus of attention, particularly Stephen's. "My name is Rosie Mitchell and I ... I . . ." she said, stumbling hoarsely, "I live up the road."

"Great!" Stephen interjected, his grey eyes alight with warmth. "We'll have somewhere for our wild student parties then!"

The others laughed and, knowing that Stephen was trying to put her at ease, Rosie smiled gratefully at him.

The others introduced themselves and then the rest of the evening was spent learning the basic procedures of watercolour painting and becoming familiar with the paint and materials. To her surprise, she enjoyed the class immensely, and couldn't believe it when Stephen announced that time was almost up.

The two hours had flown by, and almost immediately she found herself looking forward to the next lesson. Of course, Stephen's lovely easy-going manner helped greatly, and as if sensing that Rosie was overwhelmed at being there, he seemed to take that little bit of extra time in making sure she understood things properly.

"I know it's too early to tell, but I think you could have an eye for this type of thing," he said, causing Rosie to blush profusely, secretly delighted that she might be good at it.

He really was a proper dote, and had such a lovely way about him that he was the ideal person to teach an evening class, she thought, walking up the hill on her way home. She wondered idly where Stephen was from, having found it difficult to place his accent during the lesson. The South somewhere – possibly Cork or Kerry, she decided, opening the front gate.

Rosie yawned. She felt quite tired after all that concentrating, and despite her earlier intentions of coming home and relaxing on the armchair with a nice hot cup of tea and a biscuit, now she thought she might just go on up to bed. She'd better let Twix out to do her business first, though.

Letting herself in quietly, Rosie hung up her coat and almost tiptoed into the kitchen. Sheila would murder her for creeping around like that but she couldn't help it. Since David's return and his subsequent behaviour, she'd felt like a stranger in her own home and at times felt almost apologetic about being there. Anyway, it was easier to just fade quietly into the background and try not to annoy him. So, she'd just let Twix out and then …

"Mum, where on earth have you been?" she heard a voice from behind ask.

Rosie whirled around in surprise. "David, I didn't want to disturb you while you were watching television and – "

"Where were you till this hour?" he asked again, this time looking at his watch. "It's almost half ten, and it's pitch black out."

Instantly, Rosie was touched by his concern. "I was taking an evening class, love – didn't I mention it?" she said, her face slightly flushed with enthusiasm. She didn't think to tell him, assuming that he wouldn't care less as long as she was out of his way. But as David was so worried about her, she had obviously underestimated him and –

"An evening class? What kind of an evening class would you take?" he asked, his expression disbelieving. "Sure, you can barely write!"

Rosie winced, stung. "I know that, David," she said quietly. "That's why I'm taking a painting class."

"But what's wrong with the painting *I've* been doing for you?" he asked, accusingly. "Is it not good enough for you? Funny that, seeing as none of the rooms have been touched in years!"

"No, no," Rosie shook her head, her heart quickening nervously, "it's not that kind of painting, love – it's pictures, painting pictures – and Stephen – the teacher thinks I could be good at it – he reckons I have a good eye." She was babbling now but she couldn't help it.

David snorted. "Isn't it well for you? Swanning off to painting classes and leaving the place in a heap. Do you not realise how hard I have it working all day on that building site, without having to come home and clean up the kitchen before I can even start making dinner?"

The place in a heap? Clean up the kitchen? What was he talking about? She had left a plate and few pots in the sink instead of washing up straight afterwards like she usually did. But because she'd been so anxious about going to the class, and especially about what to *wear* going to the class, she'd forgotten all about it.

"David, I was going to wash up, but I was in a bit of a rush and – "

"A bit of a rush! A bit of a rush! Well, that must mean you're *always* in a bit of a rush, with the way you look after this place. The kitchen is filthy, Mum – the worktop needs a good scrub, and the oven looks like it hasn't been cleaned in months!"

"It's been difficult to clean the oven since I put my back out, David," she said carefully. "It's hard for me to bend down. But I keep my house as well as I've always done."

David snorted again, his comments wounding Rosie to the core, and making her wonder when her son – who used to put dirty leaves in his pockets and trail mud from his football boots around the house when he was younger – had turned into an obsessive hygiene nut.

"And you know I can't stand that bloody dog traipsing around everywhere," he continued, and for reasons she couldn't quite comprehend Rosie immediately felt a stab of fear. He wouldn't do anything ... would he?

Now, terrified that poor little Twix might have taken the full brunt of his anger, Rosie turned on her heel and went into the kitchen to look for her beloved pet.

"I put it outside in the shed," David informed her in bored tone.

"What? You can't do that, David. It's cold and damp out there and Twix has been sleeping inside since she was a puppy. She could catch her death!"

David murmured something under his breath that to Rosie's ears sounded like 'no bloody harm' and, if the thought of the poor creature freezing and miserable in the dark shed didn't set Rosie off, that did.

"I'm sorry, David, but I won't have it," she said, her voice rising slightly as she headed for the back door and went outside. "She's my dog, and this is my house, and I won't have you throwing the poor defenceless little animal out like some dirty rat!"

"It *is* a dirty rat," David challenged, appearing at the kitchen door. "Sniffing and mooching around, begging for food all the time. I have no peace with it."

"She's my dog, David."

"And I'm your son."

"I know you are, but Twix has been with me for a long time now, and I won't have her mistreated."

"Mistreated? I only put the bloody animal out in the shed – where it should be as far as I'm concerned."

And do you feel the same way about me? Rosie wondered then. *Should I be out in the shed too, because with the way you just spoke to me in there, it certainly feels that way.*

"Well, I'm not leaving her out here," she said, her tone defiant, belying her inner distress.

"Oh, for God's sake!" Shaking his head in frustration, David petulantly slammed the back door behind him.

Her hands shaking with a combination of nerves and unease, Rosie took a deep breath and approached the shed. Struggling to undo the lock under the faint outside bulb, she opened the door, peered inside and found the little dog cowering in a corner, obviously frightened out of her wits. Immediately recognising her mistress, the spaniel whimpered softly.

"Come on, Twix. There's a good girl," Rosie coaxed, her heart breaking at the sight of her. But still Twix didn't move, her huge eyes wide and sorrowful, her little body shaking with fear.

Rosie's stomach felt sick, and her eyes filled with tears. By the looks of things, David had done more than just throw the dog out. She shook her head dejectedly, recalling the time he had aimed a kick at Twix. This time, the aim may have met its mark.

How could he be so cruel? How could he be so cold and heartless, so different from the warm, loving David she thought she'd raised? What had happened to him that he could treat a poor defenceless animal this way?

Then again, she admitted, he hadn't exactly been generous in his treatment of his mother lately either, had he? Immediately, Rosie pushed this thought out of her head, for the moment unwilling to admit to herself that her son had been mistreating her too.

She continued persuading Twix out of the shed.

"Come on now, good girl," she said, reaching out and patting the dog's soft silky head. At this, Twix edged forward slightly and eventually made her way towards Rosie, her short tail wagging cautiously.

"Good girl." Trying to ignore the sharp pain at the base of her spine, Rosie picked her up and held her close, the little spaniel shaking all over. "Come on and we'll get you inside," she said, heading back into the kitchen.

Luckily, when they returned David was nowhere to be seen. Rosie closed the door behind her and set Twix gently back down in her basket. For a long moment, she just stood in the middle of the room, unsure what to do or what to feel. She felt like going after David and having it out with him, but yet she couldn't face another confrontation – she just wasn't able for it.

Her earlier excitement about the evening class now well and truly evaporated, Rosie sank heavily onto the armchair, and tried to stop the tears from coming.

It was bad enough that David had openly admitted he was staying around until she popped her clogs, let alone trying to make her life a misery while she was still alive. And what was all that about her keeping a filthy house? Did he not realise how much harder a simple thing like cleaning the inside of an oven was for Rosie these days – especially with her bad back?

And should she really be chastised (chastised by her own son, imagine – Rosie grimaced sadly) for not washing up the few bits she had used for her dinner earlier? What gave him the right to say that, to behave that way towards his own mother?

And to think, she reflected, letting out a low laugh, to think that only the other day one of the neighbours had stopped Rosie on the street to tell her how lucky she was to have her son back living with her again, and how lovely it must be to have him around to look after her.

"And such a lovely, friendly fellow too," Maude Hennessey informed her, blissfully unaware of the side of David his mother had the misfortune of seeing. "Myself and some of the neighbours have met him a few times since he came back, and he'd always have a big wave and smile for you."

Well, Rosie thought now, the 'lovely fellow' Maude was talking about might be a street angel, but as she herself had discovered the hard way, he was also very much a house devil.

Where had she gone wrong? she wondered despondently. How had she raised a child that could behave like this? A child that would make his mother feel like a prisoner in her own home?

Rosie didn't know. And she didn't know how she could go on living this way, living the rest of her days with a son who clearly didn't love her – or if he did, had a very strange way of showing it.

And the funny thing was, she thought now, it wasn't until David had moved back home and brought up the subject of his inheritance that she had begun to think about her own mortality, that she had begun to actually feel old.

Before then, she had done her best to enjoy and embrace life, and make the most of it, despite the fact that she would no longer be enjoying it with Martin. Her husband had always eschewed the notion of the settled, retired-pensioner type who after a certain age shied away from the world and all it had to offer. He had always believed that life was there to be enjoyed and embraced, no matter what age you were.

And up until David's return a month or two ago, Rosie had believed it too.

* * *

Rosie threw herself into her watercolour painting after that. Unlike some of the others in the class, she never missed a lesson, and perhaps because of David's hurtful comments about her abilities, she found herself almost doubly determined to do well.

But according to Stephen she didn't have to try too hard.

"You *do* have a natural eye, Rosie," Stephen had said in the last lesson when he was teaching them to sketch outlines. "Especially for composition. It takes some of my students months to achieve that."

Rosie sat back and studied her outline. They were only sketching from photographs, but she thought it was obvious that the dominant object – in this case a boat – should be positioned so that the eye was immediately drawn to it.

She smiled inwardly. Maybe she did have a natural eye.

Or maybe Stephen was just feeling sorry for her. But then again, why would he do that? He didn't know her from Adam, and yes, it had been obvious on the first night of class that she was nervous, but since then she had become much more confident – both in herself and her abilities.

And while before she might have been afraid to ask about something she didn't understand for fear of appearing ignorant, Stephen was so approachable that she didn't hesitate to ask his advice and opinions. Luckily, he never seemed to mind answering what she considered inane and obvious questions, and took as much time as necessary to help her understand.

Rosie felt enormously comfortable around him. Perhaps this was because they were around the same age, she thought, recalling how one time Stephen had let slip the year he was born, much to the amusement of some of the younger students.

That evening after class, they both happened to be leaving the building at the same time. When approaching the front door, Stephen, like a true gentleman stepped forward and opened the door ahead of Rosie, then stood back to let her pass.

"Thank you very much, sir," Rosie smiled, unused to such chivalry.

"My pleasure, madam," he said, smiling back at her.

Outside, she gathered her tweed coat tightly around her. "It's a cold one tonight," she said. She was sorry now she hadn't brought her hat and gloves.

"It certainly is," Stephen replied, putting on his own jacket. "And it looks like we could have frost too." He looked at Rosie, who stood there shivering. "Can I give you a lift anywhere?"

"Ah no, I don't want to delay you," she said waving him away. "Anyway, my house isn't far from here."

Stephen's grey eyes twinkled. "Well, if it isn't far, it won't delay me, will it? Come on, it's freezing," he urged. "Now the heater in the car isn't great, but I can almost guarantee that it'll be warmer than this anyway."

Rosie was torn. On the one hand, she didn't want to impose, but on the other, the thought of not having to walk up that steep hill – particularly in this cold – sounded heavenly.

"If you're sure you don't mind," she said finally

"No problem at all – I'd be delighted," Stephen said, leading her to where his car was parked. "Just tell me where to go, and I'll have you home in no time."

Rosie gave him short directions to the house, and then settled herself into the passenger seat.

But almost as soon as she was inside the car, she began to have second thoughts. Yes, Stephen was her teacher and seemed like a very nice man, but at the same time he could be anyone! What if he wasn't as nice as he seemed, and decided to take her away into the Wicklow Mountains and chop her to pieces or something? Rosie's heart tightened as a bout of unexplained nervousness overwhelmed her. Oh, how she wished Martin were still here; then she wouldn't have to be getting lifts with strangers in the first place, she thought, her nerves suddenly sending her fears – and imagination – into overdrive.

"Are you OK? Is that seat too far forward for you?" Stephen's calm, assured voice startled her out of her reverie.

But, of course, that's why these murderers got away with these things, wasn't it? she thought, her paranoia in full flight now. Because they seemed so nice and trustworthy. Well, she wasn't going to take anything for granted.

"No, no, it's fine," she replied absently, all the time trying desperately to think of a good escape plan, should one be required.

"I've got all this equipment on the floor behind you," Stephen was saying, as he started the car, "but I could move it out of your way if you like."

Her eyes widened at this. Equipment? What *sort* of equipment? Ropes, knives, duct-tape, maybe?

"Rosie, are you sure you're OK?" he asked again, concerned by her obvious change in demeanour.

"I'm grand," she said, as the car moved off. Then, all of a sudden, she lifted her handbag onto her lap, making sure it was in full view. She then made a great show of patting the bulge of her hairbrush beneath the leather. "Just making sure my gun is safe," she added airily.

Stephen almost rear-ended the car in front of him. "Your *what!*"

"My gun," Rosie repeated, pleased with herself. That had been a brainwave. Now he knew better than to try anything!

"O – K." There was a silence in the car for a while, as they made their way through the town and up the hill towards Rosie's house.

Then, her anxiety somewhat relieved, Rosie smiled inwardly. What had she been thinking, getting carried away with herself like that? Stephen was her teacher – her *friend*, for goodness sake! She stifled back an amused laugh. God, he must think she was an awful eejit – if not downright insane!

Eventually Stephen spoke again. "So, do you – em – carry one of those everywhere with you or – "

"Oh, everywhere," she replied, before she could stop herself, unwilling to call a halt to the charade just yet – not to mention that it would be very difficult to do that now! "Because these days you just never know."

"Right." Stephen seemed flabbergasted. He paused again. "And ... and did you have to get a permit for it, then – the gun, I mean."

A permit? Rosie floundered, her nervousness swiftly returning. Now, if Stephen *did* happen to be a murderer then he would know all about permits and things, and whether or not they were required. So, she'd better get the answer right, otherwise he'd know she was bluffing.

"I think so," she replied cautiously. "But my son sorts out those kinds of things for me, so I don't really know the details." That was a good one.

"So, your son works in the defence forces or something then, does he?" Stephen enquired.

"No, he's an FBI agent actually." Again, the words were out before she could stop herself. Perhaps that was *really* overdoing it, and maybe she shouldn't have said it, but despite herself she was rather enjoying this little bit of excitement.

"An FBI agent? I see."

Stephen was silent for the remainder of the journey and when the car eventually turned into her estate, Rosie knew she was home free.

She gave him a quick glance out of the corner of her eye and felt suddenly ashamed. Imagine thinking that this nice, mild-mannered evening-class teacher was actually a serial killer! Her imagination had really run away with her this time and, in fairness, she should just tell him the truth and apologise. Otherwise what would he think of her when she turned up for class from now on?

"Where will I drop you?" Stephen asked.

Feeling guilty then, and more than a little embarrassed about distrusting him, Rosie asked him to let her off at the nearest corner.

"No, seriously, I said I'd drop you home and that's what I'll do. So, what number?"

"Honestly, Stephen, it's fine," Rosie said. "It's one of those houses just there."

"Which one?" he insisted.

And quick as a flash, Rosie felt the earlier panic wash over her once again. Why was he so persistent in finding out where she lived? Had she been right all along?

"Well, which one?" Stephen repeated, this time with an impatient edge to his tone, she thought, and immediately her mouth went dry. Her heart thudded against her chest.

Then, all of a sudden, he reached across, as if to lunge for her and ...

Rosie quickly closed her eyes, covered her face with her hands and let out a terrified yelp.

"Rosie? Are you all right?"

A blast of cool air rushed in from somewhere and then she heard Stephen chuckling softly.

Slowly, she took her hands away from her face, and glanced towards the open passenger door. Then, even more slowly, she turned her head to look at him and as she did, a feeling of immense relief rushed through her.

He was still laughing, his big body shaking with amusement. "Rosie, you are an absolute tonic," he said, his eyes sparkling in the darkness. "Did you honestly think I was going to kidnap you, or something?"

Rosie was mortified. "Of course not," she said. "I just got a bit of a fright, that's all."

"I see," Stephen was nodding his head exaggeratedly. "And was it just myself, or do you threaten every man that offers you a lift home with a gun?" he added, in a teasing way that suggested he knew all along she'd made it up.

She bit her lip, now feeling very silly. "No, not every man," she admitted apologetically. Then she turned to face him. "I'm very sorry, Stephen – I really don't know what came over me. Here you were good enough to offer me a lift home, and here I was thinking all these terrible things about you and I got a bit carried away and –"

He waved her away. "Look, I don't blame you – and with the way things are these days, you're probably right to be concerned. But Rosie, we've known each other for a few weeks now, and I think you're a lovely person, and ... well, look, I'm not sure if I've any right to say

195

it, but I thought we were friends."

She smiled at him, thinking again how stupid she was to believe he might do her harm. Not when he'd spent all that extra time in the class making sure she'd do well!

"You're right, Stephen, and I don't know why I'm behaving like this. Of course, I know you're a lovely fellow and ... oh, I don't know, it's stupid really, but since Martin – my husband – died, I feel a bit like a rowing boat with only one oar." She sighed. "I relied on him for so much and ...oh, I know it's pathetic, but sometimes, I don't know if I'm coming or going."

"No, it's not pathetic," he insisted in a tone that suggested he knew exactly where she was coming from. "Still, I must admit I wasn't altogether sure you *didn't* have a gun in there either!" he added, laughing again. "With women these days you just never know!"

"Sorry." Rosie felt really silly now. "Well, look," she said, "I've delayed you enough and we've both had enough excitement for one night, so –"

"Is the house far?"

"Just a little further down and around the corner," Rosie admitted. "But I'll be grand from here, honestly."

"Don't be silly – I'll run you down. I have to go and turn the car anyway. Close the door."

"All right so," Rosie sat back in and closed the passenger door, not wanting to cause any more fuss.

Seconds later, he pulled up outside her front gate. The light in the living-room was on which meant that David was still up. Rosie sighed inwardly.

"Someone waiting up for you?" Stephen enquired.

Rosie nodded. "My son lives with me now."

"Oh right." Stephen was silent for a moment. "It can be hard going sometimes, can't it?" again suggesting he knew what he was talking about. "I had my daughter and her husband live with me for just a few months recently while they were waiting to move into their new house. As much as I love Miriam, it was tough going. We clash a lot and Mary, my wife, used to say it was because the two of us were so bloody alike." He smiled, as if remembering. "I suppose she was right, in a way. But it was a bit of a nightmare and, really, I thought the day would never come when they would move out so that my life could get back to normal."

Rosie nodded, understanding the feeling perfectly. "David moved home recently after living ten years in Liverpool. He split up with his wife," she added, strangely relieved that someone understood that it wasn't necessarily all fun and games having your adult son back living under your roof.

Sometimes, she felt really guilty for admitting to herself that the situation wasn't ideal, and indeed, believed herself to be a bad mother for wishing that David had never come back to stay with her. Before his return, she'd been quite happy with her life, her independence and her own little ways. Now, it was all this tiptoeing around, trying not to put him out, while all the time painfully aware that he was unconcerned about putting her out – quite the opposite.

Stephen must have seen most of this written on her face. "God knows we do our best for them growing up, and they don't all necessarily return the favour," he said. "But at the same time, it doesn't mean they don't care either," he added softly.

Rosie nodded, deciding she'd better go in, or she'd keep him here all night talking about it. But she was glad they'd had the opportunity to have this little chat. Stephen understood her situation, probably better than she understood it herself. Knowing this made her feel much better about it all.

"I should go and let you get home," she said, smiling shyly at him. "Are you living in Dublin?"

"No, no, I'm only out in Brittas," he said, referring to the popular coastal beauty spot not far from Wicklow Town. "I have one of those nice houses that look out over the sea – ideal for practising my watercolours." He grinned. "That's how I started actually. For years I lived with these fantastic views and then when I retired I decided I'd have a crack at preserving them forever on canvas."

Rosie sighed. "I'd say that would be fabulous, painting down there by the sea," she said. "Aren't you lucky? I'd love a go at that real-life stuff." Then she grinned. "Sure, maybe by the time you're finished teaching me, I might be able to!"

He laughed. "No bother to you! And look, if you're ever down my direction and you'd like to try it, give me a shout and I'll show you the kind of stuff I've done."

Rosie smiled, gratified by the invitation but fairly sure she'd never accept it.

"Although, if things go well, I won't be there for too much longer," Stephen said then. When she looked at him inquisitively, he added. "The place is up for sale. It's much too big for me, now that the family have all moved out and apparently it's in such a good location, it'll fetch an indecent price, or so the estate agent tells me."

Rosie nodded wryly. "I can imagine."

"So, I'm going to take whatever money I get from it and put it towards a nice place on the Atlantic coast, down Kerry way, probably," he said. "I've always loved it down there and, as you know yourself anywhere near the city can get a bit hectic after a while, what with all the traffic and everything."

Rosie nodded, understanding.

"So I thought slowing down, taking it easy and painting the landscape in a nice quiet spot would be as good a way as any to spend the rest of my days."

Rosie shook her head. That sounded like absolute bliss. She didn't know why she didn't think of doing something like that herself – maybe move back home to Clare. But, she supposed, because David was here and her daughter and granddaughter were living in Dublin, she wanted to be close, to be there should her family need her. But did her family need her? Did they care where she lived or if she was around for them?

Still, it was a bit late now to be thinking of upping off back home to Clare, not when the house was entangled in Sophie's mortgage and all that, not to mention David living with her too.

No, she was well and truly stuck here now whether she liked it or not. And, of course, Rosie did like it, in fact, she loved living in Wicklow, but she wondered if she were really free to make such a decision, would she move back home, back home to Clare, where her heart still lay?

Rosie didn't know. All she did know was that there was no point in wishful thinking. What was done was done and she had to live with it.

"Well, good luck with the sale," she said to Stephen. "And thanks again for giving me a lift home."

"No problem at all," he replied. "And I'd love to say it was a pleasure, but being threatened by a madwoman with a gun isn't a pleasurable experience for anyone, I'd say!" He laughed again. "All the best, Rosie – I'll see you next week?"

"You will," she replied, getting out and closing the door behind her.

Then, she walked up her front path.

As she put her key in the door and watched the tail-lights of his car move away in the distance, Rosie realised she had made a new friend.

CHAPTER 19

The following Monday morning, Dara was late for work. The train had been delayed, and as a result, so were the long-suffering rail commuters of the East Coast.

Grrr! At times like this she was half-tempted to go back to using a car, but she knew her nerves just wouldn't be able to take it. Anyway, over the weekend, she and Mark had gone to the first of what she expected would be many house viewings over the coming weeks – if not months – and if they got something near the new tramline, as was their intention, she might not need to travel on this train for much longer.

Getting out at Pearse Street Station, she tried to steal a march on some of her fellow harried travellers by taking the steps down to the street two at a time.

She made it to the office a full half-hour late, but instead of teasing her about her lateness like she usually did, Ruth simply eyed her enquiringly and smiled one of her annoying self-satisfied smiles.

"What are you staring at …?" The rest of her sentence trailed off as just behind Ruth, Dara caught sight of her desk. She gasped. There sitting on top of her books, papers, stationery etc was an immense bunch of lilies – dragon lilies, her favourite. The bouquet was so huge it hid most of the desktop.

Instantly, her throat went dry. As far as she was aware there was only one person who knew those flowers were her favourite, and that person was –

"And you tell me Mark isn't romantic?" Ruth sighed dreamily. "But what's the occasion, Dara? I thought it might be an anniversary or something, but it hasn't been that long since the wedding, has it?"

Her tongue felt like sandpaper. "No – no, it's nothing like that."

"Well, go on!" Ruth urged cheerfully. "Tell me all, or if you don't know what you've done to deserve such an incredible bouquet, then at least open the card and put both of us out of our misery!"

"Um, I don't have time now," Dara muttered uncomfortably. "I'll have a look later." She set down her briefcase, and went behind her desk.

Ruth's eyes widened. "What? Are you serious? How can you *not* look? Come on, please – for me?" She continued to plead in that silly child-like tone she often used to get round people. "Please?"

Dara bit her lip. Shit, she might as well bite the bullet. They were just flowers after all, and who was to say they *weren't* from Mark, or even from a client? The fact they happened to be her favourite blossoms was probably pure coincidence. She tentatively opened the envelope and slowly removed the gift card. There was no reason for her to automatically assume that they were from … oh God, they were.

Really enjoyed catching up the other day.
Hope we can do it again soon … N. xx
Followed by his mobile number.

Oh, great, she thought, just great. That was all she needed. Just when she'd tried to put that lunch – that conversation – out of her mind, he goes and does this. And, even more disconcertingly, the fact he'd included his mobile number meant she would have to make contact in order to thank him for the flowers . . . wouldn't she? And then … who knew what could happen then?

Nevertheless, deep down, she couldn't help but experience a tiny frisson of anticipation, but discarded the feeling almost as soon as it reared itself.

"What's the matter?" Ruth enquired. "What did he say? Oh, no, please don't tell me you two had a fight or something, and now he's trying to make it up to you? How annoyingly romantic! I must slag him about it next time he rings and –"

"Ruth!" Dara hissed quietly. She motioned her closer. God, Ruth's voice was so loud, the entire first floor would know about it!

"What?" Ruth seemed hurt.

"Listen," Dara gave her a meaningful glance, and dropped her voice to low whisper, "these aren't from Mark – they're from Noah."

Now, Ruth's eyes were out on stalks. "Noah? You mean *the* Noah!"

"Yes," Dara replied through gritted teeth. "So, please stop proclaiming to all and sundry about how romantic my husband is!"

She hadn't told Ruth about Noah's recent re-appearance in her life. She hadn't been able tell anyone. She was too busy trying to come to terms with it in her own head, and also trying to forget about it, so she could concentrate on the here and now. If Ruth knew about her lunch with Noah, or more importantly what he had said at that lunch, she would never leave it alone.

"But, but ..." For once, Ruth seemed lost for words.

"We'll talk about it later, OK?" Dara promptly lifted the bouquet off her desk and sat it down on the ground alongside her. Then, and with a final look that brooked no argument, she turned away from Ruth and began to boot up her PC.

"OK." By Dara's resolute expression, Ruth knew she wouldn't get much more out of her.

Finally, when one o'clock came around, and they were comfortably seated nearby in a different café to the one she had visited with Noah – Dara had made sure of it – Ruth heard all.

"I bumped into him recently. We had lunch," Dara informed her.

Ruth was aghast. "You bumped into the love of your life and you never told me? How could you keep something like that from me? How could you not tell me?"

"He's not the love of my life any more," Dara replied, trying to convince herself more than Ruth. "I have Mark now."

"But what happened? What did he say?" Ruth couldn't get the

questions out fast enough. "How did he look? Was he really that annoyed about the wedding dress thing? Is he definitely married himself? Did he tell you what happened after he left?"

Dara nodded ruefully. "You could say that." She went on then to put Ruth out of her misery and fill her in on most of what Noah had said, carefully omitting the part where he admitted he wanted to see her again.

When she had finished, Ruth just stared in disbelief. "But … but . . ." For the second time that day, she was tongue-tied. "But Dara, what are you going to *do?*"

Dara looked at her puzzled. "What am I going to do? What *can* I do?"

"But he's getting divorced!" Ruth declared as if the answer was obvious. "He admitted that leaving you was a mistake! He admitted he had feelings for you for ages afterwards and obviously he still cares about you. Now he's come back to you. Dara, he really *was* The One!" Ruth's idealistic heart was struck by the drama of it all, struck by the fact that Dara's one true love had indeed returned to her. But she'd missed one very important fact.

"Maybe," Dara said quietly. "But I'm married now, Ruth. I'm married to Mark."

"But you admitted yourself that it isn't perfect! You told me not so long ago that you were only marrying him because he was the closest you'd ever found to Noah. But Noah's back – the real thing is back! And from what you've told me, he wants *you* back!"

"Ruth, we're talking about a person's feelings here, not to mention an actual *marriage*. I took my vows and made promises to Mark. I'm bound to him, not only by law but lots of other ways too. I can't just walk away from that."

"But if Noah is really the one for you … and now he's come back into your life." Ruth's romantic self couldn't understand it. "It has to be fate, doesn't it?"

Dara sighed. Initially she had thought the same thing. Fate – was it unavoidable? "It's not that simple. OK, I'll admit there was definitely still something there, but who knows? Noah and I are very different people now, and we've been out of one another's lives for years. Who's to say that he really is the one for me?" But even as she said the words, she didn't believe them herself. Of course, Noah was The One – there had never really been any other, had there? But she did love Mark, just not in the same way and –

"I suppose," said Ruth, finally coming down from her romantic high and beginning to see sense.

The two women were silent for a while, both lost in their own thoughts.

Eventually, Ruth sighed dramatically. "Do you know, it's so bloody annoying!" she said, shaking her head. "You're like one of those really weird women who don't like chocolate!"

"I'm like what?"

Ruth rolled her eyes. "You're a bitch – and I'm jealous! There you are with two fabulous men fighting over you, and in my entire life I've never even come across one! Although," she added grudgingly, "the fact that you are a hell of a lot better-looking than me probably explains it."

Despite herself, Dara had to smile. "Don't be silly. And they're not fighting over me –there's no fighting to be done."

Her friend didn't reply. She simply continued eating the remainder of her salad, all the time humming an annoying tune that sounded suspiciously like that dreadful song 'Torn Between Two Lovers'.

Dara groaned. "Ruth, come off it! I'm not torn between anyone – do you hear me?"

To her frustration, Ruth kept on humming.

"I missed my chance with Noah and I'm married to Mark now," Dara persisted. "End of story, OK?"

End of story?

She certainly hoped so.

* * *

But, of course, it wasn't. Over the following weeks Noah began to phone her at work on a regular basis, asking her out to lunch or to meet with him again. When at first she refused, he got round her by insisting there was more he needed to say. She knew it was wrong and very dangerous, but she found it impossible to say no. Noah had once been a major part of her life and a very good friend at that. How could she *not* see him?

And maybe it wasn't – like Ruth insisted – that he was trying to win her back. Maybe he just wanted to be friends, to take up where the friendship left off, rather than the romance?

And despite her best intentions, there was a side of her that enjoyed seeing Noah's number come up on her caller display, in the same way that she now feared Mark's. She wasn't doing anything wrong, yet somehow it felt as though she was.

"Why do I feel so guilty?" she asked Ruth one afternoon, before leaving to meet Noah for lunch yet again.

"Why *shouldn't* you?" Ruth offered artlessly. "Be honest, you're not meeting with Noah to talk about how wonderful Mark is, are you?"

"We do talk about Mark," Dara replied, ashamed, "but most of the time we talk about old friends, old times, things like that."

And they did. She'd met him twice over the last week and they had great fun going over the past, catching up some more and talking about what had happened to all the gang since.

"It's all harmless," she added for Ruth's benefit.

"Perhaps," Ruth was unmoved, "but where does it stop? What happens when you run out of things to talk about? Where does that leave you then? On dangerous ground, that's what I say."

"Well, what do you want me to do?" Dara said, exasperated at Ruth's quick turnaround and unable to deny her own guilty feelings about the situation. "Not long ago, you were trying to talk me into dumping Mark and riding off into the sunset with Noah. Now you're looking at me with that disapproving face of yours! Which is it?"

"I just think you should be true to yourself, and stop trying to pretend these lunches don't mean anything. Of course, they mean something. And you have to decide what it is you want. You can't keep meeting Noah behind Mark's back like this. You should either tell Noah to back off for a while, while you try and come to terms with how you feel, or tell Mark straight out what's happened and that things aren't right. If you keep on going the way you are, you'll do something you regret, Dara." Giving her friend a steadfast look, Ruth continued, "This is serious shit. OK, I'll admit I was a bit flippant about it all at the beginning – but not any more. Think about it. You told me this guy was the love of your life. You admitted that Mark was second, a close second, mind you, but still second. Now, Noah's back in your life and he happens to be free. But you're not. Try and remember that."

"I do remember that!" Dara cried, stung. "I've been telling you that from the beginning! I've spent every spare second of the last few weeks remembering that! Why do you think I'm so behind on my cases? Why do you think I've passed over so much work to Nigel? Because I can't concentrate on anything else, that's why!"

"You have to make a decision," Ruth said stoutly. "And you have to make it soon."

"But I can't just walk away from Mark," Dara said gently. "Even if I wanted to. It's not that simple." She hung her head. "And I know it sounds pathetic and selfish, but I do love him too. I can't just up and leave. I don't want to hurt him."

"If you carry on the way you're going, you'll end up hurting him anyway. It's a Catch 22, Dara. Much as I joke about wishing to be in your situation, I don't think I would enjoy it that much all the same." She sighed. "Look, why don't you take some time to yourself for a while, go home to your parents for a few days or something, get your head together?"

"I can't. What'll Mark say? What if he suspects something?"

"Dara, I'd be very surprised if he didn't suspect something already. You're bad enough here, going around with your head in the clouds, or who knows where else. I'm sure he's noticed it too."

Mark had noticed something. Only the other day he'd passed comment on Dara's increasingly changeable moods.

"I know work is busy," he'd said, when Dara had snapped at him over something stupid. "But whatever's going on, either tell me what it is, or leave it at the office. Don't start taking it out on me."

It was very rare for Mark to get irritable like that and Dara was unprepared for it. "Oh, so it's all right for you to come home and bang on about strained hamstrings and swollen cartilages, is it? Yet, when *I* have a bad day –"

"I'm not saying you shouldn't talk about work," Mark said, gritting his teeth. "Actually, I'm saying that you *should*. A problem shared and all that. So what's the problem now?"

"The problem is that I've got enough on my mind without listening to you whining on at me. I'm in a bad mood, OK? Get over it!"

"What is *wrong* with you? You've been going around like a cat on a hot tin roof these last few weeks. Look, I know you have a lot on your plate with all these new cases coming up, but is there something else on your mind, Dara? 'Cos if there is, just spit it out, will you? I don't have time for all these deep sighs and slamming doors. It's bloody childish and I won't stand for it!"

"What? I don't slam doors! And what do you mean you won't stand for it? What are you going to do?"

"Oh, grow up, Dara!" Mark's tone brooked no argument, and despite her own annoyance, she was faintly shocked at his determination. He rarely faced her down like this.

Almost instantly, she relented. He was right. She wasn't being fair carrying on like this. Mark had no idea what was going on in her head. But, in fairness, she couldn't exactly tell him, could she?

"I'm sorry," she admitted eventually. "I have a few things on my mind, that's all." That was a truth of sorts, wasn't it? "And it seems that every second client I speak to lately has some reason to have a go at me."

"Just try not to let it get to you, OK?" he said, kissing her softly on the head. "There's more to life than work, you know."

"I know," Dara replied, feeling even worse now that he was being so understanding.

But the fact that Mark *had* noticed something made her feel even more guilty and Ruth had hit the nail on the head by saying she'd end up hurting him no matter what she did.

"Dara, you're concerned about other people's lives here," Ruth said now. "But think about what's important in yours. If you really feel that Noah is the one for you and he feels the same way, then you have to think seriously about that. What's the point in staying in the marriage for the sake of it? You don't have any kids to think about – yet – and I know you do love Mark, but it's not the same, is it?"

"But we haven't even been married six months ..." Dara replied, despondent.

"Exactly. So, wouldn't it be better to get out now, while you're both still young enough to get over it? Dara, you married him for the wrong reasons, you know that yourself. You married him because you thought you'd missed your chance with Noah and didn't want to be left alone." Ruth sat forward and her tone softened. "Look, despite the hard time I gave you about it, I *can* understand it. Sometimes I feel the same way. Don't think I don't get the same comments from my family, or the weird vibes from my married friends. Yes, sometimes I'm tempted to settle too, but as you know I'm too much of a romantic, and stupid as it may well be, I'd prefer to keep living in hope." She smiled self-deprecatingly. "But that's me."

"I should have listened to you," Dara said, meaning it, "but I honestly thought that Noah was lost to me, I thought I'd messed it all up. And I certainly didn't think he'd come back, otherwise I wouldn't have dreamed of marrying someone else."

"I know that. And look, while it wouldn't be me, I can still understand why you did it." Ruth shook her head and exhaled deeply. "But maybe, Dara, just maybe you made an awful mistake."

Dara looked at her, a mixture of guilt and confusion in her eyes. "But Ruth, if I did make a mistake, then how the hell am I going to get out of it?"

CHAPTER 20

Fiona shook her head and tut-tutted as she read the headline on that morning's *Irish Independent*. She and Louise were on their morning break, but as both were hung-over from yet another night out socialising, neither was in the mood for talking. Despite her protestations, Fiona had dragged Louise out to help her pursue yet another guy she was interested in. Unfortunately, the same guy had a penchant for pub-crawling, which meant that, rather than the 'quiet night' Louise had envisaged, the two girls had stayed out a lot longer and drank way more than intended. And in the end, Fiona hadn't managed to nab her man, the same one seemingly unaware that she even existed. It had been a huge waste of time – or more aptly for Louise, a huge waste of money. Fiona's pleading didn't stretch to financing her exploits, and they were each forced to cough up for a fresh round of drinks every time the object of Fiona's affection moved premises.

Louise found that lately she was tiring of all the drinking – she was tired of this continuous 'let's go out and get blotto' aspect of her social life. Yes, it was lovely having such great friends and having such fun with them but she wished they could do something else occasionally. She wished they could go to the cinema and watch some of the latest releases, or for once forget about the up-to-the-minute designer clothes, throw on a pair of comfy pyjamas, and just sit in and have a good old chat over a Chinese takeaway and a DVD. That was what the fancy surround sound-system in the apartment was for after all, wasn't it? But she didn't think it had even been used – again it was another example of Fiona's obsession with 'the best'.

It must be lovely not to have any money worries, though. Fiona must owe just as much on her credit cards as Louise did, but she didn't seem to care. Her motto was to live life to the full and to hell with the consequences.

Louise wished she possessed the same devil-may-care attitude but she'd been brought up differently. Not to mention that she'd practically grown up with this huge immovable debt.

But hopefully all that would be sorted soon, and maybe then Louise could stop worrying so much and for once she might be able to relax and enjoy herself instead of feeling guilty every time she spent beyond her means, which was basically all of the time.

"Disgraceful," Fiona was still shaking her head at the newspaper article she'd been reading, "bloody disgraceful."

"What is?" Louise angled her head to get a better look. The headline was 'Irish Woman Secures Massive Payout after Fall in Supermarket'

Apparently the woman had slipped on a spill in one of the grocery aisles and had damaged her hip and broken her ankle. She'd sued for damages and had been awarded a large sum in compensation.

"This country's gone crazy," Fiona tut-tutted again. "Raise your voice to someone these days, and off they go looking for a big hand-out. Bloody disgraceful. Why didn't the silly cow look where she was going?"

Louise felt her skin go hot all over. Fiona didn't know about her upcoming suit and judging by her reaction to this poor woman, who according to the article seemed to have suffered genuine injuries, it wouldn't go down too well. Fiona knew a little about her accident and she'd seen her scars that time on holiday, but for some reason Louise had never told her about the case her solicitor was taking. Probably because deep down she felt the same way as Fiona did, that she didn't really deserve it, that she was just looking for a handout. But she felt bad enough about it all as it was, without admonishment from an apparently unforgiving Fiona.

"I mean, whatever happened to personal responsibility?" Fiona was saying. "What happened to watching where you were going? If I was stupid enough to fall over in a supermarket like that, firstly I'd be so embarrassed I wouldn't be able to get out of there fast enough, and secondly, isn't it my own bloody fault for not looking where I was going? But no, these people see an opportunity, down they go, and then quick as you like, they have you up in court whining about how their lives have been ruined for good!"

Louise nodded absently, not wishing to offer an opinion one way or the other. Still she couldn't help but stick up for the woman. "She broke her hip though, Fi – she couldn't exactly get up and run out of there, and I'm sure she suffered afterwards. A broken hip is no joke."

"Suffered my ass! Louise, you can be so gullible sometimes – always seeing the best in everyone! Look at the smirk on her face in that picture!" Fiona cried, pointing at the accompanying photograph, which showed the injured woman leaving the courthouse. Louise had to admit that the woman did look quite pleased with herself all the same but that was no reason to suspect –

"The solicitors are worse," Fiona went on. "I remember reading about some law firm who used the same doctor in every single case. The guy was as bent as an S hook and he falsified reports, exaggerated injuries, used every trick in the book to get a big payout. And, of course, the judges always fall for it."

"But some people must be genuine, surely?" Louise said, swearing to herself that she would never ever confide in Fiona now. She drained her coffee mug and checked her watch. It was time to go back to work.

"Maybe, but these days it doesn't matter – certainly not to the solicitors anyway," Fiona replied, closing the newspaper. "They're making as much money out of it as their so-called injured clients. It's one big money-making racket if you ask me."

She and Louise left the canteen and took the stairs down to their office floor. "If I was any good, I'd get in on the act too, maybe take an 'accidental' tumble down these steps one day," she said. "But, I've more respect for myself. It's nothing but downright fraud in my opinion, Louise. Nothing but downright fraud."

* * *

"So, what'll we do tonight?" Sam asked her later that evening. "Do you fancy the pub, a movie, something to eat ...or," he added, nuzzling the side of her neck, "should we just stay in?"

Louise jerked uneasily. Fiona and Becky had already gone out for the night and Sam had called over shortly after they left. It had been his first visit and he'd been mightily impressed by the apartment, as Louise had known he would.

"Wow, some pad!" he'd enthused, taking in the state-of-the-art Bose stereo Fiona had insisted on installing, the huge wide-screen TV and the understated but chic décor. It was fabulous and, as that beer ad went, 'reassuringly expensive'. The rent was crazy really, twice as much as she'd paid on her old place, but still it was so much nicer and the three of them had so much fun together.

Well, they did when Fiona wasn't in one of her funny moods, or when Becky didn't hog the TV. The girl was addicted to soap operas. There wasn't one on any channel that she didn't watch, and while Louise enjoyed *Corrie* as much as the next girl, she wasn't really interested in the *Platt Family Special* or *Coronation Street – Hairstyles through the Years*, or whatever special they showed from time to time. But Becky was enthralled, which Louise thought didn't really suit the sophisticated fashionista image she too tried to project.

But Louise said nothing about the TV-hogging, or the mood-swings, untidiness or the fact that she had been landed with the tiniest bedroom. It was little more than an airing cupboard really, but she supposed that didn't matter so much, particularly when she'd been used to living in one room, and the apartment was so big.

Still, there were times when she missed doing what she liked, eating when she liked and watching what she liked on the telly. But not to worry, the girls were still getting used to one another. Give them a few more weeks together, and she was sure everything would be fine.

Sam was still nuzzling her suggestively. They hadn't slept together – yet. Louise was mad about him, she really was, but they'd only been together a few weeks, and she was an old-fashioned girl at heart. Not that she wasn't tempted – she had been many times, particularly when he was such an amazing kisser and could do fantastic things with his hands.

No, the real truth of the matter was that Louise didn't want him to see her naked, to see her ugly skin grafts and slash marks. She hadn't told him about her accident. She hadn't told anyone really – because it was such a long time ago, she hadn't seen any reason to. But now with the case coming up, and the fact that she and Sam were getting more and more intimate, she did feel as though she should say something. But again, she was afraid that if Sam knew the real her, the real boring ordinary Louise, that he'd lose interest. And, to be honest, talk of broken hips and shattered pelvises wasn't terribly glamorous, or indeed sexy.

But she supposed she'd better say something, otherwise Sam would think she was frigid, which, Louise thought with a grin, definitely *wasn't* the case.

"We could stay in, if you like," she replied, turning to kiss him.

"I didn't think girls like you liked sitting in." Sam put his arms around her waist and pulled her closer to him. He kissed her softly on the lips.

"I'm not that much of a party animal, you know."

"Oh? You could have fooled me," he laughed softly and bent his head towards hers.

After a short while, they moved to the sofa, and Sam's kisses deepened.

Her heart raced. Right, she had to say something now, didn't she? Otherwise he'd get some shock when he … although, she could just turn off the lights and maybe he wouldn't be able to see anything, but no, that wasn't fair. She should be straight up with him before anything happened. He was bound to spot it sometime, wasn't he? Louise couldn't hide her body forever.

"Sam," she began, breaking the kiss. "Um, this is a bit embarrassing but …"

He gave her an odd look. "What? This?"

"No, no, this is fine – very fine, actually." She smiled sheepishly. "It's just, well, something happened to me a few years ago, and it kind of affects how I feel about all this … " She trailed off when something in his face changed. Then she thought about how it all sounded. "No, don't get me wrong, I don't mean something happened to me that way – I wasn't attacked or anything."

His expression visibly relaxed, and Louise felt a little guilty. Typically she was going about this all the wrong way. She sat up, brushed her hair away from her face and turned to look at him. Sam sat up too, sensing that this was important. "Back when I was still living at home in Cork, I was involved in an accident."

His expression didn't change. "What kind of accident?"

At this, Louise felt embarrassed, although she wasn't quite sure why. "I was going along one day minding my own business, when I was knocked down by a car," she said airily, as if telling him she liked sugar in her tea. But she was trying her best not to make a big deal out it. "The driver went through a red light," she explained.

But when Sam showed no reaction, Louise began to feel a bit worried. This wasn't how most people behaved after an admission like that. Most people came out with the usual 'You poor thing! Are you OK?' but Sam looked as though she'd told him something particularly outrageous. "Ah, he was probably in a bit of a hurry," she added, trying to lighten the mood.

"Well, I really hope they got the bastard," Sam said vehemently. "Nobody should be allowed to get away with something like that!"

Louise realised then that he was one of those strong silent types, repressing his concern on the outside, while on the inside burning with fury. She swooned, secretly delighted by his evident concern for her wellbeing. She nodded. "They did. In fairness to him, although he knew he'd be done for drink driving, he stayed at the scene and called me an ambulance.But anyway, I was pretty banged-up," she continued, trying to return to the most pertinent aspect of it all. "I broke my hip, an arm and shattered my pelvis."

"The prick! Why would anyone *do* something like that?" Sam went on, and Louise wished he'd concentrate less on the accident, and more on the injuries.

"Well, look, maybe it wasn't all his fault. I probably should have checked that there was nothing coming anyway, but sure you know me," she said rolling her eyes, "I was off in my own little world somewhere."

"But you just said he went through a red light!"

"Oh, yes, yes, he did – at least that's what the guards told me afterwards. But look, we got him, so don't worry about that. The thing is, I had to have a lot of operations so – "

"Well, I really hope they locked him up, and threw away the bloody key!"

Louise felt exasperated. Could he not just listen to what she was trying to tell him?

"As I said, I had to have a lot of operations – "

"But he had insurance, surely. Oh, don't tell me," he went on when Louise looked sheepish, "don't tell me it was one of those boy-racer gurriers, and the insurance company wouldn't pay out?"

Louise waved him away. "No, no, no, the insurance company did pay out, that was all sorted. The thing is though," she tried again, "the thing is that as a result of all these operations, well, my skin isn't as, well, let's say as unblemished as I'd like it to be."

"Unblemished?"

Pulse racing, she lifted down the waistband of her trousers to show him the beginning of the scar on her hip. "It's not very attractive," she finished guiltily.

"Louise," Sam said gently, "did you honestly think that your scars would bother me? I'm more worried about *you* – about what happened to you afterwards, how you coped, how long you spent in hospital, things like that."

Relief flooded through her. "Don't mind that, it was ages ago and

I'm over it," she said as flippantly as she could. *Well, at least until the court case* – but there was no point in going into that now. "The thing is, I just wanted to let you know – just in case you get a bit of a shock if," she reddened, "you know."

"Louise, believe me, I'd never think that. I'm interested in you because of who you are, not what you look like."

Again, she tried to appear offhand about it. "Well, if I could afford it, I would probably get it all sorted in one of those cosmetic surgery places, but in the meantime I just have to put up with it."

"Would you really?" he asked.

"Would I what?"

"Would you really think about getting more surgery just to cover it up? You must have been through a lot of operations since ..."

Louise rolled her eyes to heaven. "You've been through one, you've been through them all," she said airily. "At this stage, I don't think it would make that much of a difference."

"You're very brave," Sam said shaking his head.

"I'm not brave – it was just one of those things," she shrugged.

"And do you have any lasting damage, any problems walking – things like that?"

Louise shrugged again, not prepared to admit that she could very well end up crippled with back pain when she got older. This wasn't a very attractive prospect to someone who she might very well end up getting older with, was it?

"I often get the odd twinge in my back, but not much," she replied. Then she put her arms around him again. "So, now that you know about my flaws," she began, and kissed him again.

Sam kissed her back briefly, but Louise sensed that the mood had changed.

A lot.

He sat up straight. "Thanks for telling me that. I'm sure that took a lot of courage and I respect that." He ran a hand through his hair. "I respect you too, you know."

"I know," Louise said giddily, delighted she'd finally let him into her confidence.

216

"That's why I have something to tell you too."

"Oh?"

He looked guilty. "When I met you a few weeks ago, I hadn't expected to meet anyone. I certainly hadn't expected to meet someone I'd fall for ... fall for –" he wouldn't meet her eyes, "so quickly."

Louise's heart melted.

"I should have told you right away, of course, but to be honest, I didn't know how things would go, and I wasn't sure if you'd be interested. Girls like you don't come around every day, Louise."

She wondered where this was going. What did he want to tell her?

"The thing is ..." he took both of her hands in his, "the thing is, I need to go away for a couple of weeks, with work."

"Oh." Louise was genuinely disappointed.

"I was going to tell you but I didn't know how you'd feel about it, and I didn't know if you'd be interested in a long-distance relationship – long-distance for a little while anyway."

She couldn't believe it. Sam wanted to keep going out with her; he wanted her to wait for him until he got back. How wonderful!

"Where are you going?"

"The States for a training course. It's such bad timing really but I had no idea ... Louise, I had no idea I'd meet someone like you."

She smiled. "I'm glad you told me now, rather than just head off one weekend never to be seen again. And that's no problem at all." In fact, it would be a great excuse to spend a few nights sitting in actually. This could be a blessing in disguise. Now that she had a boyfriend, the girls wouldn't expect (or want) her to go out on the town while they went on the pull. So she might end up saving a few quid in the meantime. "But when are you leaving?"

"The weekend after next," he replied, surprising her. "I know it seems a bit sudden, but it's only for six weeks, and it'll be no time at all until I'm back."

He'd be back just before Christmas then, which was good timing really. By then, her court case would be done and dusted, she'd be able to pay off her loans, and hopefully in the meantime would have saved some money too. Although she'd really miss him, this was pretty good news. But she'd better not mention anything about the case, or he'd feel awful about not being here to help her through it. She was thoroughly glad now that she hadn't mentioned anything about it earlier. No, better to say nothing and wait until it was all over. Then she could get on with the rest of her life. She grinned happily. Things were really looking up. She had great friends, a fabulous apartment, an even more fabulous boyfriend who loved her so much he could hardly bear to leave her, and in a few weeks' time there was a very good chance her money worries would be over!

She snuggled happily into Sam, who tightened his grip around her. Things were looking good.

CHAPTER 21

Rosie and Stephen became firm friends after the night he dropped her home, and often met for coffee and a bit of a chat, sometimes after class and other times in Wicklow whenever he was in town. They talked about everything and anything, and he was so easy to be with that Rosie found herself looking forward to their little chats.

Sheila teased her mercilessly about him. "You're some woman for the men, Rosie Mitchell!" she'd said, when Rosie told her about her new friend. "But fair play to you – you've still got it!"

"It's not like that, Sheila," Rosie assured her.

And it *wasn't* like that. Stephen was a lovely man but he was only a friend. And although she knew well that Sheila was only teasing, in a way she felt a little bit annoyed that her friend would even suggest something like that. Surely she knew that there had been, and *would* only ever be, one man for Rosie and that was Martin.

She still missed him desperately, even more so lately since David had begun to cut her out of his life altogether.

One day recently, she had arrived at the house to find that he had taken down the plates and ornaments in the kitchen – as he'd said he was going to do – and painted the room a horrible greeny colour. The new decor did nothing for the kitchen and if anything

219

made it look dark and cold.

Since he'd finished, there was no sign of him replacing Rosie's bits and bobs in there, and she wasn't too surprised to find that by putting his own stamp on it, David had begun to make what had once been her favourite room very much his own. So she found that lately she wasn't too bothered about sitting in there the way she used to, relaxing and reading her books. And then, of course, Twix wasn't allowed in the kitchen now, and with all the hair the spaniel shed, Rosie knew she could forget about having her in the living-room.

Soon after that, David started re-decorating the hallway, this time choosing another dark and dreary colour which Rosie hated. But, fearful of irritating him, she said nothing and just let him get on with it – let her son get on with stripping down and painting over the walls of her house – and the remnants of Rosie's old happy life there.

So, bit by bit, Rosie found herself spending more and more time upstairs in her bedroom. It was the only place where she felt at ease lately, the only place that was still truly her own. She'd moved Twix's basket up there too, and although the little dog seemed a bit put out for a while, she eventually grew used to her new 'spot' in the house and Rosie knew she enjoyed being able to hop up on the bed at night-time. Rosie liked having her there too as then she didn't feel quite so alone.

Nervous that David would, as threatened, dump her and Martin's old armchairs, she'd asked him to move them upstairs, but so far he hadn't done that, and Rosie dreaded the day when she would come home and see the two chairs thrown out on a skip or something.

But staying in the bedroom in the evenings wasn't too bad, and now her books were slowly but surely beginning to taken second place to her painting. Even though there wasn't much of a view from her front window, Rosie enjoyed losing herself for hours in her pictures. With all the practice she was getting, she could see that her technique was greatly improving, and despite her initial doubts about her talent, she began to believe that Stephen might have been right when he said she had an eye for it.

It was a lifeline really and it prevented her from having to think too much about her situation. She knew that she shouldn't let David come in and take over like that, but what was she supposed to do? He was her son and rather than face a big argument, wasn't it easier just to let him get on with it?

There were, of course, times when Rosie actually considered moving out and getting a small flat of her own down in the town or something, because she was pretty much living in one room as it was. Still, having to pay rent on a flat would put a big dent in her nest egg, and Rosie didn't want that. You just never knew when you'd need a few euro, and there was no point in handing all that money away to someone else when she had a perfectly good house here.

Well, a perfectly good *room* here anyway, she thought wryly.

There were times though, when she wondered how it had all ended up like this – with her tucked away in a small room upstairs, while her adult son took over her house. Had her mistake been in letting David simply come home without question – or had she made a mistake with him long before then, somewhere in his upbringing perhaps?

She and Martin, like the majority of parents she supposed, had muddled along between them over the years, and up until a few months ago, Rosie had always believed that they had done a good job in raising David and Sophie.

From an early age, they had tried to instil good manners and good behaviour in them, and ensured that they knew the difference between right and wrong. They didn't give them too much leeway when growing up, and although there had been a few rough patches – particularly when they were teenagers – she really thought they had done OK and, in terms of worry and trauma, had got away quite lightly really.

Unlike some of the other families in the estate, none of Rosie's children had ever been in trouble with the law, or had stayed out till all hours drinking or smoking and hanging around with the wrong crowd. No, both David and Sophie had had nice respectable friends, went on to have nice respectable jobs, and as far as Rosie was concerned would undoubtedly go on to have nice respectable lives. So what had happened?

Did bringing a child into the world, doing your best to raise them properly and going to the ends of the earth to make them happy automatically mean that you should get something from them in return?

Should she really expect David to fall at her feet in gratitude for letting him come home? Or should she just try and understand that he needed his own space and that there was no reason why he should have his mammy involved in the day-to-day goings-on in his life. Maybe that was just the kind of person he was and Rosie couldn't or *shouldn't* change that.

Even so, Sophie seemed to feel the same way about her and that hurt. It hurt Rosie that her children didn't seem to want her involved in their lives – in fact, it seemed that they no longer needed her. Not that she wanted to be in the middle of everything – she knew that David and Sophie needed to do their own thing – but after all she had done and all she had sacrificed for them over the years, surely she deserved some consideration, didn't she?

Or did she? Was she being unreasonable in believing that her children owed her something simply because she was their mother? Perhaps so, she mused. But still, whatever about appreciation, the very least any mother deserved was a little bit of respect, wasn't it?

And David didn't respect her, obviously he didn't, because if respect to him meant having his own mother afraid to simply say hello when he came home from work in the evenings, then there was something very wrong.

And, of course, because he became so annoyed by the smell of Rosie's cooking, and particularly her fondness for red meat (mince was the worst) she'd taken to making her own dinners a good hour or so before he arrived home, just so she could be sure the cooking smells were gone. She'd even gone so far as to hide the abhorrent meat in one of the under-compartments of the fridge, so fearful was she of offending her son's apparently delicate sensibilities. Anything to keep him happy – or more aptly, she thought wryly, anything for a quiet life.

But never mind her cooking, what about the smells of that soya stuff or whatever it was *he* used? It stayed around the place for days! Now, Rosie had nothing against it – in her opinion everyone was entitled to their own preferences. But she found it difficult to understand how someone who was so obsessive about vegetarianism could treat a harmless animal like Twix with such disdain!

She sighed. David had turned out a strange one, that was for sure, and thinking of it now, she understood well why poor Kelly had left him.

If he behaved towards his wife even a percentage of the way he behaved towards his mother, then of course she'd have no choice but to walk away. In the beginning, they seemed to have such a happy marriage, but somewhere along the line it seemed that David had changed. He had changed from a reasonably well-adjusted ordinary man into someone who now made a person fearful and jumpy whenever he was around. Someone who seemed to have no regard or no appreciation for anyone but himself, someone who believed that he had a God-given right to do what he pleased, and to hell with the consequences for anyone else. Sure, who could cope with a man like that?

But unfortunately, Rosie thought sadly, she had no choice but to cope with a man like that.

Because that man just happened to be her son.

* * *

Many weeks after the family moved in, Rosie finally got a chance to pay a proper visit to 'Graceland' as Sheila jokingly called Sophie's new house.

She was really looking forward to having a good chat with her daughter. She wanted to tell her everything that had happened since David's return, and get her opinion on what she should do about it all.

Sheila strongly believed that Rosie should confront David and tell him that she wasn't going to stand for being walked over in her own home, but Rosie knew she couldn't do that without some sort of back-up. She was sure that once Sophie heard about what was happening she would be horrified by David's belligerent attitude and would have no hesitation in giving her some measure of support, should Rosie decide to say something to him.

So it would be nice to be able to get it all off her chest, and try and make some sense of the confusing feelings she was experiencing since his return. Sheila was a great listener, but in fairness all she did was insist that she tell David where to go.

"There is no way you should have to put up with that kind of carry-on, Rosie. Don't forget that you did that fellow a huge favour by taking him in. Just make sure that he knows it!"

That was easy for Sheila to say though; she had always been straight and upfront and would brook no nonsense from her children or anyone else. But for Rosie, who was much more mild-mannered, this was very difficult, even more so because she hated any kind of confrontation.

Anyway, there was the small matter of David being her son, and as a good mother surely she had to give him a little bit of leeway – particularly considering everything he'd gone through?

So, it was with great anticipation that she took the early train as far as Connolly Station and then the DART out to Malahide to Sophie's house.

In fairness, the house was truly spectacular, but totally over the top, and Rosie still couldn't understand why the family needed so much space when there were only the three of them. Then again, Sophie did say that they were planning on having another child soon, so who was she to say what size of house they should or shouldn't buy? Still, she did wonder how they managed to keep up with those huge mortgage repayments, particularly when trying to run two cars, pay a childminder and still have enough to clothe and feed themselves.

Pushing the intercom button at the imposing front gate, Rosie shook her head. The young people really did have it tough these days, working like slaves trying to keep up with it all.

"Helloo – Morris Residence?" came the voice through the intercom, and Rosie wondered if her daughter had recently caught a really bad cold, as she didn't sound like herself at all.

"Em, hello, Sophie, it's me Rosie … em, your mother?" God, Rosie hated these things. You'd swear she was looking for an audience with the queen rather than visiting her only daughter, and as the gates swung backwards, she almost expected to have to pass a line of stony-faced uniformed guards on her way to the front door.

She rang the doorbell, idly wondering why getting into this house was like trying to get into Fort Knox, what with all the chains and bolts Sophie seemed to be unlocking behind the door. This was a nice respectable area, wasn't it? Rosie was feeling a bit nervous all of a sudden. Maybe there was a good reason for all this security.

"Hi, Mum!"

Sophie greeted her mother with an effusive hug, and immediately Rosie felt relieved. All this time she had thought her daughter didn't want her help once she had got what she wanted, but no, Sophie seemed genuinely delighted to see her now. Poor thing, she really must have been up to her tonsils between moving in and getting the house organised. She had taken a few weeks off work to do this, which was lovely for little Claudia, of course, having her mother around, but probably very tiring for Sophie. She just wished Sophie could have let her shoulder some of the burden, at least until they got themselves settled.

"Hello, love," Rosie warmly returned her daughter's embrace. "The place is looking gorgeous."

"Isn't it?" Sophie stood back and excitedly waved a hand around as if to say: 'Look – all mine!'

And indeed, Rosie thought, Sophie was looking very well too, dressed in a delicate dusky pink lambswool sweater, expensive-looking black satin skirt and a pair of high-heeled boots. Where did her daughter get such great taste? Certainly not from her anyway, she thought, feeling rather shabby all of a sudden in her good winter coat and ordinary skirt and top.

"Well, you seem to have settled in well," she said, thrilled that her daughter was so happy. Helping her and Robert buy this place was the best thing she ever did, she reiterated to herself – despite what Sheila seemed to think.

"Well, it was a bit crazy for a while but we're getting there! And,

Mum, I'm sorry that I haven't had you over before now, but things were just *sooo* hectic! You wouldn't believe how much work goes into finding a decent Filipina maid these days, and then, of course, making sure she actually does what she says she'll do!" Sophie rolled her eyes dramatically. "And then, of course, I've been busy with trying to find a suitable nanny for Claudia," she added, her words going a mile to the dozen, "but thankfully we found the *perfect* one. She's out with her now actually."

"A nanny?" Rosie's eyes widened in surprise. "But I'm her nanny, aren't I?" Of *course* she knew what a nanny was, but the words were out before she could stop them and –

Sophie pealed with laughter. "Mum, you're hilarious!" she cried. "You know what I mean, a *real* nanny, someone to look after her when I'm out."

"But, love, if you were stuck for someone to look after her I would have been only too delighted to help out – you know that," Rosie said, stung that all her recent offers of help with her granddaughter had been firmly turned down. And then, after all that, Sophie had gone and employed some stranger to look after her.

Sophie looked at her. "I know that, Mum, but the thing is – I needed someone I could trust, someone with the right qualifications … you know."

"Qualifications? But who could have better qualifications for looking after her than your own mother?" Rosie said, slightly amused by this. "Didn't I raise *you*?"

Sophie bit her lip. "I know that, and at the time I'm sure you did a great job with me and David but …"

But? Rosie wondered what was coming.

"But things are different these days, Mum. Children need a lot more now than just someone to mother them and I suppose we wanted someone who could help stimulate Claudia – intellectually, you know …" she trailed off slightly, vaguely realising how hurtful this could sound.

"Oh I see." But Rosie didn't see at all. What kind of stimulation did a two-and-a-half-year-old toddler need that her grandmother couldn't give her? Yes, Rosie wasn't all that well educated herself, but were they teaching two-year-olds *War and Peace* these days? And Claudia was a way off from starting school just yet, so why was her education an issue?

"I'm sorry, Mum – that came out sounding terrible." Sophie had the good grace to look ashamed. "I'm sure you'd do a great job, but there's also the fact that we wouldn't expect you to be looking after a young child, not at your age."

"Sophie, I'm not ready to be carted off in a box just yet!" Rosie couldn't keep the hurt out of her tone.

"I'm not saying that, Mum," Sophie replied through gritted teeth. "But we've already made the decision to get a nanny for Claudia, so there's no point in even having this conversation, is there?"

A terse silence fell between the two women then – the room's high vaulted ceiling somehow making the tension much more apparent, it seemed to Rosie.

Eventually, she sighed. "I'm sorry, love. Of course, you and Robert have to do what's right for you – and for Claudia." She smiled weakly, eager to smooth over the awkwardness. "Now, is there any chance of a cup of tea or –?"

Instantly Sophie perked up. "Of course! Come through to the kitchen diner," she said, her earlier irritation already forgotten. "Now, what can I get you – dandelion, elderflower, camomile?" she asked, heading for the cupboards of her fabulous Acacia kitchen. The place was huge, but at least there was a nice comfy living area over to the left – and against the wall sat an enormous brown leather couch.

"Mum, camomile?" Sophie probed. "Or perhaps you'd prefer dandelion?"

Once again Rosie felt coarse and gauche in her daughter's sophisticated world. "Em, just a cup of Lyons Green Label if you have it, please."

"Well, I'm not sure ... maybe somewhere ..." Sophie rummaged amongst the shelves. "Ah yes, here we are!"

Rosie tentatively took a seat on the expensive-looking leather sofa situated to the right of an expensive-looking kitchen table that was so huge it looked as though it could have been used to hold a high-power government meeting or something.

"So, what do you think of the sofa?" Sophie asked, while waiting for the kettle to boil.

Rosie patted the leather. "It's nice – the leather is lovely and soft."

"It's salmon skin."

"What?"

"It's not leather – it's salmon skin." Sophie informed her, her eyes shining with pleasure. Rosie instinctively wrinkled her nose and she shifted uncomfortably in her seat. "Oh ... oh, lovely."

"Our interior designer suggested it. Apparently, it's the ultimate in luxury these days but *sooo* expensive and almost impossible to get. Donald Trump had salmon-skin seats fitted in his newest Lear."

"Really?" Rosie had no idea who Donald Trump was, let alone what his 'Lear' might be.

"I know – isn't it fab? And what's good enough for Trump is good enough for us! But Nikki went mad once she found out we'd bought salmon skin, and she'd gone for boring old leather. But she can be like that, you know – so behind the times and she has such dreadfully boring taste."

"Right." Rosie didn't know how to answer. Besides, she was too busy holding her breath and trying not to get a whiff of the salmon. Wouldn't you think that Sophie had it bad enough in her youth having to put up with the smell of fish from Wicklow harbour, let alone having the very source of that smell installed in her own living-room!

"So how have you been?" Sophie asked, handing her mother a cup of tea and flicking her long dark hair away from her face. "Are you enjoying having David back?"

"Well, that's the thing," Rosie began, a little nervously, but pleased that Sophie had brought the subject up. "Things have been a little strange and – "

"Do you know something?" Sophie interjected, pouring coffee for herself. "The best thing he ever did was leave that tart. Personally I never thought she was right for him in the first place, so it was no surprise to me when he finally realised what she was really like."

228

"But David didn't – "

"And it must be just *fantastic* having him back home again, is it? Someone to do everything around the house and to look after you," she added dreamily. "You mustn't know yourself."

True, Rosie thought sadly.

"And isn't it brilliant that he found a job so quickly? Of course, you must find it much easier too, having someone else to share the telephone and the heating bills ..."

Funny, Rosie thought, that was something she'd never even considered. And now that Sophie had brought it up it, that was another downside of David's coming home. He didn't share the bills or contribute to the upkeep. In fact, hadn't he expected Rosie to pay for the paint he used to 'decorate' the house?

"Well, actually, Sophie, David doesn't – "

"Oh, Mum – you're too good sometimes! I'm sure his heart is broken trying to get you to take money off him. Well, don't be too proud to let him treat you to a nice meal out or something – you did him a big favour by letting him stay with you, don't forget."

"Well, love, I was hoping I could talk to you about that actually because – "

Just then the telephone rang, and Sophie almost leapt out of her seat. "Oops! Sorry, Mum, better get that. Just one second!"

Rosie stared into her teacup. Why did everyone automatically assume that she thought having David home was wonderful? Couldn't they see that things like that just didn't automatically fall into place, that it wouldn't be the same as it had been before?

And the truth was that Rosie was finding it hard to comprehend this herself. She had honestly believed that she and David would get on grand together, and that she would be able to help him through the tough times he was having. But David didn't seem to want that – he wanted to just move in, get on with things and behave as if his mother didn't even exist.

And while it was difficult for Sheila to understand, no doubt Sophie would be sympathetic to how she was feeling. So, when she was finished her phone call, Rosie would start from the very beginning, and tell her all about the episode with the meat and David changing the rooms around and –

"Mum, that was Nikki and I'm so sorry but I have to go out." Sophie breezed back into the room, her face apologetic.

"Oh, but I just got here, love!" Rosie couldn't hide her disappointment.

"I know, I know, and I'm sorry but I really do have to go."

"But is there something wrong? Is Claudia all right?"

"Claudia?" For a moment, Sophie looked as thought she didn't know who Rosie was talking about. "Oh, I'm sure she's fine – she's out with Frieda, so I'm sure she's fine."

"But then why –?"

"I wish I had time to explain, Mum, but I really am in a hurry. Look, come over again soon – next week or something, yes?" Sophie marched back out into the hallway. "Can I give you a lift back into town? I'm going that way."

"Well, maybe just as far as the train station," Rosie said, her tone downcast.

"Great. Now do you have everything with you?" Sophie quickly grabbed her keys and almost shunted Rosie out the door, so anxious was she to leave the house.

At the train station, and as she struggled to lift herself out of her daughter's dreadfully uncomfortable sports car, Rosie recollected herself. She was terribly selfish to expect Sophie to deal with her silly little problems, especially when there were clearly much more important things for her to worry about. Her friend must be in some kind of trouble or something.

"I'll talk to you soon, love," she said, "and whatever is wrong with your friend, I hope she'll be OK."

"Sure, Mum – see you later! Bye!"

Sophie drove off so fast she almost sent her mother spinning on the pavement.

Glancing in her rear-view mirror and seeing her mother looking a little lost outside the train station, Sophie briefly felt a frisson of guilt. Nah, she told herself, Mum would be fine, and she could always catch up with her later.

Then, sweeping back out onto the main road, she put the car into fifth gear and sped off towards the direction of the Southside, grinning in gleeful anticipation. Fair play to Nikki for giving her the heads-up like that, she thought. If the situation was reversed, she really didn't know if she would do the same.

Yes, her mother could wait, Sophie reassured herself – but an unexpected half-day Harvey Nicks sale *definitely* couldn't!

CHAPTER 22

She had to talk to Noah – properly, Dara decided. She had to find out once and for all if he *did* have feelings for her, if he still felt that there was something between them, be it unfinished business or something more. That was the only way around it.

And what if he came right out and admitted he still cared about her, that he still loved her? And if all came to all and he asked her to leave Mark for him, how would she feel then? She really wasn't sure. She did love Mark, but there was no getting away from the fact that Noah was the love of her life.

So what should she do? Should she stay with Mark out of respect for him and indeed respect for her wedding vows? But then, how could she go on knowing that she had been given another chance with Noah and had once again turned it down? How could she be happy knowing beyond doubt that she'd settled for second-best? Was there any merit in that, she wondered? Up until a few weeks ago, she'd thought so. She was happy with Mark and was prepared to give the marriage her all, but then Noah turned up and sent her into a tailspin.

Why couldn't he have appeared a few weeks before the wedding? Then at least she wouldn't have to go through all this – or indeed Mark wouldn't have to, she thought wryly. The ring on the finger and the wedding certificate made the whole situation a million times more difficult. Yes, divorce was common enough these days – but after six months?

Should she stay with him out of duty? Plenty of women did that, didn't they? Plenty of women stayed with men they didn't love, some with men they even hated. Still, such a thought filled her with dread and, as Ruth had said many times before, surely Mark deserved more.

Dara thought about it all the way to the bistro in which today she and Noah were meeting for lunch, and still she couldn't come up with a satisfactory solution.

She shook her head. Perhaps she was blowing this all out of proportion. Perhaps Noah was just trying to be friends, and had no interest in renewing their relationship and their connection was simply based on old times. Yes, their romance had been incredibly intense and had ended badly and without resolution, but it had still ended, hadn't it? So maybe they weren't meant to be together. Maybe she was barking up the wrong tree.

However, judging by the unmistakable look Noah gave her when she met him outside the bistro – a look that she knew only too well – it seemed there was very little doubt about his real feelings.

The questions and doubts were all Dara's.

* * *

"Noah, I just don't know what to do," Dara told him despondently over her barely touched lunch.

He gave her a steady look. "I can't tell you what to do. You know how I feel. You know that my feelings for you haven't changed. You're still the one I want, the one I've always wanted. I know the timing is bad but – "

"Bad? Noah, I'm barely married. How can I just turn around and leave him?"

Noah's tone was level. "I'm not asking you to."

She looked at him, incredulous. "Then what *are* you asking? That we keep meeting behind his back like this? Pretending that we're just a couple of friends catching up? Noah, that won't work. I think you and I both know that eventually things will get serious and we'll end up hurting people."

"I'm sorry. I wish I could go back in time and change how it was between us," he said, rubbing his temple. "But I can't. None of us can just wave a magic wand and make it all OK. People are going to get hurt anyway."

"Not anyone you know," Dara said petulantly.

Normally in control of her own life, she couldn't comprehend how she had ended up this way. Why hadn't she stuck to her guns and waited for Noah to come back? *'What's for you won't pass you'* – isn't that how the old saying went?

So, why did she bow to the others, bow to what everyone else thought she should do and marry a man who wasn't 'for her'? How could she have been so stupid? Why did she make a decision, a major decision in her life simply to keep other people happy? To keep other people off her back and stop them from looking at her strangely! Did it really matter what they thought? Did it matter to the point where she was forced into making a complete mess of her life?

"As I said, I wish I could make it easier," Noah said, tentatively laying a hand on hers and caressing it softly.

It was the first real contact they had had in all those years, and yes, the spark was still there.

She looked at his face, into those mystifying green eyes, hoping to find some kind of an answer to her problems. But none revealed itself. The answer didn't exist.

Instead, Dara had some serious decisions to make.

* * *

"So, of course I took it back to the shop and honestly, Gillian! You'd swear I'd gone and stained it myself!"

Well used to her best friend's petulance, and usually only too eager to get involved in a rant about bad service, Gillian would normally sit and listen to Norma's moaning before offering a sympathetic reply.

But not today.

Today, Gillian's mind was elsewhere.

Or more correctly, her *focus* was elsewhere, namely on the couple sitting at the top of the room in a quiet corner of the bistro. The couple who looked way too cosy for Gillian's liking.

She knew it! She knew it all along! That one was nothing but a stuck-up, two-faced man-eating … Gillian couldn't think of enough compound adjectives to describe the cow!

Should she go over and say something – make herself be known? Or more importantly, make it be known to the bitch that she had been caught – literally red-handed! They couldn't see her, the darkness of the café and the midday sunlight in their eyes would prevent that, but she could certainly see them! Look at her now, softly caressing his hand in public like that. Had the woman no shame? Blood rushed to her face and she couldn't remember ever feeling so angry. How *dare* she?

How dare she go and have lunch with some fancy-man behind Mark's back, let alone flaunt him around for all to see! Who the hell did Dara Campbell think she was? Reminding herself of the inexcusable fact that Dara wouldn't even lower herself to take her brother's surname, Gillian became even more angry.

"And then he just …Gillian? Gillian!" her friend snapped. "You're not even listening to me, are you?" Norma sat back in her chair and folded her arms petulantly across her chest. "Well, I'm very sorry if my experiences bore you, but you don't see *my* eyes glaze over like that when you talk about your little darlings, do you? Although not for the want of trying," she added acerbically.

But Gillian hardly heard her; she was too busy fuming at Dara.

"Everything has to come back to the kids with you." Mightily cheesed off at the fact that her friend was ignoring her, Norma was on a roll now. "Like the other night, when we were all having a laugh in the pub – trying to get a *break* from kids – and you had to start that conversation about Mikey's bloody poo! Honestly, Gillian, I wasn't going to say anything but – "

"What?" Finally her friend's words began to filter through, and

Gillian looked at Norma, her eyes narrowing.

"Remember? You were filling us in on all the gory details, the colour, the texture – and if you're not regaling us with tales of poo, it's something equally fascinating like how Lily points at her bum and says 'bum!'. Wow! Big bloody deal, Gillian! We're not all baby-mad, you know – some of us actually have a life!"

Gillian sat up, doubly shocked by all that was happening today. And to think she had just come out for a quiet lunch …

She leaned forward, fully prepared to give as good as she got. "Well, if we're being honest, Norma, then *I'm* sick to the teeth of hearing about your pathetic sex-life. Do you think I'm that interested in how little time Jim spends on foreplay, and how uninterested he is in your breasts?" She eyed her friend's chest derisively. "But sure, who'd blame him?"

"What? I thought you were my friend!" Norma gasped, shocked and more than a little embarrassed that they might be overheard. Her eyes darted to the closest table but the occupants seemed too busy with an animated conversation of their own to pay any interest.

"Yeah, well, maybe we should reassess that," Gillian replied stonily, thinking that perhaps today might be the best thing that could have happened. Gathering her belongings, she threw a twenty-euro note on the table, and without another word strode off in the direction of the ladies' at the back.

Once inside, she tried to calm her temper. What was all that about? She and Norma had been friends for years but, in fairness, the one-upmanship was becoming a bit tiring as time went on. Thinking about it now, Gillian wondered why she hadn't plucked up the courage to tell Norma to stuff her friendship years ago.

Still, she thought, studying her reflection in the mirror, would she be able to find the courage to tell Mark about Dara's behaviour and what his new wife – evidently – thought of him?

* * *

The following morning, Dara stared unseeingly out the window as the train trundled forward. It was packed again but at least today she'd managed to nab a seat. She had a busy morning ahead, but it was difficult to concentrate. Mark had been acting very strangely this morning, and not at all like his normal happy-go-lucky self. He'd barely said anything when she left the apartment just now, let alone given her his usual goodbye kiss.

There was no way he could have suspected anything, was there? she thought fearfully. How could he, when there was nothing to suspect? She and Noah had done nothing wrong – although with the way things were going, it would only be a matter of time before they did. She bit her lower lip anxiously.

She sighed softly. Ruth was right, of course. She had to do something and sooner rather than later. And at least Noah had given her the bit of space she needed to think about things. He'd told her that in order to make things easier and less confusing for her, he would stay out of her way for the coming weeks.

"Just don't take too long," he'd said, before leaning forward and brushing her lips lightly with his.

Just then, she didn't know how she'd resisted pulling him towards her and continuing the kiss properly, but the brief contact had enough of an effect to make her think about the weight and reality of her situation. Things were getting dangerous and it was only a matter of time …

So she had to do something – she had to make a decision, and quickly.

But it was so hard. On the one hand, there was the love of her life, the man she'd thought she'd lost forever, and on the other, her kind, gentle, loving husband.

It would be so much easier if the choice were simple, like it always seemed to be in the movies. If this was the movies, Noah would be the sexy, loveable and trustworthy one, played by someone like Colin Firth, while Mark would be the lying, faithless and villainous one, probably played by Colin Farrell.

But in this case, Mark was a decent guy, probably too decent, and it was difficult for her to come up with a good reason for leaving him.

And the worst part of all was that she did love him. Again, it wasn't the same as it was – or had been – with Noah, but there was still that shared companionship and great friendship that the two of them had.

To think that only a few short weeks ago, she and Mark had been talking about when they planned to start a family! She shook her head. She had really convinced herself, hadn't she? She had really believed that Mark would do, that he was enough, that she didn't need the big romance, that she could be happy with him. And in all honesty, she had been happy with him, in fact, she had been very happy – until Noah came along.

The train reached her usual stop, but this time Dara stayed on board. The Gardner case on which she and Nigel had spent the last few months working so hard was being heard that morning, so today she was heading straight to the Four Courts.

She sighed again, but this time for a different reason.

It was pretty obvious what was going to happen with this case, and she supposed she should be pleased, but really, the likes of Leo Gardner deserved some sort of punishment, be it fiscal or otherwise. Personally, Dara would love to see the smug so-and-so do a little spell inside Mountjoy – it would do him the world of good. But Gardner's privileged and well-connected position meant that this was unlikely to ever happen. She shook her head as the train pulled into Tara Street. To make the situation worse, from what Dara had gathered from the other side's solicitor, a negative judgement could ruin, quite literally, ruin the plaintiff.

But today, Dara thought, as she made her way towards the courts, this could very well be the least of her worries.

Because try as she might, she couldn't help but wonder what on earth was up with Mark.

CHAPTER 23

"All rise."

Louise stood up along with everyone else, as Judge Corcoran appeared and took his seat before the court.

It was all a bit exciting really, she thought, and although it was hardly glamorous with only one judge and not a jury in sight, it still felt like something out of a John Grisham film. Unfortunately, the barrister defending her side didn't look remotely like that dishy Matthew McConnaughey – no, this fella was a middle-aged, tubby bloke who was sporting one of those grey curly old-style wigs they all seemed to get such a kick out of wearing. Didn't those things itch like crazy? And how could grown men possibly think they looked anything other than downright idiotic – especially with that little rat's tail sticking out at the back?

Still, the barrister and his opposite number obviously weren't just play-acting here. The two of them had faces on them that would stop a jackass – as did the presiding judge. So Louise supposed she really should be concentrating on the importance of what was happening here today, rather than poking fun at the costumes, or imagining she was an extra in an episode of *LA Law*.

"We were lucky to get Judge Corcoran – he's generally sympathetic

239

to cases like this," she heard James Cahill whisper in her ear.

Louise's heart hammered. She wished she felt as optimistic as her solicitor sounded. She'd hardly slept last night, she was so worried about having to go up there in front of all these people to talk about her injuries – especially when she felt absolutely fine. God, would they all think she was one of these chancers that Fiona had been giving out about, looking for free money if someone looked at them sideways? She'd die!

But no, these guys were used to this sort of thing, weren't they? Although in fairness, they must be pretty sick of seeing all these people getting big payouts for the tiniest little thing. Maybe they'd go really hard on her and try and make an example of her, try and prove that there was nothing at all wrong with her.

"Well, of course," James Cahill informed her, at their prep-session the other day, "that's the job of the opposition, to try and defend their own client's interests. But Louise, there *is* no opposition. The guy admitted liability, so there's no case to be answered in that regard. It's merely a matter of how much we'll get from Corcoran. Now don't worry," he argued, when Louise went white, "they'll try and maintain that the insurance company covered everything at the time, but once the judge reads Dr Cunningham's medical report ..."

And so Louise was feeling confident, but not too confident. She wanted to get her part over with, and as quickly as possible, so she could just sit back and watch the rest of it at leisure.

She stole a quick look at the man who'd caused the accident, the man who'd run her down all that time ago. Leo Gardner's legal team seemed huge in comparison to her small gathering of Cahill, his assistant and the barrister. Once again, she felt uneasy. For a man who was being sued for a large amount of money, Gardner seemed incredibly relaxed and more than a little smug-looking as he conversed with one of his solicitors, an attractive, immaculately dressed woman who looked to be in her mid-thirties.Louise envied the other woman's obvious confidence, a confidence borne easily when you looked like that, she thought sighing. And she was obviously one of those hard nosed career-women types too, Louise decided. How else would anyone end up working for Gardner, who by all accounts seemed quite hard nosed himself? He never apologised, had never even sent a get-well card to the hospital at the time, Louise remembered, feeling wounded anew now that she thought about it. All those weeks she'd spent in agony at the hospital, simply because this oh-so-busy TV producer was in a hurry, and couldn't be bothered to stop at a red light. And he had never even sent a card.

Now Gardner looked as though he hadn't a care in the world – in fact, he looked as if he was enjoying the whole scenario. Yet, *he* was the guilty party, so why did Louise all of a sudden feel as though the opposite were true? Why did she now feel as though she were the one on trial here?

Probably because of what Cahill had said the other day.

"They'll try to maintain that you were suitably compensated the first time round. They'll ask about your job, your lifestyle, and will definitely try to downplay your injuries. So, Louise, when you get up there, please, don't do the job for them! I know you feel that perhaps your injuries weren't as severe as we're claiming, but don't even *think* about putting that across in court. As far as you're concerned, there isn't a day when you don't feel that back pain – it affects you constantly, and as Dr Cunningham will verify, it will affect you for the rest of your life."

"OK." Louise tried to take it all in.

"I'm going to focus in on your career, about how as a result of your injuries, you were forced to abandon your dreams of becoming a professional athlete – "

"Mr Cahill, there was never any question of my ..." But she trailed off when Cahill silenced her with a look. Shit, she must remember not to argue back like that in court – otherwise they hadn't a hope. But she didn't like all this exaggeration. It was totally unnecessary. She'd been reasonably decent at the shot-put in college and had won a few regional competitions, but it was very unlikely that she'd have gone professional! Yes, she had long-lasting injuries and, yes, she'd had to settle for a different career. But all this talk of 'dreams being abandoned' was totally over the top.

241

Still, Cahill was the expert and Louise would do well to follow his lead, rather than impose her own opinions on the matter. Otherwise the case would be lost, before it had even begun.

Which incidentally, was now about to happen.

Louise's barrister, a man called Donal O'Toole, began his opening statements. In a tone that was decidedly accusatory, he spoke about the accident itself, painted a very visual account of how Louise was innocently on her way home from a hard day's work – a part-time job she needed in order to finance her now defunct studies, he added pointedly – and how Leo Gardner had blatantly disregarded both the law and his civil duties by callously running the red light and knocking her over.

He outlined her injuries, namely the shattered pelvis, rib fractures and back injury. "Injuries that were clearly grievous, and yet, Mr Gardner's insurers saw fit to barely cover Ms Patterson's hospital stay at the time." He paused for what Louise thought was dramatic effect. "They chose to ignore the severity of her initial injuries – blatantly caused by negligence on the part of Leo Gardner – let alone consider the appalling emotional injury sustained thereafter . . ."

At this, the judge rolled his eyes slightly, and spotting the gesture, Louise began to panic. What O'Toole was saying was all very true, but did Judge Corcoran's reaction mean that he sympathised with Louise, or with Gardner? It was impossible to tell.

O'Toole was still speaking: ". . . emotional injuries that clearly affected Ms Patterson's social abilities and her confidence in day-to-day living and –"

"I've seen the physician's report, Mr O'Toole," the judge interjected wearily, "and I'm well aware of the nature of Ms Patterson's physical injuries. Emotional injuries however, do not come under the remit of the court at this time. So, Mr O'Toole, please continue, but this time with more fact and considerably less conjecture."

At this, Gardner's legal team looked mightily pleased with themselves, and Louise wished the barrister would tone down the drama about her state of mind. With the way he was talking, you'd swear she was afraid of her own reflection! Yes, she'd been a bit wobbly

242

about crossing roads for a long time after the accident, but that was only natural, wasn't it?

O'Toole went on to explain how Louise's hopes of a much-longed-for career as a Physical Education teacher had been swiftly and prematurely ended by her injuries and the subsequent loss of earnings as a result.

"Ms Patterson now works in an administrative role – a menial profession which by no means could match the gains her chosen career would have afforded her."

Menial profession? Hold on there a second, Mister! Louise wanted to say. There was nothing wrong with the job she had now – in fact if it wasn't for ACS, Louise wouldn't be able to work at all!

Which, she remembered just in time, was exactly the point the barrister was trying to get across. He had to make her job seem inferior, otherwise the claim for loss of earnings wouldn't stand up. She mentally reminded herself to focus on the bigger picture, and not take every utterance as some kind of insult. *Especially* when she herself had to take the stand.

Finally O'Toole completed his monologue, reiterating once more that Louise's financial circumstances were clearly deficient because of Gardner's actions and, as a result, he was bound by duty of care to compensate her for such losses. He returned to his seat alongside Louise and her solicitor, whereupon Cahill bestowed an admiring smile on him and she deduced that, in the circumstances, O'Toole must have done very well.

Next up was Gardner's barrister, Walter Flanagan, a tall, imposing, man with broad shoulders and a harsh, angular-looking face. But when the man began to speak, his voice was surprisingly soft, yet commanding and articulate. To her surprise, Louise almost found herself warming to him, despite the fact that he was the opposition.

But when his barrister began to outline the basis of Leo Gardner's defence, she quickly changed her mind.

"Your Honour, we accept that Ms Patterson has suffered additional injuries as a result of the accident, but not to the overstated lengths the claimant's legal team purport. Moreover, we will throughout the course of these proceedings prove to the court that she has *not* suffered resultant loss of earnings. In fact," he added, a little too cryptically for Louise's liking, "Ms Patterson's financial position should be considered more than adequate for a young lady of her age and circumstance."

What was he talking about? What did 'more than adequate' mean? All he had to do was look at her bank and credit-card statements and then he'd know all about 'adequate'! Louise looked at her solicitor for an explanation but James Cahill didn't seem remotely upset. She felt momentarily relieved. Again, this sort of thing must be par for the course, and James did explain that it was the job of the other side to defend themselves, which is exactly what they were doing. If Gardner's side didn't refute the charges, there would be no case to answer, would there? So she really should stop worrying and just let them all get on with it. She'd stick to her story – no, she reminded herself, it wasn't a story, it was the *truth* – and the rest of them could argue about it all they liked. It was cut and dried, wasn't that what Cahill kept saying? Cut and dried.

So Louise might as well just sit and back and let all the fancy talk go over her head.

"Furthermore," Flanagan was still speaking, "we will also seek to prove that Mr Gardner's initial settlement of this case was more than adequate and this fresh suit case against the defendant is not only frivolous, but downright fraudulent." His voice was beginning to get louder and take on more weight with every utterance, and all of a sudden Louise felt very, very frightened.

Fraudulent? Why would they say something like that? Gardner had never disputed that he was at fault – that he was *liable* – as Cahill was always saying. So what were they playing at, trying to suggest that Louise was chancing her arm? She had debts that needed to be paid, debts that originated with additional hospital bills and then more physiotherapy bills. What happened to 'cut and dried' all of a sudden?

James Cahill leant across and went to whisper something in her ear. "Don't worry," he reassured. "It's only a bluff. Flanagan's seen the medical report and the hospital receipts. He knows the evidence is too strong to ignore and he's just show-boating."

Louise nodded blankly.

Shortly afterwards, it was time to hear from the witnesses.

First up, the court heard evidence from the doctor's report. Louise's consultant physician Dr Cunningham spoke about his assessment of her injuries. The doctor outlined how additional complications, relating in particular to damaged vertebrae, had necessitated a further stay in hospital and additional physiotherapy. Louise would likely suffer chronic back pain for the rest of her life, he told them, and her injuries were 'significant and ongoing'. The back injury in particular had affected her manual dexterity and effectively ended her participation in most forms of sport. There was no question of her achieving a PE teacher qualification – in fact there were a number of career choices that were well beyond her capabilities as a result of her injuries, namely anything that involved lifting and carrying, or bending, kneeling or squatting. The back pain would significantly restrict her lifestyle and, as she got older, there was also the possibility of future complications.

Both sides questioned the doctor on some of the points raised, but as the independent physician had more or less concurred with Cunningham's findings, there was little to argue.

Shortly afterwards, the court broke for a short recess.

Outside in the corridor, Louise sat quietly amongst her legal team, her legs shaking with nerves, and her heart thudding at the prospect of having to take the stand and answer that scary man's questions. Apparently, she was up next.

The coffee James Cahill had thrust into her hand in the hope of settling her nerves looked like muck, and didn't taste much better, and she quickly put it aside thinking that throwing up in court under cross-examination wouldn't endear her to anyone, let alone the judge!

On the way out of the courtroom, she had stolen another look at the woman on Gardner's team. Seeing her up close, she couldn't shake the feeling that she already knew the girl, that she'd seen her somewhere before. But where? Where would an elegant, sophisticated, and immaculately dressed professional – the kind of woman Louise

245

would sorely love to be – cross paths with an ordinary, boring, *menial* office worker, like her?

Then Louise recalled her visit to the Four Seasons hotel during Gemma's hen night that time. Could she have seen her there? Come across her while on a visit to those amazing palatial toilets to fix up her make-up maybe? It was certainly possible, she decided. Then again, she couldn't remember much about that night other than meeting Sam, and for once her memory loss wasn't as a result of over-indulgence. No, it was a result of pure unadulterated lust! She relaxed slightly at the thought of Sam. He'd be back soon, and hopefully by the time she saw him, this would be all over and both the court case and Louise's long-standing debt would be nothing but a distant memory.

All too soon, they were back in the courtroom and almost immediately O'Toole called Louise to take the stand.

Take the stand! God, it was so weird, hearing it in real-life like that! She swallowed hard as she got up, her hands and legs shaking like crazy as she approached the witness stand. The witness stand! Was any of this real, she wondered as she shakily sat down, or was she simply having another one of her daydreams?

But when Louise looked up and saw all those people sitting there and studying her every move, she knew this was all very, very real. She offered up a silent prayer. *Please, please, don't let me mess up and stay something stupid!*

Well, at least O'Toole would be doing the questioning first, so that shouldn't be too bad. As she waited for the questions to begin, she tried her utmost not to look at Gardner or his team. They were all still looking way too smug for her liking. Anyway, if she looked directly at Gardner, she would probably go crimson with embarrassment, and then the judge would definitely think she was playing them. She still didn't feel she had the right to take this case in all honesty, and at that moment, if she had her way, she'd rather drop the whole thing and pay off her debts on her own. Anything but having to sit here on show like this.

O'Toole spoke quietly: "Louise, the court has been made fully aware of the extent of your injuries by way of Dr Cunningham's testimony, and also the report of the defendant's physician, so we don't wish to waste the court's time by going over it all again." He smiled in an effort to relax her but unfortunately it didn't work and Louise still felt like a rabbit caught in headlights. Which, incidentally, was exactly how she'd felt back then in that split second before Gardner had run her over.

"However, I would like to talk to you about how life has changed since your accident," he went on, glancing at his notes as he spoke. "You were twenty-one years of age at the time, isn't that right?"

Louise nodded.

"And isn't it true to say your life has changed immeasurably since the accident and –"

"Objection!" Gardner's senior counsel interjected. "The claimant has already put a measure on how much Ms Patterson's life has changed with regard to damages claimed, otherwise we wouldn't be here today."

The judge nodded. "True. Mr O'Toole, please try to use specifics rather than meaningless adverbs when trying to outline how much Ms Patterson's life has changed."

"Certainly, Your Honour." O'Toole bowed his head softly and then turned to look at her again. "Louise, I don't wish to cause any undue embarrassment, but isn't it true that for most of your life – throughout your teenage years right up to the accident incidentally – you were a rather … stout young lady?"

Louise wanted to die. What was he doing going on about her weight in front of everyone like this? What did *that* have to do with anything?

"Louise?" O'Toole was waiting for her to answer. "Would you agree with that assessment?"

Louise bit her lip. "Um … yes, that's right."

"In fact, unlike most girls your age, you never had an image problem or anything of the sort, did you? You were a healthy young lady who liked her grub and was refreshingly unaffected by today's image-obsessed society."

247

Louise gulped. 'Liked her *grub*?' Where the hell was he going with this? For a split second she was almost tempted to ask, but then she remembered her solicitor's instructions about simply answering yes or no.

So Louise just nodded softly, wishing he'd stop going on about weight and food and generally all things embarrassing. "Yes."

"And, of course, your stature suited your choice of sport and boosted your athletic abilities, didn't it?" he went on, and finally Louise began to understand. "Ms Patterson is a former shot-put medallist – a sport that generally requires its participants to be of – robust stature," he informed the court, in case they weren't aware that heavy women could actually participate in any kind of sport.

Then he paused and seemed to regard Louise very carefully.

"Yet, look at you today, practically emaciated, that strong hearty constitution that characterised your youth now totally depleted, the healthy glow in your cheeks no longer apparent."

If you say so, Louise thought, thinking she really should have applied more blusher this morning.

"Mr O'Toole, where is this going?" The judge piped up, obviously frustrated.

"Your Honour, I'm merely trying to convey to the court how Ms Patterson has without a doubt suffered severe emotional stress and strain as a result of the accident," he turned and indicated her, before adding, "as characterised by her dramatic weight loss."

Louise's eyes widened. What? She'd lost all the weight because she damn well wanted to, and it had nothing to do with the accident – indeed, it had more to do with denying herself that well-loved grub he'd mentioned earlier! What was he playing at?

"You're lost quite a bit of weight over the past eighteen months, Ms Patterson. According to my notes, about three stone, is that right?"

Louise nodded softly, afraid to open her mouth for fear of what she might say. She had been warned over and over again not to express any opinions, however much she might be tempted. And right then Louise was sorely tempted. But in a way, she supposed she wasn't telling any lies as such, she was simply confirming that, yes, she had lost that much weight. Yet, she hated the way he was making it all sound – it just wasn't right.

Having apparently made his point, O'Toole asked a few questions about her time in hospital, about the extra appointments with the physiotherapist, before returning to the subject of her 'much-longed for' career.

"You were a few years into your studies when Mr Gardner swiftly ended your hopes of completing them –" he began, before once again, Flanagan strenuously objected.

"Mr O'Toole," said the judge, "the defendant's liability for the accident is not in question here, so please discontinue such leading statements, will you?"

The judge sounded annoyed now and Louise didn't blame him. O'Toole had gone through most of this in his opening statement, so there was nothing new. She wished he'd ask about how the hospital bills had been exorbitantly high, and the additional treatment unexpected. That was what the case was all about after all.

"So Louise how did you feel about your dreams being shattered like that?"

"My dreams?"

"Yes, your dreams of reaching great achievements in your chosen sport, your hopes of teaching others to do the same and then realising after your accident, that this was no longer possible. How did you feel?"

"Well, I was very disappointed naturally ..." Louise was instinctively about to add something further – like 'but these things happen' or 'but life goes on', like she usually did when asked about it, but something in O'Toole's expression stopped her.

"Devastated, even?"

"Mr O'Toole!" The judge was getting *very* irritated now.

"I'm sorry, Your Honour. But I'm trying to convey how it deeply the tragedy affected Ms Patterson, and how it had such a bearing on her future. Your Honour will note that Ms Patterson is claiming for loss of earnings as a result of a greatly diminished earnings capacity. Not only has she been left debt-ridden as a result of Mr Gardner's negligence, but also has little hope of overcoming those debts any time soon, due to her low-earning profession. Once again – a situation she's been forced into as a result of Mr Gardner's carelessness."

'Forced into?' Now he was making her sound like a prostitute!

He went on to outline Louise's salary at ACS, how her back injury meant that she was unable to lift or carry heavy loads, how her periodical bouts of back pain resulted in frequent absences, and again the resultant loss of earnings, and subsequent difficulties in making her loan repayments. In this regard, he referred to documentary evidence from the banks in relation to her loans.

That was just the beginning – they'd get some shock if they saw her credit-card bills! Louise thought silently.

Finally, having painted a reasonable picture of a girl who had suffered physically, emotionally and financially as a result of the accident – although she'd have preferred he left out the weight loss – O'Toole finally finished his questioning and returned to his seat.

"Mr Flanagan?" the judge urged.

Louise took a very deep breath as Gardner's deceptively mild-mannered barrister approached.

"Based on the documentary evidence, I can't argue with your counsel, Ms Patterson," he said, surprising her. "You are indeed servicing a great deal of debt."

Louise couldn't believe it. By saying that, Gardner's side was basically admitting that she had been stung the first time round – brilliant!

"But," Flanagan went on and hearing his tone, her delight quickly vanished, "the suggestion that your lifestyle has suffered as a result of this accident is really quite extraordinary." All of sudden, the barrister's demeanour was that of an eagle just about to pounce on a defenceless little mouse. "Especially when the bulk of that debt stems from funding your – shall we say – rather extravagant lifestyle."

Her *what?*

"Isn't it true, Ms Patterson, that as well as a large term loan from your bank, you also have a generous overdraft, and a selection of credit cards from different financial institutions?"

"Yes," Louise answered weakly, her heart plummeting.

"Considering you yourself work in a lending agency, wouldn't you say that your current level of debt greatly outweighs the borrowings for your medical bills? That your lifestyle spending on clothes, shoes and ahem – copious socialising now makes up the bulk of this debt?"

"That's not true!" Louise blurted, stung. "I have to use my cards because my wages can't stretch to –"

"Can't stretch to weekend breaks in sunny Spain? Lavish nights out in some of our fair city's trendiest nightspots? Spending in designer boutiques, and let's not forget –" he made an elaborate show of checking his notes, "an upcoming shopping weekend in New York?"

Louise reddened, hating how it all sounded and, worse, realising how bad it looked to the judge. How did Flanagan *know* all this?

"Correct me if I'm wrong, Ms Patterson," he went on relentlessly. "Have you been in Spain recently?"

"Yes, but –"

"Are you planning a trip to New York?"

"Yes, I –"

"Have you recently spent money in designer boutiques in the city centre here in Dublin?"

"Yes." Louise's answer was almost a whisper.

"Hardly typical or indeed appropriate for someone with a 'greatly diminished earnings capacity', Ms Patterson. Am I correct?"

She couldn't answer.

"And correct me if I'm wrong, but aren't you a current resident of the Marina Quarter? That much-talked about, brand-new luxury development on the coast?"

"But it's rented!" Louise argued weakly. Oh, why had she done it? She'd known the rent was way over the odds, but Fiona had begged and begged and she couldn't let her down and –

"I should certainly hope so," Flanagan went on. "One certainly wouldn't like to think that someone who was apparently left destitute as a result of a car accident could afford to buy into one of the finest developments in the city."

"Objection!" Finally O'Toole spoke up.

But why the hell had he waited so long? When *he* was speaking, Flanagan had been objecting left, right and centre at nothing!

"Objection!" the barrister repeated. "As I'm sure the court is aware, Dublin rents are some of the most exorbitant in Europe. I might add that Ms Patterson could only find a job flexible enough to accommodate her injuries here in the capital. As a result, this is why she lives in Dublin."

Even Louise knew this was feeble. She certainly didn't have to live all the way out on the coast – as it was, the apartment was now further away from the office.

A fact that wasn't lost on Barrister Flanagan. "You honour, as Ms Patterson works in the city centre, her choice of residence is clearly not based on proximity to the workplace."

The judge growled and waved O'Toole away. "I agree. The claimant's workplace has no bearing on this."

Louise's hands shook. The judge was clearly suspicious now. Gardner's side had painted her as an irresponsible spendthrift hoping for an easy way out of her financial difficulties. She wouldn't blame him for being sceptical though. Taken together, all the things that Flanagan had said sounded awful, and she *did* come across as irresponsible. Yet, all this debt originally stemmed from having to pay off Gardner's handiwork and she'd never quite been able to get on top of it, so –

"It seems you've made a very strong argument that Ms Patterson's lifestyle hasn't been as adversely affected by her accident as her counsel would have us believe," the judge said, and Louise's blood went cold. "Do you have anything further to add? Any more questions?"

"Nothing further at this time," Flanagan replied and returned to his desk, whereby a smiling Leo Gardner patted him on the back.

"Thank you, Ms Patterson," Judge Corcoran told her and Louise looked at him, confused. Was that it? Wasn't O'Toole going to argue back – argue about how they'd twisted everything to make it sound bad? Surely they couldn't let the judge think –

"Thank you, Ms Patterson," he repeated, a little louder this time.

Somehow Louise found the strength to stand.

The judge banged his gavel. "The court will re-convene at 2.30 p m," he announced as Louise slowly returned to her seat.

"Why didn't you say anything?" she asked Cahill afterwards. "Why didn't you get O'Toole to tell them it isn't *like* that?"

"There was no point," her solicitor replied evenly, although the confident demeanour he possessed earlier had now departed. "As I said before, we expected them to try and argue that your claim is exaggerated. They were bound to question your spending habits. Still, there's no arguing that you're legally entitled to be properly compensated for your injuries and expenses. I had no idea you were in so much debt though," he added quietly and Louise could see that this troubled him. What? Was he worried he might not get paid, was that it? But hadn't he said it was on a no-win no-fee basis? Although, she thought worriedly, the other day he'd insisted that this case was cut and dried which meant that his percentage was practically guaranteed. Did this morning mean that things were no longer that way?

Louise hoped not, because the last thing she needed was her solicitor losing faith in her. Not when it was all supposed to be as good as a sure thing.

* * *

After lunch – Louise hadn't been able to touch a thing, she was so worried – they returned to the courtroom.

She wasn't sure what would happen now. O'Toole had called both his witnesses and as Gardner was the only witness for his side, it would undoubtedly all rest on how he came across to the judge. Flanagan had done his best to make Louise's claim look exaggerated by throwing a question mark on her spending, but the fact remained that he couldn't disprove her injuries. And that, Louise reminded herself once more, was what this case was really all about.

And as Gardner had already admitted liability, and had already been convicted in the criminal courts for speeding, there wasn't much else he could say, was there?

253

Flanagan stood up to call his witness, and Louise wondered what Gardner would be like. They'd never spoken, so she didn't know all that much about him, other than the fact he was a powerful TV producer with a lot of money behind him, and very well respected in entertainment circles. He had worked on all sorts of TV programmes throughout the years, including some of Louise's own favourites, apparently.

"Your Honour, we call Mr Samuel Harris to the stand," Flanagan announced.

Samuel? Louise questioned idly – she'd always thought his name was *Leo*. Oh well, she decided, perhaps it was just a stage name or something. But no, it wasn't –

"What the hell is this?" James Cahill was saying to O'Toole and the two of them were looking from one to the other with some trepidation. "Who the hell is this guy? What are they playing at?"

"What's going–?" And then Louise stopped short as she saw Sam, *her* Sam enter the courtroom and walk up the aisle.

She grinned. Brilliant! Sam had obviously come home early so he wouldn't miss the trial. He was going to stick up for her, let them know that his girlfriend wasn't this frivolous, shopaholic spendthrift – no she was simply a normal, decent, hardworking –

"Louise do you know this person?" Cahill was asking, apparently having spotted her happy smile.

She nodded. "Of course, I do – he's my boyfriend and he's come here to help us out," she said gleefully, hardly able to believe that Sam would do that for her, that he thought so much of her that he would come home early just for –

"Louise, whoever this guy is, he certainly isn't here to help us out, and, if you *do* know him, I hope to God you haven't told him anything stupid."

"What?" Louise looked up at Sam in the witness chair, waiting for him to smile, wave – something to show her that he was on her side. But no, Sam remained stony-faced and looked neither left nor right as he waited for the questioning to begin.

And then, it hit her. Sam didn't know about the trial, he didn't even know about the *case*! Or at least that's what Louise had thought. Her skin growing hot, she remembered his marked interest in her, his blatant pursuit of her, the wonderful times they had together. Then her stomach turned as she had a sudden flash of the conversation they'd had recently, about her injuries, about her accident – one of the last conversations they'd had before he had to 'go away for a while'.

"Louise," her solicitor finished solemnly, as the room began to swim before her eyes, "he's testifying for the opposition."

CHAPTER 24

That same afternoon, Rosie was wheeling her trolley around the supermarket, picking up groceries for the rest of the week. As she passed the meat counter, she couldn't help but look longingly at the succulent fresh pieces of lamb's liver displayed under the glass.

Martin had always loved lamb's liver, and Rosie was very partial to it herself. But the last time she'd had it, the strong scent of cooking had stayed around the house for days, and judging by David's deep sighs and irritable mutterings afterwards, he hadn't been very happy. So she hadn't risked cooking it since. It was the same with the mince and, as a result, it was ages since she'd had a nice homemade shepherd's pie or any of the other meals she used to enjoy. Sighing softly, she shook her head and moved on past the fresh meat display and on to the pre-cooked section.

"Hello, Rosie, how are you?"

Rosie looked across the aisle and smiled as she recognised one of her classmates from the watercolour lessons, a chatty and amiable young girl who lived a few miles outside the town.

"Grand, Emma, and yourself?"

"Not too bad. So, are you all set for the big night tonight?" she asked, referring to their last evening class, which was to take place

256

that same evening. Stephen had joked that it would be their big 'graduation'.

Rosie nodded sadly. "Unfortunately."

"It's hard to believe it's nearly over, isn't it?"

"I know. I'll really miss it," Rosie replied, taken aback by how much she meant it. What had started out as an excuse to keep her mind off things had turned into a really worthy and enjoyable hobby, and Rosie didn't know what she'd do with herself on Wednesday nights from now on.

"Well, I'll better get going or I'll miss it altogether! See you later!" Emma smiled and went on her way, leaving Rosie thinking about how much she'd miss having the chat and a bit of fun with her and the others, not to mention getting out of the house for a night. Still, these days the evenings were a bit too dark for walking up the hill on her own, so in a way it was probably a good thing.

She knew she'd miss her new friend, Stephen, a lot too. Over the few weeks they'd known each other, Rosie had come to see him as a bit of a lifeline, someone who, with his own wonderfully entertaining stories about his experiences and travels, would make her forget about her own worries.

And she'd miss him all the more now that his house in Brittas Bay had been sold and he was making plans to move back down the country.

Again, Rosie was taken aback by how homesick for County Clare she'd been feeling lately. It was stupid really, as it wasn't as though she had anyone left there now, other than the odd relation. Her real family – supposedly, she thought sadly – were here, and Sheila, of course. But listening to Stephen talk about the lovely cottage he'd bought down on the Kerry coast, and the lovely relaxing lifestyle he'd planned there – painting landscapes, planting vegetables and pretty much doing as he pleased – made Rosie yearn for her old home county.

But almost immediately, she admonished herself for being so maudlin. It wasn't as though she'd emigrated to America or anything, she thought, picking up some nice dog treats for Twix. A train from Heuston would take her down to Clare any day of the week if she set her mind to it, and it had been a long time since she'd done that particular journey, hadn't it? So, obviously County Clare wasn't the be-all and end-all, otherwise she'd be down there every opportunity she could.

No, it was probably just all the talk about Stephen's place and, of course, her own problems with David that was bringing this about. And anyway, she reminded herself as she took her place at the checkout, it wasn't possible to swan off to Clare just like that, was it? Not when everything was tied up the way it was. Granted the few euro she and Martin had saved over the years would go a small way towards buying a little place, but what would she do for the rest of it? And how would she live? There was no question of her selling her house, not now anyway, so even thinking about it was idiotic in the extreme.

Indeed, she would be much better off getting used to, and trying to come to terms with, the way things were now. She would be much better off just letting David do his own thing and, as long as neither of them interfered with the other, then things would be grand.

In fairness, he seemed a lot happier in himself these days, now that she was keeping out of his way and staying in her own room. There hadn't been a cross word between them in weeks, although in fairness there hadn't been that many words at all! She made sure she had eaten and cleaned up by the time David arrived back from work at six, and she usually stayed upstairs in her room for the rest of the evening. Sometimes she read a book, sometimes she painted and sometimes she just sat by the window relaxing with Twix in her lap. All in all, it wasn't too bad.

So, she supposed, in a way Stephen was right. It really was just a case of David and her taking a bit of time to get used to one another, taking a bit of time to find a balance.

Yes, that was it, she reassured herself, as she paid the cashier for her purchases. It was all about balance.

Desperate to come to terms with it all, and deliberately overlooking how unfairly balanced things were in reality, Rosie gathered her shopping bags and made her way out of the store.

Twenty minutes later, Rosie arrived at her front gate, tired and weary. Was it her imagination or did the hill seem to be getting steeper and steeper these days? Anyway, it was her own fault really; she had bought way too many groceries – more than enough for this week and possibly most of the next. On her way to the front door, she did a slight double-take as she caught sight of a car parked outside the house.

Oh no, David was home early! Which gave her no time to cook and eat dinner and then get out of his way. Oh well, she sighed, she could just have something small, a sandwich or something – anything that wouldn't need a whole lot of preparation.

But why was he back so early? Despite herself, Rosie felt a tiny frisson of fear. She hoped he hadn't lost his job or anything. How would she cope with having him around all day every day?

She opened the door, and stepped quietly and rather tentatively into the hallway, dragging her shopping bags behind her. Then she bit her lip. Judging by the clinking and clanking of utensils coming from behind the closed door, David was in the kitchen. Now, there was no way she was going to go in there too – she'd rather have her frozen groceries defrost in the hallway than interrupt him.

No, she'd just leave the bags down here and go on upstairs and wait until he was finished. It was such a pity though – she was famished and had really been looking forward to a bit of dinner. She'd bought one of those lasagnes that didn't need any cooking other than a few minutes in the microwave. There was a time when Rosie wouldn't touch anything of the sort but, since David's return, her eating habits and tastes had changed considerably.

Leaving her shopping bags in the hallway, Rosie crept softly upstairs, hoping that he wouldn't be much longer. Normally she wouldn't mind waiting, but tonight was the last night of her evening class and she certainly didn't want to be late for that! But sure, there was plenty of time yet, she thought, looking at her watch. And she could always pass away an hour or so by bringing Twix out for a long walk. That's what she'd do, she decided, trying to ignore the low throbbing on the soles of her feet and the back of her calves from walking up that hill. The dog would be thrilled anyway – like most dogs she loved nothing better than a good long walk and, knowing

Twix, a good long sniff of the paths along the way.

Rosie opened the door of her bedroom, and braced herself for the enthusiastic tail-wagging, energetic jumping and delighted squeals that usually greeted her return.

But this time there was nothing.

And even worse, there was nothing in Twix's basket.

Straight away, Rosie knew that there was something wrong. Where was she? Why wasn't the dog in her room, where she'd left her not two hours ago?

And if Twix wasn't here, where was she?

Then she thought of David's early return and knew instinctively that this had something – no, *everything* – to do with the dog's disappearance. Had he gone and put her out in the shed again? He'd better not, she thought, more than a little panicked. Or Twix had better not have done something stupid, like growl or even snap at him. The dog's earlier fear of David had since turned into full-blown dislike and distrust, and everyone knew what dogs could do if they felt threatened enough.

Rosie couldn't be sure that even gentle little Twix could be trusted not to attack if provoked enough.

Oh, she was stupid to be even thinking these things and running away with herself before she knew anything, she remonstrated as she went back downstairs.

Then, as much as she hated doing it – and hated herself even more for feeling as though she *had* to do it – Rosie knocked softly on the kitchen door. Knocking on the door of her own kitchen like some kind of stranger, imagine!

But the last thing she wanted to do was annoy David, particularly if there had been some kind of incident between him and the dog. Her darling son opened the kitchen door with a scowl on his face and, as Rosie suspected, not at all happy to be interrupted.

"David, I'm sorry to disturb your dinner," Rosie began, again feeling so pathetic for kow-towing to him like this. But she felt she had no choice. "But Twix seems to be missing."

"Missing?"

"Yes. She isn't upstairs in her basket, or anywhere in the room and I just wondered if – "

"I don't know where it went," David said flatly. But something passed across his expression and Rosie knew instantly that there had been some kind of episode.

"What happened, David?" she asked, heart thudding.

"It went for me," he admitted, with a shrug. "I came home and the little shit went for me."

"What? But Twix wouldn't ..." But even as she said the words, Rosie couldn't be sure they were true.

"Wouldn't hurt a fly? So you said. But I came in the front door minding my own business and the vicious little shit was here in the hall and started growling and barking its head off at me. As if I was some bloody burglar or something."

"Barking? But she was probably asleep in the hallway and got a fright when you woke her up – I must have forgotten to lock my bedroom door when I put her in." Rosie was relieved. That wasn't too bad – at least it wasn't anything else ... "But where is she now? Did you lock her up again or ..." Rosie knew that by all this questioning she risked annoying him, but she was so worried she didn't care.

By now, David was clearly irritated. "Mum, I really don't have time for this. Today I finish work early, so I come home hoping to have a nice afternoon to myself and take things easy. No sooner am I in the door that I nearly get the leg bitten off me, and then when I'm trying to make dinner, I have to listen to this."

"I'm sorry that Twix barked at you. But she just didn't expect ... and I didn't expect ..."

"Jeez, Mum, will you give it a rest," he said, exasperated. "Look, I don't know where it is now. The door was open and it ran off somewhere." He went to close the door again, as to say 'end of conversation'.

"She went out the front – out onto the road?" asked Rosie, full of dread. "But why did she run off?" She knew well that Twix would never take off anywhere without her. "What did you do? You didn't ... you didn't hurt her or anything, did you?" Her heart thudded with fear. "But she's not used to being out on her own, out without me ... not without a lead and ... how long has she been gone?"

David sighed loudly. "About an hour ago, I think. Look, it ran outside and after it had nearly taken the leg off me, I wasn't exactly in the mood for running after it. Anyway, it's only a stupid dog. I'm sure it'll be back here whingeing when it gets hungry enough."

"You don't understand, David!" his mother cried, utterly panicked now. "Twix is a house dog, she's not used to the roads, not used to the traffic, and she's frightened!" With this, Rosie turned on her heel and hurried out the front door.

CHAPTER 25

It was all over.

Louise stared unseeingly out the window as she made her way home on the train that evening, her head swimming, her heart breaking. She'd been hung.

She still couldn't believe what had happened, couldn't believe that she'd made such a mess of everything, couldn't believe that she'd been betrayed in such an awful way.

She recalled how utterly callous Sam had seemed in the courtroom that afternoon, recalled word for word how he had blithely gone about ruining her case. He'd sat there on the stand, his expression like stone, as if he didn't know her, as if he didn't realise what he was about to do.

* * *

Flanagan's tone had been neutral when he first addressed Sam, but there had been nothing neutral about the emotions Louise had felt at the time. "Mr Harris, can you describe for the court the circumstances of your first meeting with Ms Patterson," he'd asked, while Louise, still dumbstruck at her boyfriend's appearance, stayed rooted to her seat.

Sam's voice was equally neutral. "We met at the Ice Bar."

263

"Forgive us, Mr Harris," Flanagan interjected immediately, a hint of sadistic pleasure in his tone, "if some of us here today are not all that familiar with the particulars of Dublin night spots – but the Ice Bar?"

"In the Four Seasons Hotel."

"This is the *five-star* hotel in Ballsbridge you're talking about, and not some other establishment of the same name, is it?"

Sam nodded. "Yes."

"And Ms Patterson is a patron here?"

"She was that night. I was standing at the bar when she came up beside me."

At the time, Louise couldn't believe what she was hearing, she couldn't believe what he was doing! How could he do this? How could he pretend to care about her, pretend to be her friend, when all the time he was plotting against her? Who would do so such a thing?

"So Ms Patterson struck up a conversation with you?" the barrister prompted.

"No, I passed comment."

"Really? How so? Did one of the expensive designer garments Ms Patterson seems so fond of happen to catch your eye?"

"Objection!" To Louise's relief, O'Toole stood up. "How is this relevant?"

"Agreed," the judge conceded. "Get to the point, Mr Flanagan."

But Sam went ahead, and answered the question anyway. "That wasn't it, although I do remember she was wearing something nice that night, yes."

Louise cringed, recalling how Fiona had playfully ordered her into buying that bloody wrap dress!

"So what caused you to pass comment?" Flanagan probed.

"Well, she was ordering a round of drinks for her friends. An expensive round of drinks," Sam added pointedly.

Flanagan made a great show of appearing confused. "All drinks are considered expensive in our fair city these days, Mr Harris. Please elaborate further."

"She was ordering a dozen champagne cocktails," Sam explained.

"Oh." He paused for effect. "Champagne cocktails – in a five-star establishment?"

"Correct."

"*Twelve* of them?"

"Yes."

"My, oh my," Flanagan shook his head, "I must be in the wrong job. I can't remember the last time any of my friends or esteemed colleagues from the Law Library treated themselves like that."

Louise cringed, Gardner's crowd laughed and, mercifully, O'Toole objected.

"There's no place for sarcasm in this court," Judge Corcoran warned in reply.

"Apologies, Your Honour."

But it was too late. The point had been made, and even the judge looked taken aback by it all. Given that the defence had already made her out to be a spendthrift, the revelation was doubly effective.

Flanagan continued. "But perhaps she wasn't paying for them all from her own pocket, Mr Harris? Perhaps she was merely ordering them for her friends?"

"No, she paid. With her Visa card. And she told me it was her round."

"Oh, I see – one round of many then."

"Objection! Conjecture!"

"Apologies, Your Honour," said Flanagan and smoothly continued, "So, Mr Harris, champagne cocktails are Ms Patterson's drink of choice, then?"

"Apparently."

The bastard! Louise tried to conceal her upset. He knew well that she normally preferred a simple vodka and Coke. How many times had he been out with her after that and not once, not *once* did she suggest getting a bloody champagne cocktail!

"Objection – this is pure conjecture!"

"It was her drink of choice that night anyway," Sam clarified, before the judge could respond.

"So, you two struck up a conversation, then?" Flanagan went on, adding, "About the expensive champagne cocktails?" just in case the judge hadn't yet got the point.

"I mentioned how I was going to offer to pay for the drinks, but having discovered what they were, I thought better of it. We chatted for a while, and she told me that she was on a hen night – no, sorry," he clarified "a pre-hen night with her friends."

"A *pre*-hen night?"

"Apparently, she and her friends were off on holiday to Marbella the following day for the real hen-night – I mean hen weekend."

Bastard, bastard, bastard.

"A holiday in Marbella – to celebrate a hen party?" Flanagan repeated once more for maximum effect.

"Yes, she told me this after I asked her out. I had hoped to meet up with her that weekend, but she said she'd be away."

"I see. So you and Ms Patterson struck up a 'friendship' in the bar, and then spent the rest of the night chatting, perhaps?" It was obvious by the way the questioning was going that Sam had spent just as much time as Louise – if not more – being coached by a solicitor. And he was 'performing' much better up there than Louise ever could. She hung her head in shame. The problem was, she couldn't accuse him of telling lies – everything had happened almost exactly how he described it. But in view of what they'd already implied about her spending, it sounded a million times worse.

"No," Sam went on, "we only spent a few minutes chatting before her friend came along, and told her they were moving. She'd barely touched her drink."

"Barely touched her *expensive* champagne cocktail?"

Sam nodded. "She left it with me. I told her I'd never tried one so …" he shrugged, as if to imply that he was just a normal Joe Soap, unused to that kind of thing.

"So, Ms Patterson, a lady with obvious money problems, spends all this money on a exorbitantly priced drink and then *doesn't even bother to finish it?*"

The emphasis he put on the last few words made them almost palpable, and at this Louise thought she sensed even James Cahill's disapproval. But again, it hadn't been like that. She hadn't drunk it back all at once because she didn't want to come across to Sam as a raving lush. She'd been trying to impress him, and oh, how that had backfired!

"No, I drank it instead. As I said, I'd never tried one, and don't often have occasion to drink something like that so – "

"Indeed. So, after that first night – in the Four Seasons Hotel – when did you make Ms Patterson's acquaintance again?"

"She gave me her number, and I told her I'd phone when she got back from Marbella."

"Her holiday break in Marbella?"

"Yes."

"And did you phone her?"

Louise squirmed, knowing what was coming, remembering it all so well. The pathetic lies she'd spun to try and make herself appear unavailable, the stupidity of it all …

"I did, and then I asked her out again. I'd hoped to meet her for a drink that week."

"You were attracted to her, then?"

Sam nodded. "Very much so. She's a very lively, friendly, fun-loving girl – great to be around. But she was also difficult to pin down."

"Really? How so?"

"Well, she told me she couldn't see me that week because she had another girls'-night-out and some fashion thing in that shopping centre on the Southside – a big sale or something – "

"I'm sorry?" Flanagan's eyes widened as if in shock. "So, correct me if I'm wrong but you're telling me Ms Patterson couldn't meet with you then because she was going *shopping?*"

Oh God, oh God, oh God!

"Yes, and then her friend's wedding was happening that weekend, so she wouldn't be free until the following week."

"My, oh my, it seems Ms Patterson really does like to enjoy herself, doesn't she?" Flanagan replied wryly, and Louise waited for her barrister to object.

In vain.

Sam shrugged. "As she says herself, 'we're here for a good time, not for a long time'."

At this, Louise's heart almost stopped. *No, that's what Fiona says,* she argued silently, mortified.

"Really? 'We're here for a good time, not for a long time'?" Flanagan repeated, making sure the judge didn't miss it. "Those were Ms Patterson's own words?"

Sam nodded again. "Yes."

"So after that first night, you and Ms Patterson began seeing one another on a regular basis, did you?"

"Yes, she was a nice girl – as I said, very lively, great fun, always up for a laugh."

Rubbish! I was a tongue-tied idiot whenever you were around, she retorted inwardly, devastated by his betrayal and the way he was behaving now, as if she weren't in the room hearing all the terrible things he was saying about her, the inferences he was allowing – no, *helping* – Flanagan to draw. But she knew why O'Toole wasn't objecting – there was nothing to object to. Sam was just telling his story and it was the truth.

"And she was fond of the nightlife?" Flanagan urged.

"Definitely. I liked being with her, but some of the places her friends went ... well, the trendy celebrity spots didn't really do it for me. I preferred to meet her in normal, down-to-earth pubs in town, places where you didn't need to beg to get in."

And Louise had preferred those places too – after a while she'd begun to see through the stupidity of going to the ultra-trendy, girl-about-town places Fiona and the girls seemed to love.

"So, you let her do her own celebrity-hunting with the girls?"

"Usually, yes. As I said, it wasn't for me, but she seemed to enjoy it, so ..."

Flanagan nodded, and flicked through the sheaf of papers he was holding. Louise prayed that that was the end of the questions and that O'Toole would be able to tell everyone how this – this *cad* had callously inveigled his way into her life, pretending to be her friend, her boyfriend, while all the time trying to discredit her. Something he was doing very well.

But it seemed Flanagan was only just beginning.

"You and Ms Patterson got to know one another well over the course of your relationship, yes?"

"I would say so, yes." Sam shifted a little in his seat and for one brief second, Louise thought he looked ashamed.

"In that case, you've undoubtedly visited her home – her apartment in the Marina Quarter."

"I have. It's amazing."

Oh God no. Not this again!

"Yes, I'm sure it is. Please describe how amazing it is to the court – just so we can get a better picture of this poverty Ms Patterson's counsel described in his opening statement."

Sam took a deep breath and Louise held hers. "Well, it's on the third floor, floor-to-ceiling windows with amazing views looking out over the bay," he informed them. "Very spacious living room, with a huge TV and state-of-the-art stereo system, great kitchen, ensuite bedrooms, the works really."

Of course, he'd conveniently forgotten to mention that she happened to live in the apartment's shoebox, hadn't he? Louise couldn't comprehend how anyone could do this. Had the man no shame? Didn't he care how much he was hurting her with all this – and in more ways than one?

"Modest living, I'm sure," Flanagan agreed, again with a dollop of sarcasm, but this time the judge said nothing.

"So, up until a couple of weeks ago, you were very much involved in Ms Patterson's life, and had got to know her very well, is that right?"

"It is."

"Well, if that's the case, why are you here today?" Flanagan asked, surprising Louise. She'd been sure that was the tactic her barrister would take – that her side would try and establish that if he cared about her so much, what he was playing at? She wanted O'Toole to ask Sam why he had kissed her and pretended to care about her, why he had made her trust him, while all the time trying to discredit her. She wanted to find out why he had so cold-heartedly betrayed that trust, why he was hurting her so much now.

So, was Flanagan pre-empting that now by making sure they didn't get the chance to ask him those things?

"Why are you speaking out against Ms Patterson – effectively hindering her case?" the barrister continued. "Particularly if you two had a close relationship?"

Sam took another deep breath, as if this was something that weighed heavily on his mind, but Louise didn't believe it for a second. It was all an act – something that Sam was obviously very good at. He shook his head. "It wasn't like that. I liked Louise and had got to know her very well. But she told me something a while back, something I couldn't ignore – about her accident."

"Go on."

Louise's heart thudded, remembering the thrust of the conversation and, worse, realising exactly what he was about to do. Hot bile rose in her throat.

"We were talking about her scars," Sam continued blithely and just then Louise truly understood how carefully choreographed the whole situation had been. And worse, how easily she had played into his hands – into *their* hands. "Louise is embarrassed about them, ashamed of them really. She feels they take away from her looks somehow. She even talked about having cosmetic surgery done – to get rid of them."

Her stomach turned. *Oh – my – God.*

"Cosmetic surgery?" Flanagan looked astonished. "A young girl on clerical assistant's wages? However would she pay for such a thing?" he added pointedly.

"I don't know – that didn't come up. Anyway, she told me about the accident, not about the case mind you, although I knew about that from another source."

"Oh? How so?"

"My friend – he works with Leo – with Mr Gardner. But that had nothing to do with my meeting Louise. It was just the way things happened."

"So, you weren't aware of the case at the time you met Ms Patterson?"

"No, no, of course not," Sam replied, the picture of innocence, but Louise knew well that he was lying. He'd done it all on purpose. Chatting her up in the Four Seasons, asking her out, and finding out all those things, all the time silently plotting against her. Of course, she'd made it easy for him, hadn't she? Playing the busy girl-about-town, the unavailable party girl. Then, when he had enough to sink her, when he had what he wanted, he'd taken off. Busy with work, my foot!

But now she couldn't even feel angry about it, she was so hurt, so ashamed at being so easily taken in, at being so stupid as to think that this seemingly perfect guy would be interested in her. She'd been right all along. She *was* useless. Tears pricked at her eyes, but she was not going to give in to them. No, she wouldn't let any of them see her cry. No matter how bad it looked, no matter how bad he made it look, she had to remember that she'd done nothing wrong, nothing wrong at all. He was the lying, deceitful one in this room.

Sam was still talking. "No, I was mad about Louise but, as I said, one night she mentioned something about the accident, and we talked about it. I'll admit I was curious about how it all happened. My friend had told me about this girl who had taken a case against Leo, and I thought it was fairly straightforward. In fact, up until that night I was on Louise's side. And I was about to tell her I sort of knew Gardner, but I was still on her side."

Lies, lies, lies.

"So why didn't you?"

"Because I discovered that it *hadn't* all been Leo's fault," he said, delivering the killer blow and, with that, Louise stopped breathing. "She told me that it was as much her fault as it was his. She told me that she'd been in a world of her own when she stepped out on the road, and to this day she's not sure if the lights had gone red or not. The guards had told her that afterwards."

Flanagan smiled, having delivered his *coup de théâtre*. "Ms Patterson believes that the accident was as much her fault as Mr Gardner's?" he repeated, just in case somebody in the room might not have been paying due attention. "That she might have contributed to

271

her accident and subsequently her injuries – herself?"

"I believe so, yes."

Out of the corner of her eye, Louise saw James Cahill shake his head in defeat. O'Toole sat rigid in his seat, dumbfounded. It was all over.

"I see." Trying desperately to hide a smile, the barrister nodded. "Thank you very much, Mr Harris," he added before returning to his seat. "No further questions."

* * *

Shame and embarrassment burned through Louise now as she stared out the window of the train and remembered the things that Sam had said about her and her lifestyle, all of them true, but twisted and edited to make it sound as though she were a fraudster, a dishonest chancer. The shame was even worse than the certainty that she was now going to lose. They were due back in the court the following Monday for the judge's decision – a decision that would undoubtedly ruin what was left of her pathetic excuse for a life.

"If he rules against you, he'll likely award Gardner costs," Cahill informed her afterwards, while her brain was still trying to come to terms with the enormity of Sam's betrayal. The solicitor shook his head dejectedly. "Admitting to someone that you might have been at fault, someone that you barely knew ... what were you thinking, Louise?" Cahill was annoyed and rightly so, although Louise couldn't help thinking that he was more annoyed about losing his percentage than losing the case – a case that up until today had been such a sure thing. Cut and dried.

How did they get it so wrong? How could *she* have got it so wrong? She should have known better than to be taken in by someone as handsome and charming as Sam. Fiona had been right – she was too trusting and gullible – and wasn't it foolish wishful thinking that a man like him could honestly be interested in someone like her? How could she have been so bloody stupid? How could she have possibly believed that a pathetic idiot like her could seriously attract someone like him? Sam was way out of her league, had always been out of her league, and she supposed, deep down she'd always known that too. Yet, he seemed so honest, so genuine – she couldn't believe how anyone could be so heartless and so evil as to fake all that. To think that she had allowed herself to be kissed and caressed by him and had almost …

She shook her head. Would he have gone through with it? Would Sam have gone as far as sleeping with her just to find out the information he wanted? His admission that he'd been a 'friend' of Leo Gardner's all along was bull as far as she was concerned; any fool (even she, in retrospect) could see that. She recalled how Sam had told her he worked as a 'troubleshooter'. Chances were he was some kind of private investigator, someone who had been paid to get close to her, find out what he wanted, and then, without a second thought, callously mess up her life. At the end of the day, what did it matter to Sam? He could just walk away – wages in pocket. Job done.

The problem was that Louise had fallen for him, and fallen hard. It was the first time in a very long time that she'd seriously allowed herself to fall for anyone. She'd really believed they might have a future together. Sam had seemed so honest and open that there had been little game-playing once she had got over her initial 'play hard to get' phase. They had spent many a nice night just having a laugh at the pub or watching a movie and Louise couldn't remember ever enjoying herself so much. He had created such a false sense of security that his betrayal was only second to the blow of actually losing him, of realising that he never cared about her at all.

But, she thought, tears brimming in her eyes, much as he'd hurt her and broken her heart, losing Sam was now the least of her worries.

She'd lost the case – Gardner's sharp legal team and Sam's testimony had made sure of that. So there would be no magic wand to wave away her pile of debt; if anything, this was now about to become a full-blown mountain. If the judge awarded costs to Gardner, then financially she would be in serious trouble.

And what had made her think she deserved compensation in the first place? All the things her sister had warned her about, all the things that Heather had disapproved of came rushing back. Heather had been right.The fact that she was still alive should have been enough. The fact that she was up to her eyeballs in debt was just one of those things, and who was she to expect that someone else should bail her out? It was incredible how clear it all seemed now. But of course, she wouldn't hear of it at the time – no, she needed the money, needed to rid herself of the loans and credit-card bills which, no matter how hard she tried, never seemed to decrease. And as James Cahill had drummed into her often enough, she was entitled to the money, wasn't she?

But the truth was that she was a fool, a stupid, pathetic fool and it served her right for being so determined, when everyone else – well, Heather anyway – had been so sure it was all a bad idea.

She couldn't tell Heather about this. No, Heather would go crazy with worry and would probably insist on helping her pay for Leo Gardner's legal costs. And Louise knew her sister couldn't afford that. Who could? This thought once again reminded her that she was in a very desperate situation, and one that she'd brought entirely on herself.

Her eyes welled up with tears, and she willed them away, trying to block out her own worries for a moment and concentrate on something else, otherwise there was a danger she'd break down altogether.

She looked furtively around the train carriage, and noticed how everyone seemed happy and content with not a care in the world. She'd give anything to feel like that again, give anything to take back the disaster that was today, and the embarrassment of the last few weeks, when she'd stupidly begun to fall for Sam. She'd give anything to go back to being carefree and debt-free, the way she'd been long before all of this happened. She'd even go back to being overweight and friendless, as in all honesty it had been the weight loss that had got her into a lot of these troubles in the first place, hadn't it?

When she was overweight, people didn't expect her to be dressed in up-to-the-minute designer gear, or go out clubbing three and four nights a week. Back then, the girls never asked her to join them on nights out on the town, on shopping trips to New York, on expensive holidays abroad. It was only when she'd lost the weight that she'd lost her inhibitions, and become friendly with people like Fiona and Gemma – people who loved to socialise and, unfortunately, loved to spend even more.

She would have been much better off keeping her head down, and working hard to pay off her debts, rather than swanning around the town with the girls, chasing so-called celebrities. If she'd done that, she mightn't be in this mess now. She would have been quite happy in her little bedsit in Rathgar with her teeny wardrobe and only her books for company, rather than friends like Fiona and her never-ending shopping trips. Life had been much simpler back then, hadn't it?

Louise's eyes welled up with tears again She'd do anything – *anything* to make life simpler again, anything to make all this shame, hurt and utter heartbreak go away.

Anything at all.

CHAPTER 26

That same evening, Dara too returned home, her heart also heavy at today's events. .

She was used to both winning and losing, but she didn't think she would ever forget the expression on that poor girl's face when their 'star witness' appeared. Louise Patterson had looked astonished, crushed, totally defeated.

Whatever about Gardner's dirty tricks, Dara had never believed that the girl had exaggerated her injuries; in fact, she personally believed her client should have made recompense from the very beginning. The poor girl would now not only have to pay costs, but could very well face charges of her own if the court believed she willingly attempted to defraud the system. No wonder she looked crushed.

And, despite her true feelings on the matter, Dara had to live with the fact that she'd helped ruin that poor girl's life, and very possibly, her future.

She let herself quietly into the apartment, unable to shake the feeling that soon she might very well have to do the same to her own husband.

Inside, the apartment was strangely quiet. Usually Mark had the

TV or stereo on, and more often than not, he could be found singing along to his Dean Martin CD collection, something that Ruth thought was terribly endearing, and something that Dara really wished he was doing now. In view of his offhand behaviour that morning, the silence was unnerving.

But when Dara stepped into the living-room, she knew without doubt something really was wrong.

Mark was sitting on the sofa in silence, his body rigid, and his expression unreadable.

"Mark?" she queried, softly. "What's going on? Why are you sitting in the dark like that?" She switched on the overhead light.

"I know." His tone was hard.

She felt her throat close over. "What?"

"I said I know," he repeated. "I know about you and that – that guy you've been seeing."

Oh God, no. Dara set down her briefcase, and sat quietly on the armchair across from him. His eyes were downcast, his jaw set in a firm line.

"Mark," she began softly, "you don't – "

"Dara, we haven't even been married six months." The quiet way he said it – his disappointment palpable – instantly made Dara feel incredibly ashamed.

"Mark, you really don't – "

"And do you know, the crazy thing is, I think I knew it all along! I think I knew deep down you didn't really love me. I knew you were marrying me because you were afraid of being left on the shelf."

"That's not true!" Despite herself, she had to refute this. "That wasn't how it went – I did ..." she paused, "I *do* love you."

Mark laughed, a short nasty laugh that she had never heard from him before. "So how come you were caught crawling all over some bloke in town a few days ago, then?"

"What?" How ... who? What was he talking about? Who could have seen them?

"Gillian phoned me last night. She said she had something to tell me – about you."

Dara's heart sank. "So, that was why you were acting so strangely this morning – "

His sister must have seen them together in the café, or perhaps walking down the street or something. Bloody hell! Of all the people to catch them ... but still, she reminded herself, she wasn't doing anything wrong. She *hadn't* done anything wrong. And if she could just explain everything to Mark then, maybe, he might understand. But what had Gillian said?

"I didn't know for sure this morning," he continued. "Last night, all she said was that she had her suspicions. Today she told me everything she'd seen."

Dara shook her head. "Mark, there was nothing to see." She wasn't sure why she was trying to defend her meeting with Noah all of a sudden. This was what she wanted, wasn't it? To bring things out in the open, to discuss them so it would be easier for her to come clean with Mark, and stop feeling so guilty about it. And, more importantly, so she could reach some sort of conclusion. "I haven't done anything wrong."

But Mark didn't want to hear it. "When she told me on the phone that she'd seen you with someone," he continued, his tone hard, his eyes steely, "first I thought, nah, it has to be a client. But then, when I heard the two of you were holding hands, I thought to myself, well, you did say once you'd do anything to keep your clients happy. So how far *would* you go, Dara?" He looked at her scornfully.

Dara recoiled in shock. Why was he saying these things? She'd done nothing wrong!

"He wasn't a client!" she cried, astonished by his demeaning accusations. "He's an old friend and – "

"An old friend?" At this his face changed suddenly, as if unable to believe that what Gillian had told him was really true. "What kind of old friend? An old friend of the family – or an old friend you used to sleep with?"

Dara looked away, and said nothing. But her expression told him all he needed to know.

"I see." He stood up and walked to the window, turning his back to her. "So how long has it been going on?" he asked, his voice dripping with hostility. "Did we ever actually have a marriage – or had you decided from day one that you were going to have your cake and eat it?"

"No, it's just ... Mark, you must believe me, I never planned this. I never thought I'd see him again and – "

"But why, Dara? Why did you marry me if you were pining for someone else? You didn't need me – you had your own home, a good job and were well able to fend for yourself, so why drag me into all of this? Why mess up my life too?"

"I didn't – "

"It couldn't be just about sex, could it?" he went on, not letting her answer. "I mean, you're a good-looking girl and these days women don't need to get married just to have regular sex. These days it seems women don't need us at all, so what ...?" He trailed off then as if realising something. Then he turned back to face her, his expression filled with disdain. "Please don't tell me you married me because your bloody biological clock was ticking, Dara! Don't you dare tell me you wanted me to act as a goddamn sperm-donor!"

She flushed with guilt, and tears sprung to her eyes. Of course, there was a grain of truth in what he said, but, God, he made it all sound so predatory!

"Mark, it wasn't like that! I care about you a lot – we were great friends and we had a wonderful time together so I thought ... I thought that would be enough." Hearing her own words out loud, Dara finally understood how incredibly stupid she'd been, how she'd been kidding herself to believe that what they had would be enough.

And how selfish she'd been towards him.

"So you decide to go ahead with marrying me, even though you knew I wasn't the right one for you?" he asked angrily, waiting for her to contradict him.

But Dara didn't say a word. She didn't dare.

"You selfish cow!" Mark was incandescent. "The nerve of you, Dara! The nerve of you to stand up in front of all our friends – in front of our *families* – and simply lie through your teeth! How dare you make those empty promises to me, empty promises about our future! Who the hell do you think you are?"

By now, Dara was in tears. "Mark, I'm sorry. I'm so, so sorry. I thought it would be OK. I thought we'd be fine, that we'd be happy, that I'd – "

"But that's it, isn't it?" he interjected. "It was all about you. All about *you* being happy, and *you* getting what you wanted, although even now I can't figure out exactly what that was. Did you ever stop to think that *I* might deserve better? That *I* might deserve someone who considered me worthy of them? That I might appreciate the chance to find someone who loved me as much as I loved them?" With that, his voice broke, and he looked away.

Dara's hands shook. She had never seen this side to him – seen him so angry, so full of explosive rage. She'd never even imagined that Mark had an angry side. He was always so easy-going, so slow to anger and averse to conflict. She'd thought she knew him well, but seeing him like this merely brought it home to her how much she'd underestimated Mark Russell.

For the next few minutes, a heavy silence hung between the two of them.

Eventually Dara found the courage to speak. "Mark, I do love you," she began softly, willing him to try and understand. "I never lied about that. But there was – there *is* – someone else that I have feelings for too – strong feelings. We knew each other a long time ago, and I thought it was over between us."

"But it's not," Mark stated flatly, refusing to look her in the eye.

"No, no, it's not," she admitted sadly.

"So why the fuck did you marry me, Dara? If you had feelings for – for *him*, then why did you go through with it? Why didn't you stay with him, or go to him, or whatever the hell – "

"He came back into my life only recently," she interrupted, "completely by accident. We hadn't seen one another in years, and I thought I'd never see him again. A while back, I found out he was married to someone else so I – "

"Oh? It must *really* have been true love between you two then,"

Mark interjected derisively.

Dara ignored the jibe. "The marriage happened a long time after we broke up," she clarified. "And as it turned out, it was a mistake."

"I see." Mark ran a hand through his hair. "So he gets bored with the wife and then what – he comes crawling back to you, looking for forgiveness?"

"No, nothing like that," Dara replied, the accusation stinging somewhat. "We simply bumped into one another one day, spent a bit of time catching up and ... after a while, we both realised ..." she hesitated, "we both realised that our feelings for one another hadn't really changed."

"And while you were reliving these – these feelings for the guy, the fact that you had a husband at home was conveniently forgotten, was it? Jesus, how stupid was I not to notice that you were carrying on behind my back?" Then his eyes narrowed and his face paled, as if realising something. "And you must have been doing both of us at the same time! For fuck's sake, Dara!"

Realising what he was thinking, Dara's eyes widened, horrified. "No, Mark, please believe me, I wasn't ... I *didn't* do anything wrong. I didn't sleep with him or do anything with him – with Noah." She wasn't sure about mentioning his name, but at this stage, there seemed no reason not to.

"Noah!" Mark almost spat out the name. "A guy who likes things in pairs. So, not content with having one woman, the guy has to go and get himself another – to hell with her husband!" He began to pace the room. "Still, I don't suppose I can blame the man. If I could get away with having two women at once, I'd probably try it too. The problem is, I can't seem to keep even *one* happy, so I suppose that rules out my chances, doesn't it?"

"Mark, that's not true. You did make me happy – you *do* make me happy." She shook her head, feeling jaded all of a sudden. With today's underhand court proceedings and now this, everything was really beginning to drain her, and she knew that neither of them was in the right frame of mind to resolve things here and now. "Look," she said softly, "it's been a long day, and I know you're upset."

"That's putting it bloody mildly!"

"I know you probably don't believe me, but I was going to tell you about Noah coming back into my life. I was going to discuss it with you. I'm telling you the truth when I say that nothing went on between us. I've always been faithful to you, and despite what Gillian thinks, I did nothing wrong – nothing." Mark's expression was stony, and Dara knew it was pointless trying to talk to him when he was in this state. "Look, we both need some time to think about this, some time to get our heads together." She paused. "I was thinking I might stay at Ruth's tonight."

"I see."

"Mark, I just need some time to get my head together. Things aren't as straightforward as you seem to think. I still don't know what I'm going to do yet. I do have feelings for Noah, but you're my husband and – "

"What?" He laughed cruelly. "So what you're saying now is that you're going off on your own to think about it – to make a *decision?*"

Her heart leapt with fear at the dangerous tone in his voice. "Well, yes, I thought –"

"You're some tonic, Dara, do you know that? Do you really think it's all that simple? Do you really think that now – knowing what I know about you, about what a selfish, deceitful person you are – that I'll just sit around like an idiot and wait for you to come to some kind of decision? That I'll wait patiently for you to make a choice between that bastard and me?" His eyes flashed dangerously. "You've got some cheek! After everything I've heard today, what makes you think *I* want to remain married to *you?* What makes you think *I* should settle for second-best – for someone who has to *decide* whether or not she loves me enough, someone who has to choose between me and some other idiot! What makes you think I'll be a part of that? Go to bloody Ruth's! Go wherever you like! Just make sure you get the hell out of my sight!"

With that, he strode off out to the hallway, his face crimson, his muscles clenched in rage. Then he banged the front door behind him with such fury that the apartment shuddered.

Dara sat there, stunned. In the stillness of the room, her mind began to go over everything Mark had just said, the accusations he had levelled at her.

He was right, she realised then. All this time, she had never really considered his true feelings. She'd imagined he'd be hurt certainly, but she'd never really believed that he wouldn't stand for it, that he wouldn't allow himself to be humiliated like this. She had always assumed that *she* would be the one to decide if they had enough to keep the marriage going, and that Mark just would sit around and wait for her to make that decision. Naively, she had always assumed she would be the one to make it.

But having heard all he had to say, having experienced his hurt and downright fury at her duplicity, she began to view things in a brand new light. What if there were no longer two men to choose from, no longer a decision to make. What if the choice had already been made – by Mark?

CHAPTER 27

"Here, Twix, good girl!" Rosie cried out once again, but deep down she knew her frantic calling would be in vain. There was no sign of the dog. She'd looked all over the estate, walked down the hill to the main road (just in case) and had even knocked on a few of the neighbours' doors in the hope that someone might have seen her. But it was no use. It was as though Twix had disappeared off the face of the earth. Rosie's stomach churned with dread and fear. She had a picture in her head of the little dog scared out of her wits in a place she didn't recognise, unable to find her way home, or even worse, lying injured and dying somewhere. Her eyes blurred with tears as she wandered the streets in the cold, and she prayed to whoever might be listening that her dear friend would be all right. What would she do without poor old Twix? She couldn't imagine being without her.

Damn David for being so selfish!

All of sudden, Rosie felt astonishing disgust towards her son. What had happened to him? How could he be so cruel, so unmoved by the dog's disappearance? Granted there was no love lost between David and Twix, but why couldn't he understand his mother's panic and distress about losing her?

Because David didn't give a damn, that's why. In fact, neither of

284

her children seemed to give a damn about her, she admitted unhappily.

After the first half-hour of panicked, anxious searching, she'd eventually gone back to the house and frantic, picked up the phone to the first person she could think of – the only other person who might be able to help. David's car was no longer parked outside the gate, and Rosie safely assumed that he hadn't gone off to help with the search effort.

"Sophie?" Rosie cried tearfully, when many long rings later the phone was eventually answered.

"Mum? Is that you?" Her daughter sounded hassled.

Rosie sniffed. "Sophie, I can't find Twix. She's run off, and I've looked everywhere, and I think she could be hurt, and David –"

"Mum, I'm very busy here – can I call you back?"

"Oh, Sophie love, I don't know what to do!" In her panic, Rosie didn't properly register her daughter's reply. "Can you and Robert come over – maybe give me a hand to look for her? I've no car, it's so cold out and she could be anywhere, and I'm just so worried, and I –"

"Mum, it's really not a good time," Sophie interjected impatiently, while at the same time trying to keep her voice low. "I can't just take off at the drop of a hat to go looking for a dog! I have guests here!"

"Guests?"

"Yes, well …" Sophie seemed embarrassed. "We're having a bit of a house-warming tonight – just a few close friends … friends who live locally," she added quickly.

"Oh."

"So as I said, Mum, it really isn't a good time. Normally I'd love to help but … Look, I'm sure the dog will be fine." When there was silence at the other end, she went on quickly. "I'll give you a buzz tomorrow and we can look then, maybe?"

But tomorrow could be too late . . .

"Don't worry about it," Rosie replied, her voice low and hurt. "And I'm sorry for interrupting your party."

"Look, Mum, it's not like that!" Sophie was petulant. "Look, if I'd known you were – "

"Forget it," Rosie said, and with a brief goodbye, dejectedly put the phone down and let her daughter get back to her house-warming celebrations in the house she'd helped her attain.

Now, having searched for close to three long hours in the blistering cold, Rosie's feet were numb, her body ached, and her heart was well and truly broken. Exhausted, but still determined to keep looking – there was always the slim chance that Twix might have made her way back home by now – she began to make her way back up the hill.

Then, as she reached the corner of her estate, she heard a car-horn beep at her from behind.

"Rosie?" Stephen called out from the open window and pulled up alongside her. "Are you all right?"

She put a hankie to her face and blew her nose, refusing to look at him and trying to hide her tears.

"Rosie? What's wrong?" he urged, when she didn't answer straight away. "You weren't at class tonight, so I wondered ..." His voice trailed off, as he caught sight of her expression. "Rosie, please – tell me what's happened? Are you hurt? Jesus, you must be freezing ... wait." Stopping the car, but keeping the engine running, Stephen hopped out and put a strong arm around her shoulders.

"It's Twix," she told him through chattering teeth. "She ran away – David let her run away, and I can't find her."

"Rosie, get into the car – you'll catch your death if you stay out in this cold."

"I can't. I have to find Twix – she's out in the cold too."

"Look, we can still search for her in the car – we'll cover more ground that way and at least it'll be warmer."

Rosie finally acquiesced, grateful at least for some help, let alone the warmth of the car.

The two of them continued the search for another hour. They drove all over the estate, all over town, anywhere they could think of, but there was still no sign of little Twix.

"Rosie, there's always the chance she could make her own way back home," Stephen said eventually.

Rosie sighed. After four hours of continuous searching, she had

286

finally begun to admit defeat. It was dark, very late and very, very cold.

"Not when he's there," she insisted. "She hates David, and the feeling is mutual. That's why she ran away in the first place. I think he might have hit her," she added, her eyes downcast, ashamed to admit out loud that her own son could do such a thing.

Stephen patted her on the arm. "Look, you never know – she might turn up looking for you anyway. But if nothing else, you should go home and get some rest, Rosie. You'll be lucky if you don't catch pneumonia after being out in this weather all evening."

Rosie nodded quietly, although she doubted very much that Twix had returned. But her bones ached, she was cold and weary, and there was little else she could do anyway.

But, as Stephen drove along one of the back roads on the way back to Rosie's house, he caught sight of something lying very still at the side of the road. Rosie saw it at the same time and her heart leapt as she spotted Twix's familiar golden coat and tartan collar.

The car pulled to a halt, and the two jumped out, Rosie unable to believe that after all the worrying, and all the searching she had finally found her!

But poor Twix was in trouble. The little dog lay on her side, her huge brown eyes sorrowful and glassy, her chest barely rising up and down. Although clearly in pain, she managed a brief and very faint wag of her tail when she recognised her mistress.

"Oh Twix, pet – what's happened to you?" Rosie cried tearfully. Her heart racing, she bent down and gently stroked the injured dog. Although the spaniel looked perfectly fine at first glance, on closer examination there was quite a bit of blood on the ground beneath her, and she was shivering badly.

"She's been hit by a car, I'd say," Stephen confirmed what Rosie was almost afraid to admit. He was tapping numbers into his mobile phone. "Stay with her – I'll see if I can find a vet. I know a fellow who visits the farm next door to me – maybe he can help."

Rosie blinked back tears. *Please, please, let her be OK,* she whispered inwardly, all the time gently stroking the little dog's silky head and floppy ears, afraid to touch her belly for fear of injuring her further. Twix whined faintly, she was obviously in serious pain, and at that moment, Rosie felt something so close to hatred towards David that the strength of the emotion shocked her. This was all his fault.

"It'll be all right, Twix – don't worry. The vet will come soon, and he'll make it all right. Then we can bring you home, and give you a nice bit of chocolate, and tomorrow we might go for a good long walk." Rosie didn't believe her own words, but she'd stay here all night if she thought her voice was having any kind of soothing effect on Twix.

Again, the dog's tail moved slightly at the mention of the word 'walk', and her huge dark eyes held Rosie's, a silent communication passing between them. It seemed that Twix understood well that there would be no more chocolate or doggie treats for her and certainly no more walks.

The fact that her little friend was in so much pain and there was nothing she could do about it broke Rosie's heart in two. Feeling utterly helpless, tears began to stream down her cheeks. Twix steadily held her gaze, and whimpered again softly. There was so much intelligence in a dog's eyes, Rosie reflected sorrowfully, recalling all those times Twix had been there for her after Martin's death, how her excitable and playful nature nearly always lifted Rosie's spirits, and helped her get through the tough times. She remembered the first time she'd seen her peeping shyly out from under the bushes, how the little dog had followed her home, and then spent the next few days soiling every corner of the house. She thought about the wonderfully enthusiastic and excitable welcomes she'd always got from Twix upon her return to the house – even if she'd only been gone a few minutes – and what a huge comfort she'd been since David had come home. What would she do without her?

"It's all right Twix," she soothed, a huge lump coming to her throat. "I'm here – you're all right."

Then, seconds later, the little spaniel whimpered once more, and Rosie knew in her heart and soul that they were too late – there was nothing any of them could do now for poor Twix. And finally, as her mistress continued to gently stroke her injured and trembling little body, Rosie's most loyal friend slowly slipped away from her.

* * *

Afterwards, Stephen had taken her in his arms as she wept, and Rosie had no idea how much time had passed when the tears finally stopped. The vet had arrived soon after and taken poor Twix away, saving Rosie the heartbreak of having to deal with her broken body. The poor man was almost inconsolable upon arrival, and was deeply apologetic that he hadn't been able to help. But he couldn't be blamed. In Rosie's opinion there was only one person to blame – David.

"Him and the heartless bastard that hit her!" Stephen had said, shaking his head in disgust. "What kind of person would run over a poor defenceless animal, and then drive on without checking to see if he could do anything?"

But they both knew there was no point in even discussing it. Twix was gone and there was nothing anyone could do about that.

Now, they were heading towards Brittas Bay, where Stephen had insisted Rosie spend the night.

"You're not going back to your own house tonight – I won't have it," he'd said, when the tears had finally stopped and Rosie had to decide what to do next. "You're coming back to Brittas with me, and you can stay in my spare room."

"But –"

"Rosie, you're in no fit state to go home. I don't know what's going on between you and your son, but you're upset enough as it is without having to go home and face that. After all you've been through tonight, it sounds to me as though you need a friend – the last thing you need is to have to go back there and think about ... about everything." He patted her gently on the hand. "Please, let me look after you for a while," he'd said and when Rosie looked up and saw genuine concern in his eyes and the hand of friendship he'd offered – one that just then, she so desperately needed – she knew she couldn't say no.

She'd stay with Stephen tonight, she decided numbly, and then she'd get him to drop her at the train station in the morning so she could talk it all over with Sheila. She sorely wished her good friend lived nearer than she did now; if she'd known about the dog's disappearance Sheila would have been over in a shot and no doubt would have stayed out all night trying find her. More than anyone, Sheila understood how important Twix was to her, and was the only one who could truly appreciate how lost she would now be without her. But living all the way out in Blackrock as she did, Rosie couldn't have asked Sheila for help. After all, if her own flesh and blood wouldn't help ...

The evening's events having drained her completely, Rosie felt numb. All the walking around and searching not to mention the sheer enormity of the little dog's death had left her more exhausted than she'd ever been in her life. And it's not as though David would care if she didn't come home. Chances were he wouldn't even notice.

Her heart hardened as she thought about her son. She wasn't going to let him know where she was either. Let him think what he liked. She could have been the one dead at the side of the road for all he cared anyway. Normally such a notion would hurt and upset her, but right then, Rosie didn't give a damn.

Right then, she was beyond caring.

CHAPTER 28

Dara groggily awoke to the sound of the alarm clock ringing in her brain. She groped blindly for the snooze button, and let her head fall back on the pillow, just for a few minutes. It had taken her hours to fall asleep, her thoughts full of all that had been said the previous night, Mark's parting words imprinted in her brain.

Not to mention the rather unsettling phone call she'd received not long after he left. She had spent most of the night thinking about that, and feeling ashamed about how utterly selfish and unfair she'd been.

It was her dad who had phoned the apartment, not ten minutes after Mark left. Dara had been surprised to hear from him, really – it was usually her mother who phoned and often put Eddie on for a word or two afterwards. But a few minutes into the conversation, Eddie had muttered uncomfortably, "Any chance I might have a word with himself?"

Dara was taken aback. "With Mark?" This was very odd. First, Eddie was phoning her off his own bat, and now he wanted to speak with Mark.

"Yes, I want to talk to him about something."

"About what?" she couldn't help but ask.

Her dad cleared his throat, evidently uncomfortable. "It's erm … it's private business, love."

"Private business?"

"Yes. So … um … could you put him onto me for a minute? It won't take long."

Dara was flabbergasted. Her father clearly wasn't going to tell her what this 'private business' might be, and was obviously very embarrassed about it. What had he and Mark been up to?

"Dad, he's not here at the moment," she told him.

"Oh. Will he back soon? He knows I'm phoning tonight. I told him I would and – "

"I don't know when he'll be back. Dad. What's all this about?" To be honest, Dara felt a little peeved that her father and her husband were keeping some kind of secret from her. What was going on?

"Well … um … it's a bit awkward really," Eddie spluttered. "And to be honest, love – I'd rather wait until Mark gets back. Tell him to ring me when he gets in, will you?"

"Dad, I don't know when that will be," she cried then, frustrated. Frustrated not only by all this secrecy, but also about the fact that she genuinely *didn't* know when – or if – Mark would be back.

Eddie's tone changed considerably. "What's wrong, Dara? Have you two had an argument or something?"

"Oh, Dad!" The events of the last few weeks and everything that had happened yesterday were way too much for her to take, so Dara there and then broke down and told her father everything. She told him all about her initial doubts about the wedding, her long-standing feelings for Noah, and her confusion since his return. She gave him an edited version of the argument she and Mark had just had, leaving out the 'doing both of us at the same time' and the 'sperm donor' comments – the ones that had hit her the hardest. She ended it all with the admission that she really didn't know what she wanted, and that Mark might very well have left her for good anyway.

Afterwards, it took a very long time for Eddie to speak.

When he did, Dara could hear the disappointment in his tone. "Love, I wouldn't dream of interfering, but I honestly think that by letting that chap go, you could be making the biggest mistake of your life."

Dara frowned. Her father liked Mark, she knew that, but this was something more. There was something else going on with the two men that Dara obviously wasn't privy to. Something important.

"Dad, what's going on? Why did you want to speak to Mark so badly tonight? Please tell me."

After a few seconds, Eddie cleared his throat once more, and Dara could tell that whatever it was, he really wasn't comfortable telling her. So why was he telling Mark then? "Well, it's a bit embarrassing, and I thought I might get away without saying anything at all but – "

"Dad, what is it?"

It seemed to take him forever to reply. "Well, I've been a few problems lately, love – men's problems. Em ...with my prostate, you know." The mortification in his tone was palpable, and for a second, Dara was almost sorry she'd forced him into such an admission. Her father was a quiet, private man of sixty-six years of age, and to Dara's knowledge had never even changed her nappy when she was a baby – let alone discussed 'men's problems' with his daughter.

"Oh, Dad."

"Right. Well, um ... myself and Mark were having a chat one day ... a few weeks ago when the two of you were down home for a visit, and he noticed that I seemed in a bit of pain."

"He noticed you ..." Dara was shocked. "But Dad, why didn't you say anything to any of us? And if you were in pain, why didn't you go and get yourself checked out?"

"Dara, I've never had a day's sickness in my life, thank God. I'd had a few problems for a while, but there was no way in hell I was going to let a doctor near my um ... my privates."

Dara's heart went out to him. Men, especially older Irish men from a country background, could be funny like that.

"But, Mark, fair play to him, he sat me down and gave me a good telling-off. Told me that there was no point in ignoring the thing, and hoping it would go away. Told me it would go away all right – six-feet under along with the rest of me."

Dara's heart melted. She could imagine Mark doing just that – pulling no punches, making sure Eddie didn't let things go too far. But it wouldn't have been an easy task. Her father was notorious for avoiding hospitals or doctors. He'd have to be dragged into the GP for a simple thing like a prescription for a sore throat!

"So, eventually he wore me down, and got me an appointment with some specialist fella he knows up in Dublin."

"Here in Dublin?" As if there were twenty Dublins in the country, she thought, feeling stupid. But still she couldn't get her head around the fact that Mark had done this, had spoken about this to her father, and not said a word.

"Yes. So anyway, I went to see this doctor fella a while back, he didn't like what he saw, so he booked me in for a biopsy. I wasn't a bit happy about it, and if I had my way, the man wouldn't have seen me again for dust. But Mark knew what I was like, and he made me go. He went to the hospital with me too – for support." He chuckled slightly. "That and the fact that he knew I'd probably run out the door at the first opportunity – that's if I managed to get the nerve to turn up at all!"

"Mark went with you – for the biopsy?"

"Well, he didn't come in with me while I was getting it done or anything, now," Eddie was eager to clarify that. "No, he just waited in the hospital with me and tried to keep my mind off it, keep my mind away from thinking the worst. And, of course, he's so witty he had me in stitches with his smart comments about the doctors and the nurses so that I didn't have a minute to be nervous about it."

Dara was unbelievably touched. To think that Mark had done all this for her father, had made him go to the hospital and then had sat through the entire frightening experience with him ...

"When did all this happen?" she asked, her voice barely a whisper.

"We were in for the biopsy last week. The results were due back today. I'm grand, love – I got the all clear. They reckon the pains I was having were some kind of infection or something but it's gone now." She could hear the relief in his voice. "And if it wasn't for that husband of yours, I would have pretended the pain wasn't there, and I certainly wouldn't have got it looked at. So, who knows where I might have ended up?"

"Oh, Dad."

Dara just couldn't comprehend how much she admired and respected Mark just then, how grateful she was that he'd gone out of his way to make sure her father looked after himself. He really was an incredibly generous and kind-spirited person who not only loved her, but obviously cared a lot for her family too.

Mark was a wonderful person who really didn't deserve someone like her.

Now, sitting up in the bed, she wondered where he had gone last night, and what time he had returned. She must have been asleep when he came in, as she hadn't heard anything, and seeing as the space in the bed beside her was empty he must have slept in the spare room. Remembering their argument, and her father's revelations afterwards, she once again felt incredibly guilty. She'd never argued with him like that, never really argued with him at all. Yes, they bickered over silly little things, but most of the time it was light-hearted banter. You could never stay angry with Mark for long anyway, as he never really took anything seriously.

She sat up and swung her legs out over the side of the bed, trying to find the energy to stand up. She'd had two or three hours' sleep at best – not so good, she thought groaning, when the first thing she and Nigel had to do this morning was meet with bloody Leo Gardner. The man would be delighted with himself – especially after yesterday. His dirty tricks had worked and worked very well. Dara sighed as she clearly recalled the expression on poor Louise Patterson's face.

Something else for her to feel guilty about. Something else that she wished she hadn't been a part of.

Finally getting up, she gave another quick glance at her alarm clock. Shit! She'd snoozed for longer than she'd thought – and if she didn't get a move on she was going to be late.

She quickly flung on the same clothes she'd worn the day before – no one would know the difference, and for once she didn't care. Today she didn't care about much, other than what was going to happen with Mark and if he'd calmed down a little. She hoped he had because they had a lot to talk about, and she wanted to sort this out. They needed to have a good long chat, no fighting, no accusations, just sort it all out. And she wanted to thank him profusely for what he had done for her father. She bit her lip. That's if he would consent to talking to her at all and, in all honesty, she couldn't blame him if he didn't.

She crept into the kitchen in her stocking-feet, not wanting to wake him if he was in the spare room. But no, the door was wide open and the bed was unmade. Mark hadn't slept there, nor had he slept on the couch she discovered, as the living-room was empty too. Where was he? Had he come home at all?

And if not, she thought, heart pounding, where had he stayed last night – and with whom?

She tried to think rationally, tried to ignore the feeling of dread that had suddenly, out of nowhere, implanted itself in her brain. Had he gone off and spent the night with someone else, just to teach her a lesson? Recalling all that he had said the night before, about how he wasn't going to be made a fool of, she couldn't help but wonder. *Would* Mark do something like that? And if he had done it, what could she say? Hadn't she been on the brink of doing the very same thing? And hadn't she intimated to him that their marriage had been a big mistake? So who could blame him if he decided to go off and be unfaithful to her? Head dizzy with questions, she went back into her bedroom to look for her shoes.

No, no, she was being stupid jumping to conclusions like that, she thought, trying to be logical. He hadn't come home because he was upset, that's all. It didn't mean that he would automatically jump into … To her surprise, Dara found her stomach coil with jealousy at the thought of Mark, her *husband*, with someone else.

He wouldn't do that, would he?

No, Mark wouldn't do something like that, she reassured herself – he wouldn't. He had more respect for himself, had more respect for her. But the question was, did she deserve his respect? After the way she'd behaved, did she deserve anything from him?

She gave a quick glance at her watch. Unfortunately, she didn't really have time to be thinking about this; she'd was already behind time, and if she didn't leave soon, she'd miss the train.

Briefly checking her appearance in the mirror, she picked up her jacket, handbag and briefcase and quickly headed for the door. Then, remembering that she wouldn't be in court today, she set the briefcase back down on the countertop. Just as well that today would be an easier day, she thought, closing the front door behind her, considering she hadn't had much sleep and her thoughts were all over the place. No, today there were no court appointments, no surprise witnesses, just a day of endless paperwork and phone calls.

Dara hurried down the street. She couldn't help but worry about Mark, and where he might be or worse – *who* he might be with. She rummaged in her handbag for her mobile phone. She could always give him a ring, or send a text … just to see if he was OK. Then at least she'd have some idea of how he might be feeling, if he'd calmed down a little, whether he was still angry and disgusted with her …

But a quick glance at the phone told her that her battery was dead. Shit! With all that had happened last night, she'd forgotten to put the phone on charger. Oh well, she'd phone him as soon as she got to the office. Maybe today things might be better between them. She wanted him to know how much she really did care about him. Her dad's phone call last night had really got her thinking. Thinking about what a wonderful person Mark really was, and how much he really did love her. She'd thought about all the little things he'd done for her, and for those she loved. Things for which she had given him very little in return.

Things that she desperately wanted to make up to him.

CHAPTER 29

Louise hadn't slept a wink all night for thinking about it, thinking about how in a few short days her life would be in tatters. She couldn't even comprehend how she would pay off the rest of her debts, let alone pay Gardner's undoubtedly substantial legal costs. As she tried to force down a mouthful of muesli, she barely heard Fiona's chatter about some date she had that weekend.

Simple things like food and going out – things that Louise usually got excited about, seemed so frivolous and unimportant in comparison to what she was feeling just then. In a just a few days' time, an elderly man in a black gown and silly white wig was going to put an end to any frivolity and excitement she had in life. For good. Thinking about it all made her head swim, and her stomach turn.

"So, did you get your passport changed?" Fiona was asking.

Louise's brain was foggy. "Passport?"

"Duh ... for New York? I thought you said you were getting the photo updated this week. The trip is only six weeks away, remember? Didn't you get a chance to do it yesterday?"

Louise blinked slowly. "No ... no, I didn't get a chance."

Changing her stupid passport photo had been the very *last* thing on her mind yesterday – although Fiona was right; she had originally planned to make the most of her 'day off' and pop into the passport office when they finished in court. Of course, she thought, her stomach turning as she remembered Sam's shock appearance, she had no idea that things would go so badly. Afterwards, she could barely see straight, let alone pose for new passport photos. Although it was probably just as well. If she had got them done, her dazed, shocked and white-faced image would no doubt set off red-alerts at the airport, and she'd never be let out of the country again.

"Well, I hope you remembered to get to the travel agent's then."

Louise groaned inwardly. The New York trip needed to be paid for this week but the cash she'd withdrawn from the bank the other day was still sitting at the bottom of her bag. Again, something else she'd planned to do yesterday.

"Louise, are you all right? You don't look good," Fiona asked then, her face filled with concern.

"I'm fine," she barely managed in reply, but even to her, her words sounded fuzzy and unconvincing.

"I don't think you're fine at all. In fact, I really think you should go back to bed and stay at home today. If you like, I can phone work and tell them you've come down with a bug or something. I'm on the late shift today so ..."

The thought of going back to bed and pulling the covers over her head and shutting out the rest of the world sounded glorious. She could pretend none of this was happening and, when she finally did get up, maybe it would have all gone away. It was all so overwhelming that she really didn't know how her mind could cope. But much as she longed to, she couldn't take a day off – today or any other day from now on. She couldn't risk losing her wages or losing her job, because she needed the money now more than ever.

Fiona shrugged when Louise didn't answer. "Look, they can't say much – if you're sick, you're sick. And you hardly ever miss work anyway, do you? Except for that jury duty thing you had yesterday. How did it go, by the way?"

"Fine," Louise nodded slowly, her head heavy. *If only she knew.*

Fiona sat forward and took a bite of her banana. "What do you mean, just 'fine'!" she urged impatiently. "That tells me nothing! I want to know all the gory details ... like did you all vote to put the bad guy in jail or did you let him go or ..."

Louise barely heard the rest of her friend's sentence – she could only concentrate on the word 'jail'. Was that something else she hadn't considered, she wondered, and the very thought sent her head spinning and her stomach into sudden spasms.

Then, she leapt up from her seat and staggered to the bathroom, barely making it to the toilet bowl on time. And as she threw up over and over again, thinking about all that was about to come – and who knew, perhaps much, much more she hadn't even contemplated – she wondered how on earth she was going to get through the day.

Not to mention the day after that, and the one after that too ... how on earth would she cope? And what was the point?

At that moment, Louise felt so hopeless and so utterly desperate, that she really and truly wanted to die.

CHAPTER 30

Mark wished the driver of the cab would stop his incessant chattering. Normally he would be well up for a chat with anyone, but this morning he was tired, hung-over and just way too miserable for a discussion about 'that shower of gobshites in Leinster House' or the country's 'disgraceful cost of living'. After last night's argument, he'd gone up to the rugby club and drank himself stupid with a few of the regulars, and had ending up sleeping in his own treatment room.

As the car neared the apartment, Mark stole a quick glance at his watch. Eight o'clock. Dara would have left for work by now – in fact he'd probably just missed her.

Just as well, he thought, fishing in his pocket for money to pay the driver, because he wasn't sure what he'd say to her.

"Thanks, bud. Go home and sleep it off, yeah?" the driver said with a grin before he drove off.

Mark wished things were that simple. He wished it were a case of just sleeping off all his problems. He couldn't believe that it had come to this. Yesterday, he was a happily married man. Today, that so-called marriage was on the rocks, and his wife was on the brink of leaving him for someone else! How could he have been so stupid?

He'd never been so angry with her, never been so angry with

anyone in his life. The depth of his emotions last night shocked him. He'd thought the two of them were happy, had never even considered the possibility that Dara would cheat on him. She'd insisted she hadn't but still ...

When Gillian had first told him about it, he'd wanted to take that Noah guy and tear him limb from limb. The dirty bastard! Who did he think he was coming on to a married woman – ex or no ex? Didn't the man have any shame? From what Dara had said, he'd had his chance and he'd blown it, so why did he think he could just waltz back into her life like that? And to think that the two of them had talked about having children and everything ... A vice closed around Mark's heart. He'd wanted children, had wanted them more than anything, and especially with Dara. Yet, all along she'd seen him simply as a means to an end.

Was she really that hard-hearted? Had she really married him just because she thought this Noah guy was out of her life for good, that she couldn't do any better? If that was the case, then Mark didn't really know her at all. He didn't have a clue who she was – this sexy, funny woman who had stolen his heart the first time they'd met, and who'd last night trampled all over it with her admission that she didn't feel the same way. He'd always thought himself a decent judge of character, so how could he have got it so wrong? And were there really women out there who would do that? Who would marry a man they didn't love simply because they were afraid of being left on the shelf?

He loved her though, that was the problem. He loved her very much. Dara was the best thing that had ever happened to him and all he wanted, all he'd ever wanted, was to make her happy. And, if she ended up leaving him for this Noah guy, really, what could he do about it? There was no point in ranting and raving about it; he couldn't change how she felt and there was no point in trying. If he'd lost her, he'd just have to pick up the pieces and get on with it. Still, the very thought of this filled him with incredible rage. Then again, why should he make it easy for her? If she thought she could just up and leave him without a second thought, she had another think coming. Despite what Dara seemed to think, he was no bloody pushover!

With a heavy heart, Mark opened the door to the apartment. Silence. As expected, she had already left for work – who knows, she could have left for good. Well, he thought, recalling the taxi driver's words of wisdom, at least he could sleep it off – he wasn't due at the club until the afternoon. He went into their bedroom and undressed, relieved to rid himself of the clothes he'd slept in. He badly needed a shower, but first he went back out to the kitchen to get himself a glass of water, which would hopefully help to rid him of the blasted hangover.

He stopped short as he caught sight of something on the counter-top. Dara's briefcase. She never went to work without it, especially when she was due in court. And she was due in court today, wasn't she? Yes, sure, weren't they right in the middle of that TV producer's case – the one she'd been dreading. He picked up the phone and quickly dialled her mobile number. It went straight to her voice mail.

"Dara, hi, it's Mark," he said, trying to keep his voice even. "Just wanted to let you know that you've gone off without your briefcase. Um ... I'll talk to you later, OK?"

He hung up and took a deep breath. Chances were Dara wouldn't get the message until she got into town and by then it would be too late.

He stared at the briefcase. Feck it, whatever problems they were having and however mad he might be at her, he would hate for her work to be affected because of it. She'd spent months working on this case, and he knew that briefcase was important. He looked again at his watch. 8.20. If he hurried he could catch up with her down at the station before her train left. Or, having since realised she'd forgotten it, she could already be on her way back to the apartment. In which case, he'd give her a lift into town; at least make sure she got to work on time.

He sighed. Their personal problems could wait for the moment.

Changing quickly into a clean sweatpants and a hooded top, Mark picked up his wife's forgotten briefcase, and hurried out the door.

* * *

He arrived at the station just seconds before the train pulled in. Dara obviously hadn't noticed she'd gone off without the briefcase, as he'd kept an eye out for her on the drive down, in case she was on her way back. He'd originally planned on explaining the situation to one of the rail workers in the hope of being allowed through to the platform – but there was no time for that now. He'd just have to grab a ticket and rush through if there was to be any chance of catching her before she got on the train.

But when Mark reached the platform, he couldn't spot her amongst the crowds of people all trying to board different carriages at once. While he thought he'd recognised her trench coat and dark curls at one stage, it really could have been anyone. Feck it! Maybe he should just forget about it and let her off without the briefcase altogether. After all, she'd have had to do without it if he hadn't come back and spotted it, wouldn't she?

Still, it was a shame to have come all this way for nothing. And she really needed that briefcase. He could always get on the train himself and look for her, couldn't he?

Mark shook his head. Damn it, this wasn't just about a stupid briefcase! Despite himself, he wanted to see her, wanted to see if she was OK. He hated the fact that they weren't speaking, hated that they'd spent last night fighting. And he'd said some pretty hurtful things to her, some things perhaps she didn't deserve. Whatever might happen in the future, he wanted to make it up with her, and if it had to happen on a bloody train in front of a rake of people, so be it.

Seconds before the train pulled away from the station, Mark stepped into the nearest carriage, and resolutely set about finding his errant wife.

CHAPTER 31

Zombie-like, Louise left the apartment, the lovely expensive apartment in the Marina Quarter that had caused her so much trouble, and made her way down the street towards the train station.

It was a wonderful autumn day, the sky was clear and blue and the sea calm and peaceful. Yet there was a bite to the air that cut Louise to the quick, particularly as she'd forgotten to bring her hat or gloves with her. Typical, she thought – even the weather was punishing her now. Still, because of the biting cold, she was today almost eager to get on the train, and as much as she didn't want to go anywhere today, she knew that missing her lift and being late for work would only add to her worries.

She reached the station and was on the platform only seconds before the train pulled in. She piled on with all the other commuters and, luckily enough, managed to grab an aisle seat just inside the double doors. With legs that felt like jelly and a stomach that was spinning like a washing machine, she knew she couldn't trust herself to stay standing.

Her head heavy, she looked dazedly out the window at nothing in particular.

A woman in a lovely candy-coloured pink coat hurrying through the ticket barrier caught her eye. Would she make it before the train left? Yes, the woman managed to step inside the double doors just seconds before they closed. Then, as she tried to pass through the crowds standing near the door, the same woman managed to drop her handbag directly in front of Louise's seat. Louise instantly bent down to retrieve it and, even in her dejected state, she couldn't help recognising that it was a gorgeous Orla Kiely bag and admiring its lovely pink and white swirls. Fiona would go mad for one of those.

"Here you go!" she said, and couldn't resist adding, "Orla Kiely, isn't it?"

"Yes – thanks a million," replied the bag's harried owner breathlessly, giving Louise a grateful smile as she took the bag, before making her way towards a nearby vacant seat.

Louise's gaze moved back to the window, and she saw yet another latecomer hurrying along the platform. Unfortunately, this person hadn't been fast enough, and as the train pulled off, Louise felt for the unlucky commuter who would have to wait a while for the next service – the much slower Dart.

She gave a quick glance around the busy carriage. The passengers standing up were doing their utmost to retain some measure of personal space, trying not to get too close to the person next to them. Those lucky enough to get a seat were reading books and newspapers, some sitting back and listening to music, others busily texting friends or business colleagues on their mobile phones. And the rest, like Louise, were simply staring out the window or into the distance, lost in their thoughts.

She couldn't help but wonder about what was going on in these people's lives at the moment, all these people packed into a tiny carriage, each with their own plans for the day. Did any of them have the kind of worries she had? Had any of them been betrayed and hurt like she had? Did they feel as awful – as desperate as she did just then?

She stared out the window once more, and tried not to think too much about it. It was bad enough not getting a wink of sleep the night before, and if she thought about the situation any more, her brain would surely explode. She swallowed hard, trying to overcome another familiar bout of nausea, one of many that had plagued her since the disaster that was yesterday. Her heart heavy, she looked away from the window, determined to will away her worries.

A minute or two later, the connecting door up ahead opened, and an attractive man came through and began to push his way through the crowd, obviously looking for a seat. He certainly didn't look like a typical commuter, she thought, dressed as he was from head to toe in sports-gear and but, oddly, carrying an expensive-looking briefcase. No chance of a seat in here, Action Man, Louise informed him silently, before looking away disinterestedly.

Then, again out of nowhere, another strong wave of nausea overcame her, and this time it was so strong that Louise had to clutch her stomach.

She sat back and closed her eyes, trying to relax, trying to block it all out. Before she knew it, tears sprang to her eyes as all the worry and stress she'd spent all morning trying to contain, unexpectedly overwhelmed her.

Then, without warning, it suddenly felt as though all the air had gone out of the carriage. She sat up straight, her heart hammering rapidly in her chest, her stomach going into spasms. Suddenly, she couldn't breathe. Eyes wide, her eyes darted quickly around the carriage, wondering if anyone else seemed to notice how hot it had suddenly become.

Then she felt another much more intense bout of nausea, and one that she knew she couldn't hold back. She had to get off, had to get out, otherwise she'd be sick right then and there and her brain, never mind the rest of her, would surely explode. Mercifully, she realised the train was just then slowing down, preparing to pull into the next station. Could she hold on till then?

Did she have a choice?

"Are you OK, love?" a woman sitting across asked in a kindly voice. She had put down her newspaper and was now regarding Louise worriedly.

But Louise couldn't answer. She just had to get out of here, out before the carriage closed in on top of her and swallowed her whole.

She had to get out!

She stood up, her head dizzy and her legs like jelly as she stumbled to the train's double-doors. Stars appeared before her eyes then, and she knew that if she didn't get out soon, she would almost certainly …

The doors hissed open, and Louise practically slumped outside, awkwardly colliding with the hordes of commuters waiting on the platform, all anxious to board the early commuter train to Dublin, all ready for another hard day's work in the capital.

Somehow finding the strength, she wandered clumsily down along the platform, and as the train departed slowly into the distance, threw up noisily in the nearest flower-bed.

* * *

Afterwards, when the retching stopped and she had managed to clean herself up with a tissue, she sat down on the nearest bench and waited. She would have to get one of the Dart trains now. Granted, with all its stopping and starting, it would take a lot longer to get into town than the train she'd just got off, but she didn't have much of a choice, did she? Anyway, after all that she was feeling much better, and that was something. Hopefully though, no one had seen her make a show of herself, no one other than perhaps some lucky commuter who might have glanced out the window as the train moved off. They'd think she was hung-over or something. Louise wholeheartedly wished it were that simple.

She shivered, wondering how long she would have to wait for the next service. The Rail Ireland electronic display board was out of order, but that was nothing new. Anyway, as Fiona was always saying, everyone knew that the timetables meant nothing, and the display boards were only there to provide some light entertainment for waiting passengers. Thinking of her friend, Louise smiled thinly. What would Fiona think about all this when she finally plucked up the courage to tell her? And she'd have to tell her soon, because she would almost certainly need to move out of the apartment and she didn't want Fiona and Becky to be left in the lurch. She sighed, imagining Fiona's reaction. She would be furious with her, furious to discover that her flatmate was one of those compensation-seeking, money-grubbing parasites that annoyed her so much – that seemed to annoy everyone so much. So, there would be no more apartment, no more nights out on the town, and very likely, no more friendship.

Louise's life – the frenzied, fun-filled life she'd lived for the last year or so was over now, so she'd just have to face facts and get used to it.

Although she'd be lucky if she still had a life at *all*, she thought, recalling Fiona's throwaway remarks about being sent to jail. The judge could very well decide on Monday to charge her with fraud, and might throw her in jail along with all the murderers and drug-dealers. Louise shuddered at the thought of it.

She sat lost in thought for some time, before eventually looking up and realising that the platform had by now become decidedly crowded. And, she realised, quickly checking her watch, there hadn't been a train for over twenty-five minutes!

That was highly unusual – at this time of day the Darts usually ran every ten minutes – fifteen at the most! Louise gulped hard. She was definitely going to be late for work now – it was well past nine o'clock, she was due in at nine-thirty, and she was still a good half-hour away from town! What was going on?

The man sitting alongside her shook his head. "If this is what it's like when they're carrying out so-called bloody improvements," he muttered impatiently, "then God help us all if they decide to ever run a normal service."

"Probably some problem with the tracks," another passenger commented. She rolled her eyes. "It's nearly always some problem with the tracks."

But the waiting passengers were soon to be put out of their misery, as just then, there was an announcement over the Tannoy: "*This is an announcement by Rail Ireland. We regret to inform passengers that due to an incident on the line this morning, all scheduled North and Southbound trains will be cancelled until further notice.*"

"An incident?" Louise repeated.

"*Sssh!*" the man silenced her, as he struggled to hear the remainder of the announcement *"Shuttle buses will shortly be provided to transport passengers to other stations. If you wish to avail of the shuttle bus, please make your way outside and to the front of the station building. Rail Ireland sincerely regrets any inconvenience caused to passengers at this time. Thank you."*

"I don't believe this!" the man hissed. "Bloody shuttle buses! It'll take me a whole day to get into the office at this rate. I might as well go bloody home!"

"Typical!" Another woman shook her head. "And the government keep telling us to leave our cars at home to help the traffic. Well, we might just do that if they'd provide a half-decent bloody rail service!"

Louise got up and followed the crowd out to the front of the station. She'd never make it to work on time now – no way. She'd better ring the office and let them know that she'd be –

She stopped short as she caught sight of the TV screen behind the counter at the station's mini-market. The news was on, and they were showing pictures of some unimaginable, horrific train accident – probably somewhere in England, Louise deduced, as train crashes were always happening over there. She strained to hear the accompanying news report. For all her giving out, she supposed she should be thankful really that she was only slightly inconvenienced by being late. Wasn't she lucky that she hadn't been caught up in something like that?

Then seeing a face she recognised on the screen, Louise stood rooted to the spot, stunned. Almost at the same time, she identified the accompanying voiceover as that of RTE journalist Clare Rogers – the good-looking one with the lovely hair that was always in *VIP* magazine – she recognised the train carriages, that distinctive logo, the corporate colours …

And all at once Louise realised that this was no English or foreign train disaster. This was happening right now, right here in Ireland, in Dublin, probably only a few miles up the road. The wrecked carriages and scenes of horrible disaster they were showing on TV were of the train Louise – just a few minutes before – had been forced to get off.

CHAPTER 32

Having watched the rest of the TV report and overheard some more details from passers-by, Louise numbly made her way outside the station. Injuries, fatalities, devastation, catastrophe – words the news reporters had used over and over again – planted themselves in her brain.

She couldn't help thinking of all those poor passengers – like the woman sitting across from her, the one who'd asked Louise if she was all right in the seconds before she'd fled the carriage. Had she survived? Had the man in the tracksuit with the briefcase survived? And what about the woman with the lovely Orla Kiely bag? What had happened to her? And wasn't that other person at that same station, the one who *hadn't* made it on time, wasn't she a very lucky woman indeed?

Louise's mind reeled as she tried to take in the enormity of the situation, as she tried to come to terms with it all. *She* should have been on that train! Only for the fact that she'd been so sick with worry, so sick with nerves about that stupid court case ... she could very well be dead by now!

She pondered the situation for a few more minutes as she stood waiting with the other passengers for the shuttle bus into town. It was almost too much to take in – it was as though she'd been given a second chance or something and …

Then in a sharp, unexpected burst of clarity, Louise realised something. And all of a sudden, she began to see things in a very different light.

Moving very slowly at first – head bent as she went – Louise began to walk away, away from the bus stop, away from the bus that would take the stranded commuters into the city centre, and on to the rest of their lives.

But not Louise.

Her footsteps quickening as she walked down the road, she went over it all again in her head. She was *supposed* to have been on that train. She was supposed to have been injured, maybe even *killed* in that crash – if she'd been on the train. And if she hadn't got out at this station, if she hadn't felt so ill, she *would* have been on the train.

So, what would have happened if she'd been in the crash, she asked herself, her thoughts racing.

She certainly wouldn't have been able to make it into court on Monday and the judge wouldn't be able to make the judgement against her. And, if she *had* been on the train, *had* been one of the people who'd died, then there would no longer be any court judgement, any decision to make, would there?

Everyone who knew her knew that she used that particular service. Since she'd moved out to Dun Laoghaire, she'd taken the same train every morning, along with the hundreds of other regular commuters along the East Coast.

So, everyone would, reasonably enough, assume that she had been on the train that morning and that she, like so many others had likely perished, wouldn't they?

Her heart hammered in her chest and her heart soared at the chance she'd been given. In some weird twist of fate, this was a way out – a second chance.

And Louise was going to grab that chance with both hands.

Heart pounding and pulse racing, Louise dipped her hand into her bag and exhaled deeply when almost instantly she found what she was looking for. Yes, her passport was still there, nestled nicely amongst her things – along with the cash she'd withdrawn a few days ago to pay for the New York trip.

Her breathing quickened and she felt another burst of nervous adrenaline. She could do this – she really could! Who would know the difference? Who would know that she hadn't been on the train, that she hadn't been killed in the accident?

Nobody, that's who. Not Cahill, not the judge, and certainly not horrible Leo Gardner. None of the people who were about to pull the rug from under her and ruin her life for good would know. No, nobody would know the difference.

The train station now far behind her – she had made sure of that – she quickened her pace and headed further along the street towards the nearest taxi rank. She knew exactly where to go first – somewhere she could lie low for a while, at least until it all blew over and she figured out what she wanted to do.

She patted her bag reassuringly. She had her passport and a nice wad of money, so really, she could go anywhere she liked. She knew from TV that she couldn't use her bank card or her credit cards – that would give the game away entirely – but the cash would keep her going for a while.

Granted, she didn't quite know exactly what she was going to do when she got to where she was going, but she'd think about that when the time came. All she knew was that there was no going back. She'd been given a second chance!

Head bent low as she approached the taxi rank, she barely felt her feet touch the ground as she moved towards a waiting car.

Neither did she see her newly married friend, Gemma Howard, waving enthusiastically at her from across the road.

CHAPTER 33

Rosie was trying to ring Sheila, but there was no answer at Gillian's house. By rights, this morning she should be heading off on the train for her usual visit, but after all that had happened the night before, and the fact that she was still at Stephen's, she hadn't the energy nor the inclination to go on the journey today. She hoped Sheila wouldn't mind. Anyway, by the looks of things she was off out with Gillian somewhere – and not too concerned about missing Rosie at all.

She replaced the receiver, idly wondering if something might be wrong. No, she thought, shaking her head, she was fretting over nothing as usual – Sheila was probably taking a nap, and Gillian wasn't answering because she was outside hanging out washing or something. She'd try again after lunch. Sheila would be devastated about poor Twix. Granted, her friend was more of a cat lover herself, but even Sheila had gradually been won over by the little spaniel's cheery antics.

Rosie resolved to try not to think about it. Twix was gone now, and she had to get over it. She and Stephen had talked well into the night about lots of things – Twix, David, even Sophie – and as Stephen had said himself, maybe Rosie had relied on the dog a little bit too much, rather than facing up to her son's bullying.

"Stephen!" she'd said, shocked at the idea. "David has his moments, and yes he might be moody and selfish, but he's not a bully."

"If his moods mean that his mother is afraid to go about her daily business in her own house, then yes, he is a bully."

She bit her lip, not sure if she wanted to admit this out loud. "But if he is, then it's my own fault, isn't it?"

His eyes widened. "What on earth would make you think something like that?"

"Well, I'm his mother, aren't I? I raised him – well, me and Martin, of course. So, if David does have those sort of ... tendencies, then I have nobody to blame but myself."

"Rosie, he's a grown man! And grown men have to take responsibility for their own actions! As do grown women," he added, Rosie having explained all about Sophie's busy life – a life so busy she couldn't even take a phone call from her upset mother. "Look, Rosie, you can't seriously believe that your children's behaviour has anything to do with the way you and Martin raised them. You did your best, but eventually they have to make their own way in life. Not to mention the fact that they have their own personalities, their own problems and their own individual way of dealing with them. And how they do that has nothing whatsoever to do with you!"

Rosie still didn't seem convinced.

"Think about it," he continued. "I have three children, each of them so different to one another – and indeed to me – that I often wonder if they were actually switched at birth. There are some things you can teach them, lots of things you can teach them actually, but most of it they have to learn on their own. You said yourself that you and Sophie are very different, yes?"

"Yes, well, she had a lot more opportunities than I had growing up. She's well educated, and with that she's a lot more confident –"

"Exactly, you've just admitted that Sophie is different to you – not because you raised her to be, but because of her own personality, her own experiences. How can you not think the same way when it comes to David?"

"I don't know. I suppose in a way, I'm ashamed of how he's turned out," she admitted, quietly, almost afraid to say it out loud. "I'm ashamed of how he's treating me. He doesn't seem to have any respect for me, and surely that's something you have to teach?"

"Rosie, who knows what goes on inside people's heads? I've tried to figure that out for years with my own kids, with everyone I've ever met, and believe me, it's a waste of time. Look, I'll give you an example. When you walked into my class, that first day, you and everyone else in there had the same level of experience – as in none, yes?"

"I suppose."

"So, really for me it was like working with a blank slate, a blank canvas if you'll pardon the metaphor," he added, eyes twinkling.

Rosie nodded.

"So, should I, as the teacher, feel guilty because every single one of my students didn't turn out to be as good as you were? That they didn't learn as quickly as you did?"

Rosie blushed, flattered by this little bit of praise and feeling silly about it.

"Of course I shouldn't feel guilty, because people aren't simply blank canvases upon which you can imprint your view of the world," Stephen went on. "Everyone is different, unique, whatever you want to call it. David and Sophie got great guidance from you and Martin – I've no doubt of that whatsoever, but you're not responsible for the kind of adults they are now. Sophie seems very selfish certainly, but perhaps she's been mollycoddled and indulged by her husband. You said Martin never indulged her?"

"No, he always felt it was good for the kids not to have everything handed to them." Martin had been adamant about that. Sure, wasn't that his argument for not helping Sophie out with getting a house in the first place? And as it turned out, he'd been dead right. Sophie had been all over her in the weeks leading up to the signing over of the deeds, and then once she got what she wanted, she couldn't be seen for dust!

"So, how then," Stephen persisted, "can you hold yourself responsible for the fact that she's turned out selfish anyway – in the same way that David has become introverted, and as you say, less respectful. When it comes to our children we can have the greatest intentions in the world, give them the benefit of our own experiences, teach them the difference between right and wrong, but, Rosie, we have absolutely no control over what they do with that knowledge. That's up to them and them only."

She nodded, understanding. "But I made a mistake in signing over my deeds to Sophie and probably an even bigger one in giving David the run of the house."

"Rosie, you're their mother. All you did was try to help them. Just remember you did *your* best and don't beat yourself up thinking that your children's faults are your faults. They're not. But what you *shouldn't* be doing is letting them get away with it. You deserve better."

"I know that," she admitted quietly, Stephen's sensible words finally getting through to her. She'd spent so long blaming herself for her children's behaviour, it was a relief to think that she might not have been totally at fault after all.

Stephen sat forward. "Now, I need to visit the estate agent's about this place in the morning, and when I'm finished, we'll have lunch and then I'll drive you back to the house. If you want I can stay for a while, until David comes home. Personally, I think it would be better if I wait outside in the car or something – he mightn't react well to some stranger being there while he and his mother have a little chat – but I'll be there one way or the other, OK?"

Rosie nodded. She wasn't looking forward to it having 'a little chat' with David, but she knew it had to be done. "Thanks, Stephen."

"And from what I've heard about your husband, he seems like a very sensible no-nonsense bloke, and I suspect he wouldn't want you worrying like this – nor would he let David get away with upsetting you like that."

"No, he wouldn't," Rosie smiled.

"You say that David gets home from work around five-thirty …"

"I'd rather go home before then, if you don't mind – to get changed and everything," she said hurriedly.

"Of course. Well, look, I should be back from the estate agent's around twelve, so how 'bout we go and have lunch in McDaniels in the village – they do a grand carvery – and then I'll drop you back to Wicklow early in the afternoon, OK?"

Now, this morning, despite her great intentions of having it out with David, Rosie was feeling nervous about going home today. Not only that, going home meant she had to face an empty house, one that was even emptier now without Twix, she thought sadly, trying to suppress a small tear.

And the truth was, she really wasn't sure what to say to David. The disgust she'd felt for him last night after scaring the dog away frightened her. No decent mother should ever feel that way about her son. Then again, she thought, remembering Stephen's words, no decent mother should be made to. And David had treated her badly, there was no doubt about that. She'd have to confront him, let him know how much he'd upended her life with his return, let him know how much he'd hurt her. She was going to ask him to move out too – there was no way they could go on the way they were, and she knew now that there was no way she was going to be talked into doing so. She didn't know what would happen if he did move out though, and wasn't at all sure if she wanted to stay in that house on her own any longer. A tiny part of her wished she could go off to Tralee with Stephen, although that was silly, to say nothing of the fact Stephen hadn't even asked. But she liked the fact that he'd given her the courage to stand up to her son.

Well, don't get carried away, you haven't done it yet! she admonished herself. But she would. She'd tell David a few home truths and, while she was at it, she might end up doing the same with Sophie.

Rosie smiled. Sheila would be delighted that she'd finally developed a bit of backbone for herself!

CHAPTER 34

At first, Dara didn't know where the hell she was. Had she slept through the alarm clock? What was she doing in bed? This wasn't her room or her apartment or ... no, this was ...

"Hey," Ruth was sitting beside her bed, "how are you feeling?"

"I'm fine ... I think." Dara blinked and looked around her. Yes, she was in a hospital. But why? Then, little by little, it all began coming back. Going to work on the train ... lots of shaking and vibrating ... deafening noise ... screaming and then ... nothing. She had been in an accident of some sort, hadn't she? "Ruth, what happened?"

Ruth gently told her all about that morning's train derailment. "It was a bad crash, but you were one of the lucky ones," she finished. Dara had escaped with a sprained wrist and a couple of bruised ribs and minor injuries to her face. Apparently, some of her fellow passengers weren't so fortunate.

"Your mum and dad are on the way – it was all over the news, and they knew you always took that same train to work. They were frantic ..." Her voice trailed off and her eyes dropped. "They'll be here soon."

Suddenly, Dara's spine stiffened, as she thought she remembered something. She wasn't sure, and maybe she'd just been imagining it but ... "What about Mark?" she asked and her blood went cold when

Ruth wouldn't meet her eyes. The hairs on the back of Dara's neck began to stand up and an icy fear quickly enveloped her. "Ruth, what about Mark?" she persisted. "Didn't you phone him too? I hope you remembered to phone him – he is my husband after all! Ruth?"

Still Ruth didn't look her in the eye.

"Ruth, why didn't you phone Mark? Surely he'll be worried about me too?"

Say something, damn it!

Ruth seemed to be struggling to find her voice. "Dara, don't you remember? Mark was on the train too."

The room, the whole world suddenly began to spin. "What? What are you talking about?" Dara cried, although deep down she knew that Ruth was right. She thought she'd spotted him on the platform this morning just after she got on the train, but instantly dismissed it, thinking she must have been seeing things. "But why ... why would Mark be on the train?"

Ruth looked momentarily puzzled. "Well, we presumed he was with you – you were both found on the same train so – "

Found? "Ruth, who told you that? They must have mistaken someone else for him." Even as she said the words Dara knew they weren't true. She hadn't been imagining it – she *had* seen Mark at the station, she could clearly remember it now and ...but why had he got on the...? Oh dear God, he must have come after her, perhaps in order to make things up with her? Oh no, what had she done?

"Dara, I've seen him," Ruth confirmed. "They brought him straight into theatre." She paused slightly before continuing. "He's pretty bad."

"What? What do you mean 'pretty bad'? What the hell does that mean?" Dara demanded, her insides churning. What was Mark doing on the train?

"He and some other standing passengers were thrown ten feet forward in the carriage. They were all hurt badly, Dara. Mark has some broken bones as far as I know, but worse, he suffered serious head injuries, and some internal bleeding. He's been in intensive care since." Ruth gently took her hand, and looked at her, her face pained. "Dara, they don't know if he'll come through it."

CHAPTER 35

That evening, when six o'clock came and went and there was still no sign of David, Rosie began to get a little concerned. He was always home by 5.30, so why today of all days was he late getting back? Typical. The one time she'd plucked up the nerve to confront him, her recent loss of Twix greatly helping in that regard, and he'd gone off shopping or something!

She hadn't been able to contact Sheila today either. It was very strange altogether – it seemed as though everyone's normal routine had been thrown out of synch for some reason. On any normal Thursday, she'd have taken the train to see Sheila as usual and been home and had her dinner just before David arrived back from work. And he was so like clockwork it was quite disconcerting that he'd be so late. But perhaps it was only disconcerting because the entire situation was disconcerting and she was dreading having to confront him.

She jumped when she heard a key in the front door. Here he was. Rosie took a deep breath, straightened her clothes once more in the mirror, stuck her shoulders back in an attempt to appear more assertive, and quietly opened her bedroom door.

This was it.

But as she stepped out onto the landing, she heard voices. Blast it, there was somebody with him. But who?

Rosie stepped further out, praying that the creaky floorboard at the top of the stairs wouldn't betray her presence. She hadn't touched a thing in the house when she came in – had just gone straight upstairs, so David wouldn't know whether she was here or not.

He and his friends had gone straight into the living-room apparently. That was unusual. David rarely went into the living-room. Wasn't that why he had commandeered her kitchen? Then she heard a female voice – one that Rosie knew very well.

"I still can't believe it!" Sophie cried.

Rose frowned. Sophie sounded very upset. She'd better go down there and see what was wrong, see if she could help. Maybe something had happened to Claudia ...?

"Sssh, love, it's OK," a male voice soothed.

Robert? What were Sophie and Robert doing here? David and his sister didn't get on – especially since the house situation – and David hated Robert! For a brief moment, Rosie wondered if David had told the others about Twix. Or perhaps Sophie had felt guilty about fobbing her mother off last night, and had come to help with the search. Well, if that was the case, she was a bit too late!

Still, that explanation didn't sit right with Rosie. Sophie had never liked Twix, especially the dog's habit of leaving caramel-coloured hairs on her expensive clothes! So, what was going on? Please, God, let it not be Claudia . . .

She moved out further along the landing to try and hear.

"But how can they be sure?" Sophie was asking now.

"She takes the same train every single Thursday morning like clockwork," David was saying. "Since I've been here, I've never known her not to do it. She never turned up at Sheila's this morning, and the woman is beside herself with worry. And even worse, apparently someone in Sheila's family, her daughter-in-law or something, takes the very same train to work."

Train? Were they talking about the Dublin train? So, obviously David didn't even realise she hadn't come home last night, she realised, her shoulders slumping. He always left in the mornings well

322

before she did. Just goes to show how little he cared about what had happened last night, she thought despondently. Never mind Twix, *she* could have been the one dead on the road for all he cared.

"The guards weren't very hopeful either," David added then.

He sounded different, Rosie thought – agitated, worried, ashamed, maybe ...? And what was all this about guards? What was he talking about?

"I gave them her description," he went on, "but they reckon it'll be days before they get the passengers all out of the carriages, let alone try to identify them."

"Identify what's left of them, you mean," Robert added dryly and with that Sophie burst into tears.

"I just can't believe she's dead!" she wailed. "I mean, first Dad and now ... "

Rosie's eyes widened. *Dead?* Who was dead? They weren't talking about Twix – they seemed to be talking about someone who often took the train . . . She struggled to make sense of what they were saying. What – or more importantly – *who* were they talking about?

"David," Sophie cried noisily, "that means we're orphans now, you know that, don't you? Orphans!"

Orphans? What did she mean? Rosie missed David's low reply.

There was a brief silence and then a few minutes later, she heard Robert mutter something about turning on the TV. "They've been running updates since this morning," he said.

Updates on what? Mightily intrigued, Rosie began to creep further down the stairs. But she quickly stopped in her tracks as, horrified, she began to make out snatches of a news report. "*. . . this morning's horrific train derailment on the East Coast. Twelve confirmed dead, hundreds injured . . . rescue attempts . . .*"

Mind racing, she listened in disbelief. Oh, my God! The train – *her* train – apparently it had crashed! Her mind scrambled as she tried to get her thoughts in order. Then she stopped dead, shocked as she recalled the bits of conversation she'd just overheard.

"*Identify what's left*" . . . " *orphans*" . . . Oh, God! David and Sophie thought she'd been on it! They thought she'd been in the crash! Unable to move for shock, Rosie stood there for what seemed like an age, not sure what to do, what to *feel*.

Then, having finally gathered her wits about her, she went to hurry downstairs, and take her children in her arms, and tell them they were mistaken, that she was still alive and well and hadn't taken the train at all, when …

"Well, I suppose, now that she's gone, we'll have to talk about what'll happen with the house," Robert declared loudly.

Quickly, Rosie took a step backwards. Her mouth went dry. This could be interesting.

CHAPTER 36

Dara lay on the hospital bed that evening, her body bandaged, her mind sick with worry. She was an idiot, a complete and utter idiot. How could she have let this happen? Mark must have gone to the train to look for her and try and make it up with her. Why hadn't she phoned him back at the house? Who cared if she was late for work? What did bloody work matter in the scheme of things?

He wouldn't have been on the train if it weren't for her, if they hadn't had that stupid fight, if he hadn't found out about Noah!

Dara put a fist to her mouth, and tried to stifle a cry. Now, Mark was critically injured and very possibly dying in another room somewhere in this very building because of it.

The hospital staff wouldn't let her see him – in fact they wouldn't let her get out of bed.

"You were lucky to get a bed at all, love," a no-nonsense nurse informed her. "We've got people waiting on trolleys all over the place. So, if you get up and start wandering around, there'll be no guarantee you'll still have a bed when you get back."

Apparently the hospital was in chaos, what with the amount of injuries being brought in that afternoon. Dara would just have to wait and rely on what little bit of information Ruth could gather about him, from the over-worked medical staff. She longed to see him, longed to hold him in her arms and tell him how sorry she was. He should never have been on that train. It was all her fault.

And what would she do if she lost him? How would she feel then? She could hardly bear thinking about it. Her heart ached as she remembered how nervous he'd been during the wedding speeches, but how he'd got through it all – the nerves, the sickness – for her. In the same way that he'd put up with the honeymoon to Rome, had been dragged all over a city he had little interest in – for her.

Not to mention what he had done only recently for her father. Eddie would be horrified once he found out what happened, once he discovered that Dara's selfishness had led to this.

As far as her father was concerned, Mark was a good, kind, patient man, who had always gone out of his way to make other people happy, to make her happy. And yet she'd taken it all as her due, hadn't she? She hadn't really understood how much he did for her, how much he had to put up with. And yet, what did he get in return? From day one, she'd treated him terribly, openly admitting to her friends that he was second string, that he was someone who was good enough to have around when it suited her.

Then, as soon as Noah Morgan came back into her life, she'd conveniently forgotten all the wonderful things that Mark had done for her, the wonderful person he was. And he didn't deserve that. No, Mark deserved a hell of a lot better.

Later that evening, when Ruth and her parents had gone home – both shocked and dazed by the news about Mark – the root of all Dara's problems appeared with a bunch of flowers and sporting his trademark dazzling smile.

"I was so worried about you," Noah said, leaning over and kissing Dara lightly on the forehead.

Dara felt nothing. Oddly, she didn't care that he was worried about her. In fairness, he didn't really have a right to worry about her, did he?

"Mark was hurt too," she told him stony-faced. "We had an argument. He came after me this morning on the train." She wasn't sure why she was telling him this, but in a way she wanted him to take some of the blame too, for him to feel the same guilt she was feeling. Not that any of it was actually his fault but …

Noah's reaction betrayed little. "I heard. Dara, look, I hope you're not blaming yourself for this. It wasn't your fault; it –"

"Noah, of course it was my fault! He came after me! We had an argument last night – a huge argument about … about you." Dara recalled Mark's enormous hurt, thinly veiled by his enormous anger. She'd wounded him so badly with the admission that he was second-best, that she had to make a choice between the two of them.

But was that really true now? Given a choice between Mark and Noah, why *would* she choose the latter? This was a man who had deserted her for a silly childish reason, who she hadn't seen in years, and in fairness, who she didn't really know any more. The man had gone off and married someone else in the meantime, for goodness sake! Yet, the old feelings, the old attraction had kicked in instantly upon seeing him after all that time.

But maybe that was it. Maybe it was all based on the old feelings, and was nothing but the old 'one who got away' syndrome. Maybe she'd been drawn to Noah, not because of the person he was now, but because of their history. In some weird way, she wanted to prove to herself that she was his true love, that she had more power over him than any other woman. She'd convinced herself of that fact for so long that it was almost impossible to see it any other way.

"So what did he say?" Noah's voice broke into her thoughts. "Mark. What did he say when you told him about me?"

Dara looked at him, wondering why on earth he was asking such a pathetic, irrelevant question, when Mark was now fighting for his life somewhere in this very building.

And right then, Dara realised that she didn't care about Noah bloody Morgan, and she wasn't in love with him – he was simply a part of her past that she needed to exorcise, or as the Americans would say, for which she needed 'closure'.

Noah wasn't The One for her – he had never been The One. But she'd clung to that silly, immature, and supposedly romantic notion for so long that she couldn't see beyond it.

She looked at him, looked into his attractive green eyes, his perfectly sculptured face and decided that it was time to end this nonsense, this stupidity that had affected her all her adult life.

She spoke softly. "Noah, I told Mark that you were an old friend I'd met recently, and that we were catching up. I told him that there was nothing between us." The last bit was a lie, but she just wanted to get this over with.

"And did he believe you?" Noah asked warily. "Did he suspect anything?"

She looked away for a moment, remembering Mark's anger when she'd implied that she needed to make a decision. Then she looked back at Noah and spoke softly. "Noah, it's the truth. You *are* an old friend and we *were* catching up. Look, it was stupid of us both to think that we could take up where we left off. Yes, it was great when we were younger, but we're two completely different people now."

He frowned. "But I thought ... what are you saying?"

"Noah, tell me, what would happen if I *did* decide to leave Mark now? What would we do?"

He shrugged, as if he hadn't really given it much thought. "We'd be together, I suppose."

"But what would we *do*? Would we buy a house together, get married, have children?" She was particularly interested in seeing how he answered this.

He shrugged. "Well, maybe – after a while. But there are lots of things I want to do before I settle down completely. I mean, I still love travelling and there's lots more I want to see. And there's more to life than mortgages, you know that. We could go away together this time, Dara. We could go to Italy and Paris, wherever you like. You'd really enjoy it."

She shook her head sadly. She was an idiot to have seriously considered going back to him, wasn't she? Noah was no different to the man who'd left her all those years ago. He was still a drifter, still a dreamer. Noah had no concept of a normal conventional working life, had no real interest in settling down – with anyone. His marriage hadn't ended because he was still in love with Dara – it had ended because, for Noah, the drama and excitement had ended once real life

328

had crept in. Noah Morgan would never make sacrifices for Dara or for anyone else. And, she thought, with a wistful smile, she certainly couldn't picture him frog marching her father to a prostate examination!

She turned to face him. "Noah, I'm married now, married to someone who's very important to me and who I – who I love very much." As she said it, a lump came to her throat. "I'm not willing to throw that away."

"But I thought – "

"We were both being stupid," she said. "Because it all ended so weirdly that first time, we both thought there was unfinished business between us. But Noah, I don't think there was. We just weren't meant to be."

Noah was silent for a very long moment. Eventually, he sat back and sighed. "Maybe you're right. When I met you after all that time, I was so pleased to see you again, that maybe I just wanted to convince myself we still had something." He shook his head. "I've had a shitty few years and – "

"Noah, that's all it was. Seeing one another again after all this time made us both a little crazy. Yes, it was great back then, but who knows how it would be now?" Her eyes dropped to the sheet. "But it doesn't matter, because it's not going to happen. I'm not going to leave Mark for you." She tried to dispel the notion that perhaps Mark might be lost to her anyway – one way or the other.

"So that's it then?" Noah asked gently. "You don't want to stay friends, or anything?"

She smiled. "I don't think it would be right somehow. You're a good friend, Noah, and I'll always treasure our time together but ..."

He nodded. "I understand. It wasn't fair of me to come back and expect you to give up everything just for me – especially after all this time." He shrugged, and gave her another of those heart breaking smiles. "Wishful thinking, I suppose."

"Maybe," Dara smiled back and took Noah's hand in hers, feeling a strange relief at the realisation that, after all this time, they were finally saying goodbye.

CHAPTER 37

It had been a tough day at the hotel and as she approached her house around seven o'clock on Thursday evening, Heather's feet ached with the cold. She was so looking forward to getting home. Andy was on night-duty all this week, so luckily she wouldn't have to go to the bother of cooking dinner. No, this evening, she was going to just throw on an M&S ready-meal and then cosy up to the fire with a bucket of Maltesers and a good book. Bliss! Heather smiled contentedly at the thought of it.

The smile froze on her face when she looked up and saw Louise standing awkwardly in her doorway, her younger sister's face a picture of anxiety.

* * *

"Louise, you cannot do this!" Inside the house, Heather's face contorted with worry. Louise had told her all about that day's events and her subsequent 'escape'.

Heather had immediately turned on the TV to Sky News to check if there were any reports on the train crash, but other than a brief mention in the headlines about it being a particularly bad one, there was nothing major.

"Honey, I know things look bad now, but you can't seriously think you can just run away from it all. It's not the way life works!"

"But why not?" Louise replied innocently. It was a bit of shock, but Heather would come round. She just needed a bit of time to get used to the idea – that was all. Louise had had plenty of time to do that – she'd thought about nothing else since this morning. "Nobody knows I'm here. I came across on the ferry – I didn't have to give my name in order to buy the ticket. Heather, they didn't even check my passport!"

It was true. The authorities on either side of the Irish Sea hadn't asked for her passport, for identification, anything. Louise had been prepared for the fact that they might look for ID, although she knew that nothing would be entered into a computer, or on the passenger manifesto, which is why she'd taken the fast-ferry to Holyhead, as opposed to an aeroplane. After that she'd taken a bus ride down to Cardiff, and that was it. She'd done it. She'd escaped her horrible life in Ireland and was now ready to start a new one. She just needed Heather's help for a little while. OK, so her sister was in a bit of shock now, but not as much shock as she'd have been in if Louise had been on the train! So this was much better all round really.

"Louise, listen to me – you can't do this," Heather repeated slowly as though she were talking to a child. "You can't just run away. You have to go back. Look, I know you're upset about what happened in court yesterday, and I know this Sam guy hurt you very much ..." her tone softened, "but you have to go back."

"I can't go back!" Louise's voice broke slightly. "I made a mess of things – I always make a mess of everything! I thought he cared about me ... I thought he genuinely liked me." She flinched as Heather lightly touched her arm. "But I was an idiot. I'm always an idiot. I've been an idiot all my life. Now I finally have the chance to start over, to start afresh and leave that person behind."

"Honey, you'll never be able to leave that person behind because whether you like it or not that person is you! And you're not an idiot – in fact, you're one of the kindest and most loving people I've ever known. Look at all you did for me and Andy, giving up your share of the house when we needed it, thinking of us rather than yourself."

Louise sniffed. "It was the least I could do after ruining your wedding plans with my bloody accident." At the thought of the accident, her stomach turned.

"That wasn't your fault, Louise. No matter what that judge might say, no matter what that Sam guy said – you know and I know that it wasn't your fault."

"But maybe it was, Heather! You know what I'm like, I day dream about things all the time, I'm forgetful and silly and … oh, I'm just an idiot, a stupid, pathetic idiot."

"That's not true," Heather insisted. "You're just going through a tough time at the moment, a rough patch. But whatever happens, you'll get over it." When Louise shook her head, she added vehemently. "You've got over worse."

Her sister looked at her questioningly.

"What about Mam and Dad's death? We got through that, didn't we, you and me? You're a strong person, Louise, and although it might not seem like it now, you will come out of this. I know you will. And I'll help you, and I'm sure your friend – Fiona, is it? – she'll help you too."

At the thought of Fiona, Louise instantly felt guilty.

"What would she make of all this?" Heather asked, as if reading her thoughts. "How will she feel when she finds out about the accident, and thinks the worst when you don't come home this evening?"

"She won't care," Louise said petulantly. "Not about anything other than how she's going to pay for next month's rent." The deposit she'd paid would take care of that anyway, she remembered, trying to assuage some of her guilt about leaving Fiona and Becky in the lurch. They'd get over it. They didn't care much about her anyway – Fiona, Becky, Gemma, nobody. In fact, there were very few people who would give a damn whether or not she died in that crash.

When she said this to Heather, she shook her head. "Now you're being silly, and you're feeling sorry for yourself. No friends indeed! What about all those nights out and shopping trips you're always telling me about, and that lovely holiday in Spain you took a while back? You're not telling me now that you did all those things on your own, are you?"

Louise shook her head. "They're just work friends," she tried to sound offhand. "We're not that close."

Heather sighed. "Louise, I'm sorry but I won't be a part of this, and I can't let you do it. I know things might seem bad now, but I promise you everything will be OK eventually. But you have to go back home and face the music."

Louise shook her head. "Don't want to." She knew she sounded like a child, but she couldn't believe that Heather was trying to force her to go back.

Heather's temper was now beginning to fray. "Louise, this is silly! What would Mam and Dad say?"

"That's not fair."

"Fair? Fair? What about all those people who have lost friends and loved ones in that crash? Think about how fair that is! Think about how devastated and upset they are right now, and then think about how selfish and cold-hearted you are being by trying to capitalise on their grief!"

"I'm not trying to capitalise on it. I'm – "

"Yes, you are! This is a terrible tragedy, and you're trying to turn it to your own gain! Just because your life isn't going the way you want it, you've decided you're going to bow out, just like that." Heather put her hands on her hips, and her eyes flashed angrily. "You know, now that I think of it, you *are* pathetic, Louise, and yes, you are an idiot. Because what you're doing is the most idiotic thing I've ever come across, and I don't know why you felt you could involve me in it!"

With that, Heather walked out of the room and slammed the door behind her, leaving Louise feeling lonelier and more pathetic than she'd ever felt in her life.

CHAPTER 38

That same evening, in a house on the other side of the Irish Sea, another family was also trying to come to terms with the day's events.

"You stupid bastard!" David yelled at Robert, evidently enraged by his brother-in-law's callousness. "How could you say something like that? How could you even *think* about something as trivial as the house? They haven't even found my mother's body yet!"

Listening upstairs on the landing, Rosie raised an interested eyebrow. David sounded mightily unimpressed.

"Don't you dare speak to my husband like that!" Sophie snapped, sounding a lot less tearful now. "He's only saying what has to be said. And you know, David, he does have a point. With Mum gone, this house is now legally mine and Robert's. I know you've been living here too, but – "

"You selfish little bitch!" David growled. "Our mother *died* this morning, and all you can think about is how soon you can get your grubby little hands on her house! Well, you can go sing, Sophie – I'm not going anywhere until I'm good and ready – and certainly not until I've had a chance to grieve properly for Mum. She deserves that – she deserves a lot more than any of us ever gave her."

"Oh, come off it, David!" Sophie jeered. "Typical you, getting all

334

maudlin now that Mum's no longer around. You weren't too worried about what she deserved when you moved back in with her, were you?"

Rosie closed her eyes, almost afraid to breathe. It was surreal, being here listening to this. It almost felt as though she was secretly attending her own funeral.

"What are you talking about?"

"I'm talking about you taking over this place, changing things around to suit yourself, hunting her out of her own kitchen, and making her feel like a stranger in her own home!"

So Sophie did suspect something then, Rosie realised. Her daughter had after all figured out how hard her mother might be finding it, having David home again. Yet she had never said a word.

"What? I never did anything like that!" David sounded genuinely astonished. "I tried to stay out of Mum's way! I didn't want to disturb her by coming back and creating an upheaval, so I tried my best to keep out of her way. As far as I know she was happy enough in her room, with her dog and ..." With that he stopped short. "Oh, Jesus, the bloody dog!"

"That dirty little thing that leaves hairs everywhere?" Robert ventured. "What about it?"

"Oh dear," Sophie said then, and Rosie could almost picture her biting her lip guiltily, the way she always did when she was a little girl, "now that I think of it, I remember Mum rang me last night going on about the dog. I can't be sure, to be honest, I was pretty full of champagne at the time so –"

"The dog ran away last night. Mum went out to look for her. She blamed me, thought it was all my fault, but it wasn't like that. I came home early, and the dog growled at me, so I growled back. And then she nipped me on the leg. That dog never liked me for some reason."

"Really? Why ever not?" Sophie drawled.

David ignored her. "Anyway, a couple of minutes later, some guy called with a delivery for Mum from one of her catalogues. At this stage the dog was all worked up – it started barking like crazy, chased him out of the hallway, and followed him all the way down the path.

I thought it would come back after that, but by the time Mum came home it was long gone." He sounded guilty. "When she asked me about it, to be honest, I was a bit short with her, but I'd had a shit day and the last thing I needed was a row over a bloody dog. But Mum thought I'd kicked her out on purpose."

"She must have phoned me shortly after that, then," Sophie finished. "Still, it's not as though *I* could do anything – I live halfway across the city for goodness' sake! As if I was going to leave all my guests to go and look for a stupid dog!" She spoke as though it was the most ridiculous idea she'd ever heard. "So did she find the stinky little thing?" she added idly.

"As a matter of fact, I did."

All three looked up in shock as Rosie quietly entered the room – her face expressionless, her eyes sharp and wary.

"Oh, Jesus!" Robert went white.

"Mum!" Sophie pealed. "You're alive! But how … ?"

"I wasn't on the train," she told them simply. "I didn't go to Sheila's this morning."

For what seemed like an age, nobody said a word – they all just stared at Rosie, flummoxed by her appearance.

"Mum, I'm so sorry," David whispered eventually. "We really thought … we thought you'd …"

"I know." Rosie looked at the images on the television, feeling slightly outside of herself as she looked at the wreckage, the extent of the damage to the train that, on any other Thursday morning, she would have been inside. There but for the grace of God …

"Oh Mum!" Sophie leapt forward, and put her arms around Rosie. "We were so worried, we were so sure –."

"You were so sure you'd get your inheritance sooner than you expected?" said Rosie, stiffening in Sophie's embrace.

Sophie drew back, her cheeks pink, and Robert looked duly ashamed.

David, on the other hand, looked happier and more animated than Rosie had seen him in ages. "Mum, I'm so happy you're OK," he said, the words tumbling out quickly, "and I'm really sorry about Twix. I went out shortly afterwards to help you look for her. Maureen from next door told me you'd gone down the town, so I thought maybe you'd found her, but it was late by the time I got back and your light was off so … is she here?"

Rosie shook her head sadly. "She got knocked down by a car, David. She's dead."

His face went white. "Oh, Jesus, Mum! How … how are you?"

"Well, I'm upset of course," she told him tearfully. "Well, no, I'm actually devastated, but there's nothing I can do for her now. She's gone and that's the end of it."

The room was once again uncomfortably silent for a very long while.

Eventually, Rosie cleared her throat. It was now or never. "Well, I suppose I should be pleased you all got so worked up about my supposed death," she said, her heart pounding with nerves, "but I think I have a few years left in me yet." She turned to her son, who at the moment was looking subdued and suitably chastened. "David, you and I have a few things to talk about. Things aren't working out here and I think you and I both know that."

David nodded silently.

"Sophie, Robert – I'm sure you two are a bit disappointed that you won't be getting the house yet, but you'll have to get over it." Rosie couldn't believe these words were coming out of her own mouth. She sounded so strong, so assured!

Sophie's eyes widened. "Mum, I –"

"I don't want to hear it, Sophie. For once, your poor old mother is going to think of herself. I'm withdrawing my letter of guarantee to your bank." Despite her strong words, her heart ached when she saw her daughter's bewildered expression. God, she hated doing this, but she had to, didn't she? "I know this might affect your plans, but I've got my own plans too, so you'll have to make your own arrangements."

Then she turned once more to her son. "David, I don't want you living here any more – you've upset my life enough, and I think you should stop hiding away and try and face up to your own problems – whatever they might be." She coughed slightly as she looked from one precious child to the other. "Your father and I did everything for you two growing up, and we tried our utmost to give you the best upbringing possible. But," she added, her voice growing hoarse now, as emotion overtook her, "there is no denying that, through our fault or not, the two of you have grown up to be selfish individuals. So, just for once, I think I'm going to be selfish too."

With that, Rosie picked up her coat, walked out of her living-room and outside to where Stephen waited patiently in the car – her two children standing open-mouthed in her wake.

CHAPTER 39

It was the morning following the train crash. Dara swallowed hard as she entered the Intensive Care Unit. She'd been released just that morning, and although her body ached, she looked a hell of a lot worse than she actually was. Her face and body were covered in bruises and she had a patch over a black eye from when she'd been thrown forward into the side of a seat. But other than that, she was fine.

Physically, anyway.

She looked up as she realised there were other people in the room.

"Nice of you to drop by." The sardonic tone was unmistakable.

"Gillian, stop it!" Sheila admonished her daughter and gave a quick glance to where her beloved son lay barely conscious on the hospital bed.

Linda stood at his bedside, crying openly for her older brother.

"How are you feeling, Dara?" Sheila asked, her tone kind but also a little wary. "We were going to visit, but the nurses said you were being released this morning."

"I'm fine," Dara replied quietly, almost afraid to look at Mark. His face was heavily bandaged, his body still as he lay on the bed. "How is he?"

Gillian snorted, as if to say: 'What do you care?'

339

"I did nothing wrong, Gillian," Dara said, her tone hard as she turned to face her. "I know you think you saw something that day in town, but you didn't."

"I saw what I saw! You and some fellow crawling all over each other and – "

"This isn't the time or the place!" Sheila hissed, her expression pained, and Linda whirled around to face them. Dara dropped her eyes, ashamed. Sheila was right. Let Gillian think what she wanted. Nothing had happened between Noah and her, and nothing was about to happen.

Ever. Dara had made sure of that. If Gillian didn't like it – tough. She'd never liked Dara anyway.

Only then did it cross her mind that maybe Gillian had suspected all along that she wasn't being true to her brother, that she'd noticed something amiss from the very beginning. So maybe she couldn't blame the woman for being suspicious – she'd been right, hadn't she? Still, all she could do now was make up for lost time, and prove to Gillian – prove to Mark that she truly did love him, that he was the best thing that had ever happened to her.

"How is he?" Dara asked again.

Just then, Linda came over to join her mother and sister and gave Dara a mournful nod. Sheila took her younger daughter's hand in hers and slowly shook her head. "They're not too hopeful," she told Dara sorrowfully, "but they're still not sure. Even if he does come out of it, there could still be complications … with his brain, you know?" Her voice broke slightly. "All we can do now is just wait … and hope. But, Dara, love – there's very little hope."

Dara felt dizzy. She knew that it was bad – Ruth had prepared her for that, and she'd also spoken to Mark's doctor before she'd come in here.

"I'm sorry, Mrs Russell," he'd said, and Dara was startled upon hearing that. It was the first time she'd ever been called that in her life. Now, she thought sadly, there was a very real chance that it might just be the last time too. "We've done all we can for him. After that we just don't know."

340

Dara was devastated. After all that had happened, after all the time she'd wasted, worrying about bloody Noah Morgan, failing to recognise how truly wonderful Mark was, she couldn't comprehend the idea that she might lose him now. It seemed cruel. But life could be cruel, and things didn't always turn out how people wanted, simply because they wanted it, did it?

Tentatively, Dara went to the bed and took her husband's limp hand in hers. She stared down at him for what seem like an age, trying to swallow the lump in her throat.

"I'm sorry," she whispered eventually, and her eyes blurred with tears as she realised just how badly he'd been hurt, and how frail he really was. The doctors weren't mistaken – just then Mark looked as though he had passed away already. She tried to banish this horrible thought, and try and concentrate on what she was going to say. Maybe Mark couldn't hear her but she needed to say it.

"I'm sorry that I wasn't a better wife. I'm sorry that I've been such a fool." She didn't care that the others could hear everything; she just wanted him to know the truth. He deserved that. But to their credit, Sheila murmured something about getting a cup of tea and she and the girls left, to give Dara some time with him. Time that, as they all knew well, could be very precious.

Dara gulped hard, trying to bite back the tears. "I'm sorry that I made you feel second-best. I don't know why … I was blind, stupid, an idiot. Mark, you're not second-best you couldn't be second-best to anyone. You're the most honest, loving, considerate person I have ever met, and I love you very much. I know this sounds pathetic, but I really don't think I realised how much until now – now that I have some idea of what it would feel like to lose you."

Mark's eyes remained closed – his face motionless as cold stone.

"I know I don't deserve you," she added, "and maybe when you come out of this, when you get back to normal, you'll tell me to get lost. But, I just want you to know that I love you."

Tears streaming down her face, she bent low and rested her head on the bed, willing Mark to open his eyes and tell her that everything would be OK, that he would be OK. But there was nothing – no

341

response, no movement, no flicker of an eye or twitch of the hand like there always was in the movies – nothing.

Dara watched helplessly as deep down she finally understood that she would never leave him but, by some ironic and very cruel twist of fate, Mark could be leaving her.

CHAPTER 40

Monday 24th October 10.00 am

Louise felt all eyes turn to look at her, as she nervously entered the room. From behind, Heather gave her shoulder a reassuring squeeze.

"Go on," she urged her. "I'm right behind you."

Louise took a deep breath and made her way slowly to the front of the courtroom where James Cahill and the others awaited. She tried her best to avoid looking at a smug-looking Leo Gardner and his legal team. The elegant one in the power suit was missing today, Louise noticed, wondering if that meant anything as far as her own destiny was concerned.

But she was here now, and whatever was coming, she had to get it over with. Heather had finally convinced her of that.

* * *

In her living-room in Cardiff, Heather had sat her baby sister down and gone through both her finances and her options, despite Louise's protests that she had no option other than to run away and start again. But Heather wouldn't hear of it.

"Louise, at the end of the day – it's only money. And you *will* get it paid off – maybe not today or tomorrow but you will eventually.

You've always been a hard worker and you know well what you have to do. To begin with, you'll need to tone down the shopping and partying for a while and – "

"Don't worry, there'll be no more of that," Louise interjected determinedly. "That should never have happened in the first place. I'll move out of the apartment and stop seeing Fiona and I'll – "

"Louise, no! Don't do that. Of course, you can still see your friends. All I'm saying is that you have to tone down the social life. A bit – not completely! Just stop the champagne spending, particularly when you've only just about got lemonade pockets! That's part of your problem, you know," she added, shaking her head from side to side. "With you, it's either one extreme or the other."

"What do you mean?"

"Well, you got into debt because of the accident, and you said yourself your philosophy was 'Well, I'm in this deep – what's another overdraft or credit card?'. But if you'd just tried to nip all this spending in the bud, before it went so far ..."

Louise sighed. Of course, Heather was right. She'd always known she should have been more careful, more disciplined about her finances. But she'd been so pleased to finally have a social life again, and Fiona was so persuasive that she really didn't want to let anyone down.

When she explained this to Heather, her sister shook her head again. "Louise, if Fiona is really your friend, she'll understand. Nobody judges their friends by the clothes they wear or the amount of drinks they buy and, if they do, then they're really not your friends."

Then, with the mention of Fiona, Louise realised that she'd better phone and tell her where she was. She would be frantic, no doubt believing that Louise had died or been injured in the accident.

She was right.

"Oh, my God, Louise, where were you? Oh, Jesus, I can't believe you're OK! I was worried sick!" Then, incredibly, Louise heard her normally controlled self-assured and image-obsessed friend break down and sob her heart out. "I really thought we'd lost you!"

Louise was so taken aback by the strength of Fiona's emotions towards her that she too started to bawl. Eventually, and with an impatient roll of her eyes, Heather took the phone off her.

"Fiona? Hi, Heather Reeves, Louise's sister here ... Yes, yes, she's absolutely fine. Oh, it's a long story, and I'm sure she'll explain all when she comes back ... What? No, I think she just got a bit of shock. ... Yes, I *know* she's your very best friend, of course, I do. Of course, you are ... OK ... talk to you soon." Heather put the phone back on the receiver and smiled at her sister. "Well! That certainly doesn't sound like someone who doesn't give a damn about you, does it?"

Louise smiled slightly, already feeling buoyed by Fiona's depth of feeling, but at the same time desperately guilty that she had put her through so much worry.

The girls talked well into the night about the entire situation, with lots of focus on a strict budget for Louise.

"Now about all these clothes," Heather began. "It'll be the high street from now on for you, my dear. No more 'cute little boutiques' and discount evenings at department stores. You have a lovely figure, and you can wear cheaper clothes as well as anyone. Anyway, what's wrong with the cheaper stuff? It can be just as nice, if not nicer than some of those posh 'labels', can't it?"

Louise grinned. Not being a labels fan herself, her sister would probably never understand, but again Heather was right. And in all honesty, Louise had so many clothes in her wardrobe back at the apartment that she need never buy another stitch again!

The two girls continued going through some more cost-saving ideas and Heather eventually managed to convince Louise that perhaps the life she had was worth going back to. After their conversation, and particularly the phone call to Fiona, Louise finally began to come around. But there was one thing that Heather couldn't help her with, and that was her broken heart.

"He made such a fool of me," she admitted, her face burning with shame as she thought about Sam – all the great times she'd had with him, how wonderful he had made her feel.

"It's not a crime to take someone at face value, you know," Heather said softly. "In fact, it could be considered a positive thing. You're a decent, honest, open person and you expect other people to be the same. This Sam guy was a professional, Louise. He didn't just make a fool of you – he made more of a fool of himself. What kind of person can do that and still live with themselves afterwards? What kind of person can make a living out of exploiting others? Would you like to be a person like that? Louise, that guy is nothing but a weak, spineless asshole, and he's the one that has to live with it – not you."

Louise said nothing. Unfortunately, this didn't take away from the fact that she'd cared a lot about Sam. She had let her guard down and allowed herself to be taken in by him. She didn't know which was worse – the hurt or the utter humiliation at being so easily fooled.

"Someone like that doesn't deserve your respect – let alone your love," Heather went on. "I know it's easy for me to say, but I really don't think the feelings you thought you had for him were real. He played on your emotions, told you what you wanted to hear and made you feel special. That's the only reason you fell for him."

Louise nodded. Heather was right in a way, but this didn't help her devastation at being betrayed, and her embarrassment that she had made it so easy for him. But still, she'd get over it – she had to get over it and, in fairness, getting over Sam would be the least of her worries.

Now, it seemed the rest of those worries were about to be dealt with.

* * *

"All rise!"

Louise's legs felt weak, as she heard the familiar announcement in the courtroom, and she wasn't sure how she found the energy to stand up. For one very brief second, she contemplated racing out the door and running away. But she'd already tried that, hadn't she? And Heather had convinced her to come back, had convinced her that whatever happened, they'd face it together.

"We'll get over it – haven't we come through worse?" she'd reiterated once more, on the plane journey back to Ireland, a perplexed Andy having been promptly dispatched to the travel agent's the day before to buy the tickets. Heather had told her husband nothing about Louise's mess and had quickly glossed over the reasons for her sudden appearance in Cardiff. There was no point in trying to explain it.

Louise wasn't sure if she *would* get over it, but she had very little choice. And it was too late to be worrying about it now anyway.

But the weird thing was, she thought, her face burning at the realisation, it wouldn't have worked anyway. Upon her return to the apartment on Saturday when she'd told Fiona everything – everything about the claim and the money problems and her decision to run away – Louise discovered that her 'escape' hadn't been as flawless as she'd thought. She'd been spotted on the street shortly after the crash – by bloody Gemma!

"I really thought she was mistaken," Fiona informed her, still red-eyed after the two girls' rather emotional reunion. "I mean, I *knew* you had taken that train – wasn't I there that morning when you left for work? So when I met Gemma later, and she told me she'd seen you taking a taxi somewhere, when you should have been at work, I really wouldn't hear of it."

So, as it turned out, the great escape wouldn't have worked anyway. Eventually, someone would have put two and two together. Still, it was pointless thinking about that now. Louise had run away, but not for long.

And now she was back.

Now she closed her eyes as Judge Corcoran began to speak. For the first few minutes, she barely heard his words, she was so wrapped up in what might happen.

"Having carefully considered the nature of the claim ... and having listened to both sides ..."

Would he put her in jail? Lock her up and throw away the key?

"I do feel that ..."

Just how was Heather going to help her through *that*, she wondered, vivid images of a dank, grey, prison cell full of murderers and rapists filling her brain. A far cry from the glamorous celebrity hangouts full of glossy, perfect posers she used to frequent.

347

" ... having heard *very* convincing testimony from Mr Harris ..."

The judge's words were now a blur, and once more Louise felt her head begin to spin as the final decision got ever closer.

" ...not to mention Ms Patterson's extravagant lifestyle and mounting debt...."

Mounting debt. It was going to get much worse, wasn't it? How on earth was she going to pay Gardner's legal fees? Despite Heather's protests, she really couldn't take anything from her – she *wouldn't* take anything from her. She and Andy were struggling to get by as it was. This was her own problem, her own fault, and she'd just have to take it on the chin.

However bad it was.

" ...see no reason why Mr Gardner should shirk his responsibility or duty of care ..."

Duty of care? James Cahill had mentioned that phrase over and over again at the beginning while trying to convince Louise that she really had a case, hadn't he? Slowly but surely the judge's words swam into focus and, heart racing, mind spinning, Louise began to concentrate.

"... no doubt that Ms Patterson's life has been adversely affected by Mr Gardner's negligence – something that he himself does not dispute. And I personally do not feel that Ms Patterson's social life is any concern of this court. In fact, I believe that this testimony actually underlines Ms Patterson's strength of character. Instead of descending into desperation or depression, as other victims have been known to do, Ms Patterson has picked up the reins of her damaged life and continued to enjoy living it."

Louise inhaled deeply and her heart leapt into her mouth. He wasn't ... he couldn't ... was he thinking about ruling in her favour?

"Ms Patterson's lifestyle in no way takes away from Mr Gardner's culpability in this case. Indeed her lifestyle is her own concern, and the evidence clearly supports the claim of diminished earnings. So, why should she have to suffer as a result? Why should she have to alter her lifestyle because another person ignored his duty of care? Indeed, Ms Patterson has considerably altered her lifestyle and has suffered enough, both physically and financially."

As she listened, Louise realised she was still holding her breath.

"So, it is the decision of this court that Ms Patterson be awarded an amount of eighty thousand euro to compensate for her additional injuries – injuries that were caused by Mr Gardner's negligence."

Louise stood rooted to the spot, stunned. She barely heard the judge bang his gavel, barely felt James Cahill's firm handshake, Heather's enthusiastic hug.

It was over. It was all over. Her life hadn't been ruined at all. All these years, all those financial worries – it was over.

And perhaps, she thought, as she turned and saw Fiona waving gleefully from the back of the courtroom, perhaps her life – her *real* life, and not one based on lies and fantasy – was just beginning.

CHAPTER 41

December

Dara stood at the doorway and looked around the silent apartment – the place where she and Mark had spent many happy hours, many happy days. No, she thought, shaking her head sadly, they had been happy here full stop – but she'd been too much of an idiot to realise it. She'd been too blinded by her own immature ideas about love and happiness and the 'perfect man', that she couldn't see she'd had exactly that all along.

She glanced wistfully towards the couch, remembering how Mark used to massage her aching feet after a hard day's work, remembering all those lazy Sunday afternoons they'd sat there together leafing through the Sunday papers – Mark engrossed in the football, Dara doing her best not to let him know she was enjoying the game too.

And, of course, there were those times they ended up making love on that very couch – some times playful and fun, other times slow and tender but, she remembered fondly, always wonderful.

Then there was the time she'd been struck down with a bad bout of chickenpox and had been driven out of her mind with boredom lying in bed with nothing to do. Mark had gone into the bedroom, wrapped her up in a duvet and set her down on the couch in front of the television, apparently unconcerned about catching the dreaded thing, or about having to witness Dara's incessant scratching. Had she even appreciated that at the time? Or appreciated all the things Mark did on a regular basis to make her happy, all the silly little things he did to show his love for her?

No, she thought now, she hadn't appreciated any of it. She hadn't appreciated that love – real love – wasn't about excitement and all-consuming passion. It wasn't 'seeing stars' or 'going weak at the knees' – all the stupid things she'd always believed.

Real love was about the little things, the silly, seemingly inconsequential things – all the things that Mark had done so well. Things like making Dara laugh when she was stressed, massaging her feet after a hard day's work, cheering her up with a glass of wine or masses of chocolate when she was down in the dumps, cooking her favourite meal for no particular reason other than he enjoyed doing it for her. Things like being a good sport about being dragged around museums (even though he hated every minute of it), putting up with her boring solicitor colleagues at the Christmas party, making sure her father looked after his health. Real love was about being together, witnessing the minutiae of one another's day-to-day lives, forging silly little memories like these.

Dara gulped. Mark had done all of those things for her without question, never seeking anything from her in return, but she had never fully appreciated it. And he should have got something in return. He should have been appreciated. But Dara had been a blind fool – an idiot. All she had done was compare him to what had been her own pathetic, shallow ideal of what constituted true love. All she'd done, even on their wedding day, was concentrate on the things she thought her marriage was lacking, the things she thought Noah Morgan could give her.

Her heart ached as she thought about it now. What could Noah have given her – really? Could he have lived up to her impossible ideal, the romantic ideal she'd clung to for all those years? Probably not. Noah was simply a part of her past, a past that had long since dissipated, but something that up until a few weeks ago, she'd been unable to let go.

A lump came to her throat as she thought about Mark in the hospital, how frail and weak he'd been before it was finally all over. They'd understood at the time that he was close to death, of course, the doctors had explained that but, – she thought, stomach twisting – in the end none of them had any idea just how close.

"It's time to go, love." Eddie Campbell touched her softly on the shoulder. "The truck is all packed up and ready to go."

Dara smiled at her father. "Thanks, Dad, I'm just ... you know... saying goodbye."

Eddie studied her. "I know it's not easy," he said quietly, "and I know how much you loved this place. Sure, weren't you always on at your mother about how well you were doing, with your own house and your great job, when she used to get onto you about finding a husband?"

"Well, don't tell Mam, but maybe she had a point after all," Dara said with a hint of a smile.

Eddie winked. "Doesn't she always? But the new place is even better, and you'll have many a happy memory there too."

"I hope so." The new house was lovely, and Dara was really looking forward to moving in, moving on with her life and starting afresh somewhere new. Still she couldn't help feeling melancholy now. But that was only natural, wasn't it?"

"Anyway, let me know whenever you're ready. The removal guys are anxious to get moving, if you'll pardon the pun," he added with another wink.

"I'm on my way."

Eddie headed back downstairs and, although she knew he understood, Dara still felt a bit silly about getting so emotional over bricks and mortar. But he was right. Buying this place all by herself had been one of the proudest moments of her life, and it was difficult to let that go.

Still, wasn't life all about moving on and letting go? Mark had put his finger on it that time on their honeymoon in Rome when he'd commented, "What's in the past is in the past. You can learn from it, but you shouldn't let it dictate the future."

He'd said that quite innocently while referring to her own love of history, but still his words had been strangely prescient when it came to Dara's actions after that. She smiled. Yes, she would certainly learn from the past, had already learned from it, and while she wouldn't exactly let it *dictate* her future, there was no harm in reminding herself from time to time how stupid she'd been these last few months.

Dara took one last look around the empty apartment, trying to commit it to memory. Then, with a slight flourish, she finally closed the door on her past and went downstairs and out front towards her future.

As she passed, Eddie, sitting in the passenger seat of the removal truck, gave her the thumbs up. Dara smiled and waved at her father before heading to the car parked behind. Then, taking one last look at the outside of the building, she breathed deeply and sat into the car.

"Ready?" Mark asked her from the passenger seat.

It had driven him mad not being able to help with the lifting and carrying, but six weeks on, and despite his mounting recovery, he was still under strict doctors' orders not to exert himself in any way. Dara wasn't about to let him lift a finger; it was still hard to believe that he was there at all! After ten very long days in intensive care, he'd eventually got over the worst, and was now well and truly on the mend. But at one stage, before it was all over and Mark finally regained consciousness, it had been very much touch-and-go. He was 'extremely lucky', the doctors had said. "He's not the only one," his wife had told them, relieved.

Now, Dara looked at Mark and smiled happily. "I'm ready," she replied, before leaning over and kissing her still-very-sore, still-very-bandaged, but utterly perfect man on the lips.

CHAPTER 42

"As that Oprah one would say 'You go, girl!'" Sheila had laughed happily the other day when Rosie outlined her plans. Sheila was laughing a lot these days. Mercifully, Mark and his wife had made a full recovery after the train crash, and the two of them were in the process of moving to a new house. Gillian still didn't approve of the wife, mind, but Mark's brush with death had given them all a shock and brought them closer together.

Rosie was moving too. She was selling up the family house in Wicklow, and moving back to dear old County Clare in the New Year. Stephen's own plans to retire to Tralee had really set her thinking, and after the shock and utter surrealism of 'escaping' that same crash, Rosie decided to take her future into her hands. For once, instead of worrying about what everyone else might think, she was going to grab life by the scruff of the neck and do exactly as she pleased.

She'd thought very hard about it all – particularly about living so far away from her precious granddaughter, but, of course, she'd come and visit Claudia as often as she could. As it was, she didn't see the crature as often as she'd like, so being in Wicklow or being in Clare wouldn't make much of a difference in that regard! She'd miss Sheila too of course, miss her desperately, but without Martin, there was very little in Wicklow for her any more, and she longed for the peace and quiet of home.

Although, she'd have no shortage of friends down in Clare either it seemed. In the last few weeks, while searching for a suitable house at home, Rosie had run across lots of people she'd lost contact with and they all seemed pleased at the idea that she was returning to live there again. And then, there was always Stephen only a short train journey away down in Kerry. He'd made her promise to visit and join him with his painting as often as she could. Rosie couldn't wait.

Sophie was not a happy girl, and was still pouting over the fact that Rosie had removed her mortgage guarantee, but what could she do? All it meant was that Sophie and Robert had to curtail their extravagant lifestyle somewhat, which was no bad thing – the removal of the guarantee lessening their credit rating a little, but not affecting the status of their mortgage.

Anyway, Rosie thought sighing, with the ample proceeds from the sale of the family home, she'd have more than enough left over to give her errant daughter a lump sum. At least, that should keep her happy. And speaking of 'happy' …

Shortly after the train accident and the associated family upheaval, Rosie had arrived home from the shops one day to find David sitting in the kitchen, a strange dog cowering at his feet.

"I know it's not Twix, but it could do with a good home," he'd said quietly.

Rosie looked at the dog. It was a young male, some class of a Jack Russell, black with white paws – a wretched-looking scrap of thing. But judging by the dog's nervous expression and doleful eyes as it regarded Rosie fearfully, it may very well have been mistreated.

David confirmed her suspicions. "He was found tied up in a refuse bag on the side of the road," he said.

Almost instantly Rosie's heart melted and her heart went out to the poor little fellow. Now, he wouldn't replace Twix, nothing would replace Twix, but if the dog didn't mind being uprooted, it might be nice to have a bit of company starting out down in Clare all the same. And there was plenty of room out the back of the little cottage for a few more animals, if she were so inclined.

"So what'll we call you, then?" Rosie asked, dipping her hand into her shopping bag and taking out the first item she laid her hands on, remembering how Twix had ended up with her name. It was a pound of butter. "Kerrygold?" she wondered out loud. "Mmm, maybe not."

"The dog pound called him Happy," David explained. "Don't ask," he added, rolling his eyes. "I think they were being ironic."

"Happy it is then," Rosie bent down and patted the terrified dog on the head, lovingly remembering the last time she had done the same for poor old Twix.

A few days after the train crash, she and David had sat down and had a proper heart-to-heart. She'd explained how isolated and hurt he'd made her feel since moving back home, and he finally explained his reasons for doing so, as well as the cause of his anger and frustration.

"Kelly and I were trying for a baby, but it didn't work out," he admitted shamefully, his cheeks full of colour as Rosie sat there trying not to betray her surprise. "I felt so emasculated, Mum – all our friends were popping them out left, right and centre, and I couldn't do anything. We had the tests, and Kelly was fine, so we knew it was me."

He'd went on to explain that he'd read every book he could on the subject, and had decided to change his lifestyle to try and become more healthy, which was the reason he gave up eating meat. "It was making me miserable, Mum – you know how much I love my meat. But I think it also might have led to my lacking in something else too – some kind of mineral or vitamin or something, which probably made me so edgy and impatient."

He had pushed Kelly away in the process, his intensity and obsession with overcoming the problem overwhelming both of them.

"But that was probably all part of it," Rosie advised kindly, privately relieved that his recent behaviour had actually originated in something. It had killed her to think that his selfish attitude could have been 'normal'. "I'd bet if you went back to your normal eating habits, back to your normal self and tried to be a bit nonchalant about the whole thing for a while – instead of all the stressing you've been doing – that everything would work out. Kelly loves you. She's miserable without you."

Following a phone call from her husband telling her that Rosie had been in a train crash, Kelly had taken the next plane over, and couldn't believe it when Rosie's apparent demise had turned out to be a false alarm.

However, she and David had then taken their first tentative steps towards reconciliation and now Rosie knew they would be fine. He was planning to move back to Liverpool when the house was sold, and Rosie was safely ensconced in her new cottage and new life back home in Clare.

"And if it doesn't happen, what of it?" she said to David, referring to his circumstances. "You and Kelly have one another, isn't that all that matters? I'd give anything to have your father back, so don't waste what precious time you have together on wishful thinking – wishing for something that might happen, but just as easily might not."

David looked at her. "You're right, Mum. I was so caught up in what I couldn't do for Kelly that I couldn't see beyond it. I couldn't see beyond my own failure and my own misery. I was so angry and bitter that I never really gave myself a chance to think too much about it, but I suppose I was miserable without her too."

Then, mother and son smiled at one another, their long overdue discussion causing a new understanding between them. The sight of her beloved child's smile – a proper, genuine smile – had the effect of instantly reducing Rosie's recent unhappy time with him to a distant memory. Wherever he'd been these last few months, however much he'd been through, David – *her* David – was on the way back.

And wishful thinking? Rosie had been guilty of that herself. Since Martin's death, she'd existed in some kind of a void, no longer sure as to what her role in life actually was, no longer sure what she really wanted. And she'd done little else but hope that it would get better – that things would change or that *people* would change just because she wanted them to.

But Rosie understood now that wishes didn't just grant themselves. You had to take your wish, and make it happen all by yourself. Rosie smiled at the idea of her new life back home in Clare – a life of relaxation, good friends and hopefully, lots of painting by the sea. She was taking her wish and making it happen.

And she knew Martin would be helping her all the way.

THE END

Direct to your home!

If you enjoyed this book why not
visit our website:

www.poolbeg.com

and get another book delivered straight
to your home or to a friend's home!

www.poolbeg.com

All orders are despatched within 24 hours.

Published by *poolbeg*.com

THE NO1 BESTSELLER!

never say never

MELISSA HILL

*Sometimes hopes and dreams don't go according to plan –
sometimes, real life gets in the way.*

It's the late nineties and seven friends finishing college make a
pact to meet up in five years and find out whether their
predicted futures came true.

Who will be an environmentalist, and who dreams of being a
famous sports star? Will Leah be a chef, Robin an accountant and
Olivia the one who holds it all together?

But when we meet the gang years later it's clear that life has not
gone according to plan. Why is Robin in New York and
determined never to return to Dublin?

Why is Olivia grieving over a lost love? What happened to
Andrew's rugby career? And why does Leah feel so left out as she
heads towards the big three-o?

When Robin is eventually forced to return home, the friends find
themselves face to face with the past and nothing will ever
be the same again.

Sometimes it's best to *never say never*.

ISBN 1-84223-221-5